MORNING RAN RED

STEPHEN BOWMAN

A Critic's Choice paperback
from Lorevan Publishing, Inc.
New York, New York

Reprinted by arrangement with the author

ISBN: 1-55547-225-7

First Critic's Choice edition: 1988

From LOREVAN PUBLISHING, INC.

Critic's Choice Paperbacks
31 E. 28th St.
New York, New York 10016

Manufactured in the United States of America

TO HELEN AND J.W.

AUTHOR'S NOTE

What follows is a work of fiction. Because it plays upon the historical backdrop of an unsolved murder mystery, the reader may find some scenes familiar. The intrigue of the actual happening served as an outline for this work. There the similarity ends and all characters are fictitious.

CHAPTER ONE

June 10, 1912 — Monday

In the twilight of the morning when an old midwife began her "first-of-the week chores", there was nothing to indicate that life at the little village of Twin Forks would not go on in the usual way. There would always be the old families, clans whose ancestors were the first to settle there — the Porters, the Davies, the Gasts and a few others. These families held a special position of respect and, whether it was deserved or not, they would hang onto it protectively, fiercely.

And there would always be a Frank F. Gardner, owner of the giant four-story Victorian mansion which sat on the prominent high place of Twin Forks, a place reserved for the well-to-do and called "the hill" by those below it. Frank Gardner was of the new breed to come to Iowa and he wanted desperately to be accepted by the old families. But, of course, that could never be, no matter how successful or influential he became. But he would try. Sure enough, he would try.

The rest of the people that made up Twin Forks and the territory around it were farmers, businessmen, preachers, salesmen, loafers and a montage of others. They wanted most just to live comfortably with as little trouble as possible and found it mildly interesting to watch the other two, the respected old and the powerful new, fight to outdo each other. It never occurred to them that one day they could all be sucked up into the turmoil and their peaceful lives would be shattered and never put together again.

If only it would not have happened, they would say later. If only . . . but everyday things are missed when they are gone. Particularly are they missed in a small rural village like Twin Forks, Iowa. Particularly when an entire neighbor family suddenly breaks the routine of normal life. And, by nine o'clock the morning of June 10, 1912, this began to bother the midwife going about her Monday chores.

How many times she had glanced at it over her shoulder she did not know. But now Mrs. Martha Pinkerman stopped to wipe the perspiration from her brow and eyed her neighbor's home carefully.

It was so very quiet, she thought. Far too quiet.

She looked down to her Monday wash, a large tub of sopping wet clothes. She stood there with her hands on her wide hips and looked back to the small house next door. Could something be wrong over there, she wondered over and over again. Suddenly the mystery was too much for her and at nine o'clock that morning Martha Pinkerman came to the momentous decision — for the first time in fifty years of marriage she would let the Monday wash go.

Inside her own home she called to the kitchen where her husband sipped a second cup of coffee, "Elmer! I'm going to use the Mutual."

Taking the receiver from the wooden box on the wall, she gave the crank six quick turns. She stood on her toes to place her mouth in front of the speaker while she held the receiver to her ear. A sleepy voice acknowledged her ring.

"Minnie. This is Martha Pinkerman. Can you give me the ring for the Plow Store?"

Papers rattled at the other end of the line where she knew Minnie Butler sat in a small room above the Finley Hotel going through a short list of names on yellow paper. The voice came back more alert this time.

"Three longs and a short?" Martha Pinkerman repeated. "Thank you, Minnie. No, I can't talk now. I have a call to make." She pulled down the metal prong cradle of the receiver, then grabbed the crank on the opposite side of the wooden box and rang the Plow Store. As she cranked, she counted out loud, "One, Two, Three. And a short!"

A man's voice answered, "Porter's Implement Company."

"Hello," Martha Pinkerman yelled into the speaker, "Is Mr. Jas Porter there this morning?"

"No ma'am. This is Ed Borrows, his helper, and I haven't seen hide nor hair of him."

"Ain't that strange," Martha Pinkerman said into the speaker, but looked down at her husband who had come into the parlor to listen to his wife talk on the new piece of furniture. He saw the concern on her face and shook his head knowingly, but unconcerned.

"Yes ma'am, it is kinda strange! Jas is usually here by four every morning and he was suppose to bring the team down so's I could go out into the country with a delivery. I figgered he'd be up there by you people."

Her toes were beginning to cramp as she stretched to put her mouth to the speaker again.

"No. The place is still. Not a peep," she said.

"Not a peep?" Ed Borrows repeated. "You figger they went visitin' or something?"

She thought a minute. Already her husband had lost interest in her conversation and was returning to the kitchen for another cup of coffee, and the lazy voice on the other end of the line was calm. Not worried at all. She conceded.

"Yes. Maybe they did," she said finally. "Listen, Mr. Borrows, I noticed that Jas' animals ain't fed. You better come do his chores just in case he doesn't get back for awhile."

She returned to the yard and her Monday wash. It had set too long now and would require another rinse. But as she bent to pick up the heavy load, a horse nickered from the small barn behind her neighbor's house. She stopped to look at the hungry animal and the others with it. A cow bawled for her neighbor to come take the milk from its swollen teats. No, she told herself, they would not have gone away without arranging for the animals to be taken care of. No matter what kind of emergency might have come up Jas Porter would have seen that his livestock was fed. So, they must have overslept, Martha Pinkerman decided. She looked at the house once more, the small frame house where Jas and Sally Porter and their four children lived. Neighbors for fourteen years — since Jas' first child was born. Would the whole family have overslept? It was possible. But one morning out of fourteen years? It was certainly possible.

It had rained the night before — a light drizzle had started at eight o'clock and had ended sometime during the night. It was the rain that had kept her from going to church last night, she remembered now, so she had gone to bed right after doing the supper dishes. That was eight-thirty and the rain had been coming down then. But today was another bright June day, a warm sunny morning promising a scorcher of an afternoon. Even so, the windows to the little frame house across the yard were shut tight, the shades pulled all the way down. Wooden doors were closed behind the screened doors. Strangest of all, what bothered her the most, was the absence of the children.

Once again Martha Pinkerman decided to let her Monday wash go a while longer. She walked to the edge of her yard and stepped across the invisible property line thirty feet from Jas Porter's house. She did not go closer. Instead, she slowly circled the house at that distance, carefully surveying the outside of the structure, as if something there would answer her question.

She walked her circle. Each window was inspected from her distance, which for some reason seemed close enough. Every crack in the board siding, each spot of fading whitewash stared back at her. A face jumped to a window then disappeared quickly. Was it a face? No. It was the reflection of the late morning sun on the dark glass, dark because of the black shade behind it. She continued her patrol slowly, carefully —until she came to the street where she stopped in complete exasperation. Not one aspect of the house showed a sign of life. If they had left for the day, they would have fed the animals or they would have told someone else to do so. If they had overslept, the windows would have been open. It must be sweltering in there, she told herself. It was simply too much for her to understand.

Where was Mr. Borrows? She looked down the street to the west, the direction of the downtown section six blocks away. Four blocks down she saw Horseface Peterson's rig trotting away from her and, in the next block, there was Mrs. Saunders taking care of her Monday wash. From behind a row of thick Elm trees, Ed Borrows finally appeared ambling along in the lazy way of helpers. She shook her head. Ed Borrows would be of no help.

Martha Pinkerman turned back to face the front door of her neighbor's home. It was much like her own, only smaller. A short front porch flush with the living room leading to the front door. A large living room window and, above it, a small bedroom window of the second story where the roof slanted. A normal house, but quiet for the first time in a long, long while. Its stillness echoed years of memories back to the heavy midwife at the street. It sighed with her remembrances of family crisis. Laughed with her recent memory of the children playing yesterday morning before dinner. Martha Pinkerman's mind was made up. They were either home or they were not. Either way, she would find out. She would go right up to the front door and knock.

There was no answer. She pulled on the screen door. It opened — had not been latched. She grabbed hold of the inside doorknob. To her own relief, it would not turn. Inside, the telephone rang. It rang and rang without answer.

Ed Borrows would recall later how Mrs. Pinkerman ran off the porch in her long dress, perspiration streaming down her face and tears in her eyes. She said to him as she ran by, "Mr. Borrows, you feed the horses and milk those cows. I'm going to call Jas' brother. Maybe Russ has an extra set of keys. There's something wrong over there. I'm sure of it."

"What do you think, Mr. Porter?" Ed Borrows asked. Russ Porter stood in Mrs. Pinkerman's yard looking at his brothers house.

"I don't know. But I guess we better find out," he said, then walked to the front door pulling a large ring of keys from his pocket. He tried several keys before the lock would turn. Ed Borrows gasped as he crouched behind the huge back of Russ Porter, "There was no key in the lock from the inside," he whispered, "that's kind of queer." Russ Porter turned the key and stepped into the living room of his brother's house. Ed Borrows crowded at his heels.

The house was silent. A hot mustiness burned his nose as Russ Porter walked through the living room. The oaken floor creaked beneath his feet as he neared the parlor. He reached out to push the parlor room door open. Ed Borrows stood five feet behind him looking up the closed staircase that went to the two bedrooms. He did not go up them. He waited for Russ Porter to open the parlor door.

Russ Porter's hand touched the door. It moved slightly. Then he pushed harder and the door swung halfway open. As his eyes focused to the darkness of the room he saw rumpled bed sheets over sleeping bodies, but by then it had dawned on him, too, that something was terribly wrong. He wheeled and ran out of the front door, Ed Borrows still at his heels.

"Get the sheriff," he yelled to Mrs. Pinkerman. "Get the sheriff, get the doctor!" And, as Mrs. Pinkerman passed the orders along to a young boy on the street, Russ Porter vomited, although he wasn't sure why.

In a few minutes, June 10, 1912, would become a day never forgotten.

CHAPTER TWO

June 7, 1912 — Friday.   The coming storm.

Frank F. Gardner was fifty-five that summer although the darkness of his brown hair and beard and the trimness of his husky frame let it seem that he was ten years younger than that. He climbed the fifty-seven steps to his fourth-floor study effortlessly. Today, as most days, had been a busy one. Outside on the front lawn of his mansion were five hundred guests who had come to celebrate his recent nomination to the senate. It was a social gathering, a role he seldom played, which he played now grudgingly out of protocol. Later he would join the guests, but not yet.

Inside his study three men awaited him. They would be George Geldin, a lawyer from Des Moines who represented the Republican party machine there; and Fred Martin, Iowa Attorney General and an old friend from days in the legislature. They came as friends, they would have him believe, but there was no doubt in Gardner's mind why they had come. In truth, they were emissaries of his archrival, Sam Durham, who ruled southwestern Iowa politics from the County Seat nine miles away. The third man would be John Goodell, a young lawyer nephew from New York whose mother had decided it would be nice if his Uncle Frank could get him started in politics, the idea being that Iowa politics would be a softer nut to crack and provide a faster climb to the top—then back to the east. He wasn't sure what he planned to do with John Goodell, but it would be nice to have a relative around for an aide — someone trustworthy.

Outside his study door, he stopped to straighten the gray suit coat he habitually wore, along with the matching vest, a stiff white collar and bowler tie. There was a proper way to do something and there was an improper way. Gardner was proper — strictly proper — in his dress, his mannerisms, his religion. He saw everything as a test of honor. And honor was everything.

Satisfied that all was in order, he remembered that his son, Albert, still waited by the window at the end of the hallway. He decided to put off meeting the men in his study a while longer and went to his son.

"Have you seen anything of him, Albert?" he asked as he approached.

Frank noted with disgust that not only had Albert not dressed properly for the celebration, but he had been drinking also. Alcohol was specifically forbidden at the celebration. He had decided years ago that alcohol and tobacco were evil vices that worked to undermine human integrity and ambition. Never had he allowed the two to be brought into his home. It had been the devil that had driven Albert to his strange ways, he had decided. With hope and prayer, God would deliver his son back to him and once again would he have an heir to the wealth and influence he had worked to build.

"No sir," Albert mumbled. Then he added unconcernedly, "Maybe something went wrong."

Frank Gardner glared at his son, who still slouched against the window sill, thus avoiding the visual confrontation.

Albert Gardner resented having been stationed at the window. The party on the front lawn had just been getting off to a good start when he had been called away. Many young women were there. Some of whom he had had before. The fact that he was married did not seem to matter very much. Being the son of Frank F. Gardner had its advantages, he concluded, and he made use of those advantages as often as possible.

Frank Gardner stood behind the broad back of his son and looked beyond the head of thick brown hair to the window.

The Mo-Ri River valley stretched before them. In the distance they could see where Six-Mile Road came out of the eastern bluffs and crossed East Creek before it reached Twin Forks, and they could see where East Creek met the larger Mo-Ri River. It was that intersection, where the stream met the river, that caused the founder of Twin Forks to give the town its name. From their high position on the top floor of the mansion they could appreciate how prominent those land forks must have been to the old settler who first saw them from the bluffs over sixty years earlier. But they were not interested in the history or the scenery.

They watched the road for activity. Specifically, they watched for a black buggy drawn by a lone horse. They could see Six-Mile Road clearly as it twisted toward the bluffs. It was narrow and empty, shaded by late afternoon shadows. Looking at the thin line where it broke the continuity of the trees and grass, Frank Gardner could imagine the dirt road with its powdery surface of three inches of undisturbed dust blistering in the hot sun.

"He is over an hour late," he said seriously. "But Doc may have run into some complications. Those kind of things can happen in a situation like this. Don't worry about it — just remember to catch him before he comes into the house. I want him to come up by the back stairs."

"Yes sir, I'll tell him." Albert said, never turning from the window.

Frank Gardner pulled the gold chain from his vest pocket. The watch at the end of it read just past four o'clock.

"Well, I have kept them waiting almost two hours," he laughed. "That should have given them enough time to work up their venom and to come down on me as hard as they can."

He slapped his son on the back as he turned toward the study, "I am sure Doc will be here before long. And don't forget the back stairs. This will be our secret — yours, mine and Doc's."

"And the Gast's," Albert said flatly.

Frank stopped mid-step. The blood surged to his neck but he controlled his anger. "Yes Albert — and the Gast's," he repeated and started again for the study. But before he reached the door, Albert called after him,

"Sir?"

"Yes. What is it Albert? These men are waiting for me," he said impatiently.

"Sir," Albert said again while Frank Gardner felt the blood surge into his neck another time. For some reason the title, "sir" coming from his son angered him. He knew it was not intended to show respect. Albert pronounced the word in a mocking way that reminded him that it was a word that replaced "dad" or "father". He could not remember when Albert had last called him anything but sir.

"Speak up, Albert. If you have something to say, say it."

Albert had turned from the window. His huge frame filled the light behind him. Then, like an overgrown child, Albert mumbled, "I just wanted to know sir — I mean, I wanted to say, sir, that — that I am sorry."

Frank Gardner was speechless. Albert had apologized! It completely disarmed him. He looked at Albert as any father might look at a son. Albert was wide and powerful, wild and mischievous — too wild, he knew, and too powerful for a senseless twenty-eight year old man. And Albert was defiant — had been since childhood — something he simply could not understand. Lately he had been seeing Albert as another enemy, another man or organization trying to take something away from him. His power. His influence. His freedom. He had come to see Albert as a threat to the family name with his drinking and whoring. Albert had not been a son with problems that a father could help solve — he had been a force trying to undermine the Gardner empire.

But now Albert had apologized. For a brief moment he saw his son again and he was a father again.

"Well Albert, you know that I am disappointed in you. You should never have gotten involved with that Gast girl. You know that, too. Alice Gast is no good. Her father is no good and her entire family is no good. They never will be. It seems once a family like that starts sliding down hill, they just keep on going.

"Dorothy, on the other hand — well, perhaps she is not all that you would like her to be. But she is your wife and she is the most attractive woman in Twin Forks. Dorothy comes from a very respected family whose reputation is going to help us grow in this community. We cannot afford a scandal at this time. Not with the elections coming up. We have the Gardner name to think about Albert. The Gardner name."

Albert's eyes had begun to drift away. Frank Gardner realized that he was preaching and that Albert, in his silent, brooding was becoming defiant again. This is not what he wanted to say to his son. He wanted to say, look, I am your father. I love you and I can help you.

He said, "Your biggest mistake was not coming to me sooner, Albert. You should have come to me right away. It would have been easier for all of us then — for you, me and the doctor. But did you come to me? No, I didn't find out about it until Andrew Gast himself came to me and threatened me. That was wrong, Albert. You should never have put me in that position."

Defiance clouded his son's eyes. Albert returned to the window. He had lost him.

"Forget it anyway. It's over by now," he said reaching for the doorknob to the study.

"Yes sir."

"And keep a sharp lookout for Doc Stewart."

"Yes sir," he heard Albert say again as the mocking "sir" followed him into the study.

The younger man jumped to his feet when Frank Gardner entered.

"You must be John Goodell," he said curtly.

"Yes, sir. I know I am going to enjoy working with you, sir."

"We'll see about that, Mr. Goodell. We'll see about that." Without looking again at John Goodell he took the large chair behind the library table that served as his desk.

The two older men had remained seated. They looked at each other numbly as if the sudden arrival of Frank Gardner stunned them after their long wait. He looked at them in annoyance, "Gentlemen, if you are expecting an apology for my keeping you waiting, I assure you that it was unavoidable and therefore, no apologies are in order."

His old friend Attorney General Fred Martin moved uneasily in his red leather chair thinking that this was one hell of a way to begin a meeting. He had escorted George Geldin on the train all the way from Des Moines. They had waited in the hot sun at the train depot for the Gardner's carriage to pick them up and then they had wasted the better part of the afternoon waiting for Gardner in his high, but musty study. Still, Martin was more worried than he was angry. If anyone knew Frank F. Gardner, Fred Martin did, and now he sensed that after their long wait, Frank F. Gardner fully intended to give them a few minutes of his time, cut them off and cross them off his agenda.

Martin had his own reasons for keeping George Geldin happy. Although it had been at Geldin's request that he accompany him to see Gardner, he knew that being turned away like beggars at the door was not the way to keep Geldin happy. He resigned himself to the task of intermediary.

"We know you are busy, Frank. Mr. Geldin and I are busy, too. But — we are all here now, so. . ."

George Geldin had no intention of smoothing his anger over so easily. He leaned across the table, extended his arm for a handshake while he introduced himself, "I'm George Geldin, Mr. Gardner. I have come a long way and I do believe that there is a train out of Twin Forks at five o'clock. That is forty-five minutes from now. So let's get down to business."

He had never met George Geldin although he had heard about him. Geldin was a successful lawyer with large offices in the State Capitol. What his actual connection with politics was not clear, but for reasons of his own Geldin had devoted the past ten years to keeping the Republican Party in Iowa together. In this case "together" meant that everyone who wanted support of the Party would follow the strict Party line. In this part of Iowa that also meant total submission to Sam Durham's local ruling.

Gardner knew the system well. He despised most of it. He had fought it from the day he first stepped on the floor in the Legislature to present his insurance reform bill that would protect homeowners. The bill passed and took thousands of dollars away from those representatives who had been on various company payrolls keeping the previous corrupt system alive. He had won that bill and many wounds were opened that would fester over the years. He wondered now if George Geldin had lost money that day. He hoped so.

"Yes, Mr. Geldin, let's get down to business."

George Geldin cast Martin a triumphant glance that was dampened only by the knowing frown that Martin returned.

"All right, Mr. Gardner," Geldin began, "I'm sure you are aware of my position and you know that when I speak I am speaking for the Party. What I am prepared to offer you is as much support as the Party can give you for your election to the Senate this autumn. Now, we can be a great deal of help to you, Mr. Gardner. Without the support of the Party, you would have a hard time getting elected. A lot harder than need be. Now, you have just won the nomination by a considerable margin . . ."

"Yes, Mr. Geldin," Gardner interrupted, "since you brought up my nomination — where was the Party then?"

Geldin flustered, "Why, what do you mean?"

"Where was the Party support when I was running for the nomination?"

Geldin looked to Martin with a smile, "Understand, Mr. Gardner, that the Party cannot support a candidate prior to the nominations. It just isn't done. Why, we would be pitting Republican against Republican and we can't do that."

"So you wait until after the nomination. That way you know you're backing the right horse. Is that right?"

Geldin nodded stubbornly, "Yes, something like that."

Gardner rose from his chair, "And I don't suppose you backed Stan Wrigley against me, did you Geldin. You wouldn't have done that, would you?"

"Sir, I resent the implication. I don't know what you have heard, but no — in no way would we have backed Wrigley against you."

Fred Martin preceded his interruption with a series of coughs, "Gentlemen, let's stay on the business at hand. Frank, Mr. Geldin is here to help you. He knows more than most of us about politics and he is offering you help. Now, I think you should listen to what he has to say. And I think you owe Mr. Geldin an apology."

Gardner looked at the two men. Then he walked to the window.

"All right. I'll listen. And if the Party did not help Stan Wrigley and the rest of Sam Durham's underlings in the primary, then I apologize to Mr. Geldin. So, Mr. Geldin, you know whether I have just apologized to you or not. Go ahead."

"Of course, there are some minor requirements," Geldin continued, "to receive the Party support. You would be expected to con-
form more to the Party lines . . ."

That's where Frank Gardner shut the conversation off from his
hearing.

Below he could see the crowd gathered on the lawn. They were
at long tables that had been set for the food and now, before dark,
they were eating. The tables stretched across the grass like long coffins in white linen. The diners were pallbearers crowded together to
carry a heavy load.

At the end of the table nearest the mansion he could see his
daughter, Lona, and at the other end, Dorothy, Albert's wife. All
eyes were turned toward Dorothy and away from Lona. This was
usual, for Dorothy was beautiful and Lona was plain. It was good
that Albert had married Dorothy. Good for the Gardner family.

From his window he noticed with displeasure that not all of the
tables were filled. He scanned the crowd for the people he had most
hoped would be there — the Hargroves, the Wrights and the
Andersens — three old families which had not yet accepted him.

Those families were not there. He could not find them. After all
his years of work — all his power, his influence, his wealth . . . he
was mayor of Twin Forks, he founded and owned the area's only
bank, he owned the largest land holdings in the territory — and
now he had just been nominated to the Senate — and still the families had not accepted him.

"Mr. Goodell. Come here," he said disregarding whatever George
Geldin had been saying.

Goodell came to the window and followed his finger to the crowd
below.

"Do you see the young woman on this end of the table, Mr.
Goodell? That is my daughter, Lona. Go get her, please. Tell her I
want to see her."

He watched John Goodell leave the study as the quarter hour
clang from the clock reminded him that Doctor Stewart had not yet
arrived and George Geldin's voice droned on.

" . . . for instance, there is your stand on prison reform. That will
have to change. You are preaching leniency for the prisoners at the
same time your Party is coming out with a get tough policy. You will
have to fall in line on that. The boys in Des Moines are determined

there. Then, there is your idea of reducing the shipping charges for farmers . . ."

Geldin was so sure of himself, Gardner thought with amusement. Here was a man with the establishment behind him and all he had to do was lay down the laws of the majority. He could not keep the smile from his face.

"Look, Geldin, let's get something straight right now. I am well aware that winning a nomination does not mean that I will win the election. But I will not follow the Party line. For one reason, I don't happen to agree with some of your principles. For another, if I ran things around here the way you tell me to, there wouldn't be an election this fall."

Again Fred Martin came on with his fit of coughing, "Now Frank, Mr. Geldin is trying to help. He has had experience with politics and you haven't."

There it was — that surge of blood to his neck that he tried to control, couldn't, and pointed an angry finger at Geldin,

"I won the nomination because these people know that what I do is right for them. They know how much I have helped them and they will not bite the hand that feeds them. They have watched me grow from a poor schoolteacher to what I am today. Now, they have decided to grab hold of my coat tails and grow with me. That's politics, Geldin. Plain, hard politics."

Geldin remained calm, "Now, I have had quite a few years of experience with politics. I have lived in Des Moines . . ."

"You may know something about politics in the city, Geldin, but you don't know a horse from an ass when it comes to rural people."

"And I suppose you do?"

"I know an ass, Mr. Geldin. I know an ass."

He said it again, louder, as the two men escaped through the study door.

John Goodell held the door and Lona rushed into the study. She wore a long, featureless dress that seemed only to accentuate her plainness. The long, blonde hair that might have made her appear more interesting was pulled back into a bun at the back of her head and instead, it showed how pale and thin she really was.

Lona's only noticeable attributes were her sincerity and pleasantness. Unfortunately, these were seen only by the family or old friends and did her little good socially among circles of her own age group.

"Father," she pealed as she kissed him on the cheek, "it is a wonderful party. You must come down. Everyone is anxious to congratulate you."

Frank Gardner pointed toward the window, "I don't see the families."

Lona blushed, "The Overlands are here . . . of course, they do whatever the Davies do."

"I mean the Hargroves, the Wrights and the Andersens. Where are they?"

"They didn't come, Father," Lona admitted.

"Why?"

"Because the Porters were not invited. They follow the Porters like the Overlands follow the Davies."

Frank Gardner knew this. He had not invited Jas Porter and the other Porter families because Jas Porter had campaigned against him before the primaries. Jas Porter was also his only business rival. For years Gardner Hardware had been the only major tool and implement store in the area until Jas Porter had decided to use his old family name to attract clientele to a new implement store. The competition had not bothered him at first. He had been certain that Jas Porter would not make the business run. But that was three years ago and now Jas Porter's Implement Store in Twin Forks was thriving. Even that was bearable, however. What was not bearable — what made it impossible for him to associate with the Porters — was Jas' constant rivalry to his Senate seat. It would have been different had Jas Porter wanted the position for himself. But he did not run against him. He simply stated that Frank Gardner should not be elected Senator. This was a most believable and damaging statement coming from a non-candidate.

"All right, Lona. I thought they might have made some excuses. Go on back to your party."

"It's your party, Father," Lona reminded him pleasantly, "Have your guests gone?"

Frank Gardner's mood suddenly turned. "Yes. They are gone," he laughed. "Imagine that, Mr. Goodell — those fools actually thought they could come in here and tell me how to run my election in my country. As if I couldn't talk to my own people."

John Goodell shrugged his shoulders, "I wasn't sure why they were here, sir. I don't think they expected to win you over to their side."

"That's right, Mr. Goodell. They didn't expect me to change my position. They were just trying to test the water before they jumped in. You see, Geldin doesn't care who wins the election this fall as long as he controls whoever it is. Geldin has an umbrella hanging over half the politicians in this state and now he is frightened. He sees that I am the man bringing the windstorm that is going to turn his umbrella inside out. I'll do it, too."

"Can he hurt your chances, sir?" Goodell asked seriously.

"Geldin? No, Geldin can't hurt me. Nothing can stop me now."

He told Lona to take John Goodell to the party, for even as he said those last confident words, he saw Dr. Stewart arriving in his buggy. Something had gone wrong. The doctor was not alone. Beside him sat a ragged old man Gardner knew all too well. They headed for the rear door of the mansion.

Albert Gardner watched his wife at the table. She laughed and he remembered how her lilting chortle used to make him happy before they were married. Now, he resented the attention she received from the other men that seemed always around her. She didn't mind them, though. That is what enraged him — Dorothy loved the attention. She invited it.

Albert searched hungrily across the five hundred heads crowded at the tables. In someone he had to release his anger and prove his manhood. Frantically his eyes ran through the women who had come to the celebration. There were daughters of his father's friends and their wives. Some of them he had had before and he knew that he could have them again. But not now. It would be too risky for them now. They would be available tomorrow night or Sunday afternoon, but not tonight. Their husbands or fathers were too close and there was not a good place to go. They could not go into the mansion nor could they be seen walking away.

After dark, he thought. About an hour from now. In the carriage house behind the mansion. But who could he take?

At a far end of one of the tables was Gertrude Micheles, the schoolteacher. She had been sitting alone patiently waiting out the social function, which she considered her duty as a townsperson and schoolteacher, then she would silently excuse herself and return to her lonely room above the clothing store on the Square. Miss Micheles had heard of Albert's reputation and she had turned him into her only sexual fantasy. In her fantasy, he was the perfect lover — someone who would not care for her and yet make love to her when she needed it and then go away.

She had seen Albert come to the back porch of the mansion and now, as she watched him, their eyes met. Gertrude did not drop her eyes from his. Unconsciously she met the challenge with her chest aching to throw her arms around Albert Gardner and hug him as he slides between her legs.

Gertrude Micheles, Albert thought as he considered the forty year old woman. Her message transmitted to him. She needed him he knew as he acknowledged the message with a slow nod. She smiled. He sighed and stretched out his hand.

"He said you should go up the back stairs, Doc."

Doctor Stewart, a short plump man, of fity-eight, pulled his handkerchief from his trousers' pocket, removed his hat and wiped his brow defeatedly, "Thank you, Albert." Then he looked at Albert expectantly. When he knew that Albert was not going to ask the normal question, he said, "Everything went all right, Albert."

Doctor Stewart went into the mansion followed by Andrew Gast. At the door Gast stopped to cast a hateful glare at Albert. But Albert had not seen it. His attention was already back to Gertrude Micheles who had apparently decided not to return to her lonely room tonight.

Doctor Stewart came through the door alone. He leaned against the frame, took four gulps of air and limped to one of the red leather chairs where he plopped his chubby body.

"Well, Doctor, is everything all right?"

Doctor Stewart was still panting, "With the operation . . . everything went fine, I guess."

"But you don't like it, I gather."

"Like it? No, of course I don't like it. It's murder. You should have seen it."

"We agreed it was the best thing. Alice Gast didn't want the baby. In fact, her being from one of the old families could have caused quite a scandal. We did the Gast family a favor, too."

"I have a problem there."

"With Gast? I saw him ride in with you"

"Yes. He busted in on me just as I had finished. I thought he was going to kill me. He's planning on killing you. I talked him into waiting in the hall until I came to get him."

"Is Alice going to be all right?"

"Yes. She didn't say a word. Just looked at me, looked at old man Gast on the buggy seat, and then that woman closed the door."

"I suppose it wasn't easy for her — and there is probably a few days' depression," Gardner said evenly.

Suddenly the pressure of the past twenty-four hours caused the doctor to break. He pulled his hands to his eyes as he cried, "Frank, how can you just pass this off? We just murdered a living thing. A person. It was too late, Frank. Have you ever seen a human fetus? It's not what you might think. This had hands, feet, eyes — a human person in miniature."

Frank Gardner could stand no more. Anything but this, he thought as he felt his stomach turn.

"Is she or isn't she all right?" he demanded.

"Yes, she is all right."

Successful men fear a failure. They see a possible reflection of their own future.

Despite his low opinion of Andrew Gast, Frank Gardner had an uneasy respect for the bleary-eyed drunkard who stood as a scarecrow at the door. So out of place in the finery of the study in his worn out boots and pants' and long-handled underwear for a shirt. Gast walked with a broken limp to the desk. His blood-filled eyes glared at Gardner from a bent position, a stoop so profound that one would think he had just been punched in the stomach and could not straighten up.

"Hello, Andy."

Gast jumped back with one arm raised toward Gardner, "You gone too far this time, Gardner. I'm goin' tell the whole damn town about your boy. Your fuckin' money don't mean a damn thing when they get wind of this."

"She wanted the abortion, Andy."

"No, God damn you. You took my farm away from me — my father's land — his father's land. But no, that was fair. I, I didn't work it like I should. It was my own damn fault that I lost it. But now you had my little girl, my little Alice, butchered up by your God-damn bought and paid for doctor. I ain't standin' for it Gardner, you hear me? I ain't goin' to let it happen."

"Look at it from my side, Andy. Here's my son out throwing off a few wild oats with some of the whores. One of those whores, your daughter, becomes pregnant. Now, there is no good reason to assume that Albert is the father of that baby, but she comes to me knowing that it wouldn't do her any good at all to go to any of those bums she's been laying with."

"My Alice is a good girl." Gast's ferocity had turned to self-pity.

"She's a whore, Gast."

"My God! I tried to do . . ."

"You tried nothing. For three generations your family has squatted on a piece of land in the bluffs that should have been a good farm. But you watched it go down hill. Well, it's at the bottom now, Gast, and so is your family. You're a drunk. Your wife froze to death while you were gone on a drunk for two weeks in the winter. Your daughter is a whore and your son is going to end up just like you. The bottom of the barrel."

"I'm goin' leave this damn town — that fuckin' farm of yours."

"You're right. You should leave. As a matter of fact, I should run you off the place since you're no good for me or anyone else. But I'm going to let you stay. I'll give you one more chance to work that farm for me."

"Like hell I will, I won't give you the satisfaction of watchin' me grub a livin' on your land."

"You'll have to stay. That's the only way you can keep that old family name of yours and still have enough money to get stone drunk twice a day."

Andrew Gast sank into one of the winged-back chairs, "What about poor Alice?" He cried, "What do I say to her?"

"I don't think you have to say anything to Alice. She understands. She wants to keep her land, too. And don't worry about anyone else talking about this."

The study door swung open and Lona Gardner ran into the room and pulled her father toward the window.

"Come to the window, Father. They are going to turn on the lights."

Frank Gardner let her lead him to the window. Over his shoulder he saw Doctor Stewart helping Andrew Gast limp from the room. He was about to call the doctor back when Lona yelled, "Look, the lights!" Over the heads of the five hundred guests on the lawn a giant resemblance of the American flag glared red, white and blue bulbs. As if the lights marked some official beginning to the celebration, the people suddenly turned toward the mansion with their punch glasses raised high. They cheered, "Hip-hip . . . hooray! Hip-hip . . . hooray! Hip-hip . . . hooray!"

CHAPTER THREE

Beneath the red, white and blue lights there was no doubt about who was the prettiest woman at the party. Everywhere Dorothy Gardner went she trailed a string of smiling, happy men along behind her. She was not only beautiful but had that quality of vitality that lifts the hearts of all around. A private world had been created around Dorothy in the minds of those who knew her and in her own. She was a Davies. In Twin Forks of Davies county, that meant that no finer breeding could be had — the grand-daughter of one of the first, the very first, to come to the Twin Forks area. She moved comfortably in her world, partly because she loved it and partly because she hardly knew any other kind of life. It was right that men should follow her, even though she was married. They dared not touch her. It was right that she should be pampered and spoiled. She was a Davies, even now. When she married Albert Gardner, a bold break from tradition — her marriage license read: Dorothy Davies Gardner, a careful reminder to all just who Mrs. Albert Gardner really was. She was not a person — but an institution. As such, she deserved all she wanted and all that could be given to her.

When her marriage and courtship with Albert was arranged by their fathers, she thought little of it. As far as she was concerned, nothing would change, nothing should change. Only now, in addition to the respect of the Davies, she would enjoy the wealth and influence that came with being a Gardner.

Even after the marriage, Albert was afraid of her. He was sometimes boisterous, an attempt to cover up his fear, she knew, but the fear was there. Albert's fear and her pampered life ruined their marriage. In public, her public, Albert was a social introvert. When she would dance with a young man, he would watch. When she talked, he listened, and on the way home, he sulked. Worst of all for Dorothy, when they reached the bedroom, Albert was impotent.

Two years of their marriage had gone by before Dorothy began to look for other men to satisfy her. At first, she was afraid. Then afterwards, she was ashamed. But after three or four successful encounters, she saw how easy it was to have the Gardner money and lovers, too. Life became interesting again. She had many affairs. But always there was that lack of fulfillment, a giant void in her life, an empty space where this man should be whom she loved more than anything else — more than her money, more than her name. With each affair Dorothy realized despondently that she was not going to find what she was looking for in bed.

She tried everything. The entire winter was spent testing different projects. She tried to associate with Lona, but found her sister-in-law too common, too homespun and full of common sense for her to enjoy. She tried getting involved with Frank Gardner's politics, but found herself rejected. Church was her next step, but that business was so filled with petty arguments that she got nothing out of it other than Lona at her door every Sunday morning asking her to attend services with her.

It was March of this year that she found the man who filled the void in her life.

She knew little of Jas Porter at the time — other than the foul words she had heard Frank Gardner use of him. She knew he was from one of the "families", that he was outspoken against her father-in-law, he had a wife and four children and owned the Implement Store on the Square. She fell in love with Jas Porter on their first meeting. They had sat on feed sacks at the back of his store looking out into the rain. They talked. He was interesting, really interesting. It became unimportant that he was married or against her father-in-law. If she couldn't have him for her husband, she would have him for her only love.

A month later, in April, Dorothy Gardner met Jas Porter again at the back of the feed store after closing hours. He had been talking about the speech he was going to make against "Frank Gardner for Senator" the next day. In the middle of his talk she had put her arms softly around his neck, kissed him lightly, and asked, "Do you want me, Jas?"

Tonight Dorothy Gardner was happy. Her mind was made up to see her love tonight. That she would never see Jas Porter again had not entered her thoughts.

Gertrude Micheles left the protection of a group of older women and headed for the carriage house. It had not been so difficult to get away she thought, as she reached the shadows of the mansion. An excited shiver ran up her spine when she saw that the door to the carriage house was unlatched and opened a few inches. But then, why should it have been difficult to get away, she thought spitefully: they had never noticed her when she was there, so why should they notice that she was gone? She had been teaching their children for twenty years. Dependable Miss Micheles. She had given up her life to the children, to the town, and there had been no reward. God, how she hated them. She looked at the door. She realized that she was afraid, not of meeting Albert or of being caught or disgraced, but of being stopped from reaching the carriage house door and of receiving the few wild moments Albert Gardner would give her. The experience. The memory. Her reward. She ran for the carriage house.

Albert had spent many childhood days in the carriage house where it was cool in the summer, out of the wind in the winter and where he could be alone. It was his hideaway.

Sitting in the dark, he recalled days when he was a boy. He would sit on the cool leather of the carriage seats pretending to be his father. He was being driven to the depot for a business trip to the Capitol. People were on the streets and sidewalks but, like his father, he looked straight ahead pretending not to see them. When he pretended like this, he was confident and in charge of himself. In his dreams he would walk out of his father's shadow to reveal the person, the man, he knew he could be. Honor, his father had said to him, is all-important. Without honor, there is nothing. Honor is everything.

Once Albert had done a dishonorable deed. He had done it to defy his father and when it was done he realized that he wished he had not done this thing. But it had been too late to change it. He would have changed it if only he could. He ran to the carriage house before facing his father and he had cried alone with his dishonor. It had taught him a valuable lesson. And it had presented a terrible problem for which he would never find an answer: what to do with his defiance against his father: what to do with his honor.

The carriage house door swung open. He saw Gertrude Micheles silhouetted against the lights and then the door closed to leave them in darkness.

They paused until their eyes became accustomed to the light that came through the windows. She could hear his heavy breathing and felt her chest throbbing in expectation while her body became moist in honest want of receiving him. He took her by the hand and led her farther into the darkness to the gleaming carriage. Still holding her hand firmly, Albert climbed into the carriage, then pulled her up the two steps to him. He pulled her into his arms. She hugged him tightly as she allowed her knees to sink to the carriage floor between his legs. She clung to him, forestalling his next actions so that she could cherish the exuberance she was feeling. He tried to pull her from the floor but she pressed closer to him. She felt him against her and pressed harder while she felt him bend over her and tear the undergarments away. His hands squeezed her bare buttocks then moved toward her legs where he used one hand to part the flesh. She felt her body arch to meet him. Now she needed him. She could forestall no longer. When he pushed against her shoulders she rolled quickly to the floor open to receive him. He dropped to his knees between her legs then fell upon her. She wrapped her legs around his waist then reached down to guide him. It burst into her as she rose to meet it, to push it deeper and deeper until it was consumed and her body was at last given its promise and her fantasy was fulfilled. But he began working her violently. And that was better. Better than she had dreamed. And she wrapped her legs higher and clung to his neck.

Albert sensed her enjoyment. His temper rose to maddening anger as he pulled against her arched back and drove himself against her. He gave her everything he could never give Dorothy, everything his wife should have received, would never receive from him. He hated this woman beneath him and drove harder and harder to satisfy her, to degrade her to the point of having been satisfied by someone who despised her.

Gertrude leaped high onto his shoulder. Suddenly the sensation could be no better as she felt the warm flow between her legs. She collapsed beneath him, felt him leave her, and lay there glowing.

Gertrude was not sure how long she had been with Albert. When she came from the carriage house, most of the guests had gone and the lights over the yard had been turned off. When she walked past the front porch of the Gardner mansion where a group of women still talked, she jumped when Dorothy Gardner called to her.

"Gertrude, have you seen Albert?"

"No. No, I haven't, Dorothy." She lied and that was the first she realized she wished she could tell someone of her experience. She would have to see him again, she knew then.

Dorothy came from the porch and looked beyond the carriage house to a small group of men who were sitting around a fire at the back of her father-in-law's property.

Dorothy laughed, "So that's where he has been. Drinking and telling stories with a bunch of his bum friends. Isn't if awful, Gertrude?"

"Well, he is young," Gertrude said.

"Younger than his age, you mean," Dorothy said. "You aren't leaving are you?"

"Yes. It is getting late. Thank you very much for inviting me. I really enjoyed myself."

"I'm glad you came," Dorothy said absently. She was looking toward the men at the fire to be certain that Albert was among them. She didn't see him at first, then he stepped from the darkness and accepted a bottle that Burt McLean handed him. She sighed, that should take care of Albert for the rest of the night.

A small group of men were on the side porch talking to Frank Gardner about the upcoming election. Their wives sat inside chatting while Lona busily poured coffee. Lona went from one to the other, smiling when they noticed her, quiet as always. She returned to the kitchen for more coffee when she met Dorothy standing near the back door.

"Is there something wrong?" Lona asked.

"Poor Lona, you do work so hard."

"Oh, I don't mind, really. Mother needs my help. She hasn't been looking too well lately."

"Stop thinking of others all the time, will you. It embarrasses me." Dorothy smiled excitedly and clasped her hands together, "You should meet some young man, Lona. To think of your daddy with all the money in the county and you still unmarried."

"I suppose I'll never marry now."

"Of course you will. Haven't you ever — I mean, have you ever been interested in anyone?"

Lona blushed, "Well, there was a boy who showed me some attention. I was seventeen and he was a little younger. He asked me to go to a dance with him, but Albert beat him up and now he just walks by and says hello now and then."

"Lona! That was over sixteen years ago! Just think if he loves you. I mean, really loves you. A poor little country boy turning down advances with his cute little poor girls all around to pine away for the untouchable Miss Gardner."

"I doubt very much if Carl Gast is pining away for me."

"Carl Gast? You're kidding!"

"He just says hello."

"No wonder, your father would have him shot if he even found out about that."

"It's nothing. I'm too plain for anyone — not even father's money could change that."

Dorothy opened the door, "If anyone misses me, tell them I went home with a headache, will you?"

The men still talked on the side porch, but they did not see her leave. She heard laughter coming from behind the carriage house. She crept along the wall until she could see the five men sitting around a small fire. They were passing a bottle. A half-dozen empties lay on the grass by the fire. She could hear their drunken talk and, when she was certain that she had heard Albert's voice, Dorothy backed away from the corner and walked to the boulevard.

Dorothy did not turn north to head home as she had told Lona she would. Instead, she walked south along the boulevard to Third Street where she turned toward the Square.

Tomorrow was Saturday, a big day for the stores and an especially big day for the Implement Store. Unless he had changed his mind about working late on Friday nights, Jas Porter would still be at the store going through his inventory. Dorothy hurried along the street beneath the tall elms that had already leafed out to filter the moonlight onto her path. She tried to control her anxiety, but she was too used to having her own way and the idea that Jas Porter might not be there waiting for her had crossed her mind. She needed him now. She had been close to men all night. Their attention, the want in their eyes had aroused her and she knew there would be no satisfaction from Albert. By the time she reached the Square, she was running.

Dorothy stopped at the northeast corner of the Square. Across the little park area beneath four giant elms, a light shown in the Porters' Implement Store. Dorothy took a deep breath and walked toward the light.

Jas Porter was hanging a cultivator hoe in the window. Ed Borrows was loading a wagon at the back of the store.

"What is he doing here?" Dorothy whispered.

Jas Porter climbed out of the window, his huge frame towering over her, "I told you we weren't going to see each other again, Dorothy."

"So you brought your little helper along to protect you?"

"Yes. Something like that."

"Hmmm. That means you can't resist me, right?"

"Dorothy, I have no business seeing you. My wife is getting well, I have four children and this store to think of. We're not a couple of kids messing around behind the barn."

"You told me you loved me, Jas."

"I know, and I am sorry for that. But I also told you not to come back. I'm a Porter and you are a Gardner and we are both married."

"You hate the Gardners, don't you?"

"I hate what Frank Gardner is trying to do to this town. That's why I did everything to stop his nomination."

"Well, he's nominated."

"Yes. The power of numbers. But Gardner will be stopped sooner or later if I have to die to stop him."

"Oh, let's not talk about him. Let's talk about us."

"Dorothy, I told you there is no 'us' . . ."

He broke off the conversation when Ed Borrows approached them.

"The wagon is ready for you to take out sir," Ed Borrows said.

"Thanks, Ed. Why don't you sweep up the place and take off for home."

Dorothy walked to the rear of the store near the wagon, "You are going some place tonight?"

"I have to deliver some parts to Lerner's place down in Fog Hollow. Won't have time in the morning."

"Good. I'll go with you."

"No."

"Yes."

"Hey, there's old Ed Borrows. Come on, Ed, come tip a bottle of whiskey with us."

Borrows took a small sip from the bottle that was handed him and squatted near the fire.

Albert Gardner came out of the shadows pulling up his zipper of his pants, "Anybody seen my gawd-damn wife?"

It was not a serious question. He expected no answer. All the men at the fire shook their heads drunkenly, except Ed Borrows, who reached for the bottle again and said, "I seen her. She was headin' south on a wagon with Jas Porter."

"That bitch. Where's my fuckin' horse?"

When they left the Lerner farm, Dorothy suggested they return by way of the small bluffs road on the other side of the Mo-Ri River. They re-entered Twin Forks near the cemetery north of town. Dorothy jumped out of the wagon and ran home to bed. Jas Porter drove down Seventh Avenue, a dirt path along the east edge of town, to his own little home on Third Street. He did not go into the house right away. He unhitched the wagon and put the horses in the barn, then sat on the small back stoop smoking a cigar that a dealer had given him earlier in the day. He was relieved that he had not become involved with Dorothy again, although it had made her angry. He could see good years ahead for his family. His wife had become sick a year ago with some strange illness that sapped her energy to the point of total restriction to bed. Recently, however, she had begun to recuperate and in a couple more months, she would be her old self again. Business was doing so well that they had started to look around for a larger house. In their present small house, Jas and Sally slept in the smaller bedroom over the kitchen while all four children slept in the larger bedroom over the parlor and living room. The girls were fourteen and twelve, coming to that age where the body suddenly is a private thing and even the disinterested glance of a four-year-old brother constitutes a violation. They definitely would make a move before next winter, he had decided, and thought of the page in his wife's diary he had read the other night:

"Today we went to look at the Magnesun place. It is even bigger than I expected. It is a two-story house with four bedrooms upstairs, a full dining room downstairs with a parlor and a bath, a gigantic kitchen and another large bedroom for Jas and me. It is beautiful. They wanted four thousand dollars for it, so I have not told Jas I like it so much. It is a lot of money — but I do hope we get it."

As he stood to go into the house, he crushed the remaining ash of his cigar on the stoop and tossed the butt away from the house. He stopped short of opening the door. He heard an unfamiliar noise. It came from the direction of the barn. Jas Porter walked to the barn, but there was no more sound other than those of the horses eating fresh cut hay and a breeze shifting the tall grass along the sides of the outbuildings. Not even the chickens had become excited. Porter decided it was nothing, and went into the house to bed.

The bedroom door slammed open and the light flashed on.

"Get up, you damn whore."

"Albert? You're drunk. Now go away from me."

"Where the hell have you been?" Albert shouted and ripped the covers from the bed leaving Dorothy uncovered except for the gossamer gown that revealed her busts and outlined her hips.

"Albert, I won't take this from you. I have been right here. I told Lona I was coming home, didn't you ask her?"

"Ed Borrows said you were with Jas Porter."

"And you believed him, I suppose."

"I'd believe anybody before I would trust you."

"All right. Go ahead. I don't care what you think. If you were half a man you wouldn't have to wonder where your wife has been."

"Don't snub me, bitch. Your damn family name means nothing to me — not anymore."

"Yes it does, Albert. It means you can't touch me without getting permission from your daddy."

Tears swelled in Albert's eyes. "Bitch. Now you've done it."

He left the house.

June 8, 1912 — Saturday

Saturday was bright and sunny in Twin Forks. The small homes were open to receive the south breeze coming up the Mo-Ri Valley and children played in the shade of the elms, laughing and squealing in the streets, and the farm families were in from the country shopping on the Square, talking and milling in front of the stores, while everyone looked lazily forward to Saturday night and Sunday. In that happy, casual mood, a little stranger who was walking slowly down Six-Mile Road came unnoticed to Twin Forks. He stopped on East Creek bridge to survey the edge of town. A slight smile came to his feminine lips and his wide, yellowish eyes moved quickly from one house to the next in expectation of some friendly wave or greeting and perhaps an invitation to supper. That would normally be the way of things and he would normally accept.

But Linous Cleavers could not accept an invitation today even if it included a night's lodging, for he had an appointment to keep that was important to him.

He called himself the Reverend Linous Cleavers. Cleavers was a tiny man. Dressed in normal clothes his frail, four-feet-seven-inch frame would have seemed odd among the stalwart rural people. His quiet mannerisms, the slight smile, yellow eyes and carrot-top hair that stuck out from beneath his hat all would have created some suspicion as to the purpose of his coming. But dressed in the ragged black long coat and a dumpy black hat that made his red hair spring from his head in all directions, Linous Cleavers appeared very much as a traveling preacher should and seldom did the host town of his travels find out otherwise before he moved on.

The clothes were both the earmark of his trade and the costume of his problems. They worked successfully time after time, so he moved easily on to Twin Forks unworried about his reception. He knew he could rely on the traditional open attitude of the Midwesterners. It had been that way for over two hundred years. For over two centuries pioneer farmers, trappers, and hunters had little contact with the rest of the world and they had few neighbors. When a stranger did stumble upon their living quarters, it was call for an occasion. The table would be laid high with all the best food, the bottle would be hauled down from the loft, work stopped and the entire family would gather on the front porch in the summer, the fireplace in winter, to listen to the stories and tales of this traveler who could expand their scope of the world. This extra-fine treatment of strangers remained a tradition in the Midwest even after the newspapers, telegraph, radios and telephones appeared. It was this tradition that allowed a man to travel without so much as a penny to his name. And if the man happened to also be a preacher in this land where God-fearing folks felt it their duty to offer him their hospitality, then, so much the better.

It was a beautiful moment for the Midwest and ironic that while Linous Cleavers approached Twin Forks to receive its hospitality on this lazy Saturday evening, the old tradition was to stop suddenly. In less than thirty hours — and for the rest of time — people of Twin Forks and miles around would look upon strangers with suspicion.

Six-Mile Road reaches Twin Forks and becomes Third Street. Cleavers walked to the first house on the north side of the street where four children were playing on the front lawn. When they saw him they stopped playing and waited for him to speak to them.

"Come here children, " he said lovingly. The older girl picked up her baby brother and carried him with her to the street.

"Is this your brother?" he asked smiling.

The girl curtsied properly, remembering her manners, and looked to her brother, "Yes, Reverend. This is Paul and I'm Sarah — Sarah Porter."

Cleavers chuckled as she talked, so free and open. Oh, the innocence of children, he thought, and wanted to reach out and touch her. Sarah called her sister and other brother from the porch and now all the Porter children were around Cleavers.

"Herbert, Paul, Judy and Sarah," he repeated their names so gayly that they all laughed, as if they had never heard the names pronounced out loud before. "And you all are Porters?"

"Yes. Our father is Jas Porter and our mother is Sally."

Cleavers knelt to one knee and looked around at each of the children, "What a fine family." Then reaching out to Sarah, "Come dear, what is this pretty thing on your dress?"

"A brooch of my mother's."

He slipped his fingers beneath the brooch, pressing them against her breast as he pretended to admire the blue piece of jewelry. Sarah backed away uneasily, "Mother lets me wear it now and then. It makes me feel more grown up."

Cleavers smiled slightly, "You seem quite mature to me, Sarah. You are one of God's most beautiful creations. Perhaps if I am in town long you will allow me to photograph you."

"A photograph?"

Cleavers pointed to the large case he had been carrying. "I have a camera — my hobby is taking photographs of God's creations," he explained. "I want to put all of my photographs into a book some day so that all the world will see how beautiful we really are."

"Oh, that sounds so nice, Reverend. And I would be in the book?"

"Of course."

Sarah looked to the other children and they all laughed excitedly. Herbert said he wanted to be in the book, too, and they all laughed again.

"Shall I ask Mama if you can stay for supper? I know it will be all right," Sarah said.

"No child. However much I would dearly love to break bread with you, I am to spend the next couple of days with the pastor of the Presbyterian church."

"Reverend Bush?"

"You know him then. Are you Presbyterian?"

"We're Lutheran, but we know Reverend Bush."

"Good. Then can you tell me how to find his home?"

Sarah gave him the directions. When he left she called to him, "I'm sorry you can't stay with us, Reverend."

Cleavers waved to her, "I must go, really. God's work calls me and I must follow. Blessedness to you children."

Her directions took him along the north side of the Square to Second Avenue, where he turned and walked for two more blocks until he came to the large brick Presbyterian Church. To the north of the church was Reverend Bush's parsonage. Cleavers didn't go immediately to the house, however. The sun had gone down since his arrival to Twin Forks and many lights of nearby homes had come on. He knew that for most of the families of Twin Forks it was near bedtime. He walked to the rear of the church where the backyards of homes facing Third Avenue met the alley which divided the block. He walked slowly down the alley, dragging the heavy suitcase with him as quietly as he could. Then a light came on in one of the windows. A woman stepped into the room and closed the door behind her. She reached for the top button on her dress at the back of her neck, stopped suddenly to walk across the room and pull down the window shade.

A familiar surge rose within Linous Cleavers as he looked at the yellow light that came through the shade. He walked toward the window feeling as if he were floating uncontrollably, looking excitedly around for someone who might see him. There was no one. There was just him and the window and his irrepressible habit, his need for peeking unnoticed at a woman undressing routinely, openly, unaware of his intrusion. The shade had not been tied, so it swayed in and out with the breeze. There were moments when he could see the entire room, or a part of the floor, or nothing at all. The woman was plump, lily white from her knees to her neck, fleshy where her cheeks bowed out from her legs and curved in to meet the sway of her back. Ripples of fat jiggled as she sat on the bed to pull down her hair.

She stood facing him and lifted her arms high in the air and let a nightgown fall over her body. There was a moment then of suspended animation when her body was not ugly, her stomach flattened as she rose her arms and her sides stretched and her breasts bounced in the air, round and huge and firm. Outside in the darkness a warm, numb feeling came over Cleavers while the rest of his misshaped world was blocked out from his mind and he became satisfied by a series of hot, ticklish thrills that ran up and down his spine. He did not hear the screen door slam nor did he see the light from a match that Arthur Pederson struck against the porch pole to light his cigar.

"Hey! What the hell are you doing?"

His world shattered. Like a frightened rabbit Cleavers picked up his case and ran for the protection of the dark shadows of the church. There in the dark he pressed his back against the cool brick, his heart pounding in his little chest as he caught his breath. He stayed in the shadows five minutes before he found the courage to sneak a look around the corner across the alley. Arthur Pederson was on the porch talking to his wife, who stood in the doorway in her nightgown. "Some damn pervert," he heard Pederson say, "Sick! The man must be sick!"

Home free. Cleavers collapsed against the brick smiling with relief. Suddenly the world was pleasant again. He moved toward Second Avenue with the vision of Mrs. Pederson's naked body to remember for awhile and fulfill his need.

"Blessedness to you, Brother Bush."

"Reverend Cleavers? Come in. We were wondering if you were going to make it tonight."

"As was I, brother, as was I."

June 9, 1912 — Sunday   The last day.

Cool winds brought morning. Lona Gardner stood atop the high hill overlooking Twin Forks, letting the wind blow her hair loose from the tight curls. The town was awakening below her, another Sunday had arrived. Another Sunday like the other Sundays with more Sundays just like this one sure to follow. She stood in her Sunday dress, a long white dress touched off only by a little pink chiffon lace, while grey and black clouds streaked across the sky that she felt she was a part off. She dreamed she could fly, hold her arms out and let the wind carry her away from Twin Forks, not forever, just for awhile, then return her and she could be happy.

The church bells echoed through the valley. They burst her fantasy. She looked longingly toward the clouds, but the feeling would not return, so she ran down the hill towards town, through the ankle-high grass and around small piles of brush to keep her promise to Dorothy.

Lona was feeling happy even without her fantasy. It was a cool, breezy, porch-sitting, church-going day and she was on her way to meet Dorothy for church. She passed Burt McLean on the boulevard. "Good morning, Mr. McLean," she said merrily, "Are you going to see Father?"

Burt McLean was a filthy man. She knew he owned the bar down on the Square and that he came to see her father often, although she did not know their business. He tipped a ragged hat, "Yes, Miss Lona, your pa asked me to come."

"On Sunday?" she said, "Doesn't he know he's keeping you from church?"

McLean looked around him to be certain that no one had heard her, then whispered, "I ain't never bothered much with church, Miss Lona. But I got nuthin' against them that does."

Lona smiled, "Well, that's quite fair of you, Mr. McLean. But I have to go to church now and I am suppose to meet Dorothy or we'll be late. Good day, Mr. McLean."

Lona swung gayly onto the front porch of her brother's house and tapped on the screen door. Two blue jays were in the yard fighting over a scrap of paper that had blown there. She watched them take turns trying to get off the ground with the paper before the other one grabbed hold and hauled him down again. It was a great day.

There was no answer at the door. She knocked again, louder this time. "Dorothy," she called. "It's me, Lona. Dorothy?"

Still no answer, Lona opened the unlocked screen door and stepped into the livingroom. Instinctively she looked around the room at what had to be the messiest house she had ever seen. Lona shook her head, thinking that tomorrow she would offer to help Dorothy clean her home. "Dorothy?" she called and ran a finger across the top of a lamp table, shaking her head again at the line her finger had made through the dust. "Dorothy, are you asleep? Albert?" She started to go into the kitchen when she heard a low moan coming from the bedroom. "Dorothy?"

From the hallway she could see into the bedroom. The bed was empty. The covers were lying on the floor. "Dorothy," she whispered. Again the moan came from the room. Lona crept to the bed. Now she could see that the bed sheets were stretched toward the wall. With her hands and knee on the bed, Lona crawled across and peered over the edge.

First shock, then horror. Blood. Dorothy. Then reality. She screamed.

She screamed again, breathlessly, at her father's mansion. Frank Gardner was in his study. He heard Lona's screams echoing up the flights of stairs. Burt McLean was still with him.

"Something has happened, Burt. Now you go find Albert. We can't have him running around drinking and whoring with the election coming up. I'm going to put a stop to that action now. It's time he learned that he is a man."

Lona's sobs filled the stair wells.

"Mr. Goodell," he called from the hallway on the second floor. A door opened and John Goodell poked his head out. "Come with me. There's something going on downstairs."

Lona was sitting on the steps sobbing with her mother hovering over her, "It's Dorothy. I went to walk to church with her and no one came to the door. I went in and found Dorothy lying on the floor between the bed and the wall. She was beaten, Father. Her face was bruised and bloodied. Someone beat her — tried to kill her. I think she's unconscious."

Frank Gardner looked down at his daughter, his face was drawn tight and red in anger, but he lifted his daughter's chin tenderly in one hand, "Hey, this is no way for a Gardner to behave," he said evenly. "Now Mr. Goodell and I will take care of Dorothy. You take your mother to church."

Outside the door Frank Gardner told John Goodell to fetch the doctor. Mrs. Gardner watched him walk quickly toward Dorothy. She shook her head and turned to the sobbing Lona and said in exasperation, "I don't know what could happen next."

On the last day of his life, Jas Porter forced himself to visit his father. Traditionally, the six sons of the Porter family left their own families for a couple of hours on Sunday afternoons and visited their parents. Jas Porter was the eldest of the sons, followed by Russ in age, who was a farmer, and also owned a clothing store on the Square. Then came three more brothers who were farmers and then the youngest brother, twenty-five year old Bill Porter, who lived in the County Seat and worked as a tinner. He was the first Porter to move away from Twin Forks and the only one never connected with farming. But on Sunday he arrived on the three o'clock train to spend a few hours with his parents and brothers. Throughout the afternoon the six Porter boys would straggle in and out of their parent's home spending the hours with idle talk about the Titanic or the weather or listening to their father speak of the Civil War and old times. These were generally pleasant days.

But today Jas Porter did not want to visit his father. Jonathan Porter was seventy-five years old this summer. He had been one of Twin Forks' first residents. His father, Ezra Porter, had been the founder. Some of what was now the town actually sat on ground that used to be part of his farm.

Lately, however, Jas Porter had watched his father grow old. It had happened suddenly instead of spreading the aging process over a period of years. One Sunday his father seemed to be fifty years old — and eighty the next. Now each time Jas Porter left his father's home he left depressed and worried — two features that were not normally part of his personality.

Jonathan Porter's home was little more than a well-kept shack. It was the original home of the Porter family "in the wilderness" as Jonathan still referred to the Midwest, and it sat on the edge of the original Porter farm in a part of town that had become known for its poorer residents. Jas Porter loyally came through the fallen-down picket gate as much as he did not want to do it, and waved to two brothers who were walking in the field inspecting new corn shoots. He went to the porch swing near his father who sat in his rocker, while Mrs. Porter prepared lunch in the kitchen.

He asked his father how things were going. Jonathan looked at his eldest son queerly, "With me? Everything is fine with me. It's you I worry about."

Jas laughed, "You're worried about me. That's funny. I worry about you."

"I'm an old man. I don't have to be careful anymore about things I do or things I say these days." His tone was accusing and required an answer.

"You're talking about my speeches against Gardner last week, right?"

"He's not a good man, Jas. He could hurt you."

"I know what he is and I know he's not good for this town. As a Porter, I see it as my responsibility to at least try to stop him. If he's elected Senator, then I don't think anyone could touch him again. But that's politics and money, Dad, and he can't hurt me with either of those and he doesn't have the guts to meet me head on."

Jonathan stopped the rocker he had been sitting in and turned to his eldest son, seriously, "I was driving to the cemetery up the boulevard two weeks ago. I looked over to see ole Tom Sutland diggin' in Gardner's rear yard. I asked him what he was doing and he told me he was diggin' out Gardner's sewer hole. Now I figger that any man who hires someone else to clean his own sewer is no damn good for anything."

Jas Porter understood what his father was saying: Gardner would not face him in the open. He would send some of his men after him. Albert and Burt McLean and some of the others on the Gardner payroll would show up at his store some night.

"Well, I'll be careful. Does that make you feel better?"

"No, but at least I warned you. As a Porter, you have a duty to the town. But you have a lot more than that to think about, too."

Sunday evening the Porters walked to church. Herbert and Paul wore angel costumes and Sarah and Judy were maidens dressed in long, black robes. It was the night of the children's summer play.

Jas Porter stood with Sally on the front steps waiting to go into the church. They were talking with Joe and Edna Stills when Sarah and Judy ran to them with two of the Stills girls.

"Girls, you're going to be late," Sally said sharply.

"We just want to ask Vera and Clesta to spend the night with us, Mama."

Jas laughed and said to Stills, "Might as well let them. I'll drive them out in the morning."

"Thank you, Papa," Sarah said, and the four girls ran back to take their places for the play.

As they climbed the steps to the front door, Jas Porter stopped and looked at the cloudy sky. Big black clouds were rolling in from the west and a light mist filled the air.

"Looks like one stormy night ahead of us, folks."

CHAPTER FOUR

Three hours later the Porters and the two Stills girls returned home beneath the crackling of lightning and thunder. A light sprinkle of rain was coming down then, but a storm was sure to follow.

They went to bed much later than usual that night and sleep was postponed even longer by the four girls. Three times Sally had called to the girls to be quiet. For a brief moment the house would quiet. Then Sarah and Judy, who were in their own beds upstairs in the room with the boys, would call down stairs to the parlor where Clesta and Vera lay close together on the small bed in a corner of the room. They called nonsense things between them — silly things that they found hilarious at this late hour. The girls giggled and the boys complained.

On the fourth call it was Jas who told the girls to be quiet and within seconds the house became still. By midnight there were only the sounds of the rain, the grandfather clock in the living room and the breathing of eight sleeping bodies.

"Greed, brother! Yes! I say greed and money and lust are the roots of your evils. For every foul thing that happens in Twin Forks it is greed that caused it. Not your neighbors' greed and not the want of the people in the next county, although we often try to blame them for our troubles — it is you! It is your own want for power and money that brings Satan into your hearts. And for that — all hell comes down upon you . . ."

Frank Gardner did not know the visiting preacher at the pulpit. "Cleavers," he remembered Reverend Bush saying before the sermon when he introduced the little man.

He had hoped that this traveling evangelist would be better than the others. Cleavers had begun in a low, calm voice with the story of God resisting the temptation of the devil. He had told the familiar story well and Frank Gardner thought to himself that perhaps the small preacher would have something sensible to say.

Then all hell broke loose. The sound that came from out of Linous Cleavers shook the church steeple. He raved against the evil of human want. And, on cue, the boys with the collection plates entered the congregation. Each time a hand went into a pocket it was reminded of the devil's greed within us all and the hand went deeper.

When the collection plate reached Gardner, he stood, stepped into the aisle and stomped out of the church after fifteen minutes of the services. He could stand no more.

Outside it was raining. He wished he had been brought to the church in the carriage when he saw his wet horse patiently waiting for him at the post. The rain might let up, he thought, and looked back into the church. The visiting preacher was still ranting about the evils of wealth while the congregation sat frozen in their seats less they offend God by taking their eyes from the preacher. Stupid people, he thought. Ignorant, superstitious people. He would rather take the rain than listen to another word Cleavers had to say, so he tossed the raincoat over him and mounted the soggy saddle of his black mare and headed home indignantly.

His anger had not subsided when he reached the mansion. He left the mare tied to the front porch railing and stamped through the front door without noticing the strange buggy that had been left at the side of the mansion on the drive.

He tossed his dripping raincoat into the living room. John Goodell met him at the door.

"Mr. Gardner . . ." Goodell began.

"Damn those evangelists," Frank Gardner roared.

"Yes sir, but . . ."

"Mr. Goodell, if ever there was legislation needed in this county, it is on those damn two-bit evangelists. Fear and ignorance. They preach against it and all the time they use it."

"Mr. Gardner . . ."

"What? What is it you want?" Frank Gardner asked and slapped his hat onto the rack near the door.

Goodell jerked his thumb toward the staircase, "There is a man upstairs waiting for you. A big German. He said you wanted to see him tonight and asked him to come here. I didn't know anything about it, so I told him to wait in your study."

Frank Gardner looked up the stairs. In his anger he had forgotten that he had asked the supervisor of The Iowa Public Electric Service Company to meet him tonight. Now he remembered the big German and darted up the stairs toward his study.

"Klaus Hartmann," he yelled back to Goodell as he neared the first landing, "he's the man who wants to waste this town's money, Mr. Goodell. You better come along to be my witness — and maybe find out how a mayor earns his money for the town."

Gardner bounded up the remaining flights of stairs. He was delighted that Klaus Hartmann was waiting in his study. Now he would have someone to give his own fire and brimstone.

The men talked for three hours. At a quarter before midnight John Goodell's elbow slipped off the arm of his chair. As he straightened himself he realized that he had fallen asleep. The conversation between Gardner and Hartmann had begun loud enough, but it had fallen off to a quiet standoff with Gardner and Hartmann repeating their views over and over again. It was not a very interesting subject they talked about — the Electric Service wanted to bring their new light poles to Twin Forks; Frank Gardner would have nothing to do with them.

Their voices were loud again, however, and John Goodell found renewed interest in watching the two glare at each other. He watched Gardner with admiration. He felt he was getting to know Frank Gardner and sensed that Gardner was not so fiercely against the new light poles or their expense. For Gardner it was a matter of pride. He had said no — and no it would be. Even against the huge Klaus Hartmann, Frank Gardner was impressively formidable.

Neither Gardner nor Hartmann were going to budge. Gardner because he had made up his mind. Hartmann, because he had been given the duty of installing new light poles in the town of Twin Forks. That had been his orders. He intended to do his job. He did not have the authority to do otherwise.

The final conflict between these two men had to come. It was Hartmann who began the last quick trek to the point of no return:

"Look, Mr. Gardner, you asked me to come here tonight and I know you're the mayor of this town — but I got my job to do and by God I'm going to do it. You will have those new light poles."

Frank Gardner leaped to his feet, "That's right — do you hear that, John? New, expensive, unnecessary light poles."

Hartmann rose from his chair. He towered above Frank Gardner and Goodell thought briefly that it was appropriate that this man represented light poles. But Hartmann remained calm.

"In the long run, they will be cheaper. They put off better light than those hanging ones you now have that swing back and forth in the wind."

"Ha! I'll be damned if I'll let your company or anyone else push a two-thousand dollar swindle over on my town."

Hartmann responded in a pleasant tone, "Like I told you — I have been given the authority to put them in whether you like it or not. Those are our lines and we'll put them in as we want."

Frank Gardner would not calm. He walked to the study door and as he passed through it he yelled back to Hartmann,

"And I, Mr. Hartmann, have the authority to shut down the power. So put up your damn poles without my electricity and see what good it does you."

Hartmann was stymied. As he stood in the study pondering his problem, he heard Frank Gardner's steps racing down the flights of stairs. They stopped for a moment then the front door slammed. He looked dumbly to Goodell.

"He wouldn't . . ." Hartmann began.

Goodell shook his head with a weary smile, "You want to make a bet on that?"

Hartmann paused only a moment, then ran for the door.

Goodell sat in his chair. He was tired. He looked at the clock on the library table. It was five minutes past midnight.

"Well, what the hell," he said out loud and he too joined the race for the power station.

When Goodell ran from the mansion he saw Klaus Hartmann's buggy rounding the corner hazardously onto Third Street. Goodell started to run after them but before he reached Fourth Street the lights at the intersections flickered — then went black.

Goodell returned to the mansion laughing. "He did it. He really did it. That crusty old son-of-a-bitch really did it."

"Blessedness to you brother. Blessedness to you sister," he said as the congregation left the church.

Linous Cleavers beamed with happiness. It had been a success- ful night. He was exhausted. Tonight he had delivered one of those rare sermons in which he had soared to the heights of his frenzy. His imagination had risen to that point just out of grasp of reality — an euphoria where his mind, his entire body floated through space — and all the sickening, tragic parts of his life had left him.

Now he stood by the door watching the last of the congregation leave the church. His head was still dizzy from his experience. Close to God, he called it — that emotion he had had at the climax of his sermon. He glowed in numbness: a feeling he often had after performing one of his miracles.

Proof of his success lay in the hands of Reverend Bush. Money was piled high in the collection plates. Further proof lay on the Reverend's face as he grinned greedily,

"You did good work tonight, Reverend Cleavers," he said.

Cleavers noted an apologetic tone in Bush's voice, as if to say he was sorry for having doubted him. He decided not to mention it, but pardoned the reverend silently.

"It was God's work, Brother Bush. It was God's work tonight," he said meekly.

Reverend Bush was not moved by the statement. He turned to- ward the office and said merrily, "Well, God's hand certainly must have had something to do with it tonight. This is more money than we have ever collected." Then the reverend went into his office counting the money.

Two hours later Linous Cleavers was alone.

From the window of the second-story guest bedroom of the parsonage he watched the drizzling rain fall past the light over the wet street. A small gas lamp burned low beside the unrumpled bed behind him. The bed had not been slept in. An open Bible lay beside it. Cleavers stood by the window wrestling with his mind.

Gone was the satisfaction he had felt earlier. Gone was the comforting dizziness of his exhaustion. His mind teemed with anxiety. A painful expression contorted his face. He jerked away from the window to resist the overwhelming desire that had entered his tiny body.

Cleavers went to the bed where he leafed through page after page of the Bible to find some meaningful phrase or passage that would give him solace. There was no help there. He slammed the Bible back to the night table and jumped to his feet.

His need had to be fulfilled. The sensation that would drive the tingles up his spine to the back of his head demanded to be had. And as he pulled the black raincoat over his small shoulders he began already to feel better, for even his decision to search for a solution to his problem was partially satisfying to the evil strain that propelled him from within.

Linous Cleavers did not know the time when he left the parsonage. He knew it was late and that people of Twin Forks had gone to bed long ago. His chances of finding what he was looking for were very slim, he knew, but nothing could suppress the anxiety that was growing within him. He turned onto Third Street because if he had walked farther south he would have reached the Square where someone might have noticed him — and because he remembered the kindness of Sarah Porter who had been the first person to speak to him upon his arrival at Twin Forks.

Sarah Porter was fourteen years old, he estimated. Young, innocent and ripe. Soon some young man would come along and ruin her, Cleavers thought sorrowfully. God will have lost another sweet virgin. To look at her from a window — to see her and she not see him — to enjoy the innocence of the virgin undressing, uninhibited in the false security of thinking she was alone . . .

His pace quickened as he became more and more anxious to experience the thrill.

Cleavers reached the boulevard where Frank Gardner's mansion stood a block to the north. Ahead of him he saw Martha

Pinkerman's house and feared momentarily that he had made a mistake. But he continued walking and soon saw the small wood-frame home of the Porter family. He did not see a light at any of the windows, but he could see the house plainly by the glow of the street light at the intersection to the east. Usually he depended upon the inside light to help him — to assure him of seeing someone inside and of them not seeing him outside. He looked at the house concernedly, then smiled slyly. He was reminded of another night in Sioux City, Iowa, where he had been unsuccessful in finding someone and, like tonight, his urge had been driving him mad. In desperation he recalled having seen a woman entering her home near his hotel, so he went there that night. He crawled through an open window and crept into the bedroom. For over an hour he had stood over her watching her breasts rise and fall while she slept. He remembered that when his hand touched her breast she did not jump away but had smiled and breathed deeper.

Cleavers eyed the Porter home carefully. It seemed safe enough. Except for the overhead light at the intersection, everything was perfect. He crouched low to the ground and crept closer to the little house.

Suddenly, as if his worry had been heard, the light over the street went black. He waited until his eyes became more accustomed to the welcomed darkness then proceeded to the rear of the Porter home.

He approached the parlor window cautiously. He was within twenty feet of it when a strange light caught his eye. He stopped, frozen in his steps, until he was sure of what he had seen. The room was not dark. A light was on in the parlor and a black shade was pulled over the window for privacy. What he saw was a thin sliver of light escaping past one side of the shade. There was enough space there for him to see inside. Linous Cleavers smiled. How lucky could he be? He could not believe his good fortune. Then his terrible urge pushed him to the window and all other thoughts left him.

CHAPTER FIVE

June 10, 1912 — Monday. The discovery.

As on every Monday morning at nine o'clock, Doctor Pencraft was on his way to the train depot to pick up the newspaper out of Omaha. He walked with a rather sophisticated limp, which seemed to denote the kindness of the old gentleman, and even now his gold watch was snugged properly into place in his vest pocket and his white suit was well pressed, although it was a little faded. But even though his wardrobe was a sore spot in his own mind, no one could have known that he only owned two suits and he gave himself much credit for that accomplishment. As he walked he tipped his wide-brimmed hat to the ladies on the street and they returned his greeting with warm smiles.

"Good day, Mrs. Campbell," he said in passing.

"Good morning, Doctor Pencraft," she corrected him pleasantly and stopped to chat. "Is the rain gone for awhile, do you think, Doctor?"

"Rain?" he asked with surprise and looked to the sides of the freshly lain brick paving around the Square. "My word, it has rained, hasn't it?" he acknowledged. "I went to sleep early last night for a change — not much chance of that for me, you understand."

Mrs. Campbell laughed, "Oh Doctor, you should be in the restaurant business. Late to bed and early to rise — we don't miss much."

"So you saw the rain then, did you?" he asked.

"Saw it? Doctor we were caught out in it. Just after closing last night, around midnight, we were walking home and then the rain came."

Doctor Pencraft shook his head, "That is too bad. Did you find shelter?"

"No. We were halfway from the house and halfway from the restaurant. And to make matters worse, all the lights went out right at the same time," Mrs. Campbell moaned.

"The lights went out, you say. Why, that is too bad," Doctor Pencraft sympathized.

"Yes, we were walking down First Avenue towards home and . . . "

. . . But Doctor Pencraft was no longer listening to her. He was watching a young boy who had just run onto the Square and was looking frantically around at the people on the street. Then the boy stopped, caught sight of Doctor Pencraft and ran towards him shouting urgently,

"They say to come quick, Doctor!" the boy gasped when he reached him. "They got trouble. Bad trouble."

"Where boy? Who?" he asked.

"Up at the Jas Porter place." He clung to the doctor's shoulder while he caught his breath, "They got some kind of trouble. They told me to fetch you and Doc Ratcliff — and for me to fetch the Marshall, too."

Doctor Pencraft looked at the boy's face and saw the tears in his eyes, "All right, now. I'll go on up there and I'll pick up Doc Ratcliff on the way. You go ahead and fetch Sheriff Gustavson because the Marshall is out of town."

The boy went running off across the Square toward the sheriff's office and Doctor Pencraft started for Third Street.

"Should I go with you, Doctor?" Mrs. Campbell asked.

"No. No." he said, "It's probably nothing more than a broken arm or something of the like, Mrs. Campbell. You go on to your restaurant and I'll take care of my business."

It was times like this that he wondered if he should retire, but as he reached Third Street and was walking beneath the cool shade of the giant elms, he began to wonder just what emergency lie ahead of him. Sadness had not caused those tears.

By the time he left Doctor Ratcliff's house and was on his way to the end of Third Street where Jas Porter's house stood at the edge of town, he had decided that he knew what had caused those tears — it was fear. Honest, ignorant fear.

Doctor Pencraft and Doctor Ratcliff were met by Ed Borrows.

"We went in the house and Russ got scared and ran out. Me, too. And Russ has been over there vomiting." Borrows said.

Doctor Pencraft saw Russ Porter sitting beneath the huge elm in the front yard of his brother's house, a circle of vomit between his legs, and Mrs. Pinkerman was standing helplessly over him. He looked at the house. Closed doors. Windows pulled. Curtains drawn. And suffocating Iowa humidity left over from the rains Mrs. Campbell had told him about. Like Mrs. Pinkerman earlier, Doctor Pencraft knew that either the house was empty or they would find something terribly strange inside.

They waited for Sheriff Gustavson.

Why did this have to happen, Doctor Pencraft found himself wondering even before he had entered the house. He watched the dew rising from the bluffs above East Creek with the sun already high above them. Summer was officially upon them. Jas Porter's slack season was arriving after a successful spring at the Implement Store. School was out and the Porter children should have had a full three months of long warm days in which to play beneath the huge elm in their front yard. What could possible interrupt that now, he wondered. Then he looked regretfully down Third Street to see Sheriff Gustavson coming toward them in a buggy pulled by one sleepy mare.

Ten minutes later, after Sheriff Gustavson had talked with Mrs. Pinkerman and Russ Porter, and had walked around the house twice to find signs of forcible entry, but finding none; Doctor Pencraft, Doctor Ratcliff and Sheriff Gustavson entered the house.

He had anticipated the worst, Doctor Pencraft thought, but who could have imagined what he would find or the frightening effect it would have?

He reflected upon this later to detective John Morgan: "It happened here, in Twin Forks — just four years ago. Why was it so shocking? I have asked myself. And I guess that is why. It happened here, where everyone thought they were safe from these kinds of things. Why, that same year the White Star Titanic went down with all of those poor people on board. We thought it was sad — too bad — but it wasn't frightening. It didn't keep us from eating breakfast and the next morning it didn't make us go out and buy ten locks for every door in the house, as the Porter murders did. I guess that is it — here in our comfortable little homes, a family was murdered. Wiped out. Brutally. And there doesn't even seem to be a lesson to be learned unless it is don't trust anybody — and that's against nature, or maybe it isn't. I don't know anymore. I'm old and I'm glad I have retired since then."

They went through the front door off the porch. Doctor Pencraft went in first. As soon as he stepped into the living room, stale air inflamed his nostrils and he knew immediately that the smell was something more than that of a closed house. Carefully, they proceeded to the parlor door. But just as he was about to shove it open, Sheriff Gustavson tapped him on the shoulder and pointed to the windows of the living room. Squinting to help accustom his eyes to the darkness, Doctor Pencraft saw that in addition to black shades over the openings, articles of dark clothing had been spread over the sides. This puzzled him for a moment. Why would anyone go to such measures to keep the light out, he asked himself. But he recovered from his confusion with the uncomforting reality that this work had been done in the night and the articles of clothing had been a careful effort to keep light in.

There was no doubt now that what they were about to discover would not be good. How awful would it be, he wondered. Prolonging the agony of searching further, Doctor Pencraft stood at the center of the small living room thinking back to his past associations with the Porter family. He had delivered the four children and remembered how difficult childbirth had been for Sally Porter. She had suffered much to give Jas Porter their children. Sally was not a strong person and three years ago she had suddenly become very

weak. "The spirit's gone out of her!" he had said to Jas one night
after he had visited her. And he had admitted then that he did not
have the slightest idea what was wrong with her. For two years it
looked as if Sally was slowly dying. Then, less than a year ago the
illness began to leave her as mysteriously as it had entered her. The
last time he had seen Sally Porter was a month ago and she had
been in great spirits. She had even confided to him that she was
slyly working on Jas to buy a new house.

"Jesus Christ!" He heard Sheriff Gustavson gasp and rushed into
the parlor to find the men standing over a small bed in the north
corner.

There were two bodies in the parlor room. One was larger than
the other. Their heads gone — bits and pieces of bone and dried
blood and brain on white pillow cases. Doctor Ratcliff studied the
bodies beneath the blankets, then announced sadly, "Both girls, I'd
say."

Doctor Pencraft stepped nearer the bed. Whoever had murdered
the girls had then covered them completely with the bed sheets. The
smaller girl had been sleeping nearer the wall and still lay in a natural sleeping position with her hands folded across her stomach.
The larger body was farther down in the bed, as if she had seen the
murderer and had tried to squirm away. He looked at the place
where her head had been — a pile of pieces of skull, except for one
eye that had somehow missed being crushed. He shook his head in
disbelief.

Sheriff Gustavson tapped him on the shoulder and pointed to the
south wall of the parlor. There, standing on the floor with its head
resting in a pool of dried blood, was an old, battered, rusted and
now bloodied axe. It stood there innocently, foreboding of events to
come and, seemingly, to tell the story of what had taken place in
this house just eight or nine hours ago.

The boy who had run for their help had approached the porch.
Sheriff Gustavson called to him, "You stay out of here boy. Now go
get Doctor Stewart." Then he turned to the two doctors and explained, "Stewart is the County Coroner, so let him do this job!"

Upstairs the three men went together into the large, west bedroom. Nearest the door were two more girls. The boys lay in a double bed by the north window. Doctor Pencraft examined the boys
first. Their heads were smashed beyond recognition, but he had

known the two sons of Jas Porter and it was almost beyond comprehension that he now should see these battered young ones. The two girls puzzled him. He knew that the Porters had only two daughters, and if they now found Jas and Sally in the next bedroom, as he expected they would, they would have two female bodies unidentified.

"A madman," he heard Sheriff Gustavson whispering over and over again.

Doctor Pencraft took a last look around the children's bedroom. Here, too, the bodies had been covered with sheets and the window shades had been supported with additional clothing. Like downstairs, the four children still lay in natural sleeping positions, except for their crushed heads. There was no sign of struggle — not even awakeness, and if chloroform had been used, its smell would have remained in the closed house, yet he could not detect it.

They went on to the next bedroom.

Jas Porter was more brutally battered then the rest of the bodies. The murderer had not been satisfied to crush his head, but had continued with a series of blows to the chest with the blunt end of the axe until every bone of the upper torso had been smashed. Then, as if the murderer had suddenly tired before continuing with the children, he caught Sally Porter in the throat and once in the side of her face. Of the eight murdered, she was left most untouched. Her expression was one of peaceful slumber, reflecting her innocent beauty even after nine hours of death.

When they returned to the living room, Doctor Pencraft could hear many voices outside. He walked to the door where fifty or more people were standing in the street and in the yard yelling their demands for an explanation. They were about to leave the house when Doctor Ratcliff yelled from the parlor.

"Hey, come here," he said, "I got something queer here."

Pencraft and Gustavson rushed into the parlor to find Doctor Ratcliff looking at the bureau. They saw what had caused his concern: not only had the murderer covered the windows with extra clothing, but a large black skirt of Sally Porter's had been draped over the bureau mirror.

I'll check the other room," Sheriff Gustavson said. As the sheriff was on his way upstairs, Doctor Pencraft yelled, "Check the ceilings, too," Above him, in the parlor ceiling over the girls, ten wide

gashes had cut through the plaster each time the murderer had
raised the axe. The gashes confirmed that the girls had also been
murdered with the blunt end of the axe.

Sheriff Gustavson returned quickly, "Cuts in the ceilings — and
every mirror in the whole damn house is covered."

Doctor Pencraft went to check the rear door off the kitchen. It
was locked from the inside. The frightening thought began then that
the murderer had not entered forcibly, but had taken the key with
him as he left the house from the front door.

As he started back to the parlor, he stopped, called for the other
men. "Look at this," he said. "The murderer took time to wash before he left." All three men stared helplessly at a small basin in the
kitchen sink that was already becoming stained by the bloody water
it held.

With each discovery the story seemed to be pieced together. And
now the bloody wash basin put the murders in their proper, useless
perspective. The murderer had crushed the heads of eight victims
then stopped to wash his hands.

Voices came from the other rooms. Sheriff Gustavson rushed into
the living room to find twenty-five people milling about the staircase
and entry.

"You all get the hell out of here!" he shouted. "You're going to
mess up all the evidence and things." With the help of the two doctors, he managed to push the people out of the house at the same
time Doctor Stewart was trying to get in.

"Oh, sorry Doc. Come in." The sheriff pointed toward the parlor.
"There's two in there, and six upstairs." He turned and cried, "God,
I wish the Marshall was here." He stared at the crowd outside for
a moment and shrugged his shoulders, "Well, I'm going to call the
National Guard to come and help keep people out of this house."

"You better send to Leavenworth for a fingerprint expert, too,"
Doctor Ratcliff volunteered.

"Thanks, Doc," Gustavson said. "I'm going to send for Jim
Jacobs over at Nebraska City, too. We'll be needing his dogs before
too long."

When the sheriff had gone, Doctor Pencraft turned to Ratcliff, "I
suppose I had better tell Russ Porter all about this. I'm afraid what
he might do. I don't see a chance in hell of us finding out who did

this, but that isn't going to satisfy Russ or the people of this territory."

"It's too much," Doctor Stewart cried as he emerged from the house. He stood on the porch nervously pulling the lapels of his suit across his plump belly. "It's just too much," he said again. And without another word to anyone, he left the porch and hurried away to the mayor's mansion.

CHAPTER SIX

From his fourth-story window, Frank Gardner could see the Jas Porter house across the block southeast of the mansion. He could not see the house well, a tall board fence built to break the cold north winds of winter still stood between the mansion and the Porter home, but he could see the street and the people who had gathered there within the past hour.

He was amazed at how fast they had grouped and already he had begun to imagine their demands for more and better law enforcement. This concerned him. The general elections were just ninety days away. The nominations a few days ago had gone well. What he needed now was a quiet summer for the voters. If he could have that — just three months of peace — then he would be assured the election. But the three hundred people crowded around the Porter home would not remain calm, he feared. The three hundred could turn into three thousand. And if anything could take his election away from him, it would be an emotional issue such as this.

He turned from the window calmly, "They are all dead?" he asked.

"Murdered," Doctor Stewart said. "Everyone of them."

"A passing madman, I suppose."

The doctor nodded his head sadly, "More than likely."

Gardner looked down at the chubby doctor in front of him, "You found nothing to the contrary — nothing that would seem to tie it in locally?"

"Nothing at all, unless it would be how the murderer got into the house in the first place."

"What do you mean?" Gardner asked.

"There was no key in the lock from the inside when they opened the door. According to those who knew him, Jas was accustomed to leaving the key in so that another key could not be pushed through. But we found no key at all — and Sheriff Gustavson says he found no signs of forced entering."

"It was a passing madman," Gardner said, and Doctor Stewart looked up at his face to be certain if what he had heard was an order or just wishful thinking. It was an order.

"They will want an investigation, I am afraid," the doctor said.

Frank Gardner pounded a fist on the huge library table, "You are the County Coroner. Give them their investigation — give them your facts . . . eight crushed heads and the gory details. But give it to them tomorrow, do you understand? If you see anything strange but are not sure of, forget it — I want those people buried by Friday so the town can begin to forget as quickly as they can."

"But they were murdered!" Doctor Stewart protested.

"Yes. They were murdered. They were brutally murdered by a stranger — a madman. And now they should forget it. Tell me Doctor . . . is it for the good of the town that we arouse needless emotions about this — cause the people to wonder about their neighbors? Or is it for their good that we do what we can to get it over with — and go on with the business of building Twin Forks?"

The doctor squirmed under the pressure of the question. "I, I suppose . . . to get it over with, Mr. Gardner."

"That is right, Doctor," Frank Gardner said, then came around the table to him. "I will tell you something I have confided to no one, no one at all. And I must ask you to keep this to yourself after I tell you. Do you understand?"

The doctor nodded.

"Good. You see, ever since I came to Twin Forks I have seen great possibilities for our town. We have the railroad, the central location, a rich land surrounds us that is better than any in all of Iowa. We have grown to just over six thousand people now, did you know that?"

"No."

"What I have in mind for Twin Forks is to make it the new County Seat. Yes, we can do it — and within the next six or seven years. And do you know what that will mean, Doctor? That will mean Twin Forks will have a place in the future of our state — it will grow to larger proportions than anyone has ever imagined. We will have a place in history."

Doctor Stewart was staring at Frank Gardner in newly awakened foresight, "Do you really think so, Frank?"

"It is true. With a few good men, it must soon be so. And that is why this matter with the Porters must be handled cleanly and quickly. It is too bad, of course. It is awful! But we cannot let it defeat our purpose. We have a town to build, Doctor. We must bury our dead and get on with our job."

On Tuesday morning, Russ Porter drove his Auburn to the County Seat ten miles from Twin Forks. He drove through the middle of town without the normal stops one would make after a trip to the County Seat. And when it looked as if he would leave town from the opposite side of which he had come, he turned the Auburn into a long drive which brought him to the top of a big hill, and the County depot. Inside the train station he stopped at a small table and carefully lettered a telegram.

Why he did not send this telegram from the depot at Twin Forks he was not sure. He had talked with Doctor Stewart on Monday evening and had been told little of the details. The fingerprint expert from Leavenworth had found no usable prints — this was strange, Russ thought. If the murders had really been committed by a passing madman — if the murderer was mad, then would he be rational enough to conceal his fingerprints? And he had talked with the Sheriff who saw no place to turn in response to the overwhelming task that had been put before him.

But what bothered Russ Porter more than anything else were the rumors. According to the whisperings that had filtered back to him, whoever the murderer was, he was out to eliminate the entire Porter clan. Because the Porters were one of the "old families" and because they had much power and influence, it was not taken lightly when he heard that the Porter families had been marked for destruction. Last night, in the wake of terror that had stricken the family, Russ had brought the four families of the Iowa Porters onto his farm outside of Twin Forks. They would live there until the murderer was found, he had decided. The women and children would stay close to the house at all times and the men would take turns standing guard at night and during the day. Last night before bed the men went together around the house opening closet doors, checking under the beds and around the perimeter of the house.

No one in Twin Forks would help him find the murderer of his brother's family, but he could not take the chance that someone was bent on killing the rest of the Porters. Russ had influence in the community — he had wealth — and he was frightened. With or without the help of the sheriff or other locals, he would find the murderer and destroy him before the murderer destroyed the Porters.

He finished his message, read it over carefully and handed it to the man behind the counter window, "I would like to send this telegram to Kansas City. I want it to go direct," he said. "It's to the Burns Detective Agency."

At the same moment Russ Porter handed his message over to the telegraph operator, ten miles away Frank Gardner entered the Twin Forks city hall and delivered his own statement to the Coroner's Inquest and the audience of 200 people who packed the small brick building on the square.

"Thank you for setting this example for the rest of us by coming forward voluntarily," Doctor Stewart said after Frank had stated his name and position. "Can you just go ahead and tell us if you might have any information about this tragedy, Mister Mayor?"

"I'm afraid I don't. But I would like to report that this morning, in the early hours not long after midnight, I was awakened by my daughter's small dog barking at the front door. He had heard something on the front porch apparently. I opened the door, but no one was there."

"Is that all?" Doctor Stewart asked.

"Yes. I don't know if it was a prowler or the murderer, but I wanted to get my statement in the record for the convenience of this hearing. I have no other information." Frank Gardner marched off the platform to the side door, as Doctor Stewart turned to the court clerk they had borrowed from the County Seat for her legal shorthand skills.

"For the record, then." Stewart ordered as her pencil raced across the page. Frank Gardner had been witness number nine, and already the pile of shorthand pages beside the stenographer was reaching over a hundred. By the time they finished with the last witness six days later, the shorthand notes would exceed two thousand, and transcribed, they would grow to over eight thousand typewritten pages. Carefully studied, they were a remarkable recreation of the movements of almost every resident of Twin Forks over a three-day period . . .

. . . and somewhere in this mass collection of movements cross-referenced ten-fold, was the murderer. With each statement the doctor, news reporter, residents and spectators waited on edge for an inconsistency to develop. Or, for someone to slip.

The inconsistency was not long in coming.

It was no secret that Martha Pinkerman was the snoop of the neighborhood, and very little escaped her regardless of the time of day or night. For this reason she had been asked over and over again, "Are you positive you didn't see something strange over there last night?"

The questions were natural enough in the beginning, but by Tuesday morning they had become accusations. Are you protecting someone? Is there something wrong? Is there something the matter with your memory?

To make matters worse, Martha was breaking under the mental strain of the unwarranted guilt she felt, as well as the tragic loss of her neighbors.

And though theories of the psychological workings of the human mind were neither advanced nor prevalent at that time in Iowa rural communities, by Tuesday afternoon the dominate explanation for Martha's strange behavior was that she had had some kind of a memory lapse — and had somehow blocked out the happenings of Sunday night.

Against Doctor Stewart's orders, Martha insisted on testifying at the Inquest on Tuesday afternoon. This tore the crowd between listening to Martha or going to watch the imported bloodhounds attempt to trace the killer's escape route.

The room was packed when Martha took the stand to vindicate herself. An hour later, when she was finished, she realized that her appearance had only made matters worse. And for reasons she would keep to herself, she began to wonder if perhaps she really did know the killer's identity.

At three o'clock Tuesday afternoon, Martha Pinkerman walked feebly across the raised platform and sat weakly in the hard, straight-back witness chair. It was a hot, muggy afternoon without a breeze in the room. All that came through the windows was the deep, throaty echoes of the bloodhounds barking eagerly on the killer's trail.

After fifteen minutes of perfunctory questioning, Doctor Stewart decided it was time to attack the real area of concern.

"Mrs. Pinkerman, do you remember seeing any stranger in the neighborhood on Saturday or Sunday last?"

"No. No one."

"Do you recall seeing a rag picker on Saturday afternoon?"

"No."

"Do you recall seeing a paper cleaner on Sunday afternoon?"

"No. I told you — nobody at all."

Martha Pinkerman looked uneasily around at the crowd of old friends and neighbors who had suddenly begun to murmur and whisper to each other. Apparently she had contradicted previous testimony, she knew, but she also knew that she had not seen any strangers. My God, she thought, don't they think I'd say so if I did?!

Now Doctor Ratcliff took over for the panel of doctors.

"Martha, we have sworn testimony from twenty people who say that both of these strangers were in your area on Saturday and Sunday. And we have testimony from five people who saw you talk with both of these transients. Do you want to change your statement?"

"I — I didn't talk to nobody," Martha stammered.

"Is there a chance you just don't remember?" Doctor Ratcliff continued.

"I 'spose . . . No. I'd remember if I seen them. Somebody's . . ." she stopped in complete bewilderment.

Doctor Ratcliff took a drink of water, gazed at the crowd and turned back to the old woman.

"Martha, is there a chance you did see the murderer that night and now you're afraid to tell us?"

"No!" Martha yelled. "That's ridiculous! Why would . . ." Again she stopped in midsentence. Since yesterday morning when the questions began there was an image in her mind, the image of a man in wet clothes and an eerie, white face. And the man was staring at her. It was all as if in a dream. A nightmare. And now these people were part of the vague nightmare.

"Martha," Doctor Pencraft said tenderly, "you said that you went to bed when it got dark Sunday night. Did you go right to sleep?"

"Yes. I think so." Martha answered, relieved to give a simple answer to a simple question.

"And you slept straight through until morning?"

"Yes. No! I remember now . . . I got up sometime during the night to put the bedroom window down a ways."

"And then you went directly back to bed?"

The face! Is that when she saw the face? There was lightening. It was the lightening that had awakened her. She went to the window and pulled it down about a quarter of the way and as she was about to return to bed the lightening flashed again . . . there! There in the Porter's back yard a man was crouched beside the huge log that lay there . . . where Jas always used to break up cinder blocks with an old axe he kept there. It was the same axe they had found inside the house. The murder axe! But then the sky had gone black again and when the lightening flashed again there was no one there. She returned to bed and not until the questions began did the vague image of a face turned brilliant white in the lightening glare begin to pop back into her mind.

But was there really someone there, or was her imagination just playing tricks on her? Besides, if she told anyone about it they would ask who it was, what the face looked like, and she would have to tell them she didn't know. She would be under an even greater suspicion then she was now.

"Yes," Martha answered. "I went right back to bed and didn't rouse again until morning."

Martha's testimony raised more questions than it had answered. On Wednesday, Doctor Stewart told her to stay in bed and not to bother with the flood of reporters who wanted to talk to her. On Thursday, the nation's headlines were not hampered by the lack of substantial information.

IDENTITY OF KILLER MAY BE KNOWN SOON!!!

This small hamlet waits breathlessly for Martha Pinkerman, the woman who first sounded the alarm about the mass axe murders, to regain her senses and reveal what she knows about the happenings of that night. Apparently dumbfounded by the tragedy, it is believed . . .

CHAPTER SEVEN

June 12, 1912 — Wednesday.   New Mexico.

A dust cloud blew across the barren land and on the road, where the farmyard was marked by a broken gate, a lizard crawled slowly from one gate post to the other in search of insects that might lay in the next shadow. It was the third day after the murders and John Morgan had just found out about them. He was sitting on the front porch of his New Mexico two-room house listening to his friend, Al Crans, who had been trying for seven days to convince Morgan to move to Denver, Colorado. They had worked together for Burns Detective Agency in the past, but Al Crans had turned his resignation in and now encouraged Morgan to join him in a private detective agency of their own in Denver.

"You'll have to get out of Burns Agency before long, Morgan," Crans said again for the thirtieth time. "You can't get ahead working the cases they'll throw at you. Come on — come with me to Denver."

Morgan had been to Denver. It was his kind of country, he admitted. He looked around him at the low wood and adobe shack with a mud-brick fireplace. It was as stark and plain as the country that surrounded it, fitting the terrain as naturally as the lizard on the road.

"Bess would not want to go," he said of his wife.

"Is that a problem?" Crans asked honestly.

"No." Morgan admitted.

They were sitting on a wooden bench together saying much without speaking, as old friends do, but their appearances were in sharp contrast. Crans was a young man, short and stocky and his facial expressions seemed to reveal the higher education he had obtained. Morgan was long and gangly, his face was weathered and the tips of his thick moustache were bleached by the sun. He wore a bowler hat which matched his dusty black suit and vest and all of this rolled into one gave him the look of twenty years beyond his age, although he was just forty-three last spring.

On the clay step beside him lay a telegram from Burns Detective Agency with a folded newspaper. A thick banner headline across the top of the paper read, "Tragedy at Twin Forks — Heads of Eight Crushed." He picked up the telegram in his left hand and held the newspaper in the other.

"This Twin Forks case — it could get me somewhere — at Burns Agency's expense."

Crans shook his head, "They're all the same, Morgan. You work your ass off and the agency comes along to take all the publicity."

Morgan let his eyes roll across the flat land around him until he came to a strip of plowed ground to the west where his wife struggled in her garden. She'll never give it up, he thought to himself. For the rest of her life, she'll try to grow those things out of this dead ground. He tried to feel sorry for her, but she was so oblivious to her hardship that all he could find for her was pity — resentment for his years she had wasted on this broken land.

He turned to Crans, "I am not in the same position as you. You have had three successes in the past twenty months — a good record to take with you. In that same time, I have had three failures."

"None of those were your fault," Crans protested.

Morgan held a hand in the air, as if to surrender the argument, "I know. But the result is the same — three failures. I will not go into a business with you as a failure — someone to leach off you because you are a friend."

"Then you'll go to Twin Forks to work on this mass murder case?" Crans asked.

"Yes. I will leave on the train tonight and get there in time for the funeral on Friday. This Porter family believes that this wealthy man is behind the killings. If that's true, then it'll be national news."

Crans stood and kicked the dust, "How long do you think it will take you to settle that case?" he asked.

Morgan picked up the newspaper again and read it, as if it would give him the answer to his question. "I would estimate that six months should do it."

"Six months. Yes, that should do it," Crans agreed. "But what if you get into another problem — will it be another six months or a year before I hear from you?"

"Six months should do it," Morgan repeated.

But Crans would not give up. He grabbed Morgan by the shoulders and brought his face close, "Look Morgan — you and I are the perfect team. I have all the research ability — and you, why you have a nose for this kind of thing that a bloodhound would be proud of. I want you as my partner." Crans concluded, "I need you — and if we are friends, then I don't think you should turn me down to go chase around in Iowa just to solve a butchery case."

Morgan wished Crans hadn't brought their friendship into the matter. Crans was the only close friend he had and to turn that friendship into a weapon now was unjust.

"All right. I'll tell you what I'll do. I'll go to Twin Forks for six months. If I don't have anything on Gardner by then, I'll quit the case and Burns Agency and I'll be on the next train to Denver."

"That's a deal!" Crans said happily. He climbed onto the wagon he had come in a week ago, I'll see you in six months," he shouted as the horses jerked him forward.

Twenty minutes later John Morgan watched the horse and buggy carrying Al Crans disappear over the western horizon. He slowly climbed to his feet and walked to where his wife knelt in her garden. He said nothing and she did not know he was there, so he watched her dig. Her hands were as dry as the dirt clogs she was breaking between her fingers and her face was a dark red from many years of exposure to the wind and sun.

He sensed that she knew he was behind her. After a long silence, he said to her quietly,

"I have another case."

She stopped her work in the dirt momentarily, then continued clawing at the ground without comment.

A hot wind came again and with it the suffocating smell of dust. He pulled his bowler hat lower on his forehead and looked into the wind at the land where tornados of dust swirled through the brush. Saying more to the land than to his wife, he said,

"You'll not see me again. But we never did have much between us, did we Bess? If we did, it is all gone."

As John Morgan left the farm in New Mexico, he stopped at the gate for a last look at his wife; she was already back to work in her garden lurching forward and dragging the clogs toward her. If she was sorry to see him go, he could not tell it.

The wind blew harder and the lizard snapped up a bug, then lumbered beneath a stone in search of another morsel. No matter what Twin Forks is like, Morgan thought, it could not be any worse than this.

CHAPTER EIGHT

June 14, 1912 — Friday

Lona Gardner was in her bedroom watching the boulevard outside her father's mansion. She felt ashamed of her fear, yet she was afraid to leave the protection of her room. It was Friday, the day of the funeral. In two hours the Jas Porter family would be buried. And near them two little girls who had stayed the night with the Porter daughters would also be buried. She dreaded going to the funeral, but it was not the funeral itself she feared. She didn't know what it was that made her so afraid. She only knew that her hands shook uncontrollably and that she hadn't slept since Sunday morning.

Lona's nightmare of the past days had included more than the murder of the Jas Porter family.

Yesterday had been the worst: the weather had cooled and she was bringing some tea to her sister-in-law when she stopped to watch the neighbor boy playing on their front porch with her father's helper, Provo. Provo was the only black allowed to live in Twin Forks because her father had hired him in contradiction to the town ordinance against blacks. But Provo was mute and he was friendly and although the townspeople found his silence unnerving, they had come to accept him as "Mayor Gardner's mute nigger" and let it go at that. Lona felt sorry for Provo and was glad to watch the warm, silent companionship that had developed over the past two years between big Provo and the little boy.

But this day as she watched them, a crowd had gathered at the end of the boulevard near the cemetery and she heard it grow suddenly louder. She had stepped onto the porch to watch three hundred men march past the mansion. But they did not go past as she had expected. They had come into the front yard instead and stopped ten feet away from the porch. Some men she did not recognize were at the front of the mob with guns raised toward her.

"We want your nigger, Missy," One of them said. She looked at him without understanding why they wanted Provo.

"Provo?" she asked. "What on earth do you want with Provo?" She noticed the long rope one of the men carried and saw the hangman's noose that had been readied in advance.

"Miss Gardner," she heard a familiar voice say, "You best stay out of the way of these men. They mean business."

"No!" she screamed and ran down the steps to face them. "You all stay away from him. Leave my father's property now — this instant."

The men in front of the crowd were from out of town and paid no attention to her. They pushed her aside and grabbed Provo by the ankles before he could understand what had happened.

"No," Lona screamed again. A man tried to hold her back, but she scratched his face and eyes until he let her go. She ran to Provo and threw her arms tightly around his thick neck as the men dragged both her and Provo across the yard.

A gunshot sounded above the noise. And then another. The men stopped. The cheering crowd stilled. Lona looked up to the fourth-floor window of the mansion to see her father looking down upon them, a revolver in one hand and a huge law book he had been reading in the other. In his grey suit and thick moustache and trimmed beard, he looked like Moses coming down Mount Sinai with the Ten Commandments ready to punish his sinful children.

Frank Gardner sat in the window ledge and said calmly, "You have the wrong man, gentlemen."

Those of the crowd who knew him moved away quickly and the outsiders were in awe of the obedience the others paid the man in the window. They hesitated, talked briefly among themselves, then followed the rest of the men down the boulevard.

One of those who had lingered was not an outsider. He had started to leave, but now turned back to the mansion.

"Timmy," he said to the boy. "You come with me. Today, you're old enough to ride with a posse."

Timmy let go of Provo's arm to obey his father.

Lona watched him ride away with thirty men on horses toward the bluffs past East Creek.

That was yesterday. Lona shivered when she thought about it as she climbed the stairs to the only other room of the fourth floor, a small bedroom. Dorothy was faintly awake when Lona entered. She seemed worse today, Lona thought. The bruises on her face and arms were darker and her eyes were more hollow than before.

"Dorothy," she whispered, "would you like some tea today?"

Dorothy's eyes opened timidly, as if to answer yes, so Lona helped her sit more erect and placed a pillow behind her. Lona's mother came to the door.

"Poor dear," Mrs. Gardner said, "she hasn't said a word since her — her accident."

"Accident." Lona whispered. "Mother, how can you call this an accident?"

Mrs. Gardner shook her head wearily, "Well, what can you call it, then? I can't tell everybody my daughter-in-law was beaten half to death."

Lona joined her mother at the doorway. "You don't think Albert did this, do you Mother?" she asked.

"Albert? Lona, how dare you say such a thing about your brother."

"Then who, Mother? Don't we have to find out? Could it have been the same man who murdered the Porter family — the axe murderer?"

"There — you see? That's the reason your father wants no one to know about this. The first thing you know the whole country will be saying that the axe murderer tried to kill Dorothy, too."

"But Mother," Lona protested, "I found Dorothy beaten like this on Sunday morning — just a few hours before the Porters were murdered. Don't you find that strange?"

Mrs. Gardner threw up her hands, "That's just what your father doesn't want — all the people getting hysterical over speculation. Now, if anyone can find whoever beat Dorothy, your father can and it's not for you to worry about."

Lona grabbed her mother's arm and began to sob. "Mother, if anything else happens, I don't know what I'll do. I don't think I could stand it."

Frank Gardner was sitting at his table in the study when he heard Lona crying outside his door. He threw open the door.

"What's happening here?" he demanded.

"She's upset, that's all," Mrs. Gardner defended her. But Lona began to cry more violently. Frank Gardner slapped her firmly across the face.

"You will conduct yourself like a lady, do you hear me? Like a Gardner."

Lona ran to her room and closed the door behind her.

She did not wear her best dress today. Instead, Lona pulled a dark grey cotton dress over her head and let it hang loosely past her waist and thighs to her ankles. It was ugly and seemed to fit the mournful occasion that would take place in one hour. Her father and mother were not ready, so she stepped onto the shaded front porch to wait for them. Thousands of people crowded the boulevard while they awaited the funeral. She wondered why they waited here. The services were to be held at the town Square, five blocks away. Then they were to walk behind the coffins the ten blocks from the Square to the cemetery for the burials. Yet all these people milled around carts and horses or automobiles which lined the boulevard and every street in Twin Forks on both sides. She had heard that so many people had come in from out of town that pastures at the outskirts of town had been taken over to park their vehicles and horses.

She was standing on the porch watching a family walk down the street on their way to the Square when she heard a small voice crying from around the corner of the mansion. She went closer to the corner and again she heard the voice cry, "Go on — get away from me. You're no damn good. I never want to see you again." When she looked around the corner of the house she saw Timmy throwing stones at Provo who stood looking at the boy with huge tears in his eyes. Timmy ran to Lona crying as he clung to her legs.

Lona knelt and straightened him. "Say, what's the matter with you? Provo is your friend — why are you being so mean?"

The boy hugged her neck and cried, "He's a nigger. A no good nigger."

Lona wiped his eyes, "I thought he was your friend yesterday?"

The boy looked at her through red, watery eyes, "That was before," he said.

"Before? Before what?" Lona asked.

"Before I went with Papa and the posse."

Lona could hardly understand his words let alone his meaning. She asked, "What do you mean, the posse?"

"Papa took me along yesterday, I should have stayed."

Lona almost cried too now that the boy broke down again into another flood of tears, "Come on, now," she said, "It couldn't have been that bad. Tell me about it and I'll show you that we can straighten it out."

The boy sniffled and began hopefully: "We got on horses and rode east and then south to where the dogs had lost the killer's scent the day before. Another posse had gone north from there and another west — so we kept on going south down the valley. Pa said the murderer probably would try to follow the river so's not to get lost. We came up a hill and looked down to see this wagon and horse tied up in a grove of trees. We didn't see nothin' movin' so we all rode on down. When we got there this big darkie pokes his head out — and he was smilin' —" The boy began to sob again, but gained control of himself and continued. "But one of the men pulled him out of the wagon and two more men got a woman and a little pickaninny out of the back. Before I knew what was going on — I was standing there looking at the three of them hanging from a tree and wiggling all around trying to catch air. It was awful and I got sick, but Pa said they was only niggers and another one of the men turned me around and made me look and told me that was what was best for niggers. Then I came home." He hugged her again and cried until he could cry no more.

"You go home now," Lona said to him.

Seconds later she ran into her bedroom screaming and tugging at her hair with her fingers. She might have killed herself with the razor they found in her hands, but just as her mind would not allow her to understand or forget Dorothy's beating or the Porter murders or the little boy's story, it would not let her commit suicide now — and she fainted.

The funeral services were about to begin. There were few people at the train station to see Lona Gardner and her mother leave Twin Forks. Lona was unconscious when she left. Provo carried her onto the passenger car. She would not awake until the train was pulling into Chicago, a point where she would hesitate from going on to New York. To go there to stay with relatives was a way of hiding from reality, she knew. She would consider returning to Twin Forks, but New York was as far away from Twin Forks as she could imagine, and that was what she wanted more than anything else. If ever she saw Twin Forks again, it would be too soon.

Twenty thousand people crowded the Square. They filled the streets and walks and pressed beneath the shade of the giant elms until, either from emotion or the heat of the day, unconscious victims had to be carried away and lain on nearby lawns until they recuperated.

The murmur that had droned from the crowd all morning fell to sudden silence as the minister of the Lutheran church stepped onto the platform with the eight wooden coffins of the axe murder victims. The exasperating silence was prolonged when the minister stepped back down from the platform for a last-minute word with Mayor Frank Gardner, and it was magnified by the eerie cry of the train whistle which called from the distant bluffs and echoed down the Mo-Ri Valley to the twenty thousand. Finally the minister returned to the center of the platform.

"My Lord," he yelled at the top of his voice so that all could hear, "we are gathered here to commit to your hands the Porter family and the two little Stills girls . . ."

Frank Gardner only half listened as the minister reviewed the life of Jas Porter and each member of the family. He concentrated on the faces of the crowd, sadly aware that the three thousand frightened people he had feared earlier had grown to over twenty thousand. Still, his original hope remained — that the people would begin to forget when the bodies of the victims were buried. Their excitement would quickly subside and if no one rekindled the flames of fear and vengeance, he could carry on with his plan to build Twin Forks to a great Midwestern city. How could the deaths of eight people be compared with his dreams for thousands, he asked himself.

"Oh Lord, we have been robbed of our loved ones and neighbors!" the minister yelled hoarsely. "And there is not a clue to the identity of the fiend shaped like a man who performed this awful sin against your commands. But we know that soon the murderer will be revealed — that even now your instrument of justice is on its way to us and at last, in your name, murder will out."

John Morgan had arrived from New Mexico. He stood in the middle of the crowd listening to the minister. The words were spoken directly to him. He could feel them — as if the message came from God. He knew little of the case and even less of the people of Twin Forks. He had not spoken to anyone since his arrival four hours ago. Yet, there in the crowd, standing a full head taller than any of the people around him, John Morgan wanted to scream for all to hear. "Yes, I am here. I am here!"

CHAPTER NINE

The Kansas City "Star" and every newspaper large and small printed a lengthy account of the Porter/Stills mass funeral. The ink was not yet dry, however, before the drama continued. In Twin Forks, everyone made a mad rush to buy a copy of the daily "yellow sheet" which, in bold black letters, an ominous, one word headline screamed a new obstacle:

CURFEW
Mayor Frank F. Gardner and Sheriff Gustavson have announced a curfew beginning at eight o'clock tonight. Anyone found on the street within the city limits will be incarcerated at the local jail, fined $100.00, and held as a suspect in the axe murder case.

Mass confusion. Almost all of the thousands of outsiders had to leave, but very few were willing to travel the dark roads. The rush to leave town created a traffic jam never seen before in Iowa as families in wagons, buggies, on horseback and a few cars made their way to the fields outside Twin Forks. There they built huge bonfires to ward off the dark.

By nightfall Twin Forks looked as if it were a town under siege. The fires stretched from the marsh of the Mo-Ri bottomland in a half circle around the cemetery north of town to the East Creek bridge just one hundred yards away from the "murder house", as the Jas Porter home was now known by all the locals.

Detective John Morgan, a voluminous note taker, was impressed enough by the scene to enter in his log: Beat the curfew for first visit to the Russ Porter farm. From the bluffs Twin Forks looks like it's on fire. Reminds me of the battle towns along the Mexican border. The people are scared. The whole territory is scared. Everyone convinced the killer will strike again.

But no one was more frightened than the Porters. In this territory where family feuds are as common, senseless and brutal as the giant twister tornadoes, it was not surprising that Russ Porter heeded the rumor that the killer was someone on a vendetta to destroy "the whole Porter clan". Russ gathered all surviving members of the Porter families and sequestered them on his farm. Morgan had no trouble at all finding the place on the strange road. The farm yard "glowed like a barn burning". When he turned into the lane and approached the farm house, a large mound of hay, ominous in a black silhouette against the orange light of fifty lanterns, blocked the lane completely.

From somewhere behind the mound a sentry demanded, "Who goes there?" Morgan stated his name and the Burns Detective Agency, nervous that he would not be believed because he had no immediate way of proving his identity. But it must have been enough because the footsteps that had run away quickly returned. The voice shouted, "Hey — move!", and the sound of horse hooves and creaking harness was quickly followed by, first a sudden shudder of the hay, then the entire obstacle moved away.

Russ Porter met him in front of the farm house. He was, Morgan thought, a man beside himself with fear and frustration. His appearance was not unusual, but always a pitiful sight. How many times, Morgan thought, had he met men like Russ, strong and masculine and capable of facing almost anything, but who are suddenly withered by a hopeless battle against the unknown. It was in all their eyes; the brothers who stood guard at the perimeters, even the children who clung to their mother's dresses on the front porch.

Russ' handshake was strong and hopeful.

Now it was clear again. Albert had stormed out of the house, and she had gone to sleep. Then the bedroom door banged open and a man pounced on her, knees pinning her shoulders down, full weight on her chest and stomach, and blow after blow to her face as she tried in vain to ward off the fists with her own hands. But the fists just kept coming and coming.

Though it was not clear where she hurt the most and for what reason, the throb in her stomach was, she thought, from hunger. What day is it? The last she remembered was Saturday. Was this Sunday? Monday? Dorothy let her legs drop over the side of the bed and walked feebly across the room to the dressing table. The mirror was missing. All mirrors that had been in the room had been taken down and removed. One of Minnie's thoughtful touches. Or perhaps Lona's. Was her face really so horrible?

There were loud steps on the stairs. She turned expecting one of the women, so her surprise at meeting a strange man must have been obvious.

"She didn't know me at first. I had to explain that I was John Goodell, a distant relative, and new aide to her father-in-law. She seemed to recall that we had passed briefly at the party on Saturday night.

Even now Dorothy was beautiful. I told her she was lucky. Doctor Stewart had offered assurance that none of her wounds were permanent. They had passed from black and blue to yellow, and now they would begin to subside. No bone damage was evident."

Then a "terrible thing happened," as Goodell wrote in his diary. Dorothy complained of being hungry and hot and went to the window.

"Mr. Goodell, what are all of those fires doing out there? And I see people. Hundreds of people. Who are they? Why are they in the fields?"

Goodell hesitated. It crossed his mind that Dorothy might not be ready for the terrible news of the axe murders. But he told her. Perhaps he told her because "the murders were almost commonplace after five days", or because at that time he saw "nothing to indicate that Dorothy was particularly close to the Porter family."

"There was a terrible crime here Sunday night, Dorothy. Eight people were killed in their sleep by some madman with an axe."

Dorothy's shock was apparent. "That's horrible! And those people by the fires? They came for the funeral?"

"That's right. So many came that your father-in-law decided a nighttime curfew was necessary. The funeral was today, so the outsiders should start to leave in the morning."

Dorothy watched the fires. There must have been fifty of them lighting the sky, and hundreds of people crowded each circle. So many visitors to Twin Forks was difficult to comprehend.

"Who was killed?" she asked.

"The Jas Porter family and two Stills girls who were spending the night."

In the reflection of the window glass Dorothy witnessed the horror that spread over her bruised face. Horror of death . . . of hopelessness. She turned and pounced on Goodell unable to comprehend.

"All of them — dead?"

"Yes."

"The children? Sarah? Jas?"

"Yes."

"Jas — too?"

"Yes. All of them. And the Stills girls."

Dorothy fell sobbing onto the bed amidst Goodell's pleas of forgiveness for telling her of the murders at such a bad time. But Dorothy did not hear him. There was no doubt in her mind who the 'madman' was. She knew who was responsible for the deaths. It had to be Albert. And even more frightening, at the same moment, she realized that Albert would not have committed the murders himself. Somewhere out there was a hired killer settling Albert's affairs in a way only Albert could perpetrate. She could be on the agenda.

John Goodell was amazed when Dorothy suddenly regained her composure and demanded all the details. He told her all he could.

She listened intently "as if she were looking for something to key onto."

When Goodell finished, Dorothy lay back on the bed, her firm breasts protruding tantalizingly over the light nightgown borrowed from Lona's closet.

"And my loving husband — what has he been doing all of this time?"

Goodell noted the mockery in her tone, but wondered if she had not had enough misery for one evening.

"We haven't seen a great deal of Albert this week." he answered. "But, er, he's well."

"Who has he been sleeping with?"

The question was point blank, no emotion whatsoever. A lie would be pointless.

"He's been with Gertrude Micheles," Goodell stammered.

It did not surprise her, nor did it bother her a great deal. Her main concern now was to figure a way to escape from this misery. But only Frank Gardner's support would do that. He had created the monster, so it was his problem. But how would she convince him to give his unwilling support. She smiled. It was ironic. It was cruel and grotesque. But yes, she had a way.

"Can I get you anything?" Goodell asked.

"Yes. Tell Frank Gardner I want to see him. Then get me some soup, and tell Provo to come and I'll give him packing instructions."

"Are you going someplace?"

"I'm going to join Lona in New York."

"But Frank won't like that. Doc Stewart will never allow . . ."

Dorothy laughed hideously through swollen lips. "Just tell them. You'll see. By morning they'll be so glad to be rid of me that they'll carry me to the train if they have to."

"But . . ."

"Just tell them!"

On Saturday the daily "yellow sheet" was again a hot-selling item. There were three primary stories, and another small item that received little attention:

MARTHA PINKERMAN IN COMA

Possible Witness to Axe Murders May Be Investigators' Last Hope.

As was reported in this paper yesterday, Martha Pinkerman fainted during the mass funeral of the eight axe murder victims. Doctor Stewart announced this morning that she remains unconscious and may be in a coma. It is too early to determine the seriousness of her condition.

Speculation has arisen that Martha may have seen the killer on the night of the murders, but that the demonic knowledge was locked in her mind until that moment during the funeral when she fainted. This coincides with her faulty testimony to the Coroner's Inquest, when she failed to recall two strangers who are known to have been at her house on Saturday afternoon. They were a rag picker and a paper cleaner who had been questioned and released.

Another story hinted at a "Surprise Witness" scheduled to appear at the Coroner's Inquest on Monday, the final day of the testimonies. And another told of a new suspect — a man who had been found early Saturday morning floating naked in a row boat eight miles down stream from Twin Forks with blood-soaked clothes in his possession. This quickly proved to be another false lead, however: by noon the man was identified as a local farmer who had passed out on home brew while fishing. The blood was from that of a cow he had butchered. But the entire ordeal had been a sorry mess.

When the locals found the man they had immediately concluded that they had the murderer and, with total disrespect, had paraded him naked from the river through town to the local jail in front of hundreds of onlookers. They had been so certain: the blood-soaked clothes matched investigator's predictions that the killer must have been drenched in the blood of his victims; and the boat answered the question of why the bloodhounds had lost the killer's trail at the river bank on East Creek, near the mouth to the Mo-Ri. Only the farmer's wife saved him from hanging. He was released. But he swore never to show his face, or anything else, in town again.

There was another notice on the back page of the yellow sheet, hardly noticeable due to the other stories.

"Frank Gardner announced that his daughter-in-law, Dorothy, will be leaving for New York today. She will join Lona Gardner and they will stay with relatives until Dorothy is fully recuperated."

News of Dorothy's departure surprised no one. Wealthy folks can afford to avoid misery.

Sunday. The churches fill like they have never filled before. On the front lawn discussions center around Martha Pinkerman. She remains unconscious for the second full day. Rumor has now become "Fact." There is no doubt that when she awakens she will announce the name, or the description of the murderer.

Reverend Bush adds to the suspense — the misery. He announces he has discovered that investigators committed "an unholy act" with one of the dead girls' body. The crowd is shocked. They plead to know more, but Reverend Bush refuses. The facts will be brought out tomorrow at the final day of the Coroner's Inquest. He prays for the dead murder victims. He prays for those who committed the unholy act. He prays for Martha Pinkerman's life and the skill of Doctor Stewart to revive her so the killer can be revealed.

The daily yellow sheet announces a "surprise witness" will testify at tomorrow's inquest. This is met with apprehension. Surprise witnesses are plentiful.

News that Russ Porter has hired a Burns detective spreads through town in a matter of minutes. He is staying at the Widow Durham's farm a mile outside of town. The Widow Durham is young and attractive and the daughter-in-law of Sam Durham, influential politician from Kaoder, the County Seat. Jokes, rumors fly. The detective is no doubt "comforting" the widow. Isn't Sam Durham archrival of Frank Gardner?

Nightfall.

Sleeplessness. Most of the outsiders have left. The village is much more like it was just seven nights ago — except now all the doors and windows are locked, shades drawn, lights burning brightly. Remember seven nights ago when everything was so peaceful? Paradise lost.

Monday was another fine example of just how stinking hot and humid it can get in Iowa. Outside under the huge maple trees on the square the temperature was ninety degrees and humidity hung at eighty-five percent. The air was dead calm. "Tornado weather", some reminded. Across the street in the small brick building that served as Town Hall, meeting place, auditorium and winter quarters of the weekly quilting bee it was over one hundred degrees, and with the eighty or so odd bodies crammed into the audience, it may as well have been raining indoors.

John Goodell attended the finale of the Coroner's Inquest "as one of my immediate functions as aide" to Frank Gardner.

Across the room in a conspicuous bowler hat and black coat John Morgan watched the locals fill the hall. Hundreds of eyes fell on him and looked away shaking their heads pitifully or snickering at some inner joke. Some day, he thought, he would know the meaning of those looks. And he would change them to looks of respect once he handed them Frank Gardner's head. As professional as he wanted to be, he could not help hoping that the killer was Frank Gardner, as Russ Porter believed. Solving the famous axe murder would help his career. Proving that the killer was none other than Frank Gardner, mayor and future senator and wealthy patriarch, would immortalize him. Even the widow Lorraine Durham would have to eat her words, which had not thus far been kind. "I am letting you stay here as a favor to the Porters," she had said. "But I don't agree with this vendetta against the Gardners. And I don't agree with your investigation". When he asked if she did not want to see justice done, she answered with a mixture of her Boston education and Iowa analogy: "When my husband went to the Mexican border war, he carried a rifle. It shoots straight and clean. But I see you carry a double-barrelled shotgun. It's messy and hurts everyone within range. Your investigation will be like that. You'll hurt hundreds of innocent people before you are through." He regretted it immediately, but too late, when he pointed out that her husband had carried a gentleman's rifle into a war, and now the gentleman was dead. Had she argued, the remark might have passed, but tears filled her wide blue eyes, and she retreated upstairs to her bedroom before he could apologize. He lay in the parlor that night thinking that she was beautiful, educated and refined. During the day she had had her long, black hair piled atop her head, but at night in her nightgown, he saw that her hair was almost inky black as it encircled her soft white face in large graceful swirls to her shoulders. She was everything that the woman he had left in New Mexico was not. And, he thought, Lorraine Durham was correct: Before he was finished, many people would be hurt. That's the way it is. For a moment he wondered if she would be hurt, and he decided then that she would not. He would not allow it, somehow.

The Coroner's Inquest began with a statement by Doctor Stewart on the condition of Martha Pinkerman:

> Martha has been unconscious for the third day. I have managed to get liquids down her, but no solid food. It's my guess that she'll come out of it, but if she doesn't, I figure I'll have to resort to feeding her through the veins startin' about one week from today.

Doctor Stewart returned to his chair behind the examiner's table ignoring the murmur of the crowd. Feeding through the veins. They all knew that meant a high possibility of infection almost always followed by agonizing death. The procedure would not be perfected for many years. For the informal record, two more witnesses were asked to repeat rumors they had heard over the weekend implicating Martha as an eyewitness to the murders.

That out of the way, Doctor Stewart introduced Lyle Svensen, the surprise witness. State your name. Lyle Svensen. What's your occupation? I'm foreman of a railroad gang. We repair the tracks between Chicago and Omaha. Where were you working one week ago today, the morning this town discovered the mass murders? About nine miles east of here near Tillbury, Iowa. Go ahead and tell the committee why you're here and what you know that might have something to do with this investigation.

Lyle Svensen was an imposing figure. He was not tall, but he was broad as a barn and the huge hands he nervously rubbed were thick and rough, hands that have swung many a pick axe and could handle the swarthy crew that ordinarily comprised a rail gang. Now

nervous as a schoolboy, he paused to recall the speech he had practiced all weekend.

"Well sir . . . it rained some at dawn that day so I let my crew
sleep in. I was up before most of 'em trying to help Cook start a fire
for breakfast. The wood was wet, en such. Well sir . . . I look up
and sees this man from outta nowhere come walkin' outta the
weeds. He's a spooky lookin' fella. Head's almost like its been
shaved and just growin' back. A tall, skinny lookin' fella. And he's
got this big white scar runnin' from his left ear about down to the
corner of his mouth. The scar is really noticeable 'cause he's been
in the weather for some time and his face is all beet red, except for
this scar. It's white and shines on his face like a piece of chalk."

"I could tell he'd spent the night in the weeds by the way he was
soaked clean through all the way up to his shoulders. He asked if
he mightn't have a job. I told him he wouldn't get paid until we
reached Tillbury on Friday and he said that was fine."

"I told him if he could swing an axe he could split the old ties for
the other crew to replace."

"What's that? No. You don't ask for names on rail gangs. Never
get the right one anyway. But his shirt was torn at the shoulder and
a tattoo showed. It said 'Blacky' in small bluish letters, and I asked
if Blacky was his name and he said it was."

". . . He was a good worker, but he never had anything to do with
the rest of the crew. He only talked to me. The rest of the time he
stayed by himself, and he always kept the axe I gived him close by,
like it was his best friend."

"It was Tuesday morning before we heard about the murders.
One of the mail people on a passing train tossed us a newspaper.
I read the stories about the murders out loud to the men, 'cause
most of 'em can't read. They weren't all that interested or surprised.
Most of 'em have had a hard life, seen a lot of death. But Blacky
was real interested. He'd look at the paper awhile, then asked me
if I wouldn't read this or that part to him again."

"I didn't think much about it until Friday when we reached Tillbury. We got there about the time the train came in, so I was gettin'
back to the men with their pay. By the time I got back the train was
pullin' out headed east to Chicago. The men told me Blacky was on
it. He didn't even wait for a full week's pay. That's when I thought
you people oughta hear about Blacky. And that's all I know."

Doctor Stewart asked for clarification on a few points, then dismissed the witness. The audience, noticeably disappointed in the "surprise" witness' testimony was anxious to release its frustration on the nearest target, which Reverend Bush had already provided them from his pulpit the day before. Years later Sheriff Gustavson would tell a reporter, "The time of the axe murder investigation were the worst years of my life. But that time I spent on the witness stand as the last witness, that was terrible. I looked out at all those people, most of 'em old friends, and saw they was ready to hang me."

(Doctor Stewart): "You've been sworn in before so let's just say you are still under oath, Sheriff."

(Sheriff Gustavson) "Okay, Doc."

(Doctor Stewart) "There have been statements made implicating you and others in . . . ah . . . in tampering with the body of Clesta Stills on last Wednesday night. Can you explain or shed some light on this?"

(Sheriff Gustavson) "Doctor Pencraft and me, in the company of a photographer from Omaha, conducted a scientific experiment on Wednesday night."

(Doctor Stewart) "Using Clesta Still's dead body?"

(Sheriff Gustavson) "Yes, sir. I should say, a part of her body."

(Doctor Stewart) "Which part?"

(Sheriff Gustavson, after a long pause) "Her eyeball."

(Doctor Stewart) "Tell us the purpose of this experiment and how it was conducted."

(Sheriff Gustavson) "There's a new crime theory that the last thing a person sees before death — or the image of it — is forever engraved on the pupil of the eye. Theory has it that a picture of the eye, enlarged many times, can show what the dead person saw."

(Doctor Stewart) "Has this theory been proven?"

(Sheriff Gustavson) "No. But we thought it was worth a try since nothing else was working."

(Doctor Stewart) "Go on, please."

(Sheriff Gustavson) "From everything we can tell, Clesta was the only person to actually see the killer. We figure she was the first victim and since she was squirmed down in the bed and died with her eyes wide open . . . anyway . . . we took a picture of her eyeball and enlarged it."

(Doctor Stewart) "How did you position the body in order to take the picture?"

(Sheriff Gustavson) "We placed the eyeball on a white linen and took the picture that way."

(Doctor Stewart) "You plucked her eye out?"

The crowd grew louder as the testimony continued. All week long they had waited for the investigators to produce some shred of evidence, some solid lead to the killer. But there were no leads. These bumbling idiots were useless. And now this. To the last question Sheriff Gustavson answered, no, the experiment was not successful. This was the final straw. Ugly jeers and threats from the audience reached a new height, led by the Reverend Bush, who screamed at the helpless Sheriff.

"Desecration! God will punish you for the unholy act! The dead are God's children!"

Twelve thirty, June 10, 1912.

The grandmother's clock in the front parlor chimed the half hour after midnight. The closet door clicked open and the intruder stepped out of the dark hold surprised to find the house also in total darkness and silence. The street lights were out. Drops of rain fell heavy from the leaves of the giant elm onto swollen wood shingles.

He remembered that the gas lamp was at the bottom of the stairs, but he did not dare light it, nor could he grope around in the dark. He slipped the downstairs windows shut, locked them, pulled and tied the black shades.

Clesta Stills rolled in her sleep. He froze. When she lay silent he took care of both windows in the parlor. Only then did he dare light the gas lamp; a three foot high brass floor lamp. The light was brighter than he thought it would be, so he returned to the windows and covered the sides of the shades with the dark coats and costumes the children had worn to the play. Then he disrobed and returned to the closet to retrieve the axe he had found in Jas Porter's back yard. The axe was dull and rusted and nicked from years of chipping cinder blocks.

As he positioned the lamp near the parlor door so that it indirectly illuminated the room, he saw himself in the front parlor mirror. Bad luck to see yourself naked in a mirror, he remembered, and the reflection

*made the light brighter. He tossed one of Jas Porter's shirts over the
mirror and tiptoed into the parlor.*

*Vera Stills slept nearest the wall lying on her stomach. Clesta, older
of the two Stills children, lay on her back.*

*The intruder raised the axe, his shadow enlarged on the wall. To his
surprise, the axe blade cut into the plaster ceiling half way through his
back swing.*

*Clesta's eyes flew open. She saw the naked man and squirmed down
trying to hide under the protection of the clean, white sheets. She opened
her mouth to scream . . .*

"No," Morgan said. "Dammit, this is too hard to believe."

Sheriff Gustavson looked around the room.

"Seems plain enough to me."

Morgan shook his head. "Why would a man sit quietly in a closet
for at least five hours waiting for the household to go to sleep
. . . then come charging out of a closet wielding an axe? Why
didn't someone wake up screaming when they heard the commotion?"

Gustavson shrugged. "I got the same questions."

"Could they have been drugged?"

"The doctors say 'no'. And there was no such smell in the house
when we opened the door."

This was consistent with Gustavson's statements to the newspapers. Morgan stepped into the front parlor, three feet from the closet
door and three feet from the parlor door.

"Right here, Sheriff. This is where something went wrong. Over
there in the closet we have a cool customer waiting to kill. Over
there, we have a man raging around the house with an axe. What
happened?"

"Maybe he just went berserk," the sheriff volunteered.

"I don't think so. Remember, he did bring the axe into the house
with him, and after he finished he stopped in the kitchen to wash
his hands. It's almost as if there were two killers; a professional
waited in the closet while a madman went loose out here."

Sheriff Gustavson stared into the parlor as if he expected an answer to Morgan's questions. Then he shivered.

"Come on, Morgan. This place gives me the creeps."

"You promised to show me the trail the bloodhounds picked up," Morgan reminded him.

"Yeah. I'll show you. But let's get the hell out of here. I knew these people and it makes me sick just to walk by the place."

They went out to the front lawn. Gustavson lit a cigar under the huge elm tree. Morgan filled his pipe.

"It was amazing to see them dogs pick up a scent," Gustavson recalled. "We let 'em sniff the closet where the killer sat, and then we just turned 'em loose. They went runnin' 'round the house for awhile. Then they shot out the front door completely ignoring the crowd."

The dogs followed the trail to the north end of the block and turned east. At the intersection, they crossed into Frank Gardner's lawn, jumped onto the porch at the mansion's front door, then followed the trail east again.

"Did you question the mayor about the killer being on his front porch?" Morgan asked.

"Gustavson shook his head. "Didn't have to. Gardner testified a whole day before the dogs arrived. Said on the night of the murders his daughter's dog woke him up 'cause someone was at the front door. When he opened the door, no one was there."

The dogs continued east to three blocks past the square, then headed south to East Creek where they lost the trail about fifty yards from the Mo-Ri river.

As Morgan looked at the dried mud cast of the 'lone footprint' of the killer on the bank of East Creek, he knew he had to find a way to convince himself, if no one else, that Frank Gardner was responsible for the killings.

That night in Lorraine Durham's kitchen, she correctly presented the other reason why undoubted proof was necessary.

"You have seen how Russ Porter and the other farmers despise Frank Gardner. But do you realize how easily they might hang him for something he didn't do?"

Morgan protested. "Hey. Frank Gardner's the king around here. He ought to be able to protect himself if he's innocent."

"But that's the point." Lorraine said. "He is the king. And people resent him for it. He's wealthy, but not one of the old 'families'. People would love to bring him down a notch or two. But he could get hanged before they realize what they did."

Morgan and Lorraine stepped out onto the porch. The farm had the look of what it was — a once impressive farm now in disrepair because the junior Durham was dead and it was kept by a widow and temporary hired hand.

"I'll fix this place up a little from time to time if you want me to," Morgan offered.

Lorraine smiled. "I'd like that."

They shared the silence of the country. Down the valley they could see Twin Forks and from here it was easy to see how the original discovery had given it its name.

Morgan turned to Lorraine. "Look. I don't want to hang an innocent man. By the time I've made up my mind to go after him, I'll know he's guilty."

Lorraine took his arm. "I know. That's all I'm asking."

Morgan decided not to react to Lorraine's touch, a mixture of not wanting to spoil the moment and not knowing what to do with a woman of respect. He wondered if her reaction would be the same next week after she discovered that he had already worked out a plan to trick Gardner.

CHAPTER 10

Among other things John Goodell introduced as aide to Frank Gardner, was a daily appointment journal. Like his diary, its entries were meticulous, tiny letterings fit for a typesetter's metal plate.

It was June 27, at six o'clock in the evening, when he admitted Benjamin Harbin and led the way to Frank Gardner's study. He had handled many appointments for the Senate-nominee, but this was the first to really surprise him. Harbin was a newspaper reporter for the Omaha "Bee", and Frank Gardner clearly disliked reporters, particularly Harbin who was most inclined to fill his stories about the axe murders with gossip and horrific detail. Goodell had hoped to witness the meeting, but this had already been denied him. Gardner instructed him to leave the room once the guest was announced.

Frank Gardner welcomed Benjamin Harbin with the same enthusiasm that a farmer welcomes hail. Goodell was only half right. He did not merely dislike Harbin, he despised and loathed this weasel-faced little man who had so successfully made Twin Forks sound like a den of hell with evil lurking at every turn.

"I'm a busy man, Mr. Harbin. You said you had something important to tell me. I suggest you say it and get out."

Harbin took a chair in front of Gardner's library table and looked around the study with measured envy. "Nice place, Senator. I can call you Senator, can't I? I mean, it is in the bucket, isn't it?"

Gardner sensed, but could not imagine what, a lead up to blackmail. The thought of it from this individual enraged him.

"I suggest you either get to the point or get out, Mr. Harbin. What do you have to tell me?"

Harbin grinned. "I've heard you get a real temper, Senator, especially against us poor reporters. But, like I said when I called, I don't have something to tell you — I have something to give you."

For the first time Frank noticed that the reporter had carried with him a cloth sack in addition to a brief case, which he now held nervously in both hands.

"You see, Senator, a reporter gets a lot of attention. Lots of people come to me with, shall we say 'evidence', that they don't give to the sheriff. I mean sometimes it's downright embarrassing.

Frank settled back in his chair. "If you are holding evidence, then give it to the investigators."

"Oh, I don't want the sheriff to see this," Harbin said as he stuck one hand in the sack. "It's just circumstantial evidence and, as far as I can see, would just cause a lot of needless trouble for an important man like yourself."

"I can handle trouble," Frank shouted.

Harbin grinned. "Not this kind. I mean, there's plenty of people out there just itchin' to prove that Frank Gardner is a mass murderer. And you don't want them to have these." With the timing of a magician, Harbin pulled a handful of clothes out of the sack.

"Old clothes, Senator."

"This is getting tiresome, Mr. Harbin I sugges . . ."

"Excuse me, Senator, but these clothes got your name on them."

"I put my name on all my clothes."

"And do you drench all your clothes in blood? Here, take a look at this shirt. See how it's been splattered. That's blood, Senator."

Frank flipped the shirt that Harbin had tossed on his desk. He tried to pretend he was unconcerned, but the stain did look like blood. The pants in Harbin's hands were also splattered. Frank had but one thought — Albert. What had Albert done?

"Who's blood is it?" he asked.

Harbin shrugged. "A bloody set of clothes all stashed away," he paused, "in a secret place? I'd say it was Porter blood. At least, that's what everyone else will say."

Gardner's blood boiled. "You could never prove that!"

"I don't want to, Senator."

"What do you want, Mr. Harbin?"

Harbin relaxed. "I've spent a lot of money down here on this story. All I want is $500 for my trouble. Heck, Senator, you think I'd be askin' if I really thought you were the killer? Five hundred dollars and the clothes are yours. You save a lot of embarrassing questions, and I get some of my money back."

Frank stood and went to the door and shouted for John Goodell. "Pay this man five hundred dollars, then throw him out!"

Less than an hour had passed before Benjamin Harbin returned to the rendezvous spot at the stable.

"He paid me the five hundred, almost without question," Harbin announced.

Morgan saw the money in the reporter's hand with a strange sense of disappointment.

"There ain't no question now," Russ Porter growled. "Frank Gardner is the killer. I'm callin' the family together."

Morgan handed Harbin a blank piece of paper and another two hundred dollars. "Write down what happened. Date it and sign it."

He turned to Russ. "Now listen, Russ. This may convince you and me that Gardner's guilty, but a court will never convict him of murder. So let's not ruin our lead by getting ourselves into a murder trial we can never win. Remember, a man can only be tried once for the same crime."

"So what do you plan to do?" Russ asked.

Morgan knew exactly what he had to do. First he needed a copy of the Coroner's Inquest testimonies. In those statements the movements of over a thousand people over a three-day period were chronicled. Hundreds of people had heard the testimonies, and hundreds of thousands had read details in the newspapers. But they had been searching for a stranger, "a passing madman". Only he would be looking for incidents that tied Frank Gardner to the crime. He needed to study those papers, then he had to learn all there was to know about Frank Gardner. It would not be easy to prove that one of the most prominent men in Iowa was capable of mass murder.

Frank Gardner slammed the flat of his hand down on the library table as he rose from his chair.

"You're sorry? Sorry! I've just been blackmailed out of five hundred dollars to avoid the embarrassment of being questioned about blood-stained clothes — with my name on them — and you're sorry? How do I explain that my son likes to wear my old clothes? What if they arrest you as a murder suspect? You're so damned idiotic you'd probably end up in jail — or dead. Is that what's going to happen to my legacy? It goes to a bumbling fool like you?"

Albert Gardner gripped the arm of the chair and, for the first time in his life, welcomed the onslaught of insults that came from his father's mouth. I knew you'd react this way, you old fool. I even counted on it. Whether you know it or not, I am in control here.

"Can you say anything that gives hope you are sane, Albert?"

"I told you, it was a fight. I got all bloody and I threw the clothes away. I knew you'd be angry. They were old clothes so I tossed them out."

"Are you involved with the axe murders in any way?"

"Good Jesus, no. Burt McLean and I were at my place most of the night. You can ask him."

"A lot of good that would do. Are you sure you know nothing about the murders?"

"Nothing."

"Tell me now because if it comes out later, I won't disgrace the family trying to protect you. Can you account for yourself at the time of the murders?"

Albert answered calmly. "I was home. Burt was with me until two in the morning. I asked him to pick me up in his Auburn early in the morning. He drove me out to Crescent to sell some wagons." Albert rose from the chair and walked to the balcony. He placed his hands on the door frame.

"I was going to change. I was going to try to help you with the farm implement business. Burt was going to help me. He kept his Auburn out of the garage all night so he could drive me out to make some calls."

Frank Gardner looked skeptically at his son. "What brought on the sudden burst of industriousness?"

Albert paused before answering. He had to do this correctly. This was the moment he had practiced for the past four weeks. The moment when his future hung like a pendulum waiting to swing this way or that. It had to be convincing.

"It wasn't sudden, Father. I know you can't understand it because you've been your own man since you were ten years old. But for me . . . I've been thinking it's about time I got around to being . . . to being a man. Believe it or not, I've been tryin'. It just never seemed to work out the right way."

"Working a half day doesn't make you a man, Albert," Frank said. But his tone was different, and this was not lost on Albert.

"I know. I know. Let me tell this my way. A couple of months ago I decided I'd change. And I was changing. Then Alice Gast told me she was pregnant, and, well, it seemed to ruin everything. It was like the past was coming up and tellin' me I couldn't change even if I wanted to. There I was, crawling to you and Doc Stewart for help again."

"So you gave up?"

"Yes. For awhile I gave up. Then I had a fight with Dorothy, and the next day I found out that somebody'd beat her up. That did something to me. In a way it made me realize that Dorothy was weak and I was supposed to be the strong one. I started thinking that maybe Dorothy would be my wife again if I acted like a husband. So I decided to start by getting serious about the implement business. I thought if I proved I was serious, you'd eventually let me learn about the banking business, too. And then, when you got busy with your politics I could help by handling things around here."

Frank spoke stiffly, uncomfortably, wanting to believe Albert but guarding against disappointment.

"So what happened?"

Albert turned away from the balcony and sat again in the chair across the desk from his father and looked him in the eye.

"Nothing seemed right again. I'd made up my mind to work in the business . . . then found out Dorothy was in a coma . . . the axe murders ended all business thinking around the county and, well, you know where I've been."

Frank's face reddened. Yes, he knew what Albert had been doing since the Monday night after the murders. Both Burt McLean and John Goodell had kept watch on him and reported daily. He had spent most of his time, day and night, with Gertrude Micheles, and the rest of his time drinking in one of the rooms above McLean's saloon. Now Albert wanted him to believe he was reformed.

"You must learn to consider the consequences of your actions, Albert. You've lost your wife for at least a few weeks. Your reputation in the community is terrible, to put it mildly. And now, this Micheles woman will have to be dealt with."

"What do you mean; dealt with?"

"She'll have to leave the community. I'll arrange it with the schoolboard."

Albert shrugged. "I'm willing to do anything, Father. I really want to be a son you'll be proud of."

Frank walked around the table and placed a hand on his son's shoulder.

"I know you're of good Gardner stock, Albert. There's nothing I want more than to see you by my side. I've brought the Gardner name up from nothing, and I don't want to see it end with my death. But you'll be tested. This won't be easy. Starting tomorrow you'll move in here and go to work — and we'll see what comes of it."

Albert Gardner left the mansion and walked down the boulevard with a determined, bold step. Never had he felt so powerful. As he looked around at Twin Forks, he realized that a crucial part of his plan had just been pulled off successfully and he enjoyed his private secret that all of this he had once viewed as his father's kingdom was now his domain.

When he reached Third Street he stopped and looked at the Porter house. It was dark and desolate. Next door a light shone from Martha Pinkerman's bedroom window. He could envision the old woman lying there motionless, Amos beside the bed praying for her recovery, and Doctor Stewart laboring to revive her so she could identify the killer, if, indeed, she had seen the killer that night.

There was still a great deal to do.

It was two-thirty in the morning when the telephone awoke him. As Doctor Stewart stumbled to the kitchen, fumbling for his glasses, he recalled from a newspaper article that Bell was working on a refinement to his invention: a private line for households. There were nights he wished he could let the box on the wall ring. But if he did that now, everyone on the line would know it was his ring and they would soon be pounding on the door to see why he didn't answer. God speed Graham Bell, he thought as he took the listener from its cradle.

"Hello! What's wrong?" he shouted. At this hour of the night it had better be something serious. He couldn't think of any patients who might be having problems. No pregnancies. An accident, perhaps. Or Martha. Could Martha Pinkerman have taken a turn for the worse.

There was a long pause; the accepted practice to give all the curious neighbors a chance to get off the line. A number of loud and angry clicks sounded on the line, even at this hour, until the hollow sound which warned that someone was listening finally stopped.

"Doc?"

"Yes. Yes what is it?"

"It's Albert. I need to see you."

"Are you hurt?"

"No, nothing serious. I just need to see you right away. It's — it's about father. Can I come over now?"

No you can't come over now. That's what he should have said. Surely at two-thirty in the morning Albert was up to no good. It's about father. And there was no question. Of course he agreed to see Albert.

Doctor Stewart pulled on his robe and returned to the kitchen to put on a pot of coffee. Albert was usually in need of a great deal of coffee any time after dark. But as he watched the pot come to a boil, he wondered why he had agreed to see Albert. Yes, because of Frank, but it was also because of something in Albert's voice. It was different somehow. The voice on the line was not that of insecure, brooding Albert. It had been a man's voice: a calm, forceful, commanding voice that was in control of things.

It was one of life's great ironies that Albert's birth had brought Stewart together with Frank Gardner. Since then he had blessed the day he had met the Gardners, with the exception of Albert. He loved Frank and believed that he was one of the best things ever to happen to Twin Forks, Iowa, and maybe the entire country. There was no doubt in his mind that Frank would not only be mayor and senator, but governor as well, And then — the presidency was entirely possible and, if not, it would be the nation's loss. Mrs. Gardner, even in ill health, was a tiny, charming woman who always made an old bachelor doctor feel welcome in her home. And beneath Lona's plain exterior, he saw something of her father in her, a hidden strength suppressed in the shadow even Frank could not identify. But on Albert, he had given up all hope.

On the first night, when the young doctor and the young schoolteacher met, Frank had stopped him at the gate to their small country house: "you can't come in here until we've agreed on some rules, Doctor. She's having a hard time of it. She's so small. But I want you to state here and now, if there's a choice, you'll save the mother and let the baby die."

Those words were spoken in a commanding tone, a ship's skipper to the crew, but in the eyes was a pleading, helpless stare that had forced him to agree to everything that was against his code and moral custom. Albert's birth had nearly killed his mother, but he had been spared the dreadful decision. Now he wondered if he had acted correctly. Albert was alive and useless. His mother never fully recovered, physically or mentally. She was continually weak and sickly, and her mind ebbed into long spells of forgetfullness which often made her seem addle-minded.

He wondered if Frank had ever forgiven Albert for ruining the life of the only person he truly loved. And perhaps that was another reason he felt close to the Gardners. He was one of a very few persons to know bits and pieces of Frank Gardner's past — parts of the story of the boy who became a man at age ten. This understanding let him accept Frank's cold friendship, knowing that it was special and as close to warmth as Frank could allow. The understanding was also frightening. If the child grows as the tree is bent, then what twisted sense of justice might lie in Frank's mind.

Doctor Stewart realized, had always realized, that this was the reason he had not been able to say no to Albert.

There was a knock on the door. He opened it and Albert barged in and headed for the light of the kitchen.

Albert accepted a cup of coffee and looked gravely across the kitchen table at his father's friend.

"It's time to make a decision about Martha Pinkerman," Albert said.

Doctor Stewart sipped his coffee and nodded.

"Yes. I was going to contact you tomorrow at the latest if I didn't hear from you."

"Oh? Why's that?" Albert looked surprised.

"I can't let Martha go unconscious another day. If I give her another dosage, I may not be able to save her."

Albert did not toss off the problem nonchalantly, as was his custom. A cloud of concern covered his face.

"Is she that close to the brink, Doc?"

Doctor Stewart nodded.

"Albert, I never should have let you talk me into feeding her those drugs. I don't know how I have let it go so far."

You hypocrite, Albert thought. Of course you know why. I would have told everyone that you covered up the autopsy. Oh, it wouldn't have been me — not personally — but the world would have known just the same. And so goes the end of the story for the honorable Doctor Everett Stewart.

"I'm sorry, Doc," Albert lied. "I had no choice. It was either that or throw father to the wolves."

Doctor Stewart slowly dropped his coffee cup to the table and stared at Albert with the fear of a horrible premonition. He didn't even want to ask.

"What do you mean, Albert?"

Albert bent his head to his chest. Act One, Part Two, he thought. This was the second crucial moment he had practiced over the past six weeks. This was the final barricade between tragedy and unqualified success. When he looked up at his father's friend, real tears filled his eyes.

"Father found out that Dorothy was running out and meeting with Jas Porter. Everybody thinks I didn't know it, but I knew it. The thought of her rootin' around with Jas made me sick. But hell, I wasn't any better. I was worse. And I let it go on as long as Father didn't know. But he found out."

"What did he do Albert?" the doctor whispered.

Albert shook his head.

"He was mad. I mean, mad like a dog gets mad. He called in Burt McLean and ordered Burt to hire a killer. Burt did like he was told. He had a contact in Chicago, and got in touch with a paid killer out of Blue Island, Illinois."

Doctor Stewart shook his head mournfully.

"Remember that railroad gang foreman that testified? He told about a stranger with a tattoo on his arm. That was Blacky Mansell. He was father's hired killer."

It was going well, Albert thought, even better than he had expected. Doctor Stewart took it all in, his face going from grey to white as he felt his world close in around him, and Albert's stoic struggle to maintain composure making it all the more believable.

"What does this have to do with Martha Pinkerman?" Doc asked.

Albert answered, fighting back the tears.

"At the last minute Father came to his senses. He rushed to the Porter house intending to stop Blacky. But he was too late. They were all dead. He grabbed hold of one of the Stills girls and cried and got blood all over his clothes. I hid them for him the next day."

"But why — if he was going to kill someone, why not just Jas Porter? Why the whole family? And the two Stills girls?"

Albert cried, then regained composure.

"Father hired Blacky to kill Jas. It was Blacky's idea to kill everybody. He thought the investigators would think it was another of the mass murders that have happened in Colorado and Missouri. I think when Father learned that Blacky was going to kill the whole family, that's when he decided to stop it."

"But he was too late," the doctor concluded unnecessarily.

Albert nodded. "Too late. But even worse, when he was in the back yard of Porter's house, he looked up and saw Martha Pinkerman staring at him from her window. She saw him. In the lightening flashes."

"Why didn't she tell the sheriff?"

"I don't know. Maybe she was scared. Maybe she blocked it out — amnesia — like everyone said. But one thing's for sure, Doc. She can't wake up."

Horror stricken, Doctor Stewart searched for some unattainable, sensible conclusion.

"I'm a doctor, Albert. I can't kill Martha."

Albert looked at him coldly. "Not kill her, Doc. Just let her die. You said yourself, you'd have a hard time saving her now. The infection and all."

"Why?"

"Because we have to save Father. They'll be coming after him sooner or later. That detective, Morgan, is already asking questions about Father. It's only a matter of time before he and the Porters and Durhams and all of the old families come at him. We have to protect him."

Doctor Stewart felt his mind wheeling. But what about Frank, he asked. Do we let him get away with it? How does he feel about it? Is Frank aware that you are talking to me? What does he plan to do to defend himself? How can the man live with himself?

Albert answered calmly, "Father doesn't seem to remember a thing about it. And worse, he is outraged to think that anyone would dare suspect him. You know how he is. Don't acknowledge the accusation, lest you lend them credibility."

"What do we do, Albert?"

Albert stood and looked down at the crumpled doctor in the pool of light from the kitchen ceiling. "I've decided to protect him, Doc. As for you, it's up to you. My father's life is in your hands."

Albert let the front door close quietly behind him. Doctor Stewart looked at the kitchen clock. It was now three-thirty in the morning. At eight o'clock Martha would need another shot — or he could let her awake. He had almost five hours to think about it.

It was a long time before he slept.

What might have been if . . . is a question often asked but never answered. In Twin Forks the topic of conversation and worry was always the axe murders, but through August, September and October, only two events of consequence were reported in the local newspapers:

> August 5, 1912
> "FUNERAL RITES HELD FOR MARTHA PINKER-MAN"
> November 15, 1912
> "FRANK GARDNER ELECTED TO SENATE"

As Frank Gardner had predicted, the axe murders were now a part of Twin Forks' history all would have to learn to live with. Except for the Porter family who remained sequestered on their farm, and the detective who was no doubt "living in sin" with the Widow Lorraine Durham, and who charged about the country tracking down false leads, even Halloween passed in a more or less normal fashion with ghosts and goblins and pranksters knocking on doors after dark, their parents keeping a more watchful eye, but having given in to the pleas of their children.

It was almost three years later when the story began again. And it began as if only a day or two had passed.

Had that not been Saturday night when, over two hundred miles away, an old Indian habitually got drunk and thrown in jail, and had it not snowed the heaviest any of the oldtimers in South Dakota can remember for early November, it's difficult to imagine what might have happened. Some say that Twin Forks would have gone on to become a major city, and Frank Gardner would have become Governor of Iowa. Others insist he was sure to become President of the United States. It's a matter of record that his name was prominently mentioned and under consideration.

But what did happen left all of this to wonderment . . .

CHAPTER ELEVEN

It was the kind of rain that would leave late crops of corn and beans frozen in the fields and not until many nights and days of hard freeze would the dirt roads and streets be easily passable.

But two hundred miles to the north, where O. E. Jackson, sheriff of Sioux Falls, South Dakota, sat reading his morning mail, a fresh ten inches of clean, wet snow covered the ground. O. E. was behind his desk, his feet propped on the normal corner of the wood-burning stove, a cup of coffee cooling in his hand and a glass of whiskey nearby the small stack of mail on the desk. Larry was O. E.'s deputy, had been for years, and now stood a few feet away pretending to watch the few people outside on the streets who had been brave enough to break the first trails in the new snow. What Larry really was interested in was the mail, particularly a brown envelope that contained a telegram he had picked up at the train depot. Larry had been O. E.'s deputy for years and would probably be sheriff when O. E. retired, but all he could get out of Hank down at the depot was that the message had come from the Postmaster General. So what the message was, Larry did not know: and O. E.

had decided that this was as good a morning as any to play his favorite game: annoy the deputy.

"O. E." Larry said, unable to stand another moment of the strain, "a telegram is a thing of importance — this one is from the Postmaster himself. Don't you figger it's your duty to read it immediately?"

O. E. gave him a look of mock disgust, "Hey I'm gettin' to it, can't you see that? This is all mail and I'm gonna read it before you go off half-cocked about this here telegram. Now, here, get me some more coffee."

"Dammit, O. E."

"Hey, you watch your tongue. I'm not going to have a deputy of mine going around swearing and taking the name of God in vain."

"The name of God . . .?"

"Will you get the coffee?"

"O. E., sometimes I don't understand you. Here we got a telegram from the Postmaster . . ."

"All right! I'll read the damn thing if it'll make you close your mouth."

O. E. opened the telegram and read the large type slowly and silently. Larry watched him read, trying to guess what the message said by the expression on O. E.'s face.

"I'll be damn."

"What? Why, what's it say?"

"I'll be damn."

"Come on, O. E., what does it say?"

"Pornography."

"Pornography? What's that mean?"

"Dirty pictures."

"Dirty pictures? In Sioux Falls?"

"Yes, you idiot. We got a man in this town who's been sending dirty pictures and filthy words through the mails. That's against the law — federal law — so since there's no federal people around here, the Postmaster has asked us to arrest this fellow and hold him until someone can get here and take him off our hands."

"Who is it? Do you know him?"

"Yeah. It says he's Linous Cleavers and that this Cleavers likes to call himself a preacher."

"Reverend Cleavers? Sure, I know him . . . a nice little fellow — kinda strange and sneaky looking though."

"It says here that your Reverend Cleavers is a homosexual."

"Oh? I thought we all was?"

"No, you idiot. We are homosapiens. A homosexual . . . that's a queer."

"Oh. Well, I ain't that, O. E., you know that."

"You best learn the difference, boy. You could get yourself into a whole lot of trouble if you go around telling everyone that you and everyone else is a homosexual."

"Come on, O. E., I ain't a homosexual. When we gonna pick this preacher up?"

"Right now, I reckon. Did he have a room at the hotel?"

"Yup. I'll get my gun. Say, what are we gonna do with him after we get him? We have an Indian in one cell and them three white boys in the other."

"Well we can't very well put a queer in with three whites, so I guess we'll throw him in with the Indian."

"But he's white, too, O. E."

"What? You want to take him home with you? No, I didn't think so."

The door to the second floor room was not locked and Linous Cleavers was not there. The manager told them that Cleavers was in the bath. O. E. sat on the bed while Larry walked around the room looking at the hundreds of pictures that were tacked to the wall.

"O. E., did you look at these pictures? He's got every girl in town up here in the nude and doin' strange things to themselves."

"Sick. The man's sick," O. E. said.

"Hey, here's Joanne Bacher, naked as a jaybird."

"Joanne Bacher — you sure?" O. E. came to his feet to study the pictures. "I'll be damn. Say, you take these pictures down and be careful not to hurt any of them. We'll need them for evidence when this queer goes to trial."

"We're gonna keep this stuff at the office?"

"Where do you think we're gonna keep them? Now take them down before he gets here."

Linous Cleavers finished his bath and walked to his room. As he pushed the door open, he let the towel fall away from his waist and threw it over his shoulder — then looked up to see Sheriff O. E. Jackson sitting on the edge of the bed. Cleavers froze. The door slammed behind him and the deputy yelled, "Look out O. E." and pushed Cleavers across the room. The false preacher's head hit the wall with a dull thud. His tiny body crumpled in the corner, then he turned and looked back toward the door, but he didn't see the deputy. He saw a jagged axe raised high in the air, swooping down, swishing the air to a final, ugly thump on the skull of Clesta Stills.

"I confess. It was God's will. It was God's will that they should die. I killed the Porter family."

Despite the rain and morning chill, John Morgan was in high spirits when he boarded the train for Kaoder. Even Russ Porter's glum greeting and sullen attitude couldn't dampen his mood. And he looked forward to their meeting with Sam Durham for new reasons.

It was just a week ago that he was returning from Carole, Illinois, the place of Frank Gardner's childhood, when suddenly he realized he was breaking the dreary chains of his past and opening a future that would include love and warmth and security . . . parts that had been missing since his own childhood. The trip to Carole had let it all jell together. He discovered that Lorraine Durham loved him, and, for the first time, he believed that Frank Gardner was capable of ordering a mass murder. The two were a strange mix of thought.

From the Coroner's Inquest and interviews with local townspeople, it was easy to conclude that Frank Gardner had both motive and opportunity to kill the Porters. But there was always those nagging questions in the back of his mind: is the man capable of murder? — and why on earth did he kill everyone in the house? In the little village of Carole, he got his answer.

When he first reached Carole, he wondered why he had bothered to come at all. It was a half day horse-back ride from the nearest depot, and the village was almost a ghost town. From public records and an interview with Fred Martin, Frank's friend from college days, he already knew that the Gardners had left New York when Frank was four years old, and Frank's parents died in a fire when he was ten. His father, George Gardner, was a newspaper reporter for the New York Daily. He had stumbled upon a story about prominent Northern businessmen who were realizing huge profits supplying arms to the South in preparations for the upcoming war between the states. The story broke and the Gardners discovered that neither the law nor the power of the press would protect them from their newfound powerful enemies. One night a friend at the newspaper warned them that they had less than an hour to get out of New York to stay alive. Six hours later, on a train heading west they had jumped on almost at random, George Gardner read in a newspaper that the "bustling town of Carole" was looking for a publisher for their local paper. Two days later, penniless and carrying two overstuffed suitcases, the Gardners took residence in the building of the "Carole Weekly Bulletin".

So what else could Carole or its forty residents tell him about a boy who had lived here for only five years so long ago?

On one side of "Gert's Place", was a long bar with wooden stools, protected rows of whiskey bottles, a large mirror, and a painting of a naked woman. Parts of the painting were carefully concealed behind Teddy Roosevelt election badges. As if designed by a schizophrenic, the other half of the room was a cafe of gleaming tables covered by red and white checkered tablecloths. Freshly baked pies lined shelves on the wall and their smell competed almost successfully with the booze and oiled bar. To its compliment, seven local farmers were at the tables waiting for Gert to bring their noon meal. They had been talking loudly when he had stepped in, but now their conversation was a murmur interrupted by glares at the stranger in town.

Only Gert didn't seem to mind that a stranger had entered. She was a plump, graying woman whose face was always in a smile, which broke into a beautiful grin when she noticed Morgan inspecting the room.

"I know it looks a little queer, mister, but that's what happens when a town isn't what is used to be. What'd ya call that back east — consolidating? That's what we done. We consolidated."

Morgan returned her smile, liking her immediately. "I can tell it used to be a nice town."

She sat down across the table, "Still is. Good folks are still about, anyway." Then she sighed wistfully, "Yeah, we use to have a clothing store and two or three saloons, of course, and a newspaper and just about everything."

Just as quickly she jumped up, "You'll want coffee. And I'll bring you a piece of apple pie. It's the last of the season. And you look like a steak and potato man to me. Am I right?"

The food was delicious and voluminous. Steak. Coffee. Potatoes. Corn. Beans. Pie. A normal meal at Gerts. When she brought a fourth cup of coffee, Gert sat down across from him again and watched him finish off the pie.

"You said you had a newspaper?" Morgan asked.

Gert smiled. "Yep. A good one, too. A fella out of New York came and turned it into a real paper. 'Course I was just a youngster then — 'bout fourteen, but I remember everyone talkin' 'bout what a good job the new owner was doing."

"What happened to him?" Morgan tried to ask casually, but the curious glances of the men at the next table didn't go unnoticed on either of them. Gert jumped up again.

"They died in a fire, except for their son."

"Does he still live here?" Morgan asked.

But Gert was off to the kitchen not to appear again until Morgan went to the counter to pay.

"You're interested in the Gardner's?" she whispered.

Morgan nodded.

"Thought so. Yer dressed like some kind of detective. Look, the Gardners are kind of a sore subject around here. But if yer interested, there's only one person to talk to. That'd be the preacher, Reverend Faversham. Lives down in the parish next to the church."

"Will he be home?"

She grinned again. Her character guess had been correct.

"Yeah, I know he's home. He was in here not more than two hours ago. He's a queer fellow. Don't get me wrong. Its just that he spends a lot of his time diggin' up old Indian relics and talking about things that happened hundreds of years ago in these parts. Makes him seem a little rattle-brained. Tell the truth, the old coot is sharp as a whip. He knows more than anyone 'bout the Gardners. He's the only one knows it all."

Unlike most village parishes, the Reverend Faversham's was little more than a three room shack, which seemed to fit Faversham just fine. Books and old papers and Indian artifacts were spewed throughout the house. "Did you know there's a cave along the Mississippi not more than fifty miles from here where Indians used to camp almost two thousand years ago?" In his tattered work clothes and a head of moldy, grey hair, Morgan wondered if it was a first-hand recollection. Faversham was over eighty, but when he spoke of the Indians or held up a significant rock, his eyes gleamed with life and curiosity.

"So you want to know about the Gardners. Mind if I ask why?"

"Frank Gardner, their son, is mayor of Twin Forks now, and a state senator." Morgan decided to answer honestly. "I've been hired to prove that he's also responsible for the Twin Forks' axe murders you've probably heard about."

Faversham eyed him intently. "His childhood is supposed to answer that?"

Morgan explained the situation, "What I'm looking for now is something to convince me that Gardner could actually bring himself to have eight people murdered. I know I'm reaching, but . . ."

Faversham held up a hand to stop him, then picked up one of the rocks on his table and stared at it like a circus gypsy into a crystal ball.

He said sadly, "History. History is nothing but incidences being repeated over and over again. The people change. The weapons get better and deadlier. But the situation . . ."

His eyes deadened as he stared out the window at the main street of Carole, and remembered:

Frank Gardner was six years old on the night he was told the family was leaving New York, and that he had only ten minutes to pack.

"But where are we going?"

"Hush," his mother comforted him. "It's best you not know until later. I'll tell you on the train. Now you and your brother pack one suitcase. We must be able to move quickly. Robert, help your brother, please."

His older brother threw some clothes in both their suitcases and snapped them closed. They stared at each other with confused, frightened eyes while they sat on the bed and waited. Soon their father bound up the stairs to their apartment and they watched him embrace their mother.

"Your a good woman, Jessica Gardner. A good wife." His tone was loving and apologetic. It said, I'm sorry I brought this tragedy to you.

"Oh George," she moaned, "Whatever will we do?"

"Nothing to worry about," their father shouted, his normal enthusiasm suddenly returned for their benefit. "There's always work for a newspaper reporter, no matter where you go in this world."

"But you were doing so well . . . just . . ."

"Too well, I'm afraid," their father laughed. "Now let's get going before someone is writing my obituary."

They boarded the train after dark and the boys followed orders to go to sleep. When they awoke it was light again and they were travelling through open fields — such wide open spaces they had never seen. Wherever they were going, Frank thought, it must surely be to the ends of the earth.

As they entered Illinois their father took them to the dining car. After magnanimously allowing them a soda, he told them enough to satisfy their curiosities.

"I was writing a series of stories about Northerners who supply guns and ammunition and loan money to the Confederates. What I didn't know was that I was stepping on the toes of some of our most 'upper crust' families. They warned me to stop, and I didn't stop. Then, about an hour before we left New York, I received a call from your mother's brother, your Uncle James. He told me a group of hired hooligans were coming to . . . to stop me and possibly hurt your . . . your mother and maybe even you two. So, I left. And now we have to find a different place to live."

"We would have fought them, Father," Robert said. "Frank and I would have helped."

Their father smiled. "I fight with the pen, Robert, not with sword. Remember that. The sword is defenseless against the pen. What do you think created the war? The sword? No. It was the pen. And why will the North finally win? Because we have more writers and communication, not because we have more soldiers."

When they stopped in Chicago, only their father left the train. He returned an hour later bristling with energy and encouragement.

"There's a little town just to the west of here that needs a publisher for its newspaper. They have a press and living quarters in the same building, ready for us to move in."

Thirty minutes beyond Chicago the train stopped again. They rented a horse and buggy and drove north for hours, until they reached a summit overlooking a small town in a lovely, green valley. A row of buildings two blocks long comprised the store section, and a few streets reached out to embrace a population of three hundred homes. On the east edge of town a handsome white church with a full, graceful spire created a picture-card setting, and beyond that was an even larger structure, obviously the home of a wealthy family. Everything was as it should have been.

Within two days, Publisher-Editor-Reporter-Pressman George Gardner put out the first edition of the Lancaster Tribune. It was an immediate success. His writing skills, applied to the rural interests, were quickly appreciated by the townspeople and local farm families. And his encouraging, flag-waving editorials about the glory of the Union and the courageous battles, which included sons and fathers from almost every local family, were uplifting and read aloud at suppertime over and over again.

One night the mayor and owner of most of the town and a good share of the countryside around it invited the Gardners to his mansion at the edge of town, "To welcome you and show how much we appreciate your work." It was an uncomfortable evening. Mayor Bremstall never budged from his place at the head of the table, bordered on either side by his two lovely daughters and who spoke not a word, but sat there smiling patiently like two thoroughbreds at a county fair.

For two full years life at Lancaster was a pleasant, carefree existence.

Then tragedy came. And, as they say, it came in threes.

First, Frank's brother Bob left for the war, and he "will never forget the night we stood in the Chicago train yards, my father's arm around my shoulder, watching my brother disappear in the fog with hundreds of other young men in their new uniforms."

It was lonely in Lancaster for Frank without his brother. Lonlier still when, three months later, Bob's body was returned and buried near the church.

Frank began to change. Boyhood innocence was lost to the realities that life and love were brief things, and ended only in greater loss.

But if Frank changed, the senior George Gardner did a complete metamorphosis. Within hours of the funeral he was involved in secret meetings that kept him out until all hours of the night. And soon his reason was apparent: the usually uplifting editorials became barbs and innuendoes . . . "what local gentlemen, and I use the term with cynicism, are supplying arms and ammunition to the Confederates".

Over a period of weeks he plotted in print the travel of guns and bullets from Illinois to New Orleans, via river barges on the Mississippi. As if he invited the disaster that had to come, he published the articles in reverse chronology: how the guns were stored and dispersed in New Orleans; how they slipped past and bribed the border guards; when they were loaded on the barges at the Mississippi twenty miles away from Carole; how mule drawn wagons covered with tarpaulins carted them down dirt roads at night from a barn near the town of Carole itself.

There was no doubt that the series would end in the living rooms of ten or twelve Lancaster County citizens. And guns and ammunition cost a great deal of money. Already, readers were finding it difficult not to conclude that Mayor Bremstall was behind the elaborate, expensive but profitable scheme. And there was no doubt that the final story of the series could not be allowed.

On October 1, Frank was lying in his bed with the window open. It was raining on the sand-covered main street of Carole, a light drizzle, and a cool breeze brought the smell of paper and ink through the window from the pressroom below.

Frank did not look to see who was riding a horse in the rain. He listened to the hooves slowly stomp into the water soaked streets below his window. The horse stopped momentarily, a dull thud of something heavy landed on the boardwalk at the front door, the horse continued down the street at a slightly faster pace.

He heard the front door open, and then he heard his mother scream.

"Oh my God." his mother moaned, "It's Joe Pendergast. George he's dead!"

His father rolled the body over. He jumped up and ran into the building, slamming the door shut behind him.

"They cut his tongue out," he gasped.

Frank watched his father and mother stare at each other, frozen in hopelessness, suddenly realizing the consequences of the editorials.

"Joe was my informant," his father said needlessly.

At the same moment his mother noticed him on the stairs, the rumbling of many horses and riders sounded outside. His mother ran to him and hugged him and kissed his cheek.

"I know you want to help, Frank," she said with remarkable calm. "But you can't help — not here, anyway. I want you to go to the kitchen upstairs, and when the men come inside, you jump onto the roof and shinny down the drain. I know you can do it, because you've done it before. Then run to the preacher's house and tell him what's happened. He'll know what to do."

The plan for his escape worked, as his mother knew it would. As he neared the church and the parsonage he heard a barrage of gunfire. He pounded on the door to the parsonage. The preacher awoke, seemed to hurry, but by the time they entered the street again, the horses and riders were leaving on the opposite side of town. The town was silent for a few minutes, then a bright orange flame showed in the glass panel windows of the pressroom, followed by three loud explosions that shot the flames outward and upward. Within seconds the building was engulfed in fire.

The rain cooled the ashes quickly. By the following evening local townspeople had searched the ashes and scooped up those believed to be George and Jessica Gardner, though they couldn't determine which was which.

On the next day they had the funeral. Hundreds of people attended, some friends, but mostly strangers who were patiently carrying out the local custom. As the preacher read from the bible, Frank looked at the graves in bewilderment, wondering which grave held his mother and which his father.

Reverend Faversham turned and looked at Morgan with sad, old eyes. I took care of the boy for six months. Then I arranged for him to work in Princeton, Illinois. He finished elementary school and went to college there."

"Like I told you, I'm trying to find something to convince me that Frank is capable of having eight people killed. I can see how he might hate the Bremstall's, but not that he came away from it a cold-blooded killer."

Faversham sighed, then turned to Morgan. "That's just the point. It worked in reverse."

"How's that?"

"A woman came up to Frank after the funeral. Mrs. Fayne, I believe it was. She said, 'Frank, your father was a good man. You should grow up to be just like him.' He nodded and watched her walk away, then turned to me and asked, 'Why should she say that?' "

"I said, 'Your father was a good man.' But little Frank shook his head and spoke with a calm that chilled my bones. 'My father was a fool. And he was weak and now he's dead. The Bremstalls have the power. I will have that power some day, and will not end up like my father and mother under a tombstone that may not even be mine.' "

"And Frank became another Bremstall?"

Faversham shifted his gaze back to the main street "Categorically. He became educated. He married into a respected family in a small community. He took it over with money and political power."

"And became a killer?"

"Became a man who truly believes that absolutely anything is justifiable if it protects his family or aspirations."

Morgan stood up and sighed. "No one will ever believe this is possible."

Faversham pointed to an ornate stone which, compared to the others, was elegant. "That's what men like Gardner and Bremstall have counted on for centuries."

"No, it can not be done that way. And I must be definite about that." Sam Durham turned from the window and addressed his companion, the Attorney General. Fred Martin had been summoned to Kaoder from the capitol building in Des Moines and now, as for the past six hours, they sat in red leather chairs and stared at the flames of a carefully built fire while they waited for Morgan and Porter to arrive. The flames rippled gently along hard oaks, emitting just enough warmth to take the chill off the air in Durham's study.

Durham had called for Martin the minute he learned of Linous Cleaver's arrest and confession. On many occasions Martin had proven an excellent attorney in his own right and, on this occasion, he would be particularly useful. Outside the Gardner group, no one knew the mind of Frank F. Gardner better than Fred Martin. They had been friends in college at Princeton, Illinois. It was Gardner who had convinced him to abstain from the tempting, quick, but limited success of opportunities available in the East, and directed him instead to the greater, long-term success to be had in Iowa. It was ironic, he thought, that he should be sitting here plotting the destruction of the man who had been most instrumental in his career.

In business college he had known Gardner for three years; had heard the story of Frank's parent's horrible death and how their murder had been ordered by Bremstall. But not until shortly before graduation day did Martin begin to understand his friend. For three days the sky had been dark, the sun blocked by a pale of black smoke that turned afternoon into dusk. It was an eerie sight, as one of God's punishments to the Pharaoh. Toward the end of the first day a rider came to town and answered the questions about the billowing smoke that had the whole town in an uproar. The man's eyes were wide and wild and his clothes smelled of smoke and ash.

"It's unbelievable!" he said.

"What? Tell us!" the crowd demanded.

"It's Chicago. The whole damn city is burning to the ground!"

The two friends sat on the hill west of town watching the sky, trying to imagine a fire that could blacken the sky from over one hundred miles away. Toward the end of the third day the sky showed some sign of clearing and the young men talked of their futures after graduation. Fred confessed that he was planning to accept an offer they had both had from a large firm in New York. But Frank spoke with a tone that was prophetic. "Back there you are another spoke in a gigantic wheel depending on others for success. But out there, in Iowa or Nebraska, you can be a leader. Those people know nothing about education or finance or politics. In ten years time you could control most of the state. And if anyone stands in your way . . ." The sentence fell incomplete, but Fred connected it with the

Bremstall's of Carole, Illinois, and knew the meaning. It was frightening to realize how accurate Frank's prophecy had become.

"I see no alternative but to bring Frank to trial for murder," Martin repeated.

"Impossible."

"If they hang this Cleavers fellow, we'll never get the chance again to try Gardner. He'll go free. Hell, even if we lose, at least the public will know we believe he's responsible for a mass murder."

"And our entire party will be out of office," Durham growled. "If there's a murder trial he'll be found not guilty. Completely vindicated. That's worse then no trial at all."

"What do we do? Just sit around and wait until he kills someone else and hope we catch him at it? A loss would be better than no trial at all!"

"My God, man, do you realize that they are already talking about Gardner for governor? If we walk into that trial without positive proof, the entire fiasco will be discounted as a trumped up political maneuver. It will be like handing Gardner the governor's chair."

"I think the public will support us."

"What if he moves the trial to another state?"

Fred Martin did not answer. He knew that Frank Gardner would not allow a change of venue. That would be too close to admitting he didn't trust his constituents. But he didn't voice this opinion. It was a moot subject anyway. Both Durham and he knew too that a jury would not put a rope around a man's neck unless they had absolute proof, no matter how outraged they became.

Durham was first to formulate the plot when he asked, "Since you know Frank better than anyone, and considering that there is a confessed murderer in custody, what would Gardner do if he was suddenly, publicly, and very loudly accused of the murder?"

"He'd file a slander suit," Martin answered with no hesitation.

Durham nodded studiously and pulled two large cigars from the humidor off his desk.

"Yes. Any innocent man would," he smiled. "And just maybe in the process he will blunder when we've brought him out of his shell."

". . . and that about sizes it up, gentlemen. Even if we manage to prove this Linous Cleaver's innocent, it is doubtful that we'll ever have enough evidence to convict Frank Gardner of murder. Mr. Martin and I have discussed this since four o'clock this morning, and we agree that only a confession will see Gardner hang."

Russ Porter and John Morgan, the farmer and the detective, sat dumbfounded. Porter wondered where justice had gone for an honest man. Morgan's head reeled with the flood of new information: Linous Cleaver had confessed, and the world would know it in tomorrow's newspapers. They knew it now because one of Sam Durham's men at the telegraph office had intercepted the message from Sioux Falls to Twin Forks late last night. Sam Durham had been financing Porter's fees to the Burns Detective Agency all along. And now, just when he had become convinced that Gardner was the murderer, the chance of a murder conviction, or even a trial, was slipping away. He thought of Al Crans' warning to him not to get involved with the "hopeless case". He thought of Lorraine Durham. He recalled painfully why he had taken on this case; it was to be his last opportunity to reestablish himself as a worthy detective in this age of law and invention, and where a reputation was the only thing that kept an old tracker like himself in step with the new generation.

"How strong is the case against Cleavers?" Morgan asked.

Fred Martin answered. "He has confessed. And the Reverend Bush has confirmed that Cleavers was in town on the night of the murders and disappeared the next morning. Over fifty people attended a sermon delivered by Cleavers that night. No one gave him another thought in the excitement of the discovery the next morning."

"So let's say Morgan here figures a way to get Cleavers off the hook. What then? You say we still don't have a prayer's chance in hell of hangin' Gardner."

"The next step is really up to you, Russ. And to you, Mr. Morgan."

"What's that mean?" Russ asked.

Sam Durham looked uneasily to Fred Martin, found no support, and back to the two men.

"First, let me ask you a question. Do you agree that if we can't hang Gardner, it would be almost as good to ruin him politically and socially?"

Russ shrugged. "Better than lettin' him go Scot free."

"Right. So, the idea is that if we can't convict Gardner legally, we can convict him publicly. And if it makes you feel any better, that will be a fate worse than death for Frank. A living hell."

"So where do we start?"

They talked on for another two hours before Morgan and Porter left to catch the three o'clock train back to Twin Forks. When they were alone, Fred Martin put the plan in perspective.

"A clever plan, I agree. No matter what happens, you lose nothing."

Durham nodded. "And Russ has little to worry about. Public sentiment will be in his favor."

"I do feel sorry about the detective. He's the one who stands to lose the most."

Durham shrugged. "So my daughter-in-law will have to find someone else to sleep with. Morgan is expendable. I guess I knew from the beginning that it would come to something like this. The Burns Agency knew it, too. Morgan is on his last legs anyway. He might as well go out having served some purpose."

"And Gardner. Won't there be repercussions?"

"Isn't that what we are counting on?"

Fifty miles west of Twin Forks was Morton Junction: a cluster of shacks with log walls and tin roofs, one of which served as a combination depot, grocery, switchboard and telegraph station. Beneath a kerosene lamp, a woman sat huddled near a wood stove, reading a three-day old newspaper. It reported that the "Reverend" Linous Cleavers was being transferred to Kaoder to face a grand jury.

Vina Thompkins wasn't sure what was going through her mind; that it was her duty to save an innocent man; that a large reward would be given her for helping to convict the killer; or, and this she was sure of, that Blacky Mansell would soon be searching for her anyway. All because she had sent a letter to her friend in Blue Island, Judy Mansell. She hadn't kept a copy of it of course, but she could remember every word:

"Dear Judy,
We have been fooled again. Morton's Junction is just another rock farm. Lester is already gone . . . sposed to be out lookin' fer a job. I maybe won't see him ever again.

Everything we ever had is gone.

    I seen Blacky on our trip out here. He was havin' some kind of secret meeting with some men, so I didn't let him know I was there. Judy, I know Blacky ain't much, but at least you know where your man is. Maybe mine's dead. At least then I'd know where he was.

Your friend,
Vina Thompkins"

Of all the ill-gotten luck. What had possessed her to write that to Judy? It was a natural thing for most women to write to their old neighbors, but not her; not about Blacky Mansell. She knew he was an ex-convict, a killer and a thief!

Blacky Mansell had worked for the underworld in Chicago, but after some trouble he never explained to anyone, he ran from Chicago and hid in the South side of Blue Island in a collection of homes hastily built to support an influx of packinghouse workers.

Blacky was a "killer" at the slaughterhouse, which had an ironic poetry to it. Even more ironic, Vina had seen Blacky at an abandoned slaughterhouse about two miles east of Twin Forks, near a pasture where they spent the night on the trek west.

CHAPTER TWELVE

June 8, 1912 — Saturday. Thirty-one hours before the murders.

Another forty-five minutes and they would have reached Twin Forks. But night was falling and the green pastures along the upper branch of East Creek were cool and inviting. Vina Thompkins had been sitting on the hard wagon seat most of the long, hot day and now her bottom was so sore that she would have given anything to stretch out in the lush pasture grass for a few minutes. Besides that, she had to urinate.

"Let's tell the Sawyers we're going to stay the night here, George. We don't have no money for a room anyways."

And so it came to be, that two covered wagons carrying George and Vina Thompkins, and Dan and Marlene Sawyer from their poverty in Illinois, arrived at a pasture six miles northeast of Twin Forks. It was to be just another stop of many on their way to the two farms they had purchased, sight unseen, twenty miles on the other side of Twin Forks.

They drove far into the pasture to avoid strangers that might pass on the road during the night and had she not needed to urinate so,

Vina might have found it quite relaxing to bump along the grassy knolls above East Creek, for it was a paradise for weary travelers, promising a lonely pleasant night under the stars amid night sounds of the surrounding forest. So because of her need to get off by herself into the trees, and her longing for a peaceful evening by a small fire, Vina was distressed when they topped the last hill before the forest and found that someone had already taken their paradise for the night.

"Get them out of here, George. They got no right being here in our pasture."

George suggested they camp farther down the hill, but Vina would not hear of it. "I am not going to spend the night in some field with a bunch of low-down niggers. Now you tell them to pack up their things and their picaninney and get off our land."

She heard her husband explain to the black man that this was their normal stopping place when they traveled this road, as they often did, and that he wouldn't mind if the blacks moved farther down the road, but understandably so, he had no intention of letting his wife and friends spend the night in the same pasture as a "nigger" family.

When the blacks were gone and the wagons were unhitched, Vina volunteered to look for firewood and hurried off toward the tall reeds along the East Creek bottom land. At last she was able to pull up her skirts and remove her undergarments to answer her urgent call. She was squatting there with her underclothes laying across some fallen reeds when she heard the piercing crack of dried reeds. She straightened her dresses and called softly, "Who's there?"

"It's me," she heard Dan Sawyer's voice answer before he appeared out of the tall grasses and reeds. He grabbed her by the waist and pulled her dresses high so that her bare buttocks and stomach were exposed.

"No Dan, we can't. We just can't."

Sawyer pushed his rough face to her neck, "I thought you wanted me. You said you wanted me."

She pushed away and looked at him heatedly. He was much bigger than her own scrawny husband and better endowed she knew from accidental sightings along the long trip from Illinois.

"We can't, Dan. Not now. Wait until tonight when they are sleeping. I'll stay awake for you."

"Okay — tonight. We better get some firewood before they get to missing us."

They rambled northward one hundred yards picking up small sticks and logs for the fire. Finally they each had an armful and started back toward the wagons. Vina stopped suddenly.

"You coming?" Sawyer asked.

"What's that over there by the creek? Is that some kind of house there?"

"Flat roof with block sides . . . looks like an empty slaughterhouse to me. Probably failed at the turning."

"You go on to the wagons, Dan. Tell them I went to the slaughterhouse to see if there is anything for salvage."

"Won't be nothin'. There never is."

"Oh, you don't know. I'll bet I find a dandy butcher knife. Now you go on and tell them before they wonder where we are. I'll be along soon."

She wished Dan had stayed as she neared the slaughterhouse. It was eerie walking up to the abandoned place overgrown by water weeds and darkness almost fully upon her. To the east side there were no windows or doors, so she crept carefully to the north where she supposed a door would let her enter. She reached the corner of the building, stepped around it and almost screamed. Why she didn't, she wondered, but she caught the impulse to scream and the second impulse to run away as she stared at seven saddled horses that stood tied to a rail at the side of the slaughterhouse. Their riders were no doubt inside.

Vina was not a courageous woman, nor was she particularly curious to see who the horses belonged to, but she did not resist her third impulse — to see who met in this old building miles away from the nearest town.

She stepped gingerly to the dust covered window of cracked glass and eyed the inside of the slaughterhouse through a small hole in a lower pane. At the far end of the building near an open door where the blood and guts of kills were once dropped into East Creek, she found the group of seven men silhouetted there in the fading light of evening. She was too far away to hear them clearly. A word would catch her ear, or a name she did not recognize would reach her, but she could make no sense of what she heard. Nor could she see them well enough to study their features. From their shadows against the western sky she could see that two of the men were bearded and that one of those did most of the talking. Nothing was prominent about the features of the other men, except that one was perhaps a black man because his hair was cropped close to his head. She saw through this man's motions that he was going for a match to light a cigarette. Afraid that the light of the match would reveal her presence, she decided this was a good time to back away from the window and to return to the wagon. This might have ended her involvement with the meeting at the slaughterhouse, but as she stepped away, she took one last glance through the window and this was at the same time the match was struck.

Vina froze in her steps. She stared at the man whose face was lighted by the flame, terrified by the grim remembrance of the last time she had seen this man. Then she backed away, walked to the edge of the pasture, ran across it to the safety of the wagons and said nothing to the others about their intruders.

It would be another two days before she put the words and names she had heard together, and the familiar face of the man who had terrified her so.

The man with the shaved head drew hard on his cigarette. He left the match burning to reveal the long scar on his right cheek.

"I'm not going to do this alone." he growled.

Burt McLean pushed him outside the slaughterhouse door angrily, "Mansell, you can't double cross me now. Gardner has agreed to pay the price. They got money. What the hell's the matter with you?"

Robert "Blacky" Mansell held up his hands and showed his yellow teeth in a wide grin, "No trouble with the job. It's easy. But you got too many people in on this. On Monday morning they're gonna roll over six dead ones and I can't take the chance that one of you could get the incline to tell someone about me."

"By God, Mansell, you're yellar. You told me you'd do the job, so do it. You done it to your own family in Illinois, didn't you?"

"Sure I did. But I was alone then. No one knew I was gonna do it except me. Hell, McLean you got six men right here who know it all."

"What the hell do you want then?" McLean asked "You got one thousand dollars. Is that what you want, more money?"

"No. One thousand is plenty. What I want is somebody with me. Somebody who no one would touch after it's over — otherwise you can forget the whole deal."

"Okay. Forget it."

"No!" This third voice came from the dark. Albert Gardner stepped from the black of the slaughterhouse into the doorway between McLean and Mansell. "I'll meet you there at a quarter past midnight."

"You're crazy," McLean argued.

"It must be done. I'll be there and I'll have the one thousand dollars on me. I want Jas Porter out of the way — forever."

And she had written that lousy letter. How long before Blacky found out about it? And came after her? It was only a matter of time.

It was Saturday, Christmas was near, and the Square was crowded with shoppers. Morgan, feeling very much a part of the warm scene on this cold day, walked along the boardwalk thinking that he must remember to get a Christmas present for Lorraine. He had already decided to give gifts to the Porter children. They called him Uncle when they ran to greet him at the farm, as if he were their only contact with the outside world, which was almost true. The Porters didn't understand why friends didn't bring their children out to play, but kept them away lest they catch some affliction. In this mood, Morgan began to feel that he was overcoming his own affliction, as Lorraine called his obsession with the axe murder case.

Once, when he was writing notes from the Coroner's Inquest testimonies, she said, "What worries me is that you are the only one who will be hurt if the murderer never comes to trial." It was understood between them that Lorraine would not refer to Gardner as the murderer. "I know," Morgan replied, "but I'm not as worried about a conviction as I am knowing in my own mind who the killer is, why it happened, and how. That's for me. A conviction is for my career."

Lorraine understood, although their relationship had been strained as of date since his meeting with her father-in-law. True to his word, Russ Porter had called public meetings of local farmers and sympathetic residents. Publicly and loudly, Russ cried for the community to help get Linous Cleavers released and proven a fraud, and to help convict the real murderer, Frank F. Gardner, knowing full well that the message would reach the Gardner mansion within minutes after the first meeting.

As Sam Durham predicted, the meetings had their effect. Money poured in from neighbors to help finance the campaign to convict Gardner, and more people came forward with bits of details they had forgotten, or failed to bring out at the Coroner's Inquest, all of which added to Morgan's notebooks and charts plotting the movement of each person the evening of June 9, 1912. Two interesting possibilities had been unturned, one from the Inquest and one from the meetings. At the Inquest, the garage mechanic had stated that his garage opened every morning at seven o'clock. But others testified they had seen Albert Gardner and Burt McLean in the Auburn an hour earlier. Upon questioning, the mechanic confirmed to Morgan that McLean had kept his Auburn out all night for the first and only time. A coincidence? Perhaps. But Morgan had learned that a coincidence is the result of events and, in this case, the event may have been mass murder and escape.

The coincidence was brought out loudly at the first meeting, and produced the next possibility. They had just concluded the meeting at Porter's barn when one of the farmers pulled Morgan aside and asked if he would step outside to talk to his daughters. He followed the man to where two wide-eyed, nervous girls waited and shivered beneath blankets in the back of a wagon. Nancy and Susan Caldwell were twin sisters in appearance only. It was obvious which one always got into trouble, and which one would also have a bearing on the situation.

"On Monday night, the night after the murders," Nancy began, her teeth chattering, "Allan Childes was sitting on the front porch talking to us and keeping us company. Ma and Pa were in town. He told us he was leaving town to take a sheepherder's job in Wyoming. Allan talks a lot and we teased him. But he said he was going because he was scared someone was going to kill him next."

"Did he say who wanted to kill him?" Morgan asked.

Sue nodded and Nancy answered, "Frank Gardner. Allan said he had seen Mr. Gardner in the Porter yard after dark on the murder night, and Mr. Gardner seen him, too."

"Why didn't you tell this at the Coroner's Inquest?"

"We was scared. And Allan talks a lot of nonsense. We weren't sure he was tellin' the truth."

"Why are you sure now?"

"Allan's gone, ain't he? If he told the truth about leaving, then maybe he told the truth about why?"

It was a long shot, but so was everything he had on Gardner. The next morning, Morgan sent a wire to his friend Al Crans in Denver, asking him to locate Allan Childes, confirm the statement, and arrange to transport Childes back to Twin Forks at the proper time. This morning he received a wire from Crans informing him that they had located Childes and would contact him as soon as the weather permitted access to the mountain area where Childes worked.

Morgan continued around the Square and, as he did every morning when he was not out of town, he stopped in at the sheriff's office. He found Sheriff Gustavson at his desk reading a white and red handbill, a stack of them piled beside him.

"Did you know about these here notices?" Gustavson asked.

Morgan nodded. "I saw some of them down at the depot."

Gustavson sighed. "Listen to this. Just listen to this!" And he read, "Save the little preacher. An innocent man, and a sick man in need of our help, has confessed to the axe murders. But we know the killer is a prominent person of Twin Forks. We all must work, as good Christians, to save the little preacher if we are ever to bring the real killer to justice."

"Now how 'bout that? It's crazy!"

"I know," Morgan agreed, "What worries me — you know what worries me is that these people don't realize — don't they wonder what Gardner will do?"

Morgan had wondered the same thing. But the answer was simple. People follow patterns and grooves. The unsolved murder case upset the pattern and wouldn't allow them to fall back into the groove. They were willing to risk a great deal just to have things settled one way or another.

"And how 'bout you?" Gustavson growled. "You think you got problems now, just you wait until it hits the fan. You're right in the middle of all this. When the shootin' starts, you're going to find out who your friends are around here."

Morgan smiled, knowing Gustavson was trying to help. "And who will my friends be, sheriff?"

"Maybe—maybe—not a damn soul."

That night there were caroles sung by the church choir on the Square. Snow started to fall gently as Morgan and Lorraine left for home, a scene from a picture postcard; a scene, Morgan thought, as fragile and deadly as the snow.

Albert, Burt McLean, Mrs. Gardner, Doc Stewart, John Goodell. Even Provo. They were all there waiting for what was built to be an earth-shattering announcement. Doctor Stewart wondered if Frank would withdraw from the senate. The others only wondered. When Frank entered he marched to his library table and, standing, prepared as if to address a legislative body.

"It is now two days before Christmas. This Monday I will travel to Kaoder and file a slander suit against the Porters, the detective, and all of the other families who are supporting the rumor campaign against me."

He paused. Six blank faces stared back at him.

"I thought you should know so you can be prepared for the worse. It will be difficult, but I won't have my good name and reputation dragged through the mud. We must stand this together. Mr. Goodell, I want you to send a wire to Lona and Dorothy instructing them to come home. We will stand as a family."

Minnie sighed and smiled. "You see, already some good is coming of this. The girls will be home."

"As for the rest of us," Frank continued, "we should be prepared for questions. Each of us should write down every step we can remember from a week before the murders to this day. We must be positively prepared. I want you to write it all down and hand it over to Mr. Goodell who will lock the papers in the safe at the bank."

"Are there any questions?"

Doctor Stewart looked at the others and thought of the questions he might be asked about the Coroner's autopsy, and Martha Pinkerman's death. Couldn't all of this be avoided?

"Why, Frank?" Doc asked. "After all these weeks, why file a slander suit now?"

Until now Frank had been firm and calm. Now he looked at his old friend and held up a stack of cards and envelopes. Tears filled his eyes and his voice broke.

"Christmas cards. These are supposed to be Christmas cards. But they are not. They call me a killer! Me! Look! Even little children are sending cards: Merry Christmas to the killer. Here's another: the Porters will miss this Christmas because of you."

He turned and faced the wall sobbing.

"I won't stand for it. Not this! Not anymore!"

Strangely enough, it was Albert who put his arm around his father's shoulder to console him.

"Don't worry about a thing, father," he said, "everything is under control."

And in the eyes of Doctor Stewart and Burt McLean, Albert was in control. Frank was hysterical while Albert was in control. Frank's actions threatened their existence, Albert's protected them.

That evening they met in a room above McLean's tavern. Albert's message was delivered without preamble or argument:

"Burt, I want you to contact Blacky Mansell. Tell him about the slander suit. And tell him that if he has left any loose ends, he'd better tie them up. Sooner or later Morgan is going to find him, especially now that father is putting his back to the wall."

Albert left the meeting feeling quite satisfied with himself. There would be a slander suit. A lot of accusations. Embarrassment. But in the end it would all wash with only tarnished reputations to be risked. He was looking forward to Christmas and Dorothy's return. She and Lona would be home.

Little did he know that by then, due to his actions of tonight, his whole world would once again be turned upside down.

CHAPTER THIRTEEN

Five days had passed since she had arrived in Twin Forks. Three weeks since Christmas. This was 1915 and it too would pass uneventfully — unless Lona Gardner rejected the role her father had laid down for her.

It was morning. A cold, Iowa early winter day of gray featureless skies blocked the sun. Not even snow flakes broke the monotony or the overpowering spell of dreary winter.

And this was the day Linous Cleavers was to be brought to Twin Forks. Only Lona and a small circle of her father's associates knew that Cleavers was being brought to the mansion, "for his protection", instead of to the jail at Kaoder, where his trial would take place. So in spite of the cold and boredom outside, the Gardner mansion was teeming with activity as they prepared to meet Linous Cleavers.

There was a bright spot for Lona, however. Lately she had noticed the amorous gazes of John Goodell. They came at supper lately, when he thought that her father would not notice them. Quick glances prolonged hesitantly. And while she felt little for

John Goodell, his attentions were both noticed and appreciated. It was Goodell she saw first this morning as she came down from her bedroom. As usual, he wore a dark suit of thin blue strips.

"Good morning, Mr. Goodell, it seems that at last we are to see this terrible person." She spoke cheerfully lest her fear of meeting Linous Cleavers be obvious.

"Yes, Miss Lona," Goodell said. "He'll be here in a few minutes I am told. They are bringing him by coach just in case the people are watching the train depot."

"The people, Mr. Goodell? You are beginning to sound like my father. We are also 'the people'. Don't you agree?"

John Goodell blushed. "Yes, Miss Lona. I was speaking as a politician to a crowd of voters. I'm sorry."

"What will he look like?" Lona asked.

"Who?"

"Mr. Cleavers."

"I don't know for sure. I have heard he's a little disgusting in appearance."

Lona walked to the center of the bay window that curved out onto the front porch. "Riding in a coach on a day like this — it must be very cold. I hope they dressed the poor creature warmly."

"I'm sure they did." Goodell said.

"Yes. It wouldn't do for our self-confessed murderer to die enroute, would it?"

John Goodell looked at Lona in surprise. "What do you mean? You do want your father's innocence made public don't you?"

"Yes. I suppose so. It's just that this entire matter with Cleavers seems so contrived. And so convenient. Isn't it a little strange that Mr. Cleavers is being brought to my father's home rather than the County Seat?"

"It's for protection . . ."

"I have heard the reasons, Mr. Goodell. It's the purpose I was asking about."

Goodell was about to defend the actions of Frank Gardner when a door slammed up stairs and Doctor Stewart came down shouting that the coach carrying Linous Cleavers was entering the drive. They ran to the window.

Wind swept over the snow crusted boulevard. The first man from the coach put his boot down from the step and broke the crust beneath his weight, but the snow was packed firmly to the ground so that he sank only to his ankles. Then the second man climbed out. His tiny feet skidded over the surface like a young calf on ice and he would have fallen had it not been for the strong arm of the first man, which he clung to, until the third man took one arm and they began the short walk to the Gardner mansion. The first man was Marshall Harmon. The third man was Sheriff O. E. Jackson of Sioux Falls. The second man felt the wind beneath his light coat where he had his arms folded across his stomach, but he did not notice the cold bite at his face and hands and legs for they had become numbed hours ago. Now he felt nothing but the strange burning sensation of freezing.

Linous Cleavers looked at the mansion which rose above him. It was awesome in size and ghastly in appearance. He looked up at the tall spires against a dead sky. As he entered the mansion he thought he was entering an insane asylum not unsimilar to the institution from which he had escaped ten years earlier near London, England. But he was not afraid to enter the mansion. It would protect him, he thought, from the people and the cold and from his fear of himself.

Cleavers saw Lona by the window. He stopped at the bottom of the staircase to look at her. When she turned away, then brought her eyes back to him curiously, he smiled a faint, sickly, sorry smirk. Then he dropped his eyes to begin the climb to Frank Gardner's study.

Lona watched him until she saw her father at the first-floor landing. He also stared at Cleavers. The Senator's beard was well brushed, his suit freshly pressed. He stood at the stairs with his hands behind his back, looking like a stern schoolmaster scolding a pupil. "Like a sinner going before God," Lona thought as she watched them round the landing.

It took ages, it seemed, for them to reach the fourth-floor study. Finally the boots on the staircase stopped, the study door slammed and the mansion was quiet again. What was now going on in her father's study Lona could well imagine. Suddenly it all seemed very wrong that Linous Cleavers should be upstairs in the study with her father, the one man who stood to gain by Cleaver's conviction.

She had to get out of the mansion for awhile. Get away from it. Lona grabbed her coat and scarf from the kitchen and escaped the pressure of the mansion through the rear door.

Linous Cleavers sat between the two lawmen, even more tiny between their huge bulks. His face was ashen, his burning cheeks sunken below wide, pale eyes that seemed always ready to cry, but unable to do so. That kind, sheepish smirk was frozen to his lips and the rest of the men looked at him silently wondering what perverted thoughts wandered through his sick mind.

And it was at this moment that Frank Gardner realized his mistake. This was like sitting down to tea with a man you were about to execute. Gardner knew in the moment that he first saw Cleavers that the little man would surely hang for the axe murders. Cleavers was just what he had ordered — with a confession, too. Innocent or guilty, the County Attorney would have no trouble convincing a jury of twelve honest Midwesterners that Linous Cleavers the pervert, Linous Cleavers the sex deviate, Linous Cleavers the pornographer, and Linous Cleavers the false preacher, was also Linous Cleavers the axe murderer.

Senator Gardner was glad now that Cleavers had not been found by his orders. Yet a week ago the possibility of just such a thing had existed. He had given orders to find such a man. Oh, God, he thought, what is this doing to me?

"Get him out of my sight!" Gardner yelled suddenly.

When the lawmen had left the study with Cleavers, Frank Gardner turned to Dan Evers and John Goodell. "Well, gentlemen, can we convict him or not?"

Both men nodded. Dan Evers spoke first, "I think we could convict him even without his confession. Obviously the man is insane."

"With the confession there is no doubt that he will be convicted," John Goodell added.

Frank Gardner nodded. "Yes. I believe you are right." But he spoke without enthusiasm.

Evers clapped his hands eagerly. "Shall we begin proceedings immediately, Senator?"

"No." Gardner snapped. "Hold off until late next week. The longer we wait and draw this trial out, the better. As a Republican, Mr. Evers, I'm sure you can see my position."

"I see."

Gardner smiled. "Do you think Hennison and Durham will go along with that?"

"Yes sir. I'm sure they will."

Frank Gardner went to the east window of his study. Although his view was of all the East side of Twin Forks and the Mo-Ri Valley, he saw only the small wood-frame home that stood empty on Third Street. He clenched his fist and pressed his face nearer the window.

"Damn you, Jas Porter. I hope you're rotting in hell."

When Lona left the mansion that morning she went to see her sister-in-law. As she knocked on the door, Lona remembered how jealous she used to be of Dorothy's vitality and beauty. It was not until New York that she developed a love for Dorothy — the kind of love close sisters have for each other.

She knocked again. Through the frosted glass she saw a figure move, perceived the outline of Dorothy's long black hair approaching and stepped back expectantly. Finally the door opened and there was Dorothy.

Lona gasped at the transformation. "Dorothy?"

There was no greeting nor even an expression of recognition.

Dorothy held the door open silently while Lona looked at her in disbelief. Beautiful Dorothy had become an old woman. The once gorgeous black hair had gone limp. Now it hung in ratted strands to slumped shoulders that were covered by a dress that had become a dirty rag. The dancing eyes she remembered were dull. Lona had to restrain herself from running away.

Another surprise awaited inside — the house was immaculate. The oaken floors and the wooden tables gleamed in the even light that came from the windows while every piece of china in the bureau and milkglass on the tables were carefully placed. It was different and it should have seemed an improvement over the sloppiness of the house the last time Lona had seen it. But it was sterile. From the shining waxed floors to the carefully placed china, there was a lack of emotion and warmth.

Lona kissed Dorothy tenderly on the cheek. "It's so good to see you again. Your home is beautiful."

"I'll make some tea," Dorothy said and walked slowly toward the kitchen in an almost zombie fashion to do so.

Lona watched her walk away. She could have cried. What could she say to Dorothy, she asked herself. "Yes, I would like some tea," she called after her.

They sat in the livingroom with their tea. Dorothy took the straight chair beside the couch where Lona sat. "Are you feeling all right?" Lona asked.

Dorothy nodded, then looked nervously around the room as if she were searching for a spot of dust she might have missed or a scrap of paper. Lona forced herself to talk of New York and the train and the countryside — anything to emit some emotion from Dorothy. But Dorothy's face remained expressionless.

Not until Lona mentioned her father did Dorothy's eyes come alive — if only for a moment — before the slight wink of emotion passed and Dorothy subsided to her deadened state again.

"Father rules Twin Forks. I had to go away from this town, then come back to it, before I could see the reins he holds on everyone. It's just not right that he should be able to do this, Dorothy. What gives him the power to rule over other people in the middle of the world's greatest free country? He's a dictator and I can't be a part of it. All my life he taught me to do what was expected of me. I found out that that was what he expected. Anything I did that didn't in some way help him was unimportant. My life didn't matter. Albert's life didn't matter and neither did Mother's or anyone else. And that's why I must get out of here. Right after the trial, I'm off for New York and I don't think I'll ever be back."

Dorothy had listened without comment. Lona looked at her in pity. This was the woman she had admired, she thought, the example of a dream she might some day attain. Now crushed. But somewhere deep inside was the real Dorothy, she couldn't help but think. Perhaps before she returned to New York she would be able to find that person again.

Lona stood, pulled Dorothy to her feet, and led her around the room, "I just can't believe what a beautiful home you have Dorothy. You must work continually."

They stopped at the hallway door that led to the bedroom . . . Lona was afraid to move closer, but Dorothy had not become excited so she led her sister-in-law to the bedroom. It was as it had been the last time she had been in the room — except the blood was gone, the sheets were not pulled to the edge of the bed where Dorothy lie beaten near to death in a pool of blood. Now would Dorothy remember? Lona wondered.

"Who beat you, Dorothy?" she asked solidly. When there was no answer, she led Dorothy farther into the room.

"You were here — on the floor. I found you crying and covered with blood. Someone had beaten you that day, Dorothy? Tell me. You must tell me. Who beat you?"

Dorothy shook her head wearily, "I did not see his face," she said, dragging the words in staccato, like a schoolchild reading a new lesson.

"Dorothy. You must have seen his face."

"No," Dorothy screamed suddenly. "I did not!"

The outburst ended as abruptly as it had begun. Dorothy returned to the living room. At the door Lona said good-bye. "Dorothy, your son. Do you remember your son? I'll take care of him, Dorothy. Remember that if you can."

Lona realized what was happening to her as she walked the boulevard. The wind blew through her blond hair and her eyes watered from the cold and her senses awakened. She was out of the confines of the mansion, away from her father and brother and John Goodell, and now she saw the world through her own eyes again. The new-found sense of freedom was exhilarating.

When she reached the drive to the mansion, she decided not to enter. Her back straightened in defiance as she raised her head proudly letting the wind whip around her soft neck. No, she thought, to return now would be defeat. The control and comfort of the mansion; her father's rule, would soon overcome her again and she will have thrown life away. She walked on, south, toward Third Street.

She thought of New York. It was there that she became a woman and an individual. She had learned to work and to think for herself. Most importantly, she had learned that her own thoughts were meaningful and through them she could have some control over her own destiny. And she was no longer a virgin. Twice she had had sexual experiences. Although she had found neither encounter especially enjoyable, she had discovered that sex was neither filthy nor disgusting, as her Puritan upbringing in Twin Forks had led her to believe. It was not so important that she had lost her virginity. What was important was that she had lost her insecurity and had grown over the old-maid syndrome. Now she was a woman and she was certain that there was a man somewhere who could fulfill, not the void, but the space left in her for him.

And there was Johnnie. Dorothy's son of whom the world was never supposed to know.

They had been in New York for three weeks before Lona discovered that Dorothy was three months pregnant, and the father was not Albert.

"Does Father know?" she asked.

Dorothy laughed. "How do you think I bargained my way out of Twin Forks?"

The situation did not shock Lona at first. Dorothy would have the baby at their Uncle's estate. The baby would be taken for adoption. Dorothy would recuperate and when she returned, the world, Twin Forks, would be none the wiser. Not even Albert.

It was a common solution to the problem when a daughter of one of "the families" fell to indiscretion.

But three months away from Twin Forks had changed Lona. She withdrew her money from her father's bank to invest in real estate. She enjoyed spending time with people who had never heard of Twin Forks. And it bothered her that Dorothy was not enjoying the prospect of motherhood and became more and more remorse each day.

One evening she entered Dorothy's room determined to get things settled one way or another.

"I think we should tell father that we are bringing the baby home with us," Lona announced.

Dorothy looked at her with a dull stare. "That's not possible."

"Dorothy! This is 1912. Father has to come out of his Puritan ways. We can tell everyone that it's Albert's baby. We won't tell them anything. They'll assume it's Albert's!"

"Your father wouldn't allow it," Dorothy said.

Lona plopped down in a chair coyly, "Well then, we girls will just have to find a way to convince him."

"No. You don't understand," Dorothy said. "This is not some game!"

"What's to understand? Of course . . ."

Dorothy screamed, "Shut up. Just shut up. There is no happy ending, Lona. The father of the baby, you never even asked who he is. Did you wonder? The father is Jas Porter! Jas Porter! So let's just not talk about it again!"

And they did not talk about it again. Lona tried to put the situation out of her mind, becoming absorbed with real estate purchases and shopping sprees in the city, but always she could feel the fingers of Twin Forks reaching out to grab her and pull her back again.

Then a wire arrived from Twin Forks: COME HOME AS SOON AS POSSIBLE. It was followed by a letter explaining that Frank wanted his family together again during the upcoming trouble with the Porters and the detective.

That night Dorothy asked to see Lona.

"I am not putting the baby up for adoption."

Lona beamed.

"I'm giving him to you," Dorothy said.

"What?" Lona was shocked.

"We will return to Twin Forks without the baby." Dorothy said. "In a few weeks, you will return to New York, like you want to anyway. I will stay with Albert in Twin Forks."

"But Dorothy . . ."

"That's the only way my baby, and Jas Porter's baby, will have a normal life."

Lona was speechless. Her mind whirled but always came full circle to the same conclusion. Dorothy was right.

She reached Third Street. To the west was the Square. She would go there, she thought, to take a room in the hotel until it was time to leave for New York. But to the east, a half-block away, was the Jas Porter home. She could not see it from the intersection of the boulevard and Third Street because the Pinkerman's large two-story house blocked her view. But she knew it was there. It had haunted her for three and a half years from two thousand miles and now, it, the house of her nightmares, was less than one hundred yards away. Lona turned her back to the Square and walked east toward "the murder house," as everyone called it.

As she walked, she thought of her father. How could he hold such power over the people of this territory? She wondered. These were strong, hard-working men and women who had braved all kinds of challenges to make a place for themselves in Iowa. They were the same people whose ancestors had broken away from the power and control of England — and now they willingly let her father impose himself upon them. Why? She asked herself the question and wondered if she knew the answer.

Herself as an example . . . she had been most eager to please Frank Gardner and every word he uttered was law. Then she had gone away from Twin Forks to New York. At one time she had laughed at herself for the way she had been before and discounted it to youthfulness. But she had come home just a few days ago and almost immediately had fallen into the old ways of letting herself be controlled by her father's wishes. She had immediately bathed herself in the security of her father's shadow. Suddenly, no problem was significant enough to bother her. Normal everyday activities consumed her and major decisions were forgotten. Like water spreading out from a spill, she had followed the easiest course. And that same reason was what let her father take control of Twin Forks. The people were all too willing to let him have control; but, she wondered, did the people also resent him for it, as she did, and as did Albert? She was running away from it, revolting, as it were . . . so, would the people revolt also some day when the time was right? Yes, she decided, for he had set himself up as king and them as peasants and that is the way it is with kings and peasants.

The house at last was before her. She stared at it too frightened to move nearer. It was so small, she thought as she looked at it, much smaller than she had remembered, and this seemed to make it even more frightening to think that the terrible murders had happened here. They should have happened in an unusual place, like her father's mansion or a shack in a poor part of the city, but not in this small average home where average people lived and worked honestly to reach average goals.

The house was stark against winter-killed grass, and where the snow had melted from the roof, dried leaves filled the gutters and troughs. Paint had fallen away from the boards to the ground where dead weeds lapped against the side of the house like stilled waves on a rocky shore. Everything about the house was dead and sad and frightening. The terrible memories of the days before she left for New York turned and twisted through her mind. She remembered Provo being dragged from the front porch to be hanged; Dorothy lying beaten on the floor of her bedroom; the moment when she heard the news that the Porter family had been butchered; the thousands of strangers parading through town; and finally the little boy telling her of the hanging of the black family. She felt the world spin around her and the ground rise up to meet her as she fell on the hard ground.

"Lona. Lona Gardner." She heard a voice say as she opened her eyes.

"What?" she moaned. She saw the concerned face hovering over her, "Carl Gast. What happened?"

"You fainted, Lona," Carl Gast said as he helped her sit. "I was watching you from over there and you just started to rock on your feet and then you fell down. I tried to catch you but I didn't get here fast enough."

She looked around in bewilderment. Suddenly she began to cry and threw her arms around Carl Gast's neck, "Oh, Carl. I shouldn't have come home. I should have stayed in New York."

"I know," Carl said softly, "I tried to tell you that the first night you were in town."

Lona cried, "I thought I could face it. I thought I had to face it if I was ever going to forget it. Oh, Carl, I think I'm crazy."

Carl held her while she cried. He wanted to tell her that he had waited a long time to hold her, that he had loved her and no one else for the past twenty years. He put his hand to the temples of her forehead, "Maybe you're trying too hard to forget what happened. It isn't something you just forget like it never happened. You have to admit that they were murdered and then you have to live with it. That's the only way. Accept it."

Lona stopped crying and stood. "I can't seem to accept it, Carl. I feel that I was partly to blame for their murders. Responsible, somehow."

"You have to leave Twin Forks."

"I know. I thought that if I could just stand here and look at that house for awhile, without feeling frightened, I would be able to leave in peace with myself. But I couldn't do it, Carl. No, I'm not leaving Twin Forks — I'm running away."

"Once you're gone, you'll be able to work it out."

"I suppose so," Lona said and she felt better. "Say, what were you doing here anyway?"

Carl blushed. "I was walking down the boulevard when I saw you. I guess you might say I followed you here. I've been worried about you, Lona."

Lona smiled. "I'm glad. I thought about you a lot when I was in New York. You were my secret love before I left, you know."

"You were mine, too." Carl said haltingly. "I guess I'm saying that because I know you're leaving."

Lona touched his face gently with her fingers, "Some things are understood even though they are never said. Don't you think so?"

Carl looked away toward the mansion, "Yea," he said mockingly, "Like a Gast doesn't talk to a Gardner."

"Carl!" Lona said sharply.

"I'm sorry. It's not your fault, but it is true. Your old man would have me shot if he even knew we were talking now. A Gast isn't good enough for a Gardner. I might hurt your father's good name."

"You don't actually believe that my father is responsible for the murders do you, Carl?" But Carl was no longer listening to her. He was watching a car down the street coming toward them, a look of extreme displeasure on his face.

"What's the matter, Carl?"

"That car is Burt McLean's. Your brother will be with him. I better leave before he starts trouble."

"Trouble? We were just talking. What were you suppose to do, leave me in the street? No. You helped me and there is no reason for you to run."

"All right. We'll see how it goes."

Albert Gardner had his feet propped against the dash board and a bottle of whiskey pressed to his lips. He and Burt McLean had been drinking and riding aimlessly through Twin Forks and the back roads of the surrounding countryside since morning. Albert talked and drank and now he had told McLean to find him a woman, as he always did when the bottle was three-fourths gone.

"There ain't no women around today," Burt McLean was saying. "It's like I told you. You gotta wait until tonight before I can fix you up with something. Your old man doesn't like it when I get you tied into local girls, so we wait for the out-of-towners."

"Oh Christ! Find me somebody Burt, I'm going to be shot before nightfall and won't be good for no woman."

McLean sent a long stream of tobacco juice to the floorboard, "I'll try, buddy. But I ain't makin' no promises. When there ain't no cunt, there just ain't no cunt unless you want me to take you to that schoolteacher again."

Albert brought the bottle down, choking on a mouthful of whiskey, "Bull Shit! No, let's keep her for the really bad days when there's nobody. And I mean nobody."

"This might be one of those days, buddy. Might be."

They had reached the boulevard and were about to turn south to take another pass around the Square.

"Hey! Who the hell is that?" Albert dropped his feet to the floor and his knuckles turned white as his fingers gripped the bottle neck.

"It's your sister." McLean said. "Looks like Carl Gast with her."

Albert Gardner was fully alert. "Get your ass down there, Burt. I'm going to pound the shit out of that son-of-a-bitch once and for all."

McLean obeyed the order and continued down Third Street toward Lona and Carl. "Hey, buddy, I'm suppose to keep you out of trouble."

"No trouble, Burt." Albert Gardner grinned and pulled a hard swig from the bottle.

"Yea, but for no reason you're gonna . . ."

"He's a Gast, Burt. That's reason enough for me and for my old man."

Lona had decided that she would not allow her brother to embarrass either her or Carl with his sneering remarks or gestures. She stood firmly on the side of the street waiting for the car to pull up to them and fully prepared to tell her brother to mind his own business and that she was not part of his business. The car came to a quick stop beside them and Albert jumped out onto the street. He came around the front of the car to where Lona and Carl waited. He stopped in front of Carl Gast, took one quick look at his sister, then came back into Carl with a jab to the stomach that sent the smaller man to his knees. Before Gast could respond Albert brought his knee up to the jaw and Gast fell backward onto the ground of Jas Porter's yard. Lona watched these first two blows without realizing what was happening. The actions were so abrupt and unnecessary that her mind did not register the brutality of her own brother. But Carl Gast lay on his back with blood pouring from his mouth and finally her mind was forced to admit what her eyes had seen.

"Albert! No!" she screamed and thrust her arms around his neck as hard as she could. But her screams and hold could not stop her brother who continued to kick Carl Gast in the sides, and in the back when he turned, and in the chest when he tried to climb to his feet for the last time. With the ease of a bull brushing off a fly, Albert tossed Lona aside and stood over Carl Gast.

"Never again, Gast. If I catch you with my sister, I'll kill you. You hear that Gast? I'll kill you." With that Albert turned and walked casually to the car. As he climbed in Lona heard him say, "Come on, Burt, I know where we're going to get what I need now."

The car went east, over East Creek bridge, toward the bluffs.

"Where are they going?" Lona asked. But Carl had propped himself to one elbow and groaned, "My family's farm is that way."

Lona ran to him and pulled his head to her lap, "Why did he do that, Carl?"

"Because I'm a Gast," Carl grunted.

"But what makes him think he can get away with it? It's barbaric."

"He's a Gardner."

Lona knew the answer was an honest one. A man's last name was all that was needed to get away with . . . murder, she thought.

"I'm a Gardner," Lona said softly.

Carl Gast sat up holding his sore sides. His pain in moving made his statement more sincere, "That's why you have to get the hell out of here, Lona. You can't stay. It's not good for you around here."

Suddenly Lona changed. She felt the change come over her in a flow of hot blood that spread from her toes to her head. "No. I will stay in Twin Forks until I have found out who murdered the Porter family and who beat my sister-in-law half to death. And I will show my father and my brother that they cannot control the lives of others. For my family and for myself, I am going to stay. And you, Carl Gast, will be my escort to the Christmas dance this year."

"You're crazy. If I take you to the dance your father would have me murdered." Carl smiled.

Lona pulled a handkerchief from her dress and wiped the blood from his lips. "Well, if you prefer not to take me," she said coyly, "I suppose I could sit home by myself."

Carl shook his head and grinned uncertainly, "If that's the way you want it, that's the way you get it. Just one thing though."

"What's that?" Lona asked.

"You said you wanted to find out who murdered the Porters, who beat up Dorothy and teach your father a lesson at the same time."

"That's right."

"What are you going to do if you find out that it was your father who murdered the Porters?"

CHAPTER FOURTEEN

Carl Gast returned to his farm where he lay in the hayloft of the barn. He had been sleeping, but now he became aware of the sound of a rattling engine on the lane to his home. He pulled himself across the loose hay to the edge of the loft where he pressed his face against the sideboards in time to see Albert Gardner and Burt McLean climb out of the car. They were both drunk now and they laughed loudly as they stumbled against the front fender to support themselves. Soon Alice Gast stumbled from the rear seat. The two men climbed back into the car and sped away down the lane.

Instead of going to the house, Alice walked limply to the barn. From his position in the loft, Carl watched her enter and latch the large barn door behind her. Thinking that she was alone, she went to the water tank and in one quick sweep she grabbed the lower hem of her dress and stripped it over her head. Naked against the loose hay on the barn floor, her wet body shone in the dull light as she stooped to the tank and brought a handful of ice cold water to her hot body. He heard her gasp as she splashed the water into her crotch and again when she wiped the insides of her legs.

After she was gone, Carl waited silently in the hayloft. He lay there wondering how his family had become so low. But he knew the answer to his question. The Gardner family had ruined the Gasts. And, somehow, he would get even with the Gardner family, he vowed to himself. Somehow.

It was evening and he sat on the floor near the open fire with Lorraine beside him. She was quiet. The light from the fire danced in her watery eyes and bounced from her face like two soft moons of yellow. He had been gazing at her remorsely while he thought of leaving her again.

"You know that I must leave tomorrow?" he asked.

"Yes. It is something that you must do."

"I have waited here too long."

"I know."

They gazed at the fire together not having to speak until John Morgan asked a question that had been bothering him.

"I wonder if you will have the courage to stand what might happen if Frank Gardner discovers what we have been to each other." He laughed when he saw her eyes turn from warm complacence to hot defiance. Morgan moved the rough tips of his fingers gently down the side of her face, "We are going to expose Frank Gardner all the way down to his bare butt. He will have to fight back if he wants to beat us. And if he finds out about you, he will use you to fight me."

"And you?" Lorraine asked. "What will you do?"

"You mean — if it does happen?" Morgan shook his head. "I don't know. I could say that I will stand by you, but if it comes to the point where I could lose this case against Gardner — I don't know. Not a very gallant thing for me to say, is it? But our other choice is for me to stay away from you until after the trial."

"No, I wouldn't like that. I worry about being found out and maybe even losing this place, but if I know that I have your love then I can put up with anything that happens."

"You'll have my love no matter what happens."

"Then love me now."

The firelight followed them into the bedroom, illuminating the room in a yellow glow that let him watch her disrobe and suddenly it was hundreds of years ago and they were making gleeful, unrestricted love. Never had he felt the emotion that rose in him with her now. He had found strength in her. She had been his help to get along in what had once been a lifeless world to him. Now she rose and fell to meet him and he came into her violently. He would need this night to remember when the failures and disappointments of his search tried to pull him down again.

CHAPTER FIFTEEN

Attorney General Fred Martin
Des Moines, Iowa

December 26, 1915

Dear Fred,

If you have been following the recent happenings of our murder case in your newspaper, then you know that we have arrested the confessed murderer and have brought him to trial. Cleavers has described the murders accurately, and much supportive evidence as to his presence at the time of the murders — and his disappearance the morning after the murders has been established. It looks like at last we have the murderer and I am happy to say that Twin Forks can soon begin to think again about progress.

There is a problem, however, and I am asking for your help. I have filed suit against men in our town who have from the beginning tried to use the murder case to destroy my political career and social standing. First, they accused me of the murders. Although I was outraged, at the time I decided not to honor their malicious lies

with comment. When Cleavers was arrested, I thought the matter
would drop. It did not.

On the last day of trial before Christmas, I was accused publicly,
and on court record, of having hired Cleavers to murder the Porter
family. Although they offered absolutely no evidence to warrant
such an accusation, I have lost the respect from my friends and
neighbors, and my daughter has left her home.

I must take action now to regain my social standing. Will you
come to the County Seat to represent me? I know that we are both
interested in my political future in this state and hope to see you before the Cleavers' trial resumes on January 5, 1916.

> With sincerest regards,
> Senator Frank F. Gardner

Frank Gardner read the letter with the same intensity that had always been his. Only now a pair of gold rimmed glasses enlarged the
words for him and when he stroked his beard slowly he did so with
the knowledge that a long streak of gray ran through it and that similar changes in color were taking place along his brows and temples. His appearance was that of a healthy, retired, well-to-do gentleman who should be riding out life comfortably and effortlessly.
But neither age nor retirement were on Frank Gardner's mind.
There were many things he had left to do in life and if it took forty
more years to do them, he intended to work every day of those forty
years to accomplish what he had started. Only one thing could stop
him from reaching his goals, only one man could keep him from
going further and he had decided that he had had enough of the
Twin Forks axe murders and of detective John Morgan. He finished reading the letter, gave a slow nod and put his signature to the
page in heavy black ink. Carefully, he blew the ink dry and gave the
paper three crisp folds before placing it in the envelope. He started
to hand it across the library table to John Goodell's waiting hand,
but before letting loose of it, he said,

"From the beginning I have had to believe that the course I am
taking is the correct one. If I don't believe that, how can I justify my
actions to anyone, including myself?"

Goodell read his statement as a qualifying one, something Frank Gardner was not accustomed to doing, and he asked cautiously, "Will you need some help from the Party?"

An irritable glance replaced the anger that might have been expected. Frank Gardner turned to a stack of papers on his table saying unemotionally, "If I go to Des Moines, it will be to pick up some support with the Governor and other senators. They cannot offer me help, none that I can think of, but they could refrain from giving us opposition if they thought I was going to come out of this on top. I will not go begging. With Cleavers all but standing on the gallows, I won't have to. I never will."

"The men in Des Moines could be important for us," John Goodell reasoned.

"Important, yes. But I will not go begging. We have our ace in the hole."

On Friday, John Morgan moved unwilling above the covers. Beside the bed on the lamp table a half-emptied bottle of whiskey stood in victory. From the lamp, through the yellowed shade, a weak light washed the dirty wall and pooled a sick glow halfway across the room, over the oak floor covered by papers and heavy clothes and empty bottles — the sacrifices of John Morgan.

Morgan sat at the edge of the bed. From the frosted window he could see the downtown of Blue Island, Illinois. And he could see the sheriff's office where he had tried for twenty days to find a link between the Mansell murders of Blue Island the Porter murders of Twin Forks. Now Morgan wondered if the sheriff had been correct when he had said that first day: "Here we had a no-good family that got murdered — probably by the husband, Blacky Mansell, who's missing. Sure, I could track the guy down, but who cares? As far as the folks that pay my salary are concerned, I'd be wasting their money to try and find Mansell. If you run across him and bring him back, then we'll hang the bastard. Otherwise, I don't care."

And there was the difference, Morgan knew. In Twin Forks a respected family of the town had been axed to death. If it could happen to the Porters, then it could happen to anyone, at anytime. He looked above the buildings. The sky over Illinois was an ice-blue re-flection of the snow-covered ground. But the depression of hope-lessness had once again settled in Morgan's mind. Don't let this day begin, he prayed.

But the day began. He heard the outer door at the street level bang. He heard the steps as a man in heavy boots hurried up the stairs. And he heard the boots stop outside his door, and the loud knock — "Telegram, Mr. Morgan," the old messenger said. He opened the envelope and read the short message from Al Crans,

JOHN MORGAN
BLUE ISLAND, ILLINOIS

COME HOME QUICK — SLANDER SUIT FILED BY GARDNER — LUCK

AL CRANS

Luck, Morgan repeated the last word of the message. He kicked at a stack of research papers that spewed across the room. No luck.

CHAPTER SIXTEEN

January 5, 1916

John Morgan watched Al Crans pin pictures of Blacky Mansell on the wall beside Marzyek, the killer of Colorado. Crans worked slowly for there was no reason to hurry.

"How's the talk, Al? Are they suppose to pass verdict on Cleavers today?"

Crans walked over to the window and looked to the Square, "I'm guessing that the decision is entirely up to Gardner himself. He could drag it out for another couple of days or he could decide to get it over with. But I think Gardner will want to be there when the jury comes in."

Morgan grunted, "Yeah, he'll want to be there for his victory. So when Gardner takes off for the County Seat we'll know that's the day."

"Right. He won't go otherwise. There's nothing more boring than to sit in a courtroom all day knowing that nothing is going to happen."

Morgan tossed a picture of Linous Cleavers on the desk. "To think that the little queer is going to kill our case. When the jury finds Cleavers guilty, then it's almost automatic that they'll find us guilty of slander. What else could there be if they decide to hang the queer?"

Crans finished the pin up job and turned to Morgan seriously, "I hate to bring this up, but you should be thinking about your own defense. If the verdict is already guilty then you should be finding ways to mitigate your sentence."

Morgan heard the words but his mind was far away searching for the answer to his question: how could he get Cleavers off? If Linous Cleavers goes — Morgan goes. The Gardner case goes. His career goes. Cleavers must be found not guilty. But how?

"I'm going out, Al." He pulled on his heavy black coat and stepped out of the headquarters onto the Square. He wasn't sure why, but he walked directly to the hotel where he knew Lona Gardner was having breakfast in the dining room.

"Miss Gardner?" he asked, then became embarrassed at his own excitement when she looked up at him apprehensively.

"Yes. I am Lona Gardner," she answered brightly.

"I'm John Morgan, Miss Gardner."

The smile faded and her eyes dropped to the table. "I have nothing to discuss with you, Mr. Morgan."

"I didn't think you would, Miss Gardner. But I did want you to know how sorry I am if my case against your father had anything to do with the trouble you have had."

"It did not. I left home for personal reasons that would not help your case, Mr. Morgan. If they would, I would not give them to you."

Her loyalty to her family pleased him. "I never asked you to help me, Miss Gardner. I'm just a detective trying to. . ."

"Trying to hurt my family. And I won't help you," Lona interrupted.

"Trying to bring a murderer to justice."

"They have Cleavers."

"Yes. They were given Cleavers," Morgan said. He did not see Lona jerk her head defiantly toward him when he spoke those last words as she turned to leave. Before he was across the dining room he was sorry for what he had said — that he had said it to Lona.

There had been no reason to bother her and he did not like the idea that she had opposed him. As he crossed the room, Morgan was glad that he could not see her staring at him, but he could feel the daggers of her glare digging into his back.

When he left the hotel, Morgan walked directly to the Jas Porter home. It attracted him this morning, the place of the crime, the location of the murders that could now be the end of his career almost four years later. The front door had been tied with rope to keep the blowing snows out of the house because the key had not been found and the lock had not been changed. No one lived there now and he wondered as he entered if anyone would live there again. In the kitchen he remembered the bowl full of bloodied water and in the parlor he recalled the testimony of the doctors in the Coroner's Inquest to the position of the bodies of the two Stills girls on the small bed that was no longer there . . . it had been burned along with all other items in the home as if they too had been diseased by the act of murder and could contaminate a neighboring house to a similar tragedy. He climbed the stairs, empty also and echoing his foot steps, to the two bedrooms where the entire Porter family had been slaughtered. He recalled pictures of Herbert and Paul and Judy and Sarah, and the parents he had never known, Sally and Jas. Stains on the walls, hidden failingly by dust, revealed which way the heads had lain and recounted too clearly the findings of the doctors.

Morgan returned to the downstairs parlor where he propped his back against a wall near the door, just two feet away from where the bloodied axe had rested that morning. He was very close to the scene now. Perhaps if he stayed there long enough, a ghost of Jas Porter or of the children would contact him and reveal the secrets that only they knew. But no news came from the blank walls or the silent creaking of the house. He sat there for two hours staring at the northwest corner of the room where the Stills girls had lain. Over and over again he imagined unwillingly the exact position of the murderer as he raised his axe to the ceiling and dropped it again to the innocent head of Vera Stills and Clesta.

It was after noon, he supposed, for he had been there a long time. The front door of the house flew open and Al Crans came running into the parlor, "I've been looking all over for you Morgan. Frank

Gardner took off for the County Seat over an hour ago. They are going to pass sentence on Cleavers today."

"So what am I supposed to do about it?" Morgan asked.

Crans groaned and called out the door, "Bring her on in," and Russ Porter walked through the door followed by a third woman. "I want you to meet Vina Thompkins," Crans said. "She saw Blacky Mansell and Gardner make the deal for the Porter's to be killed."

At the same time John Morgan ran from the Porter home, Frank Gardner was entering the County Seat. He rode in a new Auburn driven by Burt McLean. Beside him John Goodell read from a ream of paper on his lap: "We have witnesses who said that they saw Reverend Cleavers in town the night of the murders and that Cleavers disappeared around midnight. We have testimony that Cleavers is a homosexual, a rapist and a solicitor of pornographic pictures, along with author of a queer book of love. We know that Cleavers was expelled from the school of ministry in Omaha three years before the murders and we have Cleaver's own confession to the murders. That should do it, I should think."

For Frank Gardner, today was to be the end of all his problems. In one fell swoop he would not only get John Morgan and Russ Porter off his back forever, but with a guilty verdict in for Cleavers, he would close the books on the Twin Forks axe murders forever. His town could begin growing again.

The road to the County Seat swelled with people on their way to the trial. The Christmas break had been long enough and now, with renewed interest, they came to watch the demise of Linous Cleavers. By the time Frank Gardner and John Goodell reached the courthouse, the streets around it were filled by lines of spectators waiting to be let inside. They went to a side door where County Attorney Evers let them in.

"Mr. Martin is waiting in the conference room, Senator," Evers informed them.

Frank Gardner climbed four flights of the marble stairs that brought him to the second floor where the courtroom was still closed to the public. He stopped at the door to watch an old man and woman work to clean the floor once more before the trial resumed for the afternoon. The smell of the disinfectant they were using was refreshing — proper that the room should be cleaned on the day that his life was to be renewed, he felt. John Goodell came running up the stairs to join them. He took a last look at the courtroom, slapped Goodell on the back and headed across the second floor lobby to the conference room.

Attorney General Fred Martin was a man much like himself, Gardner knew. In appearance, Martin was tall and slim with broad shoulders that belied his thinness and, in the past couple of years, his full head of hair had lightened in color, and just here and there, a tuft of gray hair accented the brows and sideburns and temples. Inwardly, Gardner knew that Martin was also much like him. Martin was a man who believed only in his own convictions. Like Gardner he protected them fiercely and, like Gardner he saw that the success of Iowa was the success of Fred Martin.

"So, today's the day," Martin said as he rose to greet Gardner.

"Fred, I'm glad you could make it," Gardner said, and shook his hand warmly.

"I thought I should be here for the last day. I want to see the audience when the jury calls Cleavers guilty."

"What's the difference? If they find Cleavers guilty, then obviously I have been slandered."

"Right, from a legal standpoint, there is no problem. But from a political view, it is important that at least most of the people believe for themselves that Cleavers is definitely guilty and that justice is done today."

"If they don't believe it, then I lose the support of the party?"

"I'm afraid so, Frank. If it hadn't been for this Cleavers fellow, you were going to be ousted two months ago — they couldn't take the chance that you'd come out of court with a bad name even if you won the contest."

"They should be happy now, then. Today we convict Cleavers and Friday we begin the trial against Morgan and the others."

Three loud knocks came from the door and County Attorney Evers put his head into the room, "They're bringing Cleavers in now and the courtroom is filled. I managed to get three seats for you in the front row behind my chair."

"This is it," Martin said.

Frank Gardner nodded then frowned at John Goodell who said, "Let's hope to hell Linous Cleavers is actually guilty."

It was a festive mood in the courtroom. They took the seats Evers had reserved for them paying little attention to the crowd. But Gardner enjoyed the enthusiasm of the audience and wondered if they supported him and saw that he was also about to win his slander suit, or were they simply anxious to hang Cleavers and get this thing over with?

The audience quieted in their chairs, stood, and Judge Elmer Woodruff of the Fifteenth Judicial District court walked slowly to his chair, nodded to the foreman, A. P. Pearson, who told the audience to be seated again. A low murmur rose and fell, then all was quiet again.

"County Attorney Evers?"

"Yes sir."

"Do you have more witnesses to call, or are you ready for a summation?"

"Summation, Your Honor. We have no more witnesses. All of our evidence has been submitted."

"Mr. Schrank, are you ready for summation?"

"Yes, Your Honor, the defense is ready."

"Proceed," the judge mumbled.

"Pardon me, Your Honor?" Evers asked.

"I said get on with it, Mr. Evers."

Dan Evers quickly glanced over some papers he had placed on the table, then stepped to face the juror's station: "Ladies and gentlemen, it has been a long time since the Jas Porter family was murdered. Most of you were friends and neighbors and none of us will ever forget that terrible Monday morning when we were told that this good family and the two little Stills girls had been axed to death in their sleep. Now, by his own confession, the man responsible for this tragedy, our tragedy, sits here in the same room with us.

"I submit that no penalty other than death would bring justice to the Porters, but we are not here on a vengeful purpose. No, it is not for revenge that I ask that Linous Cleavers suffer the punishment of death. It is for justice. The same justice he would deserve had none of us know that Porters or the Stills. He still must hang for that is justice by the law, the law of man, as surely as his acts of murder were contrary to the law of God and man."

Frank Gardner looked at Attorney General Martin, who had been watching the people in the juror's box and the audience. Martin turned to him shortly and with a quick, tight smile nodded his approval.

Thirty minutes later Dan Evers still droned on about the mass amount of evidence against Cleavers and still the jury was watching and listening to him alertly. A good sign Gardner thought, and he remembered the day of "The Great Chicago Fire". As he stood there looking to the sky, a slight breeze came from the south and there, alone on the hill, he swore he saw the finger of God reach down to the black clouds and whirl them around until suddenly a large patch of blue sky showed through for the first time in five days. The depression of the overcast had been lifted, the awesomeness of the unknown black clouds had been erased.

He sat back in his courtroom chair feeling that once more the world had been lifted from his shoulders and he could breath fresh air again.

He knew that the young County Attorney Evers would go on with his summation for another thirty minutes, and he knew that Schrank would offer summation for the defense, so he settled into his chair comfortably to wait out the end. His mind had drifted to that point where one could be awake and yet not be bothered by happenings around him when he noticed the judge was pounding is gavel at the bench, the jurors heads were turned toward the back of the room and the audience around him was standing. He turned to see detective John Morgan entering the courtroom, his face red from the wind and cold, his heavy coat still buttoned around him. Gardner's heart pounded as he watched John Morgan march through the gate at the end of the aisle and approach the judge's bench.

Morgan did not walk to the bench. He closed the small gate behind him and spoke to the judge from fifteen feet away, so that the jurors and the audience could hear. Morgan's eyes were red, and the iced evaporation on his moustache glistened in the courtroom lights which added to the fierce look of the detective.

"If you hang this man, Your Honor, you'll be hanging an innocent man. I can prove that Linous Cleavers did not murder the Porter family."

County Attorney Evers walked toward the bench and smirked, "If Mr. Morgan has some new evidence, Your Honor, I suggest he present it here and now."

"I will do that, Your Honor. You must agree to hear the testimony of one more witness."

"We have entered our summations, your honor," Evers argued.

The judge shook his head. "This is a Grand Jury with serious implications. We will hear the testimony."

With a last look at Frank Gardner, John Morgan walked back down the aisle, descended the stairs and returned with Vina Thompkins. She was sworn in and told her story.

The crowd in the courtroom remained quiet for only a few seconds. Then they went wild with excitement over Morgan's display. Fred Martin tried to pull Frank Gardner back to his seat, but Gardner was oblivious to him. Suddenly Cleavers was going to be found innocent and he was left with the slander suit he had already filed. He walked out of the courtroom followed by John Goodell. As they reached the outer doors to leave the courthouse, he turned to Goodell and asked calmly, "Mr. Goodell, did you find out what there is to know about John Morgan?"

"Yes sir."

"Anything we can use?"

"Yes sir."

"Good. They'll be throwing a lot of dirt at me next week. We'll fight them with their own poison."

It was warm, calm and safe at the farm. Too comfortable because of John Morgan's overwhelming desire to stay there forever. Let the mind rest. Feel the warmth of the fire and the heat of the woman cuddled under one arm. The heart throb.

"You may not get rid of me this time," he said.

"No. You will go," she answered.

"I don't see why. Now that I have made my big show to get Cleaver's case thrown out, I'm stuck with a slander suit on my head that I can hardly defend myself against."

"Well, you kept an innocent man from hanging for something he didn't do. Doesn't that make you feel good?"

"Sure. I don't suppose God appreciates those little ironies — I, John Morgan, pulled one over on fate."

"What happens to Cleavers now? Do they just let him go?"

"No. They are going to ship him back to New York for commitment into an insane asylum."

"I love you, John Morgan."

"If it means anything from a man who is about to die — I love you, too."

Later, when the fire had burned to a low glow in the morning darkness, Lorraine knelt by the hearth and pulled her dress over her head. She fell backwards onto the thick fur of the rug that had been warmed through hours by the fire and waited for her man to climb onto her. Normally she would not understand the sexual inhibitions of this man, but tonight she felt closer than the inches that swelled within her. The tension that ran through his body came to her with a plea to drive them away and she responded in the only way she knew how. She spread herself wider and pulled him tighter, as if she could put all of him inside her and thus protect him.

Morning came to reveal a lone set of horse tracks in the fresh snow leading to the farm home, but not away again. Inside, the flames in the fireplace rose high above the new wood and the smells of sausage and fresh coffee mixed with corn-meal filled the house.

"This has got to be the coldest morning on record. Even my spring well was iced over this morning," Russ Porter said.

"Then why the hell didn't you stay in bed? I don't like to see you freezing your ass off on my account," Morgan sneered across the table at his client.

"Hey, what's the matter with you?"

"Nothing. Can't you see that? You fill me with no end of cheer and good will."

"I thought you'd be in high spirits after getting Cleavers off. You went up against Senator Gardner and you won. The whole town was talking about it last night."

"Great. I don't suppose anyone has bothered to mention the slander suit?"

"Of course. And you know what they're saying? They're saying that maybe detective John Morgan has a case against Frank Gardner after all. They're pretty mad at Gardner right now. They think he tried to push Cleavers off on them, and now they are wondering why he would do that if he wasn't involved with the murder of my brother and his family."

"That's fine. But they are wrong about one thing: I don't have a case against Gardner. I may never have a case against him. On top of that, if I did have a case against Gardner, I'd have to reveal everything to win the slander suit. Then it would be almost impossible to use the same evidence to convict him for murder later."

Russ Porter was excited. He leaned across the table, "I have been thinking of that. I think we should concentrate on winning the slander suit, like Sam Durham said. Without that, we lose all support of the people around here anyway."

John Morgan looked up at Russ, appreciating the sacrifice the man had just made. "In other words, you'd be satisfied if we showed everyone that Gardner is guilty by winning the slander trial — even if we blow our chance for a murder trial?"

"Let's face it — this is Twin Forks. What matters is what people think. If we get you off that slander suit, then Frank Gardner pays for the murders for the rest of his life. For a man like Frank Gardner, that would be worse punishment than hanging."

"The compromise. Always a compromise." Morgan was pensive. It occurred to him that there was no such thing as loss or victory. Only compromise. He had never considered this middle ground in regard to the Twin Forks axe murder case.

Russ Porter put his coffee on the table, "At any rate, I didn't come here to talk about the trial. This morning a messenger from the County Seat came to me with a message for you. Sam Durham wants to see you."

"Durham? Why in hell's name would he want to see me?"

"I wondered about that, too. But why would the boss of our County Attorney want to see the one person who could destroy our Republican senator? Sam Durham wants to make a deal — he wants to buy you off so you'll leave Gardner alone. You won't let that happen, will you?"

Morgan smirked, "Right now, he can have me for a dollar."

"You weren't very nice to Russ. He's just a frightened man depending on you to help him," Lorraine said when they were alone.

"I'm not feeling particularly nice today. In order to win a slander suit I'm not going to be able to afford the luxury of being either nice or honorable. This whole thing already smells like an over-worked shit house in the middle of July."

"You can always come here when you need to get away from it all. We don't even have to mention the case if you don't want to."

"I don't know. You're the first person I have met for a long time that meant something to me. Now I might have to lose you."

"Why?" Lorraine laughed, "to protect me from evil forces?"

"If Gardner finds out about you, he'll use you until you are ashamed to show your face in town. I don't want to see you lose it because of me and an egotistical maniac like Frank Gardner."

"As long a I have you, I can lose nothing. Without you, I can have nothing."

Morgan slammed his hand on the table. "No. I won't let your name be dragged through the dirt of Frank Gardner's trial. When they start, they won't stop. Maybe when this is all over we can start together again, but let's not fool ourselves. Not us."

Lorraine touched his face softly, "Just remember, I am here and I will love you tomorrow, next month, next year or ten years from now. Can you do that?"

"I think so."

He looked at her. He smiled but it quickly faded and he said concernedly, "I don't know for sure. After seven months on this case, I am really just beginning. And now that it is starting, I see everyone getting hurt — and no winners."

The door to the law offices of Hennison and Durham was open. Morgan walked into the lobby where he had first met County Attorney Dan Evers for the conversation that he supposed prompted his return. The lobby was empty. The desk was in pin-neat condition with the typewriter covered and a small pile of white paper stacked efficiently on the table. Ever's office and that of Hennison were dark with their doors opened. The door to Durham's office was three-quarters closed, but through the opening Morgan could see the edge of a large desk and it was evident that a desk light from the opposite side had been left on.

"Who's out there?" a voice called.

"Morgan."

"Yes, yes, come in Morgan. I have been waiting all morning and half the afternoon for you."

It was a heavy door, carved in deep panels of rose design engulfed by thorns of the same plant that produced the lovely flower.

Morgan took a deep breath and pushed against the door. It swung easily on its hinges.

Why it is necessary for a serious partner of a successful law firm to surround himself with an office that bespeaks nothing but sophistication, fine manners and a stately attitude is unexplainable by anyone other than a psychiatrist. But such is the case. One senses a deep hidden emotion of insecurity that is supported by the "how the hell are you" attitude of the lawyer.

Two men were in the room. The silver-haired gentleman behind the oak desk was Sam Durham. He looked at Morgan with sparkling, mischievous eyes that totally enjoyed the bewilderment they saw on Morgan's face. Durham waved toward a low, brown leather chair which placed Morgan beside the other older man he did not know. The older man nodded politely with the same sparkle of secrecy in his eyes. So they really are going to try to buy themselves a detective, Morgan thought as he stared at the lively face of Sam Durham across the desk.

"I am here," Morgan announced into the silence.

"And we are pleased," Sam Durham smiled. "This old fossil beside you is Amos Potters. I talked Amos into coming here today also. Amos is our territories' oldest and most respected attorney. Amos was practicing here before the town even had a sheriff — before it was even a town, just a settlement this side of Omaha."

"I have heard of you." Morgan looked at the old man who nodded again silently.

Sam Durham continued, "Old Amos has gained more respect from the people of this territory than any lawyer I know. Everyone is acquainted with him or his reputation. He has taken on some cases for people, poor people, that everyone knew he was never going to get a red cent for. And he has had his share of battles against the aristocracy — and won!"

"Durham, did I freeze my ass off today to hear your opinion of Amos Potters, or do you want something from me?"

Durham's smile did not fade. "I see. Well, to the first part, yes, I want you to know all about Amos Potters. To the second part, no, I don't want anything of you — I want to give you something."

"And what could that be — a train ticket to California?"

"No," Durham spoke seriously. "I am offering you a most precious commodity. I am offering you Mr. Amos Potters."

Morgan laughed. "And how much money do I get if I use Mr. Amos Potters as my counselor?"

"I am afraid you misunderstand my intentions, Mr. Morgan. Amos is willing to act as your counsel — to defend you to the best of his ability — to give you the benefit of his years of respect and experience in order to help you win the slander suit. He is the only good counselor you'll find in these parts willing to help you. Don't throw it away because of some foolish notion you have that I am trying to help Senator Gardner."

Morgan pulled his bowler hat from his head and tossed it on the desk. "All right, let's say that Amos Potters is going to bestow all of this on me out of the goodness of his heart? Why? Why him? Why you? You and Gardner are suppose to be on the same team."

Durham looked from Morgan to Potters then walked to the window and pulled the shade. The light of a bright, overcast afternoon came into the room and the downtown storefronts of the County Seat nestled beneath them as in a painting framed by heavy drapes.

"We want you to win this case, Mr. Morgan. Potters is willing to come out of retirement to represent you. He dislikes Senator Gardner and believes that Gardner is definitely behind the murders of the Jas Porter family."

Durham paused. He was speaking matter-of-factly and gazing out the window. "As for myself, I have learned that Attorney General Fred Martin has come here from Des Moines to help Gardner. I am against Gardner. More importantly, I am against Martin. They are two of a kind — out to get every scrap of power and success they can lay hands on. I'm not usually against that, understand, but in this situation I am certain that both of these men will be detrimental to the Republican Party in Iowa — possibly for the entire nation if they continue to climb."

"Do you believe Gardner is responsible for the murders?" Morgan asked.

"No not really, and I suppose that shocks you. But understand that I am a man of issues and politics. Right now I want you to put Frank Gardner and Fred Martin out of politics and your slander trial. The Jas Porter murders are the issues that can achieve that. If everything goes well, Fred Martin will go down with Gardner and this state will be safe from those men forever."

For some reason Morgan felt that he could trust Durham and Potters. For a moment the decision to trust them all the way or tell them to go to hell wavered back and forth in his mind. In the next moment he made his decision with the supportive reminder that nothing could hurt his position at this time. "We seem to agree that if Gardner loses the slander trial he will be automatically found guilty of involvement in the murders by the people."

"Yes . . . by the voters in this case."

"I don't like the idea of intentionally missing the chance to convict Gardner of murder," Morgan said truthfully.

"Perhaps you are right, Mr. Morgan, but if you don't win the slander suit, then nor will you win a murder trial. I think we can agree on that point. Let's have a drink."

While Durham poured three scotch and waters from a bookcase cupboard behind the desk, Morgan turned to Potters, "I don't have a case against Gardner — not one good enough to convict a man of murder."

The old man who had not yet spoken shrugged his shoulders with a pleasant smile. "Mr. Morgan, it will be your duty to discover evidence against the Senator. I will present the evidence. You must look at me as simply another tool at your disposal. Nothing more."

"That's great. What advice do you have for me right now — other than to leave the country?"

Potters chuckled, "My advice to you now is that you remember we are defending you against a charge of slander. We are not charging Senator Gardner with murder, at least not as far as the jury is concerned."

Sam Durham returned with the drinks. He sat again behind his desk with a deep contemplating look fixed upon Morgan. "John, do you realize how popular you are going to be when you are found innocent of this slander? You'll be a hero."

"Yeah. A dead hero."

"Oh, I don't think Gardner will try anything physical when the whole town would know he was behind it. He's too smart to do that. But what I was getting at, John, is that you could go a long way in politics. Maybe with a little bit of my help and possibly this year. Does that appeal to you?

"Appeal to me?" Morgan laughed. Then he became serious. "Yes, I suppose it does. But I better find a case against Gardner first. That's my main worry. I need to develop an iron-clad case."

"Where do you start?"

Morgan was at the door. He turned. "Hell if I know."

In late January the temperature in Iowa can drop forty degrees in a very short time. It can be thirty-eight degrees above zero at four-thirty at sunset and ten below an hour and a half later. By the time he reached headquarters on the empty Square of Twin Forks, Morgan's face was frozen beet red and ice particles an inch long dripped from his moustache. He was still stomping the cold from his feet when he noticed that Al Crans was at the stove at the back of the room . . . and another man was also there.

Al Crans came to meet him, "Where the hell have you been? Russ said you were going to the County Seat to see Sam Durham. Who is he?"

"Keep it down. I'll tell you later. Who's that back by the stove?"

"Oh, that's Hermann Heinsfurther. He's so upset that he decided to wait here for you if it took a month — and I was afraid maybe it would."

Morgan smiled warily, "Hermann Heinsfurther. Just what I need on a cold winter's eve."

"Mr. Heinsfurther, this is John Morgan. Would you tell him what you told me?"

Heinsfurther was a baldheaded little man with excited rabbit eyes. He puffed his chest three times and began his story. "Vell, I vas into Twin Forks in nineteen un fourteen. It vas July, the tenth, and I vas from the east. From Germany. In Germany, unterstant I vas brewmaster und it vas naturlich for me to become brewmaster here in America. Vell, next to best thing vas tavern keeper, vich I became vhen I bought a good tavern from Burt McLean. It vas a good tavern and for it I paid him two thousand dollars. Many people come from all over the country to me now un business is good."

"Mr. Heinsfurther, tell Mr. Morgan about Burt McLean."

"Oh, ja, ja. I get excited. Vell, it vas last day for Burt McLean un he vas cleaning his personal items from behind the bar un he vas drinking. Many of his friends var with him un they all had been drinking much. Then Burt McLean pulled this box from below the counter. He placed his hand in, and out of the box he pulled a large piece of bone. Ugly. He yelled to his friends un held the bone high, 'Look,' he says, 'This is no ordinary bone . . . this is hunk of Jas Porter's skull.' "

Morgan leaned forward, his face almost touching the burning stove, "Did he keep the bone, Mr. Heinsfurther?"

"Ja. I thought that strange that a man should find it important to keep such a thing. I thought he would throw it avay but he vrapped it in a red handkerchief un placed it in his pocket. I vas new here and decided it vas some crazy custom. I thought little of it until I heard you vas accusing Senator Gardner of those murders. Vell, Frank Gardner is close to Burt McLean. Friends. Un I put the two with each other and thought I should come to you."

Morgan sat back in his chair with his pipe glowing red hot, "We're glad you did come to us, Mr. Heinsfurther. Did you write this all down, Al?"

"Word for word."

"Good. So you thought McLean was a little strange — you saw the bone and you paid two thousand dollars for his business. That's interesting, very interesting. I'd appreciate it if you told no one about our conversation."

"I hope I helped. In my country this thing happening all the time. In America we stop the tyrants, eh?"

"I hope so, Mr. Heinsfurther."

"What do you think?" Al Crans returned from the door to the stove where Morgan still thawed.

"It may be something. Even if it is nothing, maybe we can use Heinsfurther's testimony to tie Gardner closer to McLean. McLean's about as low as you can go and that will mean a lot on the court record. What do you know about McLean right now?"

"We know he plays nurse to Albert Gardner quite a lot. And we know he owns the only automobile dealership in this territory."

"That's right. He owns those automobiles. Quite an inventory for a man like him and one helluva lot more than the two thousand dollars he got for the bar. Let's see if we can tie Gardner to the money it took to get McLean started."

"Maybe we should take another look at McLean's moves on the night of the murders, too."

"Right. If Gardner did give McLean the money, he was probably smart enough to do it through the bank instead of his own pocket. But who knows, maybe the big man was getting careless by nineteen fourteen."

"It's worth a try. Now are you going to tell me about Durham?"

"Not much to tell. As it turns out, Durham wants Gardner out of the way and he's willing to help us get to Gardner."

"Do they think Gardner is guilty?" Crans asked.

"Amos Potters, who will be our lawyer, thinks Gardner is guilty. Durham could care less. He wants Gardner out and is throwing in Potters to help make sure it works."

"I'll be damned. Doesn't Durham have the County Attorney working for him?"

"Evers is his nephew, but I get the impression that even his nephew isn't to know anything about this. Durham's a silent partner from here on out — which reminds me, the first thing tomorrow you ride out to Russ' place and tell him to keep the wind out of his mouth about Durham. If Gardner found out about that he'd accuse us of buying off the County Attorney and have the case thrown out."

Crans looked at him expectantly, "Is that all? Didn't Durham offer you anything?"

"No. Nothing." Morgan thought about telling his friend about the political future Durham had briefly drawn for him. The idea was tantalizing. But he decided not to tell Crans. Al would see "payola" immediately and that would be all he would hear about for the next two weeks.

It was Crans, however, who put the big question into the air. "I take it you have agreed with Russ that we should win the slander suit — at any cost?"

"Yes. I see no other way. If there was another way, I would take it. But I guess we all have to swallow some dirt now and then."

"Hey, why so down? Gardner will get his dues either way." Crans slapped Morgan on the back.

Morgan was staring through the small open diamonds in the stove at the fire blazing inside. "I guess Amos Potters made the point earlier. It didn't sink in until I was almost to Twin Forks tonight."

"What's that?"

"If we were preparing a case for a murder trial, we'd have a hard time getting Gardner convicted even if we had three witnesses who swore they saw Gardner swinging the axe. But this is not a murder trial. The jury is to decide if we slandered Gardner. And if we present a half-ass case, we might get let off. In the long run, Gardner is found guilty of the murders without getting a chance to defend himself, and yes, there is that outside possibility that Senator Frank Gardner is not guilty of murder."

John Morgan wrote notes Sunday evening while Al Crans read from newspapers published before and immediately after the murders. They were both nervous, but neither would reveal such to the other. Morgan looked at the short list of witnesses he had compiled for Amos Potters and was glad that the prosecution would be up first. He assumed that Martin would begin Tuesday with their charges and proceed to produce witnesses who would testify to Gardner's good character throughout Friday. Maybe the following Monday, Morgan prayed, he would have a case for Mr. Potters to present.

"Hey! What are doing over there, Morgan?" Crans asked.

"Listing all of our witnesses and possible witnesses."

"Oh, Christ, do you want to borrow another postage stamp?"

"Funny, funny, Al."

Crans laughed, "All right, listen to this: I've been reading up on our man Gardner through these old papers. Here, this is about a week before the murders. Remember, this paper is written out of the County Seat: 'It had been called to our attention that the feud in our neighbor city of Twin Forks, between Mayor Frank F. Gardner and the Iowa Public Electric Service Company has been fed new fuel as of lately. It seems that the electric company has announced their intention of putting up new corner lamps and posts throughout the town. Mayor Gardner has said that the town has no intention of paying the costs for these posts and the old center hanging lamps are good enough. The electric company, however, says they are going ahead with the project and will bill the town. Mayor Gardner, in turn, says that if they attempt to erect just one new lamp, he will turn off the power, and it is his right to do so.' "

"I'll say one thing for Gardner," Crans laughed, "he's a hard-nosed old bastard."

Morgan laughed, too. It was good having Al with him, now just two days before the trial. He didn't want to be alone and he didn't want to take care of anyone either. Crans was perfect — he was there to talk to, joke with or just ignore. Morgan went back to his notes, tomorrow he would talk with Doctor Pencraft about Doctor Stewart's examinations of the bodies and before that he would talk with the hotel manager. He had not give up on Lona. He sensed that she knew something that might be important to the trial, although he couldn't imagine what Lona . . .

Suddenly he stopped the notes. He swung around in his chair, "Al," he yelled. But Crans was already on his feet searching for the page in the newspaper that he had just read.

"Are you thinking what I'm thinking?" Crans asked excitedly.

Morgan spoke up, "Mrs. Campbell testified at the Coroner's Inquest that the street lights went out just after midnight. Cleavers said the same thing. They blame it on the rain and wind. Do you suppose Frank Gardner himself pulled the switch?" .

Crans found the story and read it again, "Yes. He used this trouble with the electric company to cover it up."

"If he did it, then the watchman down at the power station would know, right?"

"God, could we be so lucky?"

"I don't see how — but I'm going to find out. Keep the coffee hot. We may have to celebrate."

Morgan reached the power station half an hour before dark. Beside the power plant was a small building where the watchman stayed. It was warm inside and smelled of tobacco juice and whiskey. He was not surprised to find that the watchman was a plump old man in a railroad man's hat, but he was surprised to find Merle Sorenson reading a book.

"Yup, I remember the night before the murders. I've been on guard here every night since we got 'lectric power."

"Do you remember seeing Senator Frank Gardner that night."

"Nope."

Morgan's hopes sank as he saw his first piece of good luck disappear with a wad of chewing tobacco.

"He weren't a senator then. He was mayor. I seen Mayor Gardner that night."

Morgan came alive. He could feel his eyes trying to leave his head as they opened wider and wider. "What time was it that you saw Mayor Gardner, Merle?"

"It were just after midnight. The mayor had been having some kind of trouble with the 'lectric company and he came stormin' through here like the devil was after him."

"Was there anyone with him?"

Merle Sorenson chuckled, "Yeah. This superintendent fella from the 'lectric company chased him all the way down here. Gardner went in and pulled the switch. Everything all over town went black. Then Gardner stomped off towards the mansion. That superintendent fella was plenty mad, I'll tell you. He threw his hat down in the mud and yelled every kind of foul name you can think of back at Gardner."

"Do you remember the superintendent's name?"

"Eh? His name? Let me think — Hartmann. That's it, Hartmann. That's all I know though. No first name."

Morgan could hardly contain his excitement, "Will you testify to this if you are called to court to tell what you saw that night?"

"Don't know why not. Weren't my fault Gardner was crazy. I probably should have stopped him from throwin' that switch, but he was the mayor. Besides, there ain't too many people who get in Frank Gardner's way."

"So you will testify?"

"Sure I will, it's my duty ain't it?"

"Good. And how about Hartmann, do you know where he is?"

"He's probably still workin' with the 'lectric company — but he hops around a lot and will be hard to find. I haven't seen him since the calamity of that same summer."

"All right, we'll try to find him the hard way. In the meantime, will you try to remember anything you can that you might have heard either Gardner or Hartmann say that night?"

"Sure. Say, this won't get me into any kind of trouble will it?"

"No. Just tell your story the way you remember it and don't add anything you're not sure of. Gardner won't be able to hurt you after we get finished with him, Merle. He'll never hurt anyone again."

They were laughing. Morgan watched Lona. Her eyes gleamed when she looked at Carl Gast, a small disgusting man to him, a man who made her happy. Morgan envied Carl Gast for the affection he received from Lona. Then she saw him looking at her and the sparkle in her eyes faded as she glowered at him. He nodded. At the desk he left a note for the hotel manager, Alex Dunbar, to come to the headquarters.

"Have a cup of coffee. Hell, we're celebrating — take two," Crans laughed as he handed Morgan a cup of steaming hot coffee.

"I guess we're celebrating. I've never felt like kissing a sixty-five year old tobacco-chewing drunken watchman before."

"So it was just as we said it was?"

"Right down the line. Gardner stormed into the place, broke the damn door down and threw the switch. Pretty good acting, I'd say."

Crans clapped his hand excitedly. "No jury in the world is going to believe it was a coincidence."

"Coincidence? Gardner had that scene planned for weeks. Hartmann's showing up, the newspaper stories — the whole route. Gardner threw that switch, got rid of Hartmann and went down the street to kill the Porters. That's why the bloodhounds followed him to the front door of his mansion. He must have thought about the hounds later and ran to the river."

Crans poured himself another cup of coffee. "That's something that has been bothering me since I got here: why didn't Gardner get questioned about the bloodhounds at the time? They ran straight to his front door."

Morgan smiled. "Gardner thought of that, too. He testified at the Coroner's Inquest that he heard his daughter's dog barking at twelve-thirty. When he went to the door, there was no one there."

"But they accepted that?"

"They heard Gardner's story first. After his statement at the Inquest, everyone would have been surprised if the hounds had not gone to his front door. But now they'll have to look twice at that — and add it to the fact that Gardner blacked out the town shortly before the Porters were murdered."

"It's perfect."

"Not quite. It would be perfect if we could find Hartmann to back up Merle Sorenson's story."

"You're right. Hartmann should be easy to find, shouldn't he?"

John Morgan looked out to the Square, as if he expected Klaus Hartmann to suddenly appear at the window. "If Hartmann is still on the electric company's payroll, we'll find him right away. But no matter where he is, we'll have to find him."

For the most part, Lona Gardner was happy with her new existence. In that strange comfort she found by shutting herself off from the rest of the world, she glowed in the new attention given her by Carl Gast. Compared to her father and brother, Carl was calm and deep. His moods changed from quiet ramblings of lovely places and things to hours of silence. During these times, Lona would lie beside him on the bed in the afternoons and together they would gaze at the cracked ceiling of the hotel room and listen to the outside noises of the Square. She felt closest to him in the silence, closer than she had ever felt to any other person. Sometimes during those hours she would remember what she used to imagine her future husband should be — he should be loving like Carl, and affectionate like Carl, but there the similarities stopped, for long years of being a Gardner had trained her to look for wealth and security and social standing. It had taken thirty-four years to train her — and in thirty days Carl Gast had broken the leash. It was love and affection that made a woman, a person, and the other values could go to hell. She smiled and rolled over to him on her side.

"I love you, Carl Gast."

He opened his eyes. A smile came to his thin lips, then he closed his eyes again. "I love you, Lona Gardner."

Lona stretched her arms behind her head, "Oh wouldn't it be nice if we could go on like this forever?"

"I thought we were."

Lona shook her head. "No, even now I'm trying to imagine what my father wants to say to me. I'm wondering should I go to see him today, or should I wait a few days to see how the trial goes."

"I don't think you should see him at all."

"I know. But I will. He is my father and I know I'll never be able to live in that house again. But I don't believe he hired anyone to murder the Porter family. He is not ruthless."

In Carl's mind there were memories of his sister coming home after Albert Gardner had finished with her. And another memory of his father crying at the kitchen table when Frank Gardner had taken his farm away from the family. No, your father isn't ruthless, he wanted to say, your father is worse than ruthless and your brother is worse than your father. But he did not say that. He closed his eyes.

"Look," he said, "When we first came here I didn't care if I hurt you or not. I liked you, but my real reason for being here was to hurt your father and brother. It must drive them crazy to think that a Gardner is sleeping with a Gast night after night. But I don't want to hurt you now. I still want to get at your father and brother somehow, but I don't want to see you hurt in the process. Not anymore."

"Why do you hate them so?" Lona asked.

"I can't say. Things they have done to my family. It goes deep."

"You do love me, don't you?" Lona whispered.

"Yes. I suppose I do. But I'll do what I must do Lona. I only tell you all of this now because I want you to know I'm thinking of you when I tell you not to return to your father. He is a dangerous man."

"I know you are trying to protect me. I love you for that."

"Then you will stay away from the mansion?"

"I'll do what I must do, Carl. See. We're not so different from each other."

"You may hate me when this is over."

"I'll never hate you."

Carl raised himself to one elbow and faced Lona. "I wish you would go now, before you do have to hate me. Some day I'm going to have everything that your father has, then I could care for you and we could start over. If you stay, it will finish us."

Lona rolled to her back. There were tears in her eyes. She set her jaw firmly and said to the ceiling, "No, I cannot leave. There is too much here that bothers me. I won't leave until I know for sure who murdered the Porters and who beat Dorothy out of her mind. I have to learn the answers to those questions or I'll never have a life of my own. There was something missing in New York. I was happy there, but always there was this empty feeling. Now I know what it was and the only way to get rid of it is to find out who is responsible for those things."

"So you are staying."

"Yes. I'll go to see my father in a couple of days. From there — we'll just have to see."

"You are sounding like a Gardner again."

"I am a Gardner. That's one thing this has all done for me. I am ready to admit that I am a Gardner."

CHAPTER SEVENTEEN

By noon Monday the spring like temperatures had been replaced by cold, and a black cloud-bank from the northwest promised snow by nightfall. John Morgan pulled his coat tight at the neck and continued his walk up First Avenue until he came to the small house where Doctor Pencraft lived. Morgan introduced himself to the distinguished looking old gentleman who answered his knock and followed him into two of the most cluttered rooms he had ever seen. There was a living room and a dining room, both of which had been taken over by dust and papers and journals so that every chair in the house was in use.

Doctor Pencraft briskly poured two cups of coffee and packed his pipe for a discussion with his house guest. John Morgan took a sip of his coffee and looked to the doctor, "I suppose you know why I am here, Doctor Pencraft?"

"Of course. The Porter murders. But I'm afraid there is little I can do to help you — unless you haven't read the transcripts of the Cleavers' trial or the Inquest."

"I have read them both quite a few times," Morgan frowned.

Doctor Pencraft laughed. "Yes, I'll bet you have at that."

Morgan liked Pencraft. The doctor was an easy man to trust, and this seemed to contradict the reason for his being here. "What interests me," Morgan continued, "is a statement you made in the Coroner's Inquest. I believe the County Attorney had asked you about the bodies and the condition of them. After your description, he asked you if you thought the Coroner's examination had been properly conducted . . ."

"And I said I thought it was done awfully fast," Doctor Pencraft volunteered.

"Right. Could you tell me more about that?"

Doctor Pencraft packed his pipe until the tobacco glowed in the bowl, "In my opinion, my professional opinion, it takes much longer than two or three hours to properly examine eight bodies of that horrible condition. It's as simple as that."

"You had the axe and their heads were crushed. Wasn't it self-explanatory what the cause of death was?"

"Everyone agreed that they had been axed to death."

Morgan pulled his own pipe from his pocket, "Everyone except you, I take it?"

"I wasn't certain. I have learned that the obvious isn't always what it seems — especially in death."

Morgan nodded. Doctor Pencraft should have been a detective, he thought. "In the Coroner's Inquest, after the discovery of the bodies, you said next that you thought you had seen some cuts or gashes that might not have come from the axe."

"That's right." Doctor Pencraft sighed and closed his eyes as he remembered the worse day of his life. "There were some cuts, thin cuts, I thought I had seen. They were too clean to have come from that jagged old axe of Porter's — more like knife cuts."

"You saw them?"

"That's just it. I think I saw them. I should have looked into it closer, but I didn't. Doctor Stewart was there and he was taking over as County Coroner. Quite honestly, I was happy to get out of that house. I ran away from that responsibility. That's why I quit doctoring a few months later. It has never been the same since that day." Doctor Pencraft hung his head and for a moment Morgan thought that the doctor would cry. But he remained silent.

"I wonder, Doctor, what prompted the County Attorney to ask that question in the first place. Was there some reason to believe that there might have been something wrong with the investigation?"

Doctor Pencraft raised his head wearily. "There was some talk of foul play. Mrs. Pinkerman, the woman who actually discovered something wrong at the Porter home that morning, was telling everyone that she thought the Gardners were behind the murders in some way and that Doc Stewart was covering for them. She was pretty loud about it."

"And you agreed with Mrs. Pinkerman?" Morgan asked.

"No. Not at first — not for certain."

"When?"

Tears swelled in Doctor Pencraft's eyes. "One month later Mrs. Pinkerman died. She became ill a week after the murders and grew worse — until she finally died. The townfolks say she died from being heartsick over her discovery of the Porters."

"How does that tie in with your opinion?"

"Look, Morgan, Mrs. Pinkerman was a strong woman. She was one of our pioneers and was used to fear and hard work and death. It was a shock when she discovered her neighbors' bodies, no doubt, but it would not have killed her. I think she died for two reasons."

"Two reasons. What are they?"

"One — she knew something about the Porter murders and was touching upon something that would have pointed a finger at Frank Gardner. Maybe she had seen something and had forgotten it and now Gardner feared she might remember. Or, maybe she saw Jas with Dorothy Gardner, if you believe in rumors."

"You said there were two reasons she died. What is the other reason?"

The old man placed his pipe by the coffee cup and folded his hands on his lap. He looked around the room as if for the last time, then his eyes came back to John Morgan.

"Mrs. Pinkerman's doctor was Doc Stewart. I think he killed her."

Doctor Pencraft agreed to appear as a witness for the defense.

The telephone rang four short blasts and from the back of the room Al Crans saw that Morgan's face was drawn tight as he listened at the receiver.

"What's up?" Crans asked.

"That was Amos Potters. It seems our connection with Sam Durham is starting to pay off already. Dunbar has received word that Gardner's attorney is going to pull a fast one on us. He knows we are not ready to present our defense — so he's going to wrap his prosecution by Thursday noon."

"What's the deal?"

"He'll catch Potters with his pants down. We'll have Thursday afternoon and Friday and not one star witness. It will look bad."

Crans shook his head. "So what do we do?"

Morgan looked into the black clouds of coffee that swirled in his cup. "Send a wire to Montana. Have Allan Childes back here by Wednesday night."

Morgan exchanged glances with Crans and walked to where Alex Dunbar stood pointing at the Blue Island collection. He was pointing to a military convict picture of Blacky Mansell.

"That's Robert 'Blacky' Mansell," Morgan said curiously.

"Maybe so, Mr. Morgan. But he signed my hotel register as Mr. Drummers. I remember because he had that long, ugly scar down his left cheek. Yes indeed, that is Mr. Drummers — his hair was longer then."

Morgan wheeled around. "Al, when did Mansell get out of the army?"

Crans thumbed through a stack of papers on the desk and pulled one out. "He escaped from the military prison in February of 1911."

Morgan grabbed Dunbar by the shoulders. "Now, Mr. Dunbar. Alex. I want you to think. When did you see this man. Was it before or after the Porter murders?"

"Oh, before. I'm certain of that. But not very long before the murders. No, I'd say that it was just a couple of weeks before that terrible night. If you want to know the exact times, I'll have to look them up in my old registers."

"Times? Do you mean he was here more than just once?"

"Mr. Drummers stayed with us three or possibly even four times. I assumed he was a salesman."

"Alex. I want that register here in this office tonight. Understand? And don't tell a damn soul what we have said tonight — not even your wife."

"Al, how can we be so damn lucky?"

Crans danced across the room. "I don't know — just two super detectives sitting around the office." He laughed.

"We have a helluva lot of work to do."

Crans stopped dancing. "You mean I have work to do. You have to sit there in court all day."

"Yeah, you're right. God, I wish we had another week."

"Hey, we're lucky, but don't push it. Tomorrow the trial starts whether we're ready or not."

"I know, but how are you going to track down Mansell and Hartmann at the same time?"

Crans held a piece of paper in his hand. "I have taken care of that. Tomorrow morning the boys back in my office in Denver get a new assignment — find Klaus Hartmann. In that way, I can devote full attention to Mansell."

Morgan shook his head, "I hate to get your agency involved."

"No problem. Maybe it will remind them just who their boss is. Have you got any ideas on where I should look for Mansell?"

"He was a slaughterhouse worker in Illinois."

"Great. We have a slaughterhouse every ten miles in Iowa and Illinois. He could be anywhere."

"I don't think so. Let's assume he is working for a slaughterhouse and he also wants to conceal his identity. So where is he?"

"Chicago. Denver. Kansas City or St. Joseph."

"Right. And I'll lay odds on Chicago or Kansas City. They are the biggest. Take that a step farther — he wants to get the hell out of the state where he murdered his wife and family . . ."

"That leaves Kansas City."

"I'll bet on it."

"You just did."

CHAPTER EIGHTEEN

The courthouse for the county of Davies is of Missouri brown limestone erected in the year of eighteen hundred and ninety. The cornerstone was laid on July fourth of that year before a crowd of ten thousand. Below its red slate roof are three commodious floors all supported by steel beams. But the most impressive aspect of the courthouse is the red stone tower that rises another three stories above the structure with a great clock on each of its four sides looking in all directions over the County Seat. Each hour the great clocks chime, so that all for miles around can hear the turning of the hour. The courthouse sits at the center of a square block and is surrounded by tall elm trees and sweeping birches and a well cared for lawn.

Across the street is the only hotel in town. It's called the Page and is by far the best hotel between Des Moines and Omaha. Here the lawyers and judges and others close to the trial spend their nights. During the day there is a steady stream of people flowing between the courthouse and the hotel to eat or sleep or for private conferences.

On the street many horses and horse-drawn buggies pass. There are a few automobiles, but they are as "scarce as hens' teeth" still. There are more bicycles than automobiles.

It is a cold day, but the snow that threatened has not arrived. It is early. The people are crowded into the huge dining areas of the Page. The courthouse doors will not open for another thirty minutes. Everyone is hoping to finish breakfast by the time the doors open. There is a small crowd in front of the courthouse. They hope to get front-row seats either on the main floor or in the balcony. There are many farmers in town with their wives. They are obvious, for they look uncomfortable in suits that no longer fit. They are very proud and outspoken. Everyone is in a happy, festive mood. This is a big day and the outcome of the trial is not yet in their minds. They are anxious for the courthouse doors to open; they look forward to the battle.

At the end of the second-floor corridor of the hotel, the men of the Gardner camp have gathered to await the trial. In the room are Frank Gardner, County Attorney Evers, Attorney General Fred Martin and Doctor Stewart. They are nervous — Evers is pacing across the floor while Frank Gardner is staring out the window in the direction of the courthouse. He remembers the day the cornerstone was laid. It was exciting then, but not so exciting as now. He had come to the courthouse twice in the past week to inspect the jury members that had been selected. Only one was rejected. A farmer who lived near Twin Forks and was of one of the old families, had been sent home. He'd be damned if he'd have one on his jury. Most of the jurors were from the opposite side of the county — an attempt to appoint persons most impartial to the crime and the man.

"I'll be back. I have to go again," Evers said.

Fred Martin smiled. "Relax boy. Did you deliver the message like I told you to?"

"Yes sir, about thirty minutes ago."

"Good. That ought to give them something to worry about for awhile." Fred Martin laughed and slapped his client lightly on the back. Frank Gardner looked over his shoulder. He gave a weak smile to conceal his nervousness, then returned his attention to the courthouse. The crowd at the front doors was growing.

On the third floor in another room, room 310, John Morgan waited with Russ Porter for Amos Potters to arrive. They were not quiet. Russ rambled nervously about the value of Allan Childes' testimony and that of Merle Sorenson; Klaus Hartmann, if they found him, and then of their need to capture Blacky Mansell.

Morgan half listened to Russ. If it made Russ feel better to talk, then talk, he thought.

The room had electric ceiling lights. They had been installed long after the hotel had been built, as evidenced by the round conduit pipes that hung from the ceiling and ran to the fixtures. In the room were two beds, a small table with an electric lamp, three straight chairs, a window that faced the courthouse that was covered by a straight, brown curtain that pulled from the center and tied in the middle of each side. The walls were papered in a tiny rose design. It was peaceful enough there to spread out on the bed. Much more comfortable than the courtroom would be later.

Finally the door opened and Amos Potters stepped in. "I am sorry I'm late. Something has come up."

Morgan sat up on the bed while Russ asked the question: "Come up? The damn trial hasn't even started yet."

Amos Potters pulled a long, folded piece of paper from his inner coat pocket. "As of eight o'clock this morning, Senator Gardner is no longer bringing charges against Russ Porter, the Stills or the Burns Detective Agency."

"What? Why did he do that?" Russ asked.

"He is out to get Morgan," Potters answered, "the suit is revised to be filed only against John W. Morgan."

They both looked at Morgan who sat quietly on the bed with a sarcastic smile.

"It's not fair," Russ said to him, "we're all guilty."

Morgan laughed sardonically. "You got that wrong, Russ. We are all innocent."

There was a sharp knock at the door. Russ Porter answered it. "Telegram for Mr. Morgan," the boy announced. As Morgan inspected the envelope and tore one end open, Amos Potters replaced the paper in his pocket and continued, "It was a good move for Gardner. Pretty shrewd, too. Now there won't be any sympathy for Jas Porter's surviving brother to worry about — and all the friends of Russ and the Stills. It's going to be a head on battle between Senator Frank Gardner and detective John Morgan."

Morgan fell back on the bed holding the telegram out for Potters to read. "Ex-detective," he said with emotion. "I have been fired."

Potters read the telegram: "AFTER THREE AND A HALF YEARS ON THE TWIN FORKS AXE MURDER CASE WE HAVE DECIDED TO END OUR INVESTIGATION — STOP — CONFIDENT NO SOLUTION TO CRIME IS AT HAND — STOP — YOUR SERVICES NO LONGER REQUIRED — STOP."

Potters shook his head. "I suppose Gardner knows about this. It will look bad in court."

Morgan put his hands behind his head smiling at the way his world was crashing down on him. "Well, I hope you're good, Potters. I hope you're damn good."

The courthouse was a landmark both because of its size and because of the special meaning it held for the people who built and paid for it. Iowa had been settled in the mid-seventeen hundreds and almost one hundred years later (1846) it was admitted into the Union. But to be recognized as something other than a buffer to the great frontier was a goal almost every Iowan shared. They took great pride in their state, their capital, and when it came time to finally decide where the county courthouse should rest, it, too, became a point of immense local pride and rivalry.

There was a time when the county seat was almost stolen from the present holder. It was in the autumn of eighteen eighty-seven — the town of Dove Bank was a booming settlement then, just as large as the County Seat, and it felt every right to the courthouse, then a small wood-frame building hastily constructed to meet the rules of statehood. It was felt, and rightfully so, that the town marked as County Seat would be assured of a long, secure life. Emotions ran high on this dispute until finally, at wits end with the courts, a band of horsemen from Dove Bank showed up late one night with their ropes and a long sled — and stole the county courthouse. They dragged it five miles before riders out of the castrated County Seat caught up with them. The two groups were going to meet head on and settle the dispute then and there. But a local preacher, who thought this was one hell of a way to make such an important decision, borrowed a torch from one of the riders and within ten minutes the property in question was gone. Three years later the problem was settled by rational men and the present edifice of justice was erected.

CHAPTER NINETEEN

The day had come. The day of reckoning. John Morgan felt his stomach churn. He looked to Amos Potters for similarities but Potters' face was solid, his actions calm, as if the old man was bored with the happenings. For a moment Morgan was sorry that this old man was representing him. What were the chances of physical or mental failure for Amos Potters, he wondered? Could this old man stand up to the routine for which he had volunteered. In the same moment he was glad that Amos Potters was not against him and decided that he was grateful for his help.

Behind them five-hundred spectators found seats on the main floor and another one hundred perched in the balcony, while still another one hundred and fifty found standing room at the back of the courtroom. The crowd chattered like crows on a spring morning as they waited for the trial to begin.

The battlefield, a half-circle of clean mosaic tile floor, was bordered by a carved wood railing which separated it and the jury box from the crowd. There were the table and chairs for the prosecution and an identical set for the defense at the opposite of center. Below the bench was a small table where the foreman sat with his hands patiently folded in front of him. Beside him was another small table that held a large stack of papers. The courtroom stenographer sat rigidly at the table arranging and rearranging the papers and a box of sharpened pencils. She wore a light gray dress that covered her ankles. A tan sweater hung around her shoulders and was pinned at the neck by a silver clasp that matched the barrette in her hair. If her instructions had been to make herself as unnoticeable as possible, then she had succeeded admirably.

The bench where Judge Erwin would reside stretched across the east side of the room. Made of plush cherry wood with deep carvings of olive branches, it was three boxes which pyramided up from each side to the bench where the judge's empty chair ominously waited fourteen feet above the mosaic floor. To the far corners of the east wall were two large windows. They were the only windows in the courthouse and were heavily barred. Morgan thought the bars senseless when he first noticed them. Who would jump out of a window from the third floor of this tall courthouse? Then he remembered that he was the defendant in this trial. Presumably, he thought, the bars were for him.

In the lower step of the pyramid, closest to the juror box and in front of the defense table, was the witness stand. Morgan looked at it with new respect. He saw the whole world with new respect today.

Morgan looked toward the table for the prosecution. County Attorney Dan Evers was busily writing notes to himself on a large clean pad of yellow paper. Evers would take quick glances at the bench, pause ponderously, then duck his head again to scribble furiously. There was much Dan Evers lacked in experience and self-control, Morgan thought, but the young County Attorney made up for it with energy and enthusiasm. There was much at stake in this trial for Dan Evers. If he was to have a future with the Republican Party in Davies County, then to win this law suit would be the perfect way to begin it. To lose the trial might end any chance he might have had. Surely it would delay success for a number of years, and what could an ambitious young attorney fear more than loss of time.

Frank Gardner paid little attention to Evers. The Senator stared straight ahead to the judge's bench. He wore his customary gray suit. His beard was neatly trimmed. He appeared comfortable in his role as claimant. Behind him was Attorney General Fred Martin.

Judge Thomas Erwin entered the court from an anteroom. At the foreman's instructions, everyone in the courtroom came to a standing position. The courtroom throbbed with anticipation. John Morgan watched Dan Evers hurriedly toss his notes to one corner of the table when they were all seated. Evers bubbled with enthusiasm. He'd come on with a strong presentation, Morgan thought.

When the court had come to order, Amos Potters, the old warhorse, made his first strategic move: in a very conversational tone he told Judge Erwin that he thought the trial would be a lengthy one. The judge agreed and asked the jury if an extended trial would cause them any undue hardship. There was no reply — but the jurors, who had been sitting on the edge of their seats, slumped back into relaxed positions in preparation for hours of testimony. John Morgan smiled. He felt the pressure of the crowd behind him slacken. He imagined each one of them realizing that it would be long, drawn-out conversations with minor witnesses. Even the County Attorney seemed less enthusiastic as boyish excitement left him and the film of a professional lawyer methodically spread across his face. He had a gold mine in Amos Potters, Morgan decided.

Senator Frank F. Gardner vs. John W. Morgan. The foreman read the charges, took his seat and the judge nodded toward Dan Evers at the table for the prosecution. Evers stood. He walked slowly to the juror's box and looked each one of them in the eye. Apparently satisfied with whatever he had been trying to discover, Evers turned half toward the spectators, half toward the jury, and spoke in a crisp, clear voice.

"The charge here is slander, ladies and gentlemen. This means that my client, Senator Frank Gardner, is charging the defendant, detective John Morgan, of speaking publicly in such a manner as to defame his character and, in this case, to maliciously accuse him of low moral value. Ladies and gentlemen, this lays a most heavy burden upon you. You must decide if my client is worthy of the thirty thousand dollars in damages he has asked for. Indeed, you must decide, based on the testimony and evidence you will see here in this courtroom, if Senator Frank F. Gardner is the murderer of the Porter family."

Amos Potters did not rise. "Objection Your Honor."

"Yes, Mr. Potters."

"I would like to remind the County Attorney that this is not a murder trial. The accused here is my client, John Morgan, and the charge is slander. We are not trying the Senator for his part in the Porter murders."

"Now I object, Your Honor."

"Mr. Evers, what is your objection?"

"My opponent has taken this opportunity not only to interrupt my presentation but to imply that my client has had a 'part' in the murder of the Porters."

Judge Erwin looked at his folded hands ponderously. "I see we have a problem that will plague us throughout the trial. The charge is slander, but the slander is a charge of murder. I will ask the prosecution, the defense and the jury to remember that in no instance is the Senator required to prove his innocence of murder. Rather, the prosecution is to prove that the slander did indeed occur, that it was false and of malicious intent and finally, that it did prove damaging to the claimant. The purpose of the defense is to either deny that slanderous words were spoken, or, if spoken, to deny that they were false and of malicious intent. As jurors, your duty is to determine whether the defendant is guilty beyond a reasonable doubt, or whether he is innocent of the charge of slander."

The jurors and the spectators listened with blank faces. Yes, in theory this is true, they said each to oneself. But did Frank Gardner murder the Porters? That is the real question, isn't it?

Dan Evers nodded to the bench. "We are prepared to begin our case with testimony from many witnesses of good character who will support our case that Senator Frank Gardner is of high moral character and religious dedication. We are also prepared to prove beyond doubt that the defendant John Morgan did speak words of slander against the Senator on many occasions and that under his direction slander was spoken publicly in planned gatherings. I would close now with the reminder that not only is this slander, but slander of the worst kind. The worst possible kind. It is the seriousness of this slander that makes it so important that justice is done in this courtroom. It will be made more difficult because the slander involves the murder of the Jas Porter family of Twin Forks, the most terrible crime ever to face Iowans. Your responsibility to find the truth in this case is great. Your decision will be historic."

Dan Evers returned humbly to his chair.

It was proper then for the defense to also make a presentation. Judge Erwin now nodded to the table for the defense.

Standing before the jury, Amos Potters said: "The County Attorney did a good and fair job of informing you of your responsibility as jurors. Therefore, I will not waste your time reshaping or retelling the obvious. I do want to say a couple of things about the charge and my client's plea of not guilty."

"You might say that my client would have been better off if he would have pleaded guilty to the charge of slander and asked the jury to award a very small amount of money in damages. In that way, any amount less than thirty thousand dollars would have been a victory for my client. But this is not the case. My client has pleaded innocent. Our stand is that Senator Frank Gardner is not worthy of one red cent in damages — he is one of the foulest creatures on two legs walking the face of the earth and it is time that we cleanse ourselves of him. It is not an easy task my client has chosen. John Morgan is a detective doing his job. But he is more than that for you and for me. He is our servant, yes, our public servant, trying to save us from tyranny and oppression of men who would take over our lives with influence and education and money as if they had a license to rule the lives of others. Now, in trying to help our community, John Morgan has been accused of slander. He might have walked away from this case. He might have pleaded guilty, as I have said. He might have let his own self interest take him away from this county months ago. It is lucky for you — for me and our children that John Morgan is with us today and that he has decided to fight the tyranny of Senator Frank Gardner to the end."

For the rest of Tuesday, Wednesday and most of Thursday the County Attorney brought witnesses before the jury to testify, some in length, others briefly, to the character and moral value of Senator Gardner. When the testimony seemed to build Gardner to the point of a shining knight on a white horse, Amos Potters would briefly mitigate the importance of this or that statement. For instance, on

Wednesday, Reverend Bush of the Lutheran Church stated, "Senator Gardner was always ready to help the church. He took many trips for us. He found and brought home the new organ we now have." Amos Potters stood: "Reverend Bush, who paid for the travel expenses of Senator Gardner's travels for the church?" "The church," Reverend Bush answered. "And where does that money come from?" "The people," the Reverend answered. "Thank you. No more questions."

Then on Thursday, it became obvious that County Attorney Dan Evers was coming near the end of the presentation for the prosecution. Even the spectators sensed the change of attitude in Ever's manner. They became nervous and fidgeted in their seats and coughed. The big question was what would the defense do now. Unfortunately for Morgan and Potters, the defense was asking that same question. They would be able to stall for awhile — but not for long. They needed a key witness. Whether Allan Childes would arrive soon enough to be that witness was uncertain. For all they knew, Childes had not even received their message to come back to Twin Forks.

CHAPTER TWENTY

"Mr. Evers, does that conclude the case for the prosecution?" the judge asked.

"Yes it does, Your Honor."

"Then tomorrow, Mr. Potters, we shall begin the case for the defense. This court is adjourned until ten o'clock tomorrow morning."

They met at the hotel.

"What do you think, Amos? Are we going to swing this or not?"

Amos Potters was not a man to give false encouragement, even when it was needed. Instead he said, "I will say that the prosecution has not presented us with any great problem. About all that they have accomplished this week is to confirm that you accused Frank Gardner of murder and that Gardner has a few friends who will testify in his behalf."

Morgan smiled worriedly. "Spoken like a true lawyer, Amos. Now do we have a chance or not?"

"Yes, we have a chance, if you produce the witnesses."

"Yeah." Morgan slammed a fist down on the table. "Where the hell is Childes?"

As he spoke, three loud knocks came from the door. Morgan threw it open. There, in a new suit and with his flaming red hair well-groomed, was the sheepherder, Allan Childes. Russ Porter pushed him into the room.

"I found this bastard walking around the Square. I could have killed him."

Childes whirled around angry and hurt. "Look, I'm here, ain't I? I'm not a damn prisoner. I'm a witness ain't that right, Mr. Morgan?"

John Morgan was so happy to see Childes that nothing else mattered now. He laughed and slapped both Russ and Childes on the back. "He's right, Russ. We have no legal right to lock him up. He can walk out this door right now if he wants to."

Russ' face went red with rage. "He could have blown our whole case. Besides, if Gardner knew what he was going to say in court tomorrow, I wouldn't give two cents for him making it through the night."

"He's right, Allan. We have kept your secret all these months, but we don't know about anyone else you might have told."

Childes plopped down on the bed. "Forget it. I'm tired out anyway. I'll stay right here until it's time for court — then I'll go meet some of my old friends. That's all I'm really here for anyway."

Morgan sat at the end of the bed. He felt like a mother hovering over a sick child. "Do you remember your story?"

"Yes."

"Do you want to read your statement? It has been a long time since you signed it."

"Nope. I got my lines straight. How about bringing some food up here. I'm starved."

Russ followed Morgan into the corridor. "I don't trust that little bastard. What if Gardner got to him? He's the type who'd sell his own sister for a piece of cake."

Morgan continued down the corridor, "He's all we have right now. Besides, if Gardner had got to him, he wouldn't be here now."

"I still don't like him!" Russ yelled.

"Neither do I," Morgan laughed, "but I'm getting supper for him."

Lona was in a gay mood when court adjourned for the day. Before going to the train, she walked to the Square. She remembered the happy days she had had as a little girl when her mother would bring her to the County Seat for a day of shopping. It was always a big outing. The stores were gigantic compared to those in Twin Forks, and the selection of dresses and bonnets were fifty times better. They would always end the day with dinner or supper at the Page before returning and Lona would have a new bonnet to show Provo when he met them at the train.

Today she bought a bonnet. A childish whim. It matched nothing in her wardrobe, but it recalled memories of happy, carefree days.

The train ride home was cold and pleasant, for it was snowing, just little flurries, enough to renew the white blanket over the countryside to make it beautiful again. She was anxious to see Carl tonight.

At Twin Forks the flurries continued on a heavier scale. Lona ran to the hotel and into the lobby where she saw Carl at the top of the stairs.

"Lona, you better get up here," he said, then disappeared toward the room.

She met Carl outside the door. Her expression must have asked what was the matter because before she spoke Carl jerked a thumb toward the door.

"Dorothy."

Dorothy was standing in the corner of the room away from the window. Her face was more vibrant and her eyes had come alive. She met Lona with a hug, then sat on the bed.

"I expected you long ago," Dorothy whispered. "Now I'll be in trouble for being late."

Lona saw that Dorothy was truly frightened. She sat on the bed beside her and put her arm around her sister-in-law.

"What's wrong, Dorothy? Did father send you?"

Dorothy shook her head, "No, Albert came home tonight with your father. I heard Albert tell your father that you would come to the mansion tonight. That's when I decided I had to warn you — don't go there Lona. Never go there again. Please," she said crying.

"Why, Dorothy? I'm not afraid."

"You should be. That's why I came here — to tell you."

"Tell me what? What is it?"

Broken with sobs, Dorothy bent forward to reveal the secret she had kept to herself, "That day you found me — beaten. I said I didn't know — who it was. I lied. It was — your father. He found out I was meeting — Jas Porter — and he beat me."

"Oh, my God," Lona said numbly as she tried to visualize her father hitting Dorothy as she remembered the horrible bruises on Dorothy's face. "He really did that to you, Dorothy? You're sure?"

"I've never told anyone. After he was finished with me he said he'd take care of Jas Porter once and for all. I didn't know what he meant — until the next morning when I heard your mother telling someone about it over the telephone."

"My God. Oh my God. Dorothy, why haven't you said anything to the sheriff, to me — someone?"

"Who would believe me? This town thinks I'm crazy now. They'll put me away somewhere. The only proof I have is a key."

"A key. Who's key, Dorothy? What kind of key?"

Dorothy stifled her cries and became calm again, "There's a key in your father's desk drawer. I saw it there once. The next time I looked he had moved it, but it's still there behind a partition, It's Jas Porter's key. I remember because he had it made for the front door. Jas Porter's house key, Lona."

"The house key," Lona repeated in a whisper. "I can't — no. Please, no."

The mansion was very quiet. Fred Martin had gone to talk with a local congressman and John Goodell had not yet returned. So, after dinner Frank and Albert Gardner went into the front room to await the arrival of Lona.

The Senator picked up the newspaper and scanned the pages for bits about the trial.

"Hardly a thing in here about yesterday."

Albert sat forward, his elbows on his knees, "Maybe they are already losing interest."

"No. The crowds are still showing up at the courthouse. I don't suppose the newspapers get too interested in a slander trial until the defense goes to work. That's when the accusations begin and the prosecution starts to tear witnesses apart."

"You think it's going good then?"

"Yes. Everything is fine, son. And wait until Thursday. That's when the headlines show up — in our favor. The trial almost assures me of reelection. It has to."

Albert looked at his father. He thought of the times late at night when he would find his father working over the library table in the study to catch up with new bills he'd have to vote on in the legislature and before that, when he was a boy, he remembered how Frank Gardner worked to get ahead, whether it be on account ledgers of other farms, in the bank, the legislature, or whatever. His father deserved to be senator now, he thought. Or governor, if that is what he wanted.

"Father?"

"Yes, Albert?"

"I'm sorry for all the trouble I've caused you in the past. I really am."

Frank Gardner dropped his paper to his legs to look at his son, "It's over now. Besides, hasn't it brought us closer together?"

The two men looked at each other, realizing that these were the first kind words they had spoken to each other for many weeks.

He was still reading when they heard Lona on the front porch. Albert started for the door but it flew open as Lona came into the mansion. She stopped above her father.

"You bastard. You no good bastard!" she screamed, tears streaming down her cheeks.

Frank Gardner jumped to his feet and slapped her across the face. Lona fell against the sofa where Albert sat.

"That's right, beat me, too. Like you beat Dorothy. Come on, hit me you coward."

"Shut up!" Albert screamed and grabbed her by the neck. "Shut up! You damn tramp. Shut up!"

"Albert, that's enough!" Frank yelled. "Leave her alone. Let her talk!"

Lona climbed back to her feet holding her neck, "Bastards both of you. What's so great about the Gardner name now? Go on, tell me. First you beat Dorothy — drive her crazy, then you murder the Porters. Why? For the Gardner name? For a piece of trash not worth caring about? That's how I feel about the Gardner name. I spit on it. I'm ashamed to have you for a father. It makes me sick!"

Lona fell on to the couch. She held her face in her hands and cried.

"Lona," Frank Gardner said, "You are awfully excited. How can you believe such a thing?"

"I believe it. I believe you would do anything to protect your precious name."

Albert walked away from her, then turned, "I suppose Carl Gast is more to your liking, eh? What has he been telling you — that bum doesn't even have a job."

"A job? What does that have to do with anything? He's the only man I've met since coming back here. He and detective Morgan. Maybe Morgan has the right idea — they should hang you."

"You bitch. If you go to Morgan with this, I'll kill you myself," Albert screamed.

"Albert, let her alone. She's upset," Frank Gardner said calmly. "Lona won't go to Morgan. Will you Lona?"

"No."

Gardner took a deep breath, "Good. Now let me tell you about Dorothy . . ."

"No. I don't want to hear anything from you. I'll find out the truth in my own way. When I know the truth, I'll go back to New York, but not until then. And if I find out that any of this is true, I hope you both rot in hell. And I advise you not to touch Dorothy again. Then I will go to Morgan — and I will testify."

"They would never believe you," Albert sneered.

"Maybe not — but that would be a black day for the old family name."

Lona started for the door but Albert grabbed her by the arm, "I want Gast out of that hotel by tomorrow."

She wrenched her arm free, "I don't give a damn what you want. He's twice what you are. He doesn't have to pretend he's God before he can be a man."

The door slammed and the house was quiet again. Frank Gardner turned the page of his newspaper to a full spread story of an interview with a British soldier. He read the first two lines, raised his head. My own daughter, he thought. I wonder how many more will turn against me before this is over?

"All rise."

Judge Erwin came from chambers. His black gown hung heavily on his shoulders. Today the case for the defense would begin.

"Be seated — the court is now in session."

"You may begin the case for the defense," the judge rasped.

Amos Potters moved the papers on his desk as if he were searching for something. The audience waited while the old man completed his task. Finally, when he was ready he looked up and said quietly, "The defense calls Nancy Caldwell to the stand, Your Honor."

CHAPTER TWENTY-ONE

Nancy Caldwell wore a light pink dress. She was nervous, but when she answered the routine questions her voice was clear and calm. Nancy smiled often for no apparent reason, probably because of her nervousness. Potters knew she appeared flighty to the jurors and was glad now for his last minute decision to bring Nancy to the stand before Mary Luntree. Nancy was pretty, and she would have less credibility with the jury. Mary would support her.

"Now, Nancy, about the time of the murders, did you know the Porters very well?" Amos Potters asked the question off-handly.

"No sir. Not well."

"But you did know them?"

"Yes. We knew the girls and we'd been in Porter's Implement Store before that time."

"Where did you live the summer of nineteen and twelve?"

"Four miles east of East Creek Bridge."

"Did you attend school at Twin Forks?"

"No sir. We walked to the school at Six-Mile Corner."

"Were you at your home when you first heard about the murders?"

"Yes. We were on the porch and a neighbor stopped to tell our folks about it. They didn't think we heard because they were out by the road. But we heard and got scared. We didn't tell them we heard though because they would think we were listening."

"Did anyone else tell you anything about the murders?"

"Lots of people after that."

"I mean, did anyone tell you something about the murder night in particular? Did someone indicate to you that he knew something about the murders?"

"Yes. Allan Childes said he saw someone at the window of the Jas Porter house on the night of the murders."

"When was this?"

"When did he tell me?"

"Ah, yes. When did Allan Childes tell you this?"

"About two weeks after the murders. He came out to the farm. Mary Luntree was with me and the folks had gone to town. It was a Saturday night."

"Go on and tell us in your own words how Allan Childes came to tell you this story."

"We were on the porch. Allan Childes came to see us often then and we were talking. And we were talking about the murders and how awful they was. Suddenly Allan Childes says he was driving from the meeting he had with an older woman and he went past the house. The Porter house. He said the street lights were out and he looked at the Porter house because he saw a light. He said it was a light at the back of the house and that he saw a man that looked like he was trying to climb into the house."

"Did he say what time this was?"

"He said it was after midnight."

"Now, Allan Childes said he saw a man that was about to climb into a window. Did he indicate who he saw?"

"He said he saw Frank Gardner."

The spectators exploded. Judge Erwin brought the gavel down twenty times. Potters continued as if there had been no interruption.

"You are sure? You are absolutely certain that Allan Childes said he saw Frank Gardner at that window on the night of the murders shortly after midnight?"

"He said he did."

"Why didn't you tell someone about this sooner?"

"It didn't seem important. Lots of people were telling things that weren't true. Then last summer Mary Luntree came back to Twin Forks and we got to talking about the murders again and what Allan Childes said. We knew by then that detective Morgan was on the case and that so far there were no suspects. That's when we decided to tell Russ Porter about what we heard. Just in case it was true, we thought we should better tell someone."

"Did you tell anyone else about what Allan Childes told you?"

"No. Russ Porter asked us not to tell anyone."

"And you didn't"

"No. No one."

"No more questions. Thank you, Nancy."

Dan Evers walked to the bench. He looked down at the floor before looking at the witness. When he did, he smiled.

"How old are you, Nancy?"

"I'm twenty-one."

"So you were seventeen when all of this occurred?"

"Yes. I believe so."

"Allan Childes came to your farm. Did you know him well?"

"Yes. He came out many times."

"Tell us again exactly what Allan Childes said to you that night."

John Morgan looked across the room to where Frank Gardner was sitting. The Senator had not blinked an eye when the girl told her story. He listened, as if he was just another spectator in the courtroom. Morgan pulled a notebook from his pocket and scribbled a quick note to Potters.

"What's going on? How come Evers isn't tearing her up?"

The note came back: "?"

"Now I would like to call Mary Luntree, Your Honor."

Mary Luntree was larger than Nancy and not as pretty. She was sturdier in appearance and looked like a young lady who had a lot of common sense. These were the two reasons Amos Potters had decided for her to appear second to Nancy. She confirmed all that Nancy had said for Potters and reconfirmed it when Evers went through the motions of his cross-examination. When she left the stand, the audience mumbled. They were disappointed with Evers' lazy questioning. Why didn't Evers dispute what the girls had said, they wondered, as did Potters and Morgan.

Suddenly the audience quieted. Allan Childes would no doubt be the next witness. Surly Evers would not let his testimony go by unchallenged. It was time for the next witness.

"Now would be a good time for lunch," Judge Erwin said. "This court shall reconvene at two o'clock."

Each of the men ate rabbit.

Amos Potters had reserved a private dining room at the hotel where they could be away from the crowd, but even the oaken double doors could not keep out the exalted chatter that filled the large dining room where most of the audience were lucky enough to find a table to eat lunch.

They are expecting a lot, Morgan thought, as he rolled his fork through a huge pile of mashed potatoes and picked at the crisp rabbit meat on his plate. He looked at Amos. The old man was carefully slicing the meat from the bone, approaching his lunch in the same methodical matter in which he did everything else.

Russ, who held his rabbit in both hands, tore it ravishing oblivious to the silent communication that was passing from Morgan to Amos and back again. Russ was happy and now he brought the subject into the open: "It's really going great, isn't it? Evers didn't know what the hell to say. He might as well have gone home."

Morgan let a mouthful of rabbit slide down his throat and then put his fork down on the table. "What do you think, Amos? If I'd been the defense attorney, I would have done everything possible to tear their stories down. Through them, I would have discredited Childes to the lowest person on earth."

Amos leaned back in his chair, "Evers wasn't terribly competent this morning. Some lawyers are like that on the first day against the defense — they figger we have a long trial in front of us and they might as well save most of the bartering and bickering for the final couple of days."

"Oh hell, Amos," Morgan growled. He pushed away from the table and walked to the wall, wheeled around, "Evers might as well be on our side if that's the way he's going to conduct his cross-examinations."

"Hey," Russ Porter yelled. "What's wrong? I thought everything was great!"

"Yes, great — too great. Amos, what's he got?"

"I don't know." Amos had stopped eating and was staring at his fork as if it could tell him something.

"But he's got something! Right?"

"It would appear so."

Morgan slammed a fist on the table then turned back to the wall. "God, here's our key witness and Gardner isn't even worried. Maybe we should have brought our less important witnesses in first — to let us feel out Evers' case. For all we know they have twenty people bought and paid for to swear that Gardner was at a party that night."

"Yes, they may have someone. I don't think so, however. We could cross them up too easily based on Gardner's testimony at the Coroner's Inquest. Remember? He said he was home and in bed when he was awakened by the dog barking. No. They must have something else. At any rate, we've taken this too far to pull Childes. We'll have to get him up there and find out what Evers does to him."

Morgan shook his head. "This is one helluva way to run a trial."

"At least we'll have his statement on record."

"Yea. For better or for worse."

Seats rattled. Boots scuffed. A few coughs.

Then silence.

"The defense calls Allan Childes to the stand, Your Honor."

Bailiff: "State your name for the court, please."

"Allan Childes."

"Allan Childes, do you solemnly swear to tell the truth, the whole truth and nothing but the truth, so help you God?"

Hand on the Bible, "I do."

"You may take the stand."

"What?"

"Sit up there."

Amos Potters stood before the bench. Allan Childes looked down at him nervously.

"Allan, we have had testimony from Nancy Caldwell and Mary Luntree that you told them you saw Frank F. Gardner at the Porter house on the night of the murders. Did you hear that testimony?"

"Yes. I heard it."

"And do you now agree that their testimony is true?"

"Yes. They said what I told them."

"And three years later, did you sign this statement for the defendant, John Morgan, stating again what you saw and that all the girls said you told them was true?"

"Yes. I signed that statement."

"And you now state that this is true?"

"Yes."

"You so state?"

"Yes."

"Go ahead. In your own words, tell this court what you saw on the night of the murders."

Allan Childes' nervousness disappeared as he began telling his story to the jury and the spectators. While Childes talked, John Morgan watched the faces of Dan Evers and Frank Gardner. Gardner's face was expressionless, as it had been since the beginning of the trial. Morgan wondered if anything would effect this man. Evers was smug. This bothered Morgan. When Evers was nervous, his face showed it. When Evers was excited, his eyes all but shone. When he was frightened, his face revealed the secret. Now his face was smug — and did it reveal some knowledge that all that was taking place was not really important?

Thirteen minutes later Allan Childes finished his story. He had enjoyed his role and the attention it gave him.

"Tell me why you did not come forward with this information years ago, Allan."

"I was afraid to."

"Why?"

"Frank Gardner was mayor at Twin Forks, then. I didn't think anyone would believe me if I told them what I saw — at least, not right away would they believe it. That would have given them time to kill me, too."

"I see. You were afraid for your life."

"You bet I was."

"Thank you. No more questions."

County Attorney Dan Evers stood in front of his chair. When the crowd quieted, he remained there frozen in his position. When the courtroom had been silent long enough, he walked to face the witness stand defeatedly. Without looking at Childes he said, "Your name again, please."

"Allan Childes."

"Do you realize the seriousness of what you have said today?"

"Yes sir. I believe I do."

"You have been sworn before God."

"Yes sir."

"And you were sworn to tell the truth, the whole truth and nothing but the truth, were you not?"

"Yes sir."

"The Bailiff administered the oath to you?"

"Yes sir."

"When did you return to the County Seat from Montana?"

"Yesterday."

"You came in by train?"

"Yes sir."

"And did you talk to anyone when you reached town?"

"I went to the hotel to meet Mr. Morgan and Russ Porter."

"You didn't talk with anyone else?"

"Yes. I stopped up on the Square and found some of the old friends and I talked to them awhile before going to the hotel."

"What did you talk about?"

"All kinds of things. Montana mostly."

"You talk any about the trial?"

"No sir."

"You didn't talk to anyone about the trial?"

"Oh, I guess the trial was mentioned."

"You guess it was mentioned?"

"It was mentioned."

"Mentioned?"

"Yes. Some of the boys talked quite a bit about it, I guess."

"You guess they did?"

"They did. That's a fact."

"But you didn't tell them why you were here? You didn't say you were here to testify at the trial today?"

"I think I said I was here to testify."

"Did you or did you not say you were here to testify at the trial for the defense?"

"I did. I remember now — I did."

"Where were you when John Morgan found you this summer and asked you to sign the statement which the attorney for the defense just showed you?"

"I was in Montana."

"And what were you doing in Montana?"

"I was keeping sheep. I moved there about October of nineteen and twelve and kept sheep for a rancher until last week."

"And John Morgan contacted you there?"

"Yes. He came to see me on the mountain."

"And when next did you hear from John Morgan?"

"I believe it was Monday. I got a wire asking me to come to Twin Forks as soon as possible to testify."

"Did you receive travel money?"

"Fifty dollars."

"Any other money?"

"No."

"There was never any other money?"

"No."

"No promise of money?"

"No."

"Now, Mr. Childes, last night on the Square of this town you told two men that you were going to testify today in court. You told them that you were going to tell a lie today. You told them that you in fact did not see Frank Gardner or anyone else at the window of the Jas Porter house that night. You told them you actually were never near the Porter home on the night of the murders. Did you say that?"

Allan Childes looked at John Morgan then quickly moved his eyes to the jury, and then let them fall on the cherry wood in front of him. Dan Evers waited four minutes before prodding.

"Allan Childes, did you or did you not tell the men on the Square last night that you were going to lie today in court?"

Another long pause.

"What's the matter?"

"I don't remember."

"You don't remember? How could you not remember?"

"It'll come to me."

"Would you like us to wait until you have the answer?"

"Yes. Let me think a minute."

(Forty-five minutes pass) — (Stenographer's note)

"Have you had time to think?"

(no answer) — (Stenographer's note)

"We are waiting, Mr. Childes. This court wants to hear the truth and nothing but the truth. Did you see Frank Gardner at the Porter home that night?"

"No."

"Nor on any other night?"

"No."

"And in June of this year you lied to the two girls about what you saw on the night of the murders?"

"I lied."

"And this summer you lied when you told John Morgan that you saw Frank Gardner at the window?"

"Yes."

"And the paper you signed was a lie?"

"Yes."

"What? I don't think everyone heard you."

"I lied."

"You lied today when you testified under oath, too, didn't you?"

"Yes."

door. He loved her, he told himself. She was a totally different person than his wife had been. She held all the love and affection that a man could want. She offered much more than he could return.

Yet, for a few fleeting moments only, his mind had wandered to Lona Gardner. Then he remembered her again at the dining table of her hotel. Next, the last time, he saw the vicious stare she had given him melt momentarily, imaginarily, to a round, innocent, helpless shape.

"I don't think so," he said and wondered if he lied.

Russ Porter pushed the door open. A cold wind met Morgan in the face.

"I'm starved." Russ said. "Who's for supper?"

"Not me."

"I'll go with you," Amos Potters said. "Tomorrow is going to be pretty cut and dry. I'm going to call Doctor Stewart and Sheriff Gustavson to rehash the day of the discovery of the bodies. Then I'm going to call on Doctor Pencraft to bring up his theory about the knife cuts. That ought to give the people something to think about over the weekend."

"Where are you going to go, John?"

Morgan turned toward the carriage house, "I got an idea last Tuesday when Evers brought the tenth witness to the stand to confirm Albert Gardner's whereabouts on Monday. I think now is a good time to check it out."

"Then I'm going to see a lady about a supper."

Russ Porter laughed, "And after supper?"

"After supper?" Morgan called back over his shoulder, "Dessert — what else?"

Morgan reached Twin Forks an hour after dark. There were many people in town for a cold Friday night. Horses and carriages and automobiles lined the Square. Campbell's restaurant was open. He could see the people at the tables and along the counter as they ate super in town.

Outside the pool hall he could see a crowd of men through the window. He imagined that most of them had come home from the County Seat for the night and were now discussing the trial. He wondered what they were saying about Allan Childes' testimony. Could Amos Potters be correct, he asked himself. He answered, yes, to himself and felt better for it. In addition to Potter's reasons why people would believe Childes had told the truth about seeing Frank Gardner at the window, Morgan had his own theory — Frank Gardner was king; Frank Gardner was a tyrant; Frank Gardner was, therefore, resented and, if it was possible to believe that he had bribed Allan Childes not to testify, the people would choose to believe it. Kill the king. Long live the peasant!

He wanted a drink. He'd been looking forward to a drink and deserved it now. But he snapped the reins across the horse's back to take him away from the temptation.

When he reined the horse to a stop he was sitting in front of Bambaugh's Garage. It was late for a business to be open, but he was lucky tonight he hoped. A thin slice of light shone through the crack where the wide garage doors met. It invited him inside to enjoy the shelter of the barn and that comfortable loneliness of a man working late amidst the fumes of gas and oil and sweat.

He entered through the small sidedoor. To his surprise there were over thirty cars along the two alley ways down the center of the barn. They rested in their rows, some cold from sitting all week, some hot and still melting from the heat of the lanterns and stove. In the quiet of the barn, periodic thumps sounded as frozen slush beneath the wheels melted again and fell away to the earthen floor.

A clicking noise of metal against metal came from the rear of the barn. Morgan walked down the west corridor until he came to where an older Auburn had been pulled out of its night stall with a lantern hanging above it and a pair of human legs sticking out from beneath it.

"With you in a minute, mister," the voice rang out through the motor. Soon the body that was attached to the legs squirmed into the open and a happy, smiling man sat up in the dust.

"E. M. Nelson." he volunteered, "Can I help you?"

"I'm John Morgan."

Immediately E. M. Nelson's eyes widened, "So, you're John Morgan the detective — don't think I've ever met a detective before."

Morgan liked E. M. Nelson. The mechanic was thin, but stood firmly on the ground in an easy manner. He'd make a good witness, Morgan thought, one whom everyone would like.

"Have you been following the trial?" he asked.

Nelson shook his head violently, "Naw. I don't pay much mind to things of that sort. They don't effect me here so I mind my own business."

"I thought you might be able to help me in my business, E. M."

Nelson waved his arm in a half circle, "I work on automobiles. That's all I do — and I suppose that's all I know."

Looking around at the cars, Morgan said, "You do quite a business. Probably everyone in town keeps their car here?"

"Just about everyone," E. M. said proudly.

"How about Burt McLean. Does he keep his car here?"

Nelson grinned, "No. McLean sells cars now so he's not keeping his here anymore. He used to though."

"When?"

"Back before September when he opened his store."

"Were you here at the time of the Porter murders?"

"Yup. I'd been here about two months at that time."

Nelson was looking at him suspiciously. Morgan was afraid the little mechanic would close on him.

"Now listen, E. M., it has become very important that I find out exactly what Burt McLean did that night or the next morning. Do you remember if you saw McLean that night?"

"Yup. I saw him. You see, McLean was one of a few people I knew at that time. I remember him coming in about eleven o'clock that night — a Sunday night — and asking for his automobile."

"Did he always have to ask you for his automobile?"

"Yup, we keep all the keys over there in the office. Everybody has an extra set, but they ask us for our set mostly. Why? Is that important?"

"It's important that you remember if you saw Burt McLean that night — that night for certain."

E. M. Nelson scratched his head frowning. Then he burst into a wild smile, "Yup, it had to be that same night. I remember, because the next morning everybody was excited about the murders. I was on my way over to Campbell's to get a bite to eat and Burt McLean yelled to me from across the Square. His Auburn was over there in front of the pool hall and he asked me to come get it. I remember it like it was yesterday."

"Was anyone with McLean when he took the Auburn out or brought it back?"

"Nope. He was alone."

"Didn't it make you curious why he was going out at eleven o'clock at night?"

"No. I stick to my own business."

Morgan looked again at Nelson. He envied the little mechanic — his carefree life. To be so simple and happy, that nothing but an income mattered. Would he — no, it would not be nice, he thought, not for himself anyway. Who would move the world if no one tried? Who would bring a murderer to justice? It was up to the doers of the world to force the contented to react.

But where was the value of E. M. Nelson's testimony? There was no crime against a man driving his own automobile out of a garage. There was no crime against keeping the car out all night. To a jury the testimony of E. M. Nelson could seem quite ordinary. But not if he got the correct answer to his next question:

"Was Burt McLean in the habit of taking his automobile out at night, E. M.?" Morgan asked as casually as he could.

E. M. Nelson scratched his head again thoughtfully, "No. No, I'd say he only did that once. Just the one time."

Correct. So there it was. A man broke with his pattern just once. Never before had he acted in such a way, and never after. But on the eve of the murders, Burt McLean did something uncommon — he took his car out of the garage for the night. And that, the night of the murders. Coincidence? Is there such a thing as coincidence? What would be the odds of McLean's strange act coinciding with the tragedy? Ask the jury these questions. Repeat them until the jury asks the same questions. Pray they come up with the correct answer.

"Will you testify in court next week?"

"No."

"I can have you subpoenaed."

"Would you do that — force me to testify?"

Morgan nodded solemnly, "Yes. Your testimony is important enough to my case that I would subpoena you."

"Maybe I'd get up there and lie." Nelson pouted.

"I don't think so."

"Neither do I. I guess I might as well be on your side."

"Good. I'd hoped you'd say that," Morgan smiled.

"And I might as well tell you another thing I saw while we're at it," Nelson said as he kicked at the hard dirt floor with his boots. "A couple of weeks after the murders I had done some repair work for Burt McLean. I made out a bill and old man Bambaugh told me to run across to the pool hall and deliver it to McLean.

When I get there they sent me up to one of the rooms upstairs, where they play poker and things. I opened the door to the room and walked in on Burt McLean and Frank Gardner. They were sitting at a table drinking beers."

Morgan's mind flashed back to a conversation he had had with Al Crans. They had agreed that it would be good if they could tie McLean to Gardner. Al was suppose to find out if Gardner had given money to McLean for the new car business he had started. Now Nelson tied them still closer together at a time nearer the day of the murders.

"I just gave McLean the bill and walked out," Nelson was saying "That's what I saw. Maybe it's nothing."

"It's something." Morgan assured him and slapped him on the back. "Now listen, E. M., Amos Potters is my lawyer. I want you to do whatever he says. He'll let you know when he wants you to testify. He may send Russ Porter after you."

"I never thought I'd be doing this," Nelson said proudly. "If we lose, you know that I'll have to leave town?"

"You're a good man, Nelson. You can't let this go by without trying to stop it — Gardner. People will never know how much you've done for them once you've testified. But, you'll know. And that's enough isn't it?"

"Yup. I guess that's why I'm agreeing to testify. But I hate to think of what happens if you lose. I'll be run out of town."

Morgan held the door before opening it. He looked back at the little mechanic. Yes, you may lose your job, E. M. Nelson, he thought, but we'll all sacrifice to beat Gardner — all of us.

"We lose if we let Gardner go, E. M. And that's the only way we lose."

He was gone into the cold night.

A wide moon froze in the eastern sky and lighted the snowy earth. Shawdowless, the hills and the trees lay exposed in the night-time brightness of a cloudy day. It was colder on the road but the wind had died and the air was dry, making it more comfortable to ride the buggy seat. Morgan was anxious to see Lorraine again, but he let the horse pull the buggy along at its own lazy pace over the frozen ruts while he leaned back in the seat and relaxed for the first time in what seemed a thousand years.

The moon swelled as he gazed at it. Any sound, if there was a sound, was muffled long before it reached the lone horse and buggy and driver silhouetted against the strange horizon.

Beside the road was Russ Porter's two-story farm house. It glowed against the black line of evergreen trees and formed a windbreak around it because every light in the house had been left on for the night. Five Porter families crowded the large house in fear that whoever murdered their brother's family was also planning to exterminate the Porter clan. It was not a ridiculous assumption — not in Twin Forks — not in 1912. Morgan had lived in Twin Forks long enough to not discount the possibility. He knew that here the family name was everything. To smear the name was a sin — and leaders of the family were fanatical on their protection of the name.

Honor of the name was reason not to do business with a neighbor for three generations of the clan. Honor was reason to murder . . . it was reason enough for anything . . . reason enough for Frank Gardner to destroy eight sleeping persons.

He smelled the burning wood from the fireplace before he saw Lorraine's home. Light came from one window, a yellow square against the gray hills, a lamp turned low. He was glad she was not yet asleep and slapped the reins across the horse's rump to hurry it down the hill.

She met him at the door. Never before had he seen her cry. She smiled when she let go of him, "Put your horse in the barn," she said as she wiped the tears from her eyes, "I'm not going to let you go this time."

He led the horse to a stall in the barn and threw down some hay. He turned the lantern to smother the wick and pulled the bar across the door. As he walked from the barn to the house he heard the far away sound of an engine. There were no headlights on the road, but the sound was unmistakable. Lorraine heard it, too. She stood in the open doorway eyeing the hill.

"There," she said, pointing toward the south end of the hill.

Morgan looked. A piece of metal reflected in the moonlight and he saw the machine. It was a light automobile — a roadster, he guessed, but could not be sure. It must have been sitting higher along the road where a tree had shadowed it from the light of the moon. Whoever drove the car had waited there until they were sure of his actions. When it was obvious that he was to spend the night, they left — to report to someone, he wondered? To report to Frank Gardner, he imagined.

The car moved across the horizon then disappeared behind the hill towards Twin Forks. Morgan walked on to the house. Lorraine said nothing but when she had closed the door he looked at her longingly.

"I'll leave if you want."

She shook her head, "It's not necessary."

"That was somebody working for Gardner. They'll try to use us now. I've never wanted that — you to be pulled into this mess."

"I know."

It was late. They had made love. A new log caught fire sending high flames up the chimney. It heated the two motionless figures who sat watching it thoughtfully. There had been a conversation, a few ideas exchanged, that had broken off many minutes earlier unfinished.

John Morgan felt the fire hypnotize him. The gentle licking of the flames on the new log were as soothing to his thoughts as the soft touch of her fingers whispering tenderly across his forehead, as warming as the bare insides of her legs against his face while she held him in her lap. The blanket she had pulled over her shoulders draped each side of his view so that all he could see was the fire in front of him and her loving, questioning face above him.

At other times when they had been together nothing else had mattered. For the few moments or sometimes hours when they had lain back satisfied with each other, either in front of a warm fire or on a summer morning listening to the rest of the world awaken, while a cool morning breeze that would soon be gone swept across their bodies, they had been alone and deep within each other.

Tonight they lay there. Like a gun shot beside the ear, outside problems disturbed the silent meanderings of the mind that had been theirs.

Morgan knew his mind had wandered away. It thought about Frank Gardner and Allan Childes and Amos Potters and Doctor Stewart and eight dead people. He wondered where Al Crans was tonight and if he had located Blacky Mansell. He thought about Lona Gardner, too.

Lorraine could feel his alien vibrations, he knew, and this he regretted. He had come here to find the past protection of their reclusive moments together. He resented the thoughts that intruded the lovemaking, but could not rid himself of them. They were forever with him now. He had lost his last refuge.

"What happens in court Monday?" Lorraine asked finally in a defeated tone of voice that said she, too, had given up trying to find that past peacefulness and now tried to at least share his other thoughts.

Morgan heard the question. By the time it registered, the partial cloud that had drifted over his mind snapped away with a pop of green wood in the fire. He rubbed his eyes.

"Monday we stall. We're going to make everyone relive the whole scene step by step."

"Is that all?"

Morgan paused before answering. "No. We are also going to begin a new approach to discredit Frank Gardner. I wasn't too sold on the dirt-throwing idea — thought we could manage without it. But Gardner got to Allan Childes somehow. Bought him off so Childes would deny the statement he made to me last summer. I thought that was about the worst thing that could happen to our case, but Amos Potters thinks he can turn it around again. Many people around town already are believing that Gardner must have gotten to our witness. Now we have to give some kind of evidence to support that."

"Do you have evidence?" Lorraine asked.

"No. We don't have 'evidence' as such. But if we can show the jury that Gardner is a bastard, then that'll be enough to let them assume our witness was paid for."

"What do you know about Dorothy Gardner? I have records as far back as nineteen twelve of people gossiping about her having a love affair with Jas Porter. I've always excluded them for nothing but rumors."

"Until now . . ." she said coldly.

Morgan sat up facing her. He was angry at her implication and madder still that she may be correct.

"Yes. Until now," he said. "What do you know about them?"

Lorraine shrugged her shoulders and pulled the blanket around her. "I have heard the rumor before. I never believed it."

Morgan did not want to look at her eyes. He turned again to the fire and lay back again in her lap, although it was not so welcoming.

"Rumor or not, I have to check it out. It may be true. If it is, then we'll be able to put the whole Gardner situation in another perspective."

She squeezed his shoulder as if to say listen — I ask this to help you see yourself, not to hurt you.

"Why would you do this? I mean, the real reason. Is it because you need to expose Dorothy Gardner because it would help you in your case against Frank Gardner? Like daughter-in-law, like father-in-law? I don't believe that. It seems you are losing the case and now you're trying to grab at any root you can cling to. Your case against Gardner is falling through so you are going to hurt him any way you can."

"Maybe you're right," Morgan said cruelly.

"Yes. Maybe I am. I didn't think you would do such a thing. I would expect something like this coming from Frank Gardner, but not you."

"I'm not different than most people."

"Yes, you are, or you were. I used to admire you for the way you stayed on this case. It was something you had to do because your conscience forced you. But now you're bringing innocent people to the witness stand — a chopping block you can use to leave the Gardner family in a graveyard of dead secrets. Why? Is it just to save your career? Are you that far down that you would do this for a little money and attention?"

"No, damn you!" Morgan screamed. Then in a calm voice he said to the fire,

"I am convinced that Gardner either murdered those people himself or he hired someone to do it — probably Blacky Mansell. Why would a man murder another man — business, politics, money. There are hundreds of reasons. But why would a man like Gardner murder an entire family — only because his family had been hurt or dishonored."

"If Dorothy Gardner was having an affair with Jas Porter, and Frank Gardner found out about it, then Frank Gardner might have had all the reason he needed to counterattack in the awfullest way possible."

"And that's the only reason?" she asked.

"No. That's not the only reason. The real reason is the children. When I first came here, this case was important to me — my career. I suppose it's even more important to my career now. But the money and fame and future are no longer the things that keep me on this case.

"I think of the Porter children. Every time I look at Frank Gardner across that courtroom, I imagine him with an axe crushing their lives out, smashing their brains on the pillows and walls. It makes me sick. And sicker still to think that he might get away with it."

"If it's possible that Frank Gardner murdered those children because his daughter-in-law was having an affair with Jas Porter, then I want to know about it. And I want the rest of the world to know about it. I won't be satisfied until I see Senator Frank F. Gardner hanging from an old rope outside of town."

"It's not a question of do I or don't I expose Dorothy anymore. It's only — how do I expose Dorothy — or anyone else that might be connected."

"What if there is no way?" Lorraine asked.

"There has to be."

"Maybe not."

"If there was a romance going on, then somebody knows about it. All I have to do is find that person and get him to testify."

She hugged him from behind. She was warm once more. She opened her blanket and pressed her breasts against his back and pulled the blanket around both of them.

"You'll do it," she said. "If there is a way, you will find it."

"I must," he said.

A half hour later he lay beside her. She slept. Soon he would be asleep, he knew. It was good that he had come here — so good to be away from newspapers, telegrams, telephones and people . . .

CHAPTER TWENTY-THREE

Moments before wakefulness, when the mind races through years of past, future and present, complexities become simple and inhibitions remain faded behind a clinging cloud of sleep. Time was endless. In those few seconds he searched the vast storage of his unconscious memory for a solution to the problem. He sat up wide awake,

"Minnie!" he yelled, "Minnie Butler!" He jumped up reaching for his clothes.

Lorraine sat drowsily on the bed recuperating from the sudden awakening. "What? What are you talking about?"

"Minnie Butler," Morgan said joyfully, "She's the one person in Twin Forks who might help me. The one person who might know if Dorothy Gardner was having an affair with Jas Porter."

Lorraine fell back to her pillow. "All right . . . so who's Minnie Butler?"

"It's perfect. I should have talked to her a long, long time ago. Minnie is the telephone operator . . . she lives over in the hotel and operates the switchboard from there. It's so obvious that I missed it. The perfect witness." He pulled on his coat and jerked his wide-brim hat over his forehead, but Lorraine was still confused,

"Do you mean that to solve a mass murder case, you just go over and talk to the telephone operator?"

Morgan laughed, "If you're in a town as small as Twin Forks, you better do just that. Too bad it has taken me so long to learn that for myself. You see, Minnie is not only an old snoop, but she probably listens to every call that goes through her switchboard. What the hell, she's got nothing else to do."

"Do you think she'll have some information?"

Morgan was halfway out the door, "I don't know, but if she doesn't, she isn't the snoop I think she is."

A man on horseback rode out of town. The ground was frozen, but he rode hard, foolishly.

Morgan had reached the east side of the bluffs. He had not pushed the mare that pulled his buggy, for he was not in a hurry. It was a Sunday morning. Most of the townspeople would be in church. He knew Minnie Butler would be at her station by the switchboard in her room in the hotel. There was no reason for him to hurry.

The mare began the long pull up the side of the bluff, picking her way expertly over the hard ruts. Morgan let her take her own course. He loosened the reins and relaxed on the buggy seat, thinking of what he might learn from Minnie Butler. He knew that the possibility of her having any kind of helpful information was a long shot. Perhaps, he thought, she would be able to add to the rumors that had already begun about Dorothy Gardner and Jas Porter. That would be damaging to Frank Gardner. No, he reversed the thought — even if Minnie testified to overhearing a conversation between Dorothy an Jas, even if they had spoken openly over the telephone about their affair and Minnie testified to that — even then, Minnie Butler's testimony would not be solid. It would not be believed fully. Always in the back of each jurors mind there would linger a doubt. Is it more rumor that we are hearing now, they would ask themselves, or is it true?

Why worry about it now, Morgan thought, shaking his head. The first thing to do was for him to ask Minnie what she knew. She should know something. Next to barbers in a small town, telephone switchboard operators were the closest to being professional snoops. Every call was monitored. She listened mostly for the lack of nothing else to do, and because there were not that many phone calls anyway. People lucky enough to own a telephone still looked upon it as part of an emergency aid kit, not as an outlet for hours of socializing or small talk. So, in addition to the other reasons, almost every call was for some kind of emergency, and well worth the listening.

If Dorothy Gardner was having an affair with Jas Porter or anyone else, Minnie would know, Morgan decided. How else would they have lined up their secret meetings without arousing suspicions? At least once they must have used the telephone. If they did, Minnie would have heard them. Four years later it would give their secret away.

Knowing that Minnie's testimony would not be extremely valuable, Morgan still was anxious to talk to her. No matter what Minnie says or doesn't say, in court he would hear her and he would be able to decide for himself the truth of her statements.

The mare broke the crest of the bluff. When the buggy rounded the top, Morgan saw the lone horseman on the narrow road below. He reined the mare to a stop so not to meet the rider halfway down the steep bluff. Damn fool, he thought as he watched the horse and rider speed across the dangerous road. Morgan looked away and waited.

The rich Mo-Ri valley spread before him. Soon it would turn green and lush, but now it was white across the open lands. Streaks of dark ran through it, indicating the roads that came and went through Twin Forks, and he could see the river and the stream from which the settlement first got its name. To remain here — to accept Sam Durham's offer to help give him a start in politics — be with Lorraine — no, he would think about those things later. But not now. If he beat Senator Frank Gardner, let it be simply because Frank Gardner is a murderer and John Morgan is a detective; no other reason. But would those other reasons be there always? Yes, he supposed they would be. Then could they effect him? He wondered.

Hooves on the road sounded clearly now. He eyed the horseman with annoyance — then recognized Russ Porter with concern.

"What the hell are you doing?" Morgan yelled when Russ Porter brought the horse up next to the buggy. "You're going to kill yourself."

"If you're not on the noon train for Kansas City, I will kill myself!" Porter yelled back as he dismounted.

"You heard from Al?"

"Yes" Russ said, then tied his horse to the back of the buggy. Morgan waited until Russ sat beside him then headed the mare down the west side of the bluffs toward Twin Forks.

"What did he say? Has he found Mansell?"

"The telegram was short: he's found Mansell — wants you to meet him in Kansas City tonight. He's staying at the Fellman."

"Never heard of it."

"I know of it. It's a dirty little shack down by the slaughter-houses."

Morgan whipped the mare to a light trot, "So I was right — Mansell stayed with the slaughterhouse."

"Looks like it. Now all you have to do is go down there and pick him up."

Morgan nodded, "That's the easy part. Then we have to make him confess. A man could hold out a long time with eight murders over his head — or twelve, if you include his own family in Blue Island."

"I'm glad I'm not going to be there. I don't think I could be near the man that did that to my brother and his family. Mansell must be a monster — inside — a monster."

Morgan gave Russ an encouraging slap on the back, "We'll have him pretty soon right where we want him. He'll lead us to Gardner. The end of the road."

"When will you bring him to the County Seat?"

"Let's say Mansell confesses tomorrow — then I'll have him back here by Tuesday evening or Wednesday. Amos is going to have to run things here while I'm gone. I want you to meet me at the head-quarters after you get me a train ticket. Tonight, take a message to Amos for me — I've got a new witness."

"A witness — who's that?"

"Nelson over at the garage. He remembers McLean checking out his car the night of the murders. McLean kept it out all night."

"That's a witness?"

"It is when you consider that the night of the murders is the only night McLean ever kept his car out all night. Was it just coincidence? — something for the jury to ponder, I'd say."

"Okay, I'll get your tickets. What are you going to be doing?" Russ asked.

"I'm going to talk to the switchboard operator. I'll be honest with you Russ. I'm hoping she can prove that Dorothy and Jas were having an affair."

"She won't," Russ said. "That was all rumor."

They had entered Twin Forks. Morgan stopped the buggy in front of Jas Porter's vacant home. It seemed even more lonely in the bleak of winter and this emphasized the haunting reminder it had always held for John Morgan.

"We're closing in," he said to the house.

"What did you say?" Russ asked.

"I said get your horse. We've only got an hour."

Sunday church bells echoed throughout the Square calling stragglers to service.

As he climbed the stairs to the third floor, he saw the door to Lona Gardner's hotel room. He stopped in front of it and found himself wondering how hurt she would be if Minnie Butler did testify to prove the past rumor.

At the end of the hall was Minnie Butler's door. He blocked Lona from his mind. A few moments later he tapped on the door at the end of the hall.

A cute little lady not more than four and a half feet tall opened the door.

"Detective Morgan! Imagine, you comin' to see me. Ain't you a church goer?"

He tipped his hat with a smile, as a man would to any little old lady in a polkadot dress with a braided bun wrapped around her tiny head,

"Mrs. Butler, I've been meaning to talk with you a long time," he said as he followed her into her room.

"Me? I can't imagine why. Would you lie a cup of tea, Mr. Morgan?" she asked in a pleasant, crackling voice. Before he could answer, a loud buzz came from an adjoining room. Mrs. Butler scooted for the door, "Excuse me, I have to take a call." He followed her into what should have been a bedroom, but unlike any other bedroom, in addition to the small single bed pushed over to one corner was a soft-padded rocker chair positioned in front of one of the first switchboards "the Bell" ever produced. "The Park's place? Yes, Mrs. Good," she said in the same crackling voice, "Say Mrs. Good, ain't you goin' to church this mornin'? Without waiting for an answer, she pulled a wire from a small hole and moved it to another. That's three longs and a short and a short," she said. Morgan watched with satisfaction while Minnie Butler stayed on the line long after the connection has been made. "Oh!" she blushed when she noticed Morgan, "was just a . . ." her voice trailed off.

Nosey old gal, he thought, then he smiled, "Please Mrs. Butler, don't explain. I'm glad to see you have curiosity. It's a sign of intelligence."

"Oh? You think so?" she asked hopefully.

"Of course I do. What kind of person could sit here all day with calls going through and not wonder what was going on?"

Minnie breathed easier, "It is lonely sometimes. You'd be surprised of some of the things I find out about first now and then. Why, do you know what I learned just yesterday? Sarah Luther's little girl; she's pregnant . . . fifteen years old, unmarried and pregnant."

Morgan pulled a chair near to her and sat down, "I wondered if you would have some information about the Porters or Gardners that I could use. Anything you might have heard lately, or back around the time of the murders, that might throw some light on the reasons for this thing?"

"I don't know anything," Minnie Butler said, shaking her head, "I mean, no calls about late meetings or anything like that."

"How about calls to Gardner, perhaps from Chicago or Denver?"

"No. Only from Des Moines, but he's always getting calls from Des Moines."

Well, she wasn't going to volunteer the information he wanted. All that he could do was ask. "Mrs. Butler, did you ever learn anything strange about Dorothy Gardner, the daughter-in-law of Senator Gardner?"

Minnie rubbed her hands nervously. She walked to the other room where she put a pot on a hot plate to boil water for tea, then she sat at a simple wooden table in a bentwood chair and put her face in her hands, "Yes. You see, I always liked Dorothy. That's why I listened to her calls . . . I worried for her."

"What kind of calls?"

"Well," she paused, "gentlemen callers. She was never happy with Albert, you know. It was one of those marriages arranged by the parents and such."

"Did Jas Porter call Dorothy?"

"Yes. She was in love with Jas Porter, I'm afraid. He'd call her now and then, but mostly she'd call him and ask him to meet her."

"And did he meet her?"

"Sometimes he'd meet her, but usually he would refuse. He had a wife and family and a business reputation to think of. But that was the worst time for Dorothy. Because then . . . " Minnie Butler's eyes moistened — she fumbled for the pot of hot water.

"Then what, Mrs. Butler?" he had to ask.

She sniffed and pushed on her braids, "Well, she'd be feeling pretty low in those times when Jas wouldn't see her and defiant, I guess you would call it . . . hated the world, you might say. At those times, she would call a local bum and tell him to meet her and they'd go out in the country for a few hours. I know what they did there, but she was a nice girl, believe that. It was only that marriage that changed her. Anyway, she would return home late at night and get into another fight with Albert."

"You said that Dorothy would call a bum. Who would that be, Mrs. Butler? Is he still in town now?" Morgan watched Minnie pour the tea and then accepted a cup from her, "You won't believe me when I tell you," she said, "but along with just a couple of times with another man, she would usually call Carl Gast."

Morgan almost spilled his tea as his reflexes pulled him out of his chair, "Are you sure . . . Carl Gast?"

The tiny head nodded sadly, "Positive. The same Carl Gast who is living with Lona Gardner right now."

Morgan could see that this little lady had given up much to talk to him. A secret she had kept to herself for years had just been divulged and her statement was final. "Will you swear to that on the stand if you are ever called to testify?"

"Yes, I won't lie over a Bible. It was Jas Porter . . . and Carl Gast."

CHAPTER TWENTY-FOUR

"Remember. We're suppose to take him quietly, right?"

Morgan nodded nervously to Al Crans. He wondered if the excitement he felt showed. A shiver ran down his spine. It was just the cold that caused it, he told himself.

It was six o'clock. The sun lighted the sky over Kansas City's slaughterhouse district. Across the local area of slaughterhouses, holding pens and rows of employees' shacks, an eerie morning mist rose from manure piles and innards of fresh kills. Stench of burning hair and of cattle remains caused Morgan to hold the gag reflex as both he and Al Crans watched with envy as Charles O'Neil vomited.

Charlie O'Neil was a reporter from the Kansas City Post, an old friend of Morgan's. He had called O'Neil from the train station. Their bargain worked two ways — it would give O'Neil the opportunity to break one of the biggest stories of his career — and Morgan could be certain that the story would receive the attention it deserved.

Having O'Neill join them had caused its problems, however. Crans did not like the idea. He had accused Morgan of having hired a press agent. The argument might have developed had it not been for O'Neil's practiced show of deep hurt and his insistence that he was an honest, objective reporter.

The three of them waited outside one of the large slaughterhouses. It had taken Crans six days to find Blacky Mansell in the maze of nameless streets and numberless shacks. Then it was by accident. There was not a better place on earth for a man like Mansell to lose himself.

The mistake Blacky had made was that he had kept his name and he had married a woman from out of the district. Crans had little hope of finding Mansell on any kind of official records. But he did look. And was surprised when Mansell's name appeared on the records of the marriage license bureau. And then Crans did not find Mansell — he found his wife. Through her, Mansell's only homing spot, Crans found Blacky and followed him to his night shift at the slaughterhouse.

Morgan, Crans and O'Neil were not alone. Behind trucks lined along the street were four police cars. As Crans had told him earlier, the police wanted the arrest to take place as discreetly as possible. The workers had an amazing loyalty to each other, and most of them had reasons of their own for hating the Kansas City police department. If the workers saw Mansell being pushed to a car by policeman, their reaction could be violent — and Mansell could have a chance to escape in the melee.

If Mansell escaped this time, Morgan knew that he would never find him again.

The shift was changing.

At 6:15 the doors to the slaughterhouse opened. Groves of men covered with blood stains began to leave.

"There he is," Crans said.

Out of the doors with five men walked Robert "Blacky" Mansell. He had long brown hair now. All that Morgan had seen of him was his military convict picture taken in 1911. Was it really the same man? He thought for a moment that Crans had made a mistake. He could not believe the fear that gripped his chest then. Mansell was his last chance.

As they had agreed, Crans approached Mansell. The other five workers stopped a few feet away. He saw Mansell jerk his arm away from Crans.

Morgan saw the long scar on the left cheek. He took a deep breath and moved to help Al.

"Mr. Mansell," he said, taking his arm, "my name is John Morgan. I'm a detective and I have a business proposition for you."

Mansell's face was twisted with anger. "Yea, what the hell kind of business?" he growled.

"It's like this — you get your ass over to that taxi without causing any trouble, and I won't blow it off."

Thirty minutes later. Through a glass door Morgan saw Mansell. Five burly police guards surrounded him.

"He was out drinking Saturday night," Crans said to Morgan. "And he worked the late shift. That means he's probably had four hours sleep in the past fifty-two hours."

"Good. Maybe we can be on our way to the County Seat sooner than I thought."

"How long do you think it will take?" O'Neil asked.

A guard offered Mansell a cigarette. He spat on the pack, snarling like an animal.

"As long as it takes."

Over and over again Morgan asked Mansell the same questions about the murder of his family in Blue Island. Only now and then did he bring up the subject of the Twin Forks axe murders. At noon a guard brought food and water to the room for both Morgan and Mansell. They had been going since six forty-five. Watching from the door most of the time, Crans and O'Neil wondered which of the two men seemed more tired. Each time Morgan accused Mansell of the murders, he denied it, then the questioning would begin again. The guards had changed at eleven o'clock, but those of the first shift remained in the hallway. They had never seen such grueling questioning before. They began to feel sorry for Mansell. "Then you think he is innocent?" O'Neil had asked one of the guards. "No. I think he's guilty, but even a dog gets to sleep."

"Not this dog," Crans said sadly.

Four o'clock, Monday afternoon.

Morgan left the room for a cup of coffee.

"Look at that bastard. He's tough as nails — but he's about ready to break. I can feel it."

O'Neil pulled a pocket watch from his vest, "I hope you're right. Two more hours and I miss tomorrow's deadline."

Al Crans whirled around, "Jesus Christ. This is suppose to be a murder investigation, not a three-ring circus. I'm going to get the hell out of this. I have a business in Denver."

Morgan caught Crans by the arm, "I'll need someone to take him back to the County Seat, Al. I was counting on you."

Crans looked into Morgan's face. "All right, I'll do it — but only because I'd like to see that bastard live long enough to stand trial."

"Good." Morgan started for the glass door, then he turned to O'Neil, "You better come in too, Charlie. I want you to hear the whole confession."

"Okay, Blacky — let's start from the beginning. Why did you kill your wife and daughter and your mother-in-law and father-in-law?"

"I didn't. I told you that," Mansell muttered.

"Oh you didn't? Then why didn't you go back?"

"Why should I — they was all dead?"

"How did you know that? If you didn't murder them, how did you know they were all dead?"

"I read it in the newspaper."

"No. The newspapers didn't report that they were all murdered. It said that your wife and her parents were murdered — but the report didn't mention your daughter. How did you know your daughter was dead?"

"A friend told me."

"What friend? How long ago? What did he say exactly and where did you meet him?"

"I don't know his name — a couple of weeks ago, I guess."

"A couple of weeks ago. Why didn't you try to find your daughter when you read about the murders?"

"I don't know."

"Why didn't you go to the funeral?"

"I don't know — I didn't want to. I was separated from my wife anyway — I hated her and her folks. I didn't care if they was dead."

"Did you hate your daughter, too?"

"No."

"Why did you kill her, too?"

"I didn't."

"Why didn't you return? The house was yours. It was worth $3,000. Don't you need $3,000?"

"I don't know — I didn't want it."

"And your wife's life insurance policy — that was worth $10,000. That's $13,000, Blacky. Don't you need $13,000?"

"Yes. I don't know — I just didn't want it."

"Because you murdered them?"

"No."

"The Porter family. Remember them, Blacky? June 10, 1912, you murdered them too. You took an axe and chopped your way through the house."

"Who's house?"

"The Porter house in Twin Forks, Iowa. You smashed their heads with an axe."

"No."

"No what?"

"Not an axe — not an axe."

"What then?"

"Ah — yes. An axe."

"You used an axe?"

CHAPTER TWENTY-FIVE

June 10, 1912

The house at last was quiet.

At ten o'clock the Porters had returned from church. The girls were giggling as they entered. Sarah and Judy led Clesta and Vera Stills to their upstairs bedroom where they could be alone.

"Do you want the boys to sleep downstairs?" Jas Porter asked his wife.

Sally's headache had returned. Jas had noticed that she had not felt well during the recital. He had hoped it would not last long this time — that she would have a headache and it would go away within an hour like most people could expect. Didn't the doctor say she was getting better? What then did "better" mean?

"Heavens no," Sally almost cried. "If those girls are in the same room, they'll stay awake talking all night."

"I'll tell the Stills to sleep in the parlor. You better go to bed, Mother."

"I will. As soon as I do the supper dishes. Can't leave them 'til morning."

"Go to bed. I'll have the girls do them."

"I can do it. They have their friends with them."

Jas led his wife to the stairs. "Go to bed. The girls can all do the dishes. Besides, isn't that what daughters are for?"

"You better lock the door."

He could hear the girls talking and laughing in the kitchen. There would be eight now instead of six.

Beside the three wooden steps to the back door was a small pile of cigar butts. The rain had been coming down steadily for the past hour, but a southerly wind had accompanied the rain and now blew harder than before. From the shadows toward Seventh Street, Jas Porter could see that the street light hanging over the intersection was swinging in the wind. It crossed his mind that the new pole lamps that Mayor Frank Gardner was so violently against were not such a bad idea.

Because of the wind, the steps were dry. He sat on the top step with his back against the screen door. The smoke from his cigar rose lazily in the heavy air before it was caught by the wind.

The four girls giggled.

"Hey! Are you girls about done in there?"

Silence. "Yes Papa," he heard Sarah say. Sarah was the oldest. She was calm and confident — like himself. Judy was their second child and more like her mother. If there was an illness going around, Judy would get it. And she, too, had been having headaches. The cause for these was a mystery for the local doctors. "God works in mysterious ways," they would say. Then Jas would grow remorseful wondering why God had chosen to punish his wife and daughter so.

Jas Porter hoped Sally would get better. He didn't love her like he wanted to love his wife. She was the mother of his children — his devoted wife — when she was not ill. He would never have the passion for her that he felt for Dorothy Gardner. Sometimes he longed for that passion — to be with a woman who was bright and cheerful and willing to give herself to him. But he did not fool himself — a life could not be built around simple passion. What he felt for Dorothy could not last a lifetime. On the other hand, if he stuck it out with Sally, then, in a few years, theirs would be a normal relationship between two people growing old together. He had decided not to see Dorothy again. Even if she forced herself on him as she had Friday, he would reject her.

It would be for her own good if he refused to meet Dorothy, he told himself. And without her, it would be easier for him to accept his situation with Sally.

There was the family name to think of. It would be dishonorable to divorce. A divorce would disgrace his parents and his brothers. Business would fall back — it was out of the question. Besides, there were the children . . .

"Are you done yet?" he yelled through the screen door.

"Yes. We're all done, Papa."

"All right — get some fresh sheets for the parlor. I want Clesta and Vera to stay there tonight. Your mother isn't feeling well."

"Yes, Papa."

It was eleven thirty by the time the lights in the bedrooms finally went out. Jas looked at the kitchen. It was spotless and nothing was out of place. Sally would be pleased in the morning. Jas wondered if she appreciated her daughters. It was so easy to take children for granted.

He stepped into the living room. It was not in such good order. The white angel costumes Herbert and Paul had worn were heaped on the couch. The black costumes the girls had worn and the long, black slips that had been worn underneath were draped over a chair back.

If it had been earlier he might have opened the closet door. The clothes should have been put away. They would be folded and placed in the large trunk that filled the top shelf in the closet. Probably the costumes would stay there until they were useless. Then Sally would use the material to sew new clothes for the girls. It was a good system and the material would be used for three or four different sets of clothes before it went to rags. The trunk at the top of the closet was heavy and the large grandfather clock across the room was striking midnight, he decided to let the trunk wait until morning.

At the bottom of the steps he turned the switch that put out the ceiling light in the livingroom.

Jas Porter took a last look around the livingroom. At first, light from the street lamps came through the windows and he could see the room clearly. Suddenly the light was gone. The storm had put out a light, he decided.

There was a gas candle light at the bottom of the steps which he could have used. But he knew the house well and he would not have to check on the children tonight. He turned and climbed the stairs. He was tired. Jas Porter went to bed.

Fifteen minutes passed. Then half an hour. Except for the clicking of the old clock and the rustling of bedsheets as one of the sleeping people stirred, the house was silent. Outside the rain had stopped. Only a few drops of water hit the roof as they fell from the old elm tree on the front lawn.

The doorknob turned slowly. There was a sharp "click" as it pulled the bolt free from the slot. The closet door cracked open and Blacky Mansell was alone in the house with eight sleeping people. It was twelve thirty-five in the morning.

Carefully, confidently, Blacky Mansell pulled his pants off and his suitcoat and shirt. He tossed them onto the closet floor. Then, naked, he stooped to his knees and fumbled through his suit vest. It took him a long time to find the inner pocket in the dark. He moved his coarse fingers along the lining until he revealed the opening of the pocket. Then he felt the cold, bone-handled knife which he pulled free. He felt along its edge — it was a narrow blade over eight inches long. It had a point as fine as a sewing needle and the edge was sharper than Jas Porter's razor. But he could not see. One thing that Blacky Mansell had not counted on was the street light going dark. He cursed himself for not having thought of it before. He should have brought a candle with him. If his plan was to work, he could not be fumbling around in the dark, particularly when he reached Jas Porter upstairs or the bedroom with the four Porter children. This could not be a clumsy operation. Each cut would have to be expertly completed, an ability his years of working in the slaughterhouses had given him.

It would be an added risk to light the house after everyone had gone to bed. But it was necessary.

He pulled some matchsticks from his coat pocket and struck one against the wall. It lit the dark room like a torch. He found one glass lamp stand and soon it glowed evenly. Then he stepped carefully around the livingroom and kitchen pulling down the black shades and tying them securely.

When he came to the parlor, he left the lamp in the livingroom. There were two windows there, one at the foot of the bed on the north wall and one beside the headboard to the west. He pulled and tied the shades quietly. The girls did not awaken. They slept peacefully. Blacky took his knife from between his teeth and bent to inspect the first girl with professional interest. Clesta was lying on her back, her head sunken into a soft pillow. He eyed her face and the firm, square chin of her ancestors, then his eyes fell on the neck which curved up towards him. He held the knife firmly and slashed her throat.

The girl jumped as blood squirted from her wound. Her eyes opened. She saw the naked man above her. She opened her mouth to scream but received no sound. Blacky placed one hand on the wound to keep the blood from squirting and another on her stomach to stop her from squirming and to awaken her sister. Within moments Clesta stilled. She was dead.

Blacky had not expected the violent reaction. The blood, yes, but not the struggle. It was not this way with the cutter in the slaughter plant. Obviously, he needed to find a faster way to cause death. He would need to go directly to the brain, he decided, and was glad that his knife was long and narrow.

Vera Stills stirred. Mansell held the knife patiently above her. She rolled to her back. He brought the sharp blade into her left eye at an upward angle to reach the brain. She stirred no more.

There were only two small windows upstairs, one in each bedroom. He was not concerned with these. If he left the lamp in the hallway, between the rooms, little light would reach the windows and even then no harm would be done since they faced away from the neighboring homes.

Systematically, Blacky went from Jas Porter to Sally Porter, then to Sarah, Judy, Herbert and, at last, little Paul. It had gone perfectly. Except for Clesta, not one of the victims had moved. Mansell pulled the shades of the two upstairs windows then returned to the living room where he left the lamp. He went to the kitchen where he filled a bowl with water and washed his hands and face and upper part of his body. He unlatched the back door off the kitchen and returned to the closet to dress.

Albert Gardner stood in the doorway between the kitchen and livingroom.

"It's finished?" he asked.

Mansell pointed to the parlor. "Take a look."

Albert walked into the room. It was dark in the corner where the bed was. He could just make out the two forms of two sleeping bodies. The thought that they were dead was numbing and he was glad that he could not see them.

Mansell came around the corner. He pushed the burning lamp ahead of him, "Here. Want some light?"

The red blood at Clesta's throat gleamed. Her eyes stared innocently up at Albert as he looked back to them. Why was this done to me, they asked. It was shocking enough to paralyze him and keep him from fully realizing the meaning of the ghastly sight. He looked to Vera. She was perfectly whole, except for the place where her eye used to be. A small red and yellow stream went from her eye down her cheek to her neck. That was too real.

Albert screamed, running from the house.

He ran from the back door. It was too awful, too horrifying. Too real and simple, he, Albert Gardner, had ordered the destruction of eight human beings. In life they had been enemies. In death they were the simple remains of eight fragile persons. They could have died one hundred different ways, but he had said, no, they die now. And the hired killer carried out his orders. They should have been beaten and tortured and effaced — death might have been welcomed. To leave them there, sleeping yet dead, one simple eye poked out — it was too easy.

He ran into the back yard. He stumbled and tumbled forward against an old log Jas Porter had used to chop wood over. As he stumbled to his feet his hand touched upon a smooth handle of a tool. Albert lifted it — Jas Porter's axe — the jagged axe Porter had used to break cinder. Dumbly he carried the axe back to the house. Mansell followed him into the parlor.

"What the hell are you doing?"

Albert raised the axe. The sharp edge chipped into the plaster ceiling but that did not soften the blow of the horrible descent.

Clesta's head splattered onto the walls. Then Vera — her face collapsed into the pillow. Again and again the axe dug into the ceiling and crashed down upon the victims.

When he was finished with the Stills, he pulled the sheet across them. He went upstairs.

He went into the children's bedroom first. Their young skulls crushed easily. When he covered them, they seemed to be sleeping again, only their heads were missing.

When he came to Jas Porter, all the rage that was in him came to the surface. He chopped away at Jas Porter's head until not a single piece of face or bone fragment was identifiable. Brain tissue still warm from life clung to the walls amidst splatters of blood. The slanted ceiling behind him was torn to shreds by the axe.

But when he came to Sally, he became sad. Whether he knew it or not, the axe handle had turned in his hands so that when he brought it down onto Sally, it stuck in her forehead. He wrenched it out — stared at the clean split he had left in her skull, and hurried from the room. He went back into the children's room. Paul was not covered well — he tossed another sheet over the pillow. He stood. In the window he saw his reflection. It bothered him so he turned away only to find his reflection again in the mirror. He covered the mirror with one of Paul's shirts and ran to the parent's bedroom to do the same thing, and again the large bureau mirror in the livingroom.

"Mirror don't tell no stories," Mansell said.

Albert ended his rampage where it had started — in the parlor. "Who are they?"

Mansell looked at him curiously, "I thought you'd know — you're the one who wanted them killed."

Albert felt his right arm tugging at him. He looked at it — the axe was still there. He propped it against the wall.

"Let's get out of here," Mansell said. "You still got your key to the front door?"

Albert nodded.

"Good. I found another key in the bureau. Remember we're going to lock the back door — the screen, too — and leave from the front."

When they reached the front yard Albert began to run. Blacky chased him, but Albert was like a jack rabbit to Fourth Street where he turned and ran to the front porch of the mansion.

He banged on the door. "Father, Father, I need your help."

"Yes. I used an axe!" Mansell screamed.

"So you confess to having murdered the Porters?"

"Yes."

"And you confess to having murdered your wife, daughter, and your mother-in-law and father-in-law in Blue Island?"

"Yes."

"Now — back to Twin Forks. Did a Frank F. Gardner hire you to murder the Porters?"

No response.

"Did Frank Gardner hire you?"

"Yes."

"How much did he pay you?"

"One thousand dollars."

Morgan turned to a clerk. He placed a typed piece of paper in front of Mansell.

"This is your statement," he explained. "All you have to do is read it and sign it."

Later, in the corridor, Morgan was on his way to the stairs. "There's your story, O'Neil. Will it be in the morning paper?"

"Sure thing. I've already called my editor — front page."

"Only one restriction, Charlie — don't use Frank Gardner's name. Say, 'a prominent Twin Forks citizen' instead. Everyone will know who it means."

"You're the boss. Is it all right if I go up to Twin Forks with you? I'd like to follow up on this story?"

"We can use all the publicity we can get. The train leaves at one o'clock tomorrow morning."

"You're kidding. That means the paper will be in Twin Forks seven hours before we get there."

"That's the idea. I want a nice warm reception for Mansell."

KANSAS CITY POST — FEBRUARY 16, 1913

TODAY IN ONE OF THE MOST EXCITING CRIMINAL IN-VESTIGATIONS OF OUR TIME, ROBERT "BLACKY" MANSELL, AN EX-MILITARY CONVICT AND A WORKER AT A SOUTHSIDE SLAUGHTERHOUSE, CONFESSED TO THE MURDERS OF THE JAS PORTER FAMILY AND TWO NEIGH-BOR GIRLS IN TWIN FORKS, IOWA, JUNE 10, 1912.

MANSELL, WITH AN IDENTIFYING FOUR-INCH SCAR ON HIS LEFT CHEEK, WAS CAPTURED BY DETECTIVE JOHN MORGAN. DETECTIVE MORGAN HAS BEEN ON THE FAMOUS TWIN FORKS MURDER CASE SINCE THE DAY OF THE MASS FUNERAL OF THE VICTIMS IN 1912. NEVER HAS HE STRAYED FROM THE TRAIL OF THE MURDERER OR THOSE INVOLVED.

THANKS TO DETECTIVE MORGAN'S SUPER SLEUTHING, THE WOMEN AND CHILDREN OF TWIN FORKS, WILL ONCE AGAIN BE ABLE TO SLEEP SAFELY TONIGHT. FOR THE FIRST TIME IN ALMOST FOUR YEARS, TOTS CAN GO TO BED WITHOUT WONDERING IF THE BRUTAL FIEND WHO SO PUNISHED THEIR CLASSMATES AND NEIGHBORS IS OUT THERE WAITING TO STRIKE AGAIN.

TEN HOUR QUESTIONING — GUARDS FEEL SORRY FOR MURDERER.

FROM SIX-THIRTY, MONDAY MORNING TO FOUR O'CLOCK MONDAY AFTERNOON DETECTIVE MORGAN RELENTLESSLY FIRED QUESTION AFTER QUESTION AT MANSELL. EVEN THE PRISON GUARDS WHO ARE LONG EXPERIENCED AT THIS SORT OF THING AND DEALING WITH MEN OF THE UNDERWORLD SAID THEY WERE SORRY FOR MANSELL. THESE CALLOUSED MEN, SOME OF WHOM HAD REASON TO ASSIST MORGAN IN THE CAP-TURE OF MANSELL, STAYED ON EVEN AFTER THEIR SHIFTS WERE OVER TO WATCH MORGAN EXPERTLY BREAK DOWN EVERY DEFENSE MANSELL HAD TO OFFER.

PROMINENT CITIZEN OF TWIN FORKS IMPLICATED.

AT FOUR O'CLOCK MANSELL CONFESSED TO THE MURDERS AT TWIN FORKS. WHEN ASKED IF A PROMINENT CITIZEN OF TWIN FORKS HIRED HIM TO DO THE FOUL DEED, MANSELL ANSWERED WITH AN AFFIRMATIVE AND SAID THAT HE HAD BEEN PAID $1,000 FOR THE MURDERS. THE PROMINENT CITIZEN WILL REMAIN NAMELESS IN THIS ACCOUNT IN ORDER TO LET THE COURTS DECIDE THE TRUTH OF THE MATTER AND NOT TO HINDER DETECTIVE MORGAN IN HIS INVESTIGATION.

GOVERNOR OF IOWA PRAISES MORGAN.

OVER THE WIRES TODAY, THE GOVERNOR SPOKE TO OUR PAPER. HE THANKED THE KANSAS CITY POLICE DEPARTMENT FOR THE ASSISTANCE THEY GAVE MORGAN IN CAPTURING THE DANGEROUS AND DESPERATE CRIMINAL MANSELL. MOST OF ALL, HE HAD GREAT PRAISE FOR DETECTIVE MORGAN. TO QUOTE THE GOVERNOR'S WIRE, "NEVER HAVE SO MANY PEOPLE OWED SO MUCH TO ONE MAN."

(BLUE ISLAND, ILLINOIS) MANSELL CONFESSES TO MURDER OF WIFE AND FAMILY.

MANSELL, WHO HAS BEEN ACCUSED OF THE MURDER OF HIS WIFE, DAUGHTER AND HIS MOTHER-IN-LAW AND FATHER-IN-LAW ALSO CONFESSED TO THESE CRIMES. THE BLUE ISLAND POLICE FORCE SAID THEY HAD BEEN LOOKING FOR MANSELL SINCE THE MURDERS BUT SAID THEY WOULD NOT PRESS FOR EXTRADITION IN ORDER TO ALLOW JUSTICE TO BE DONE IN IOWA. THE SIMILARITY OF THE BLUE ISLAND MURDERS AND THE TWIN FORKS MURDERS PUT MORGAN ON THE TRACK OF MANSELL. LIKE A LOYAL BLOODHOUND OF THE PEOPLE, MORGAN GOT THE SCENT OF THE MAN WITH BLOOD ON HIS HANDS AND DID NOT LET UP UNTIL HIS SEARCH ENDED HERE, MONDAY MORNING.

CHAPTER TWENTY-SIX

Frank Gardner slammed the paper to the table. His face was afire.

"Damn."

Around him were Fred Martin, Doctor Stewart, County Attorney Dan Evers and Sam Durham.

"Imagine. The Governor supporting this pack of liars. Listen to this, 'Never have so many owed so much to one man.' God, the stupidity of our Governor is astounding."

Martin smoked a cigarette. He was calm. "The important thing now is, what are we going to do about it?"

"I could have him extradited."

"That would seem a little odd," Durham offered. "Do you have a better idea?"

"Perhaps I do," Martin volunteered. "The newspaper account was quite prominent in pointing out that Morgan hounded Mansell for over ten hours. As soon as Mansell reaches the County Seat, I think Mr. Evers might talk with him about denying his statement.

It is obvious that the man was under extreme duress. His statement could be rendered useless."

"Evers — what do you say?"

"It is worth a try."

Sam Durham tapped his pipe over the fireplace hearth, "Gentlemen, I doubt that Mr. Morgan is going to be willing to let us talk with his chief witness just like that."

"Not just a witness, Sam, Mansell is also classified a criminal. That means the County Attorney has every right, indeed, duty to speak to the man."

Sam Durham bowed cordially, "I shall leave both the meeting and the discussion up to County Attorney Evers and his conscience."

Frank Gardner came around the library table to face Sam Durham. "What would you have me do — let Morgan hang me for something I didn't do? He has taken this trial outside the courtroom. Now I have to prove to this entire state that I am innocent. If Morgan wants to get dirty — we'll get dirty, too. These people think he's some kind of demi-god — wait until they see what I'm bringing to this town. Then we'll see what kind of man they think Morgan is."

Sam Durham went to the door. The other three followed him. Durham held the door for the others. Before he left, he looked back at Gardner,

"While you're thinking about it, Senator, you might wonder why the people are so willing to believe you're guilty."

"Because they're selfish, ungrateful fools."

"Well, Senator, if you impose a kingdom on peasants, then you have to expect a peasant revolt. England couldn't handle us."

"Get out of my home, Durham."

"Certainly, King. Kill the king."

Alone in his study, Frank Gardner watched the men leave the drive in front of his mansion. He looked around him. This mansion, this room and everything in it testified to his accomplishments.

To have them taken away, even marred by scandal, was a thought unbearable to him.

"King," he repeated the word to himself. No, he was not a king. He saw himself as a general of an unruly army. All they needed was someone to bring them together to create the finest soldiers in the world. It was a lonely role to play. He recalled a saying from Napoleon, "A great leader has few friends." Yes. This is true, he thought.

He recalled another book. It read, "For God so loved the world that he gave his only begotten son."

"My son," he whispered. "Is that my price? Will I have to turn him over in order to save all that I have worked for? The people, so many, will be lost without me. Twin Forks will reduce itself to nothing. The fate of an entire population is more important than one man. But could I, when all else fails, turn him over?"

He sat in a chair before the fire. It burned low as he pondered the situation. Suddenly he stood and went to the typewriter. He pulled a piece of paper from the table drawer and placed it on the typewriter. On the top of the page was his letterhead.

Frank Gardner took a deep breath, then let his fingers fall,
TO THE SHERIFF OF BLUE ISLAND.

CHAPTER TWENTY-SEVEN

(headline) FEBRUARY 16, WEDNESDAY SLANDER TRIAL HELD UP WHILE GRAND JURY QUESTIONS CONFESSOR — MANSELL.

(headline) FEBRUARY 17, THURSDAY MANSELL PLEADS IN-NOCENT TO GRAND JURY — SIGNED STATEMENT UNDER DURESS.

(headline) FEBRUARY 18, FRIDAY GRAND JURY TO MAKE MANSELL DECISION OVER THE WEEKEND.

(headline) FEBRUARY 21, MONDAY GRAND JURY DIS-MISSES MURDER SUSPECT. MANSELL EXTRADITED TO IL-LINOIS — SLANDER TRIAL RESUMES TOMORROW.

"How can they do it, Amos?"

John Morgan was in the Page Hotel room. He watched the court-house across the street. There, Robert Mansell walked across the lawn between two deputies. County Attorney Evers walked directly behind him. The ground sank beneath their weight. An early thaw had taken the frost. It was a bright, sunny day. Mansell was happy. Morgan could see Mansell joking with the deputies and as he climbed into the car for the drive that would take him to the train which would carry him on to Illinois to stand trial for the murders of his own family, Mansell turned to Evers, gave him a wide smile and a warm handshake.

Morgan turned away from the window, "I bring Mansell back — right here to the County Seat — and they let him go."

"They outsmarted us, John."

"You don't seem to be damn upset about it."

Potters gave him that same curious smile he had seen on the first day of meeting with the old man in Sam Durham's office.

"I'm an old lawyer, John. These things happen in a courtroom. It wasn't your fault. Our mistake was our failure to anticipate it."

"Christ, you're supposed to be the most respected man in this territory. Isn't anyone interested in justice?"

"You and I think that we are interested in justice. Perhaps Evers and Martin think they are fighting for justice. By this very conflict, justice becomes secondary. Most importantly, we want to win. Right or wrong, we want to win."

"We're right, Amos. This time we're right! Frank Gardner is responsible for the murder of eight people and he is running around free."

"And that bothers you?"

"You're damn right that bothers me. Why in the hell doesn't it bother you?"

"That was uncalled for, John. I've been fighting men like Gardner all my life. I've watched them take land from hard-working families and then I've seen those same families turn around and work the land for the new owner like indentured servants. To me that is the worst offense Gardner or men like him commit. They murder thousands of people — it just takes longer for the people to die, with more suffering. Myself — I'd rather be staked out on an ant hill.

"But I'm not going to let a setback like this bother me. I can't afford to — there are too many setbacks in my business. If you let each one take a little bit of yourself each time, then there isn't going to be anything left. That's your problem, John. You die a little everytime you lose."

"There's enough of me here to beat Frank Gardner — and I'll do it without your help if that's what you're coming to."

"No. That's not what I'm saying and I have preached enough."

"Thank God for that."

"Can we still work together?"

"Yes."

"What's the next step?"

"We use Dorothy Gardner. I've got no choice now. I didn't want to drag her story through the court, but it will hurt Gardner — so I guess it is worth it. I'm suppose to meet Al this afternoon to work on that."

Potters stood to leave. The weather outside was pleasant, but he wrapped a scarf around his neck and buttoned his huge overcoat securely. "I'm not giving up on the Mansell angle. Our jury wasn't convinced that Mansell is guilty — but I think they must wonder. They let him go only because they knew Mansell would stand trial in Illinois for the same crime. With all of the confusion, they passed the buck."

"So what does that do for us?"

"We'll use it. If we can play on their guilt — make them wonder if they let a murderer go free — then maybe they'll take it out on Gardner."

"Amos! The newspaper said that Illinois would not extradite Mansell until we were done with him. Do you suppose Gardner had something to do with that?"

Potters laughed. "I'm way ahead of you there, John. Russ Porter left for Blue Island two hours ago."

"You're not as senile as I thought."

"Where are you going?"

"Back to Twin Forks. One way or the other, Gardner is going to be found guilty of those murders. We've got Mansell, if you're right. And we have Dorothy Gardner's affair with Jas Porter — and others."

"Do you think that's enough?"

"What do you think — would Frank Gardner have a family murdered if he knew that his daughter-in-law was cheating on his son?"

"Yes, I think he would." Potters answered.

"And so do a lot of other people. I think we'll win the case if we can make everyone aware of it. Like you said, legally we're not convicting a man of murder — we're proving I did not slander him."

Potters held the door for Morgan. The two stepped into the hallway. Potters said, "We're back where we started — win the case — with or without justice."

Morgan walked into the sun on the front porch of the hotel. "If we win this case, Amos, justice will have been done."

It was noon when Morgan reached Twin Forks. He headed for the power plant hoping to catch the watchman before he left for lunch. This visit was to be routine. He trusted Merle Sorenson as one tends to trust lazy old men who have little to lose in hard times, and even less to gain in the good times. The jury would trust Sorenson, too. For the same reason, they would believe him.

Morgan knocked on the door to the small building that served as the watchman's shack. He knocked again, there was no answer. Lunchtime, he thought as he started to leave. He was ten paces away when he heard voices behind him. He turned back to the shack but there was no one there. Again he heard the voices and finally the mystery was solved when he saw Merle Sorenson's boots sticking out from under the corner of the back of the shack.

Morgan opened the door to the shack and went on to the door that led into the small, fenced compound around the power plant. He stepped through the rear door without knocking and found Merle Sorenson sitting on an old bent-wood chair worn smooth by use and faded white by the sun and weather. Another old man was there beside him. The two of them had brought their chairs to the west side of the shack to catch the afternoon sun and escape the breeze that came out of the northeast.

"Hey, I was wondering if I'd see you again," Merle Sorenson said without changing positions.

"I told you I'd let you know when we needed you," Morgan smiled. "Well here I am. We need you tomorrow."

There was a long pause as Merle Sorenson pulled a chew from his tobacco plug. That accomplished, he rested grim in his chair and said sleepily, "What do you need me for?"

The old man was insane, Morgan thought.

"I need you to testify. I need you more than ever now."

"Testify? Testify to what?"

Absolutely crazy.

"Mr. Sorenson, you said you would testify against Gardner when I was ready for you — you would tell the jury about how Gardner came down here and turned off this town's electricity on the night of the Porter murders. Now I need you to do that tomorrow. You promised me that you would."

Sorenson sent a stream of tobacco juice across the compound. "Well, young fella, if you'd of come got me last week, I'd of done it. After all, a promise is a promise. But I've made other promises and I'll have to keep them — promises that got in the way of yours."

"What promise — were they to Frank Gardner?"

"Nope. They were to my daughter. I promised her that if I could I would go back to Pennsylvania and visit her for awhile. But I never had no money so I never went. Now I've come into some money — and now I'm goin'."

"This money — did Frank Gardner buy you off?"

"He called it a bonus — a well deserved bonus. He said that the community had to take care of its older folks. That Gardner is a good person."

"Yea, real fine person. Sorenson, don't you give a damn that he murdered the Porters and the Stills girls?"

"Now I don't know that he done it."

"You saw him black out this town on the night of the murders. Doesn't that make you think he had something to do with it?"

"I saw nothing of the kind."

Well, that was that. Now it would be up to the contractor, Klaus Hartmann, to prove that Frank Gardner pulled the switch that night. Merle Sorenson had sold his pride for a few dollars. Morgan looked at him. No, perhaps he didn't sell his pride — perhaps old men like Sorenson had no honor left.

"Goodbye, Merle. I hope you have a good trip."

It was evening. As soon as the sun disappeared from the sky, the temperature dropped to a cold twenty degrees.

Morgan sat on a bench in the Square watching the hotel across the street. Behind him he could see the light coming from the window of their headquarters, but that was the only light coming from the store windows. The streets were empty.

On the second floor of the hotel a light came from the room of the northeast corner. Lona Gardner and Carl Gast were there now. He had seen both of them move past the window and remembered, when they embraced each other, how he had felt like a peeper. They had pulled the shade and all he could see after that were shadows in the room.

It was cold and getting colder. Morgan would have to talk to Carl Gast tonight, he knew. But he did not want to involve Lona if he could help it. If he was lucky, either Carl or Lona would leave the hotel — then he would make his move. If he wasn't, then he would have to go up there and knock on their bedroom door. Patiently, he waited.

Lona Gardner threw herself onto the bed. She laughed and rolled to one side.

"Hey, do you know that I'm happy? I mean, I am really happy."

Carl stretched out beside her, "That's because you're a spoiled brat and I've been doing everything you want."

"That's right, honey." She smiled promiscuously, "You're just lucky I've only been asking one thing from you."

"Well, I manage to work you in with the rest."

Lona laid her head back onto the pillow. She became serious suddenly and reached out to Carl's hand.

"Carl, what are we going to do?"

"What do you mean?"

"The trial will be over soon. I'll have no other reason to stay here."

Carl squeezed her hand lightly, "Then you'll leave."

"Come with me, Carl." She cried as she pulled his head to her breasts, "Come to New York with me. I know we can be happy. Back there it doesn't matter if you're a Gardner or a Gast. We'd be just two people in love."

"I love you," Carl said. He kissed her on the forehead.

"Oh, Carl. Don't let me go without you. You can't survive in this place any longer. You're too much of a man to put up with all of this."

"Maybe I can change it."

"No. No one can change it. Don't you think I can see how my father has taken control of people? He's not the only one. Some of the families are just as bad or worse. But they are all wrong and no one is going to change that."

Carl stared at the ceiling. He searched his mind for words that would explain what he felt. Yes, he loved Lona. He had fallen in love with Lona Gardner, the daughter of the man who had ruined his family, the sister of the man who had disgraced his family further.

"Since I was a boy I have dreamed of a way to fight all of this. I dreamed one time that I had thrown the Gardners out of Twin Forks, and I owned the mansion. It's difficult to forget something — after so many years. There was a time when I wondered if the only reason I was here with you — well, I wondered if this was just to hurt your father."

"But you love me — don't you?"

"Yes. And if you want me to go to New York with you after the trial, I'll go."

"I love you, Carl Gast. Come on, make love to me."

"Later," Carl said jumping off the bed. "I'm going out for a drink. I have to think about what I just said."

"You'll be back?"

"Sure, I just have to think a little. That's all."

Lona laughed, "All right. Go ahead. Think. See if I care."

Carl Gast stopped at the lobby door to button his winter coat. His face was serious, pensive, as he thought of all he had just said to Lona. He was not lying when he told her he loved her. Nor had he forgotten his hatred of her father and brother. Could the two, the love and the hate, exist together he asked himself. Or perhaps his love for Lona outweighed the hatred of Frank and Albert Gardner. Hadn't he told Lona that he would go to New York with her? — and didn't that answer the question?

Carl Gast left the hotel. As he stepped into the freezing night air and headed for the pool hall, Carl teetered on the edge of his decision.

"Carl Gast."

Carl heard his name spoken. He turned to see a tall dark shadow of a man in a long overcoat and bowler hat. The man said no more and Carl could not recognize him.

"Yes. What do you want? Who are you?" Carl said boldly.

The shadow stepped forward. At five feet the light from the corner street lamp revealed Morgan's frozen face.

"I'm John Morgan, Carl. I have been waiting for you."

"Why? What do you want from me?" Carl asked.

Morgan did not answer the question. He continued, "I didn't want to upset Lona with this. I thought that we could talk quietly, over at my headquarters, and Lona wouldn't have to know."

Carl stepped back, a man with a secret found out.

"Tell me now, Morgan. What do you want to talk about?"

"Your involvement with Dorothy Gardner just before the murders."

The words hung in the air. Frozen there.

The three of them, John Morgan, Carl Gast and Al Crans, sat near the wood stove. Morgan shivered and Al Crans poured three cups of coffee. Carl Gast accepted his with a scowl.

"Well, Carl," Morgan began, "I have already told you why I brought you here — we have learned that you had been meeting Dorothy Gardner quite a bit before the murders. In fact, once or twice a week either she would call you or you called her to set up the meetings."

"What about it — that doesn't prove a damn thing!" Carl Gast muttered.

"No it doesn't. You're absolutely correct. But do you think a jury would believe that?"

"I don't care what a jury thinks. What jury — hey, you guys aren't going to try to hang those murders on me now, are you?" Gast had set his coffee on the stove and now crouched in his chair ready to spring should he have to.

Morgan stood near the stove. He did not want to force Carl Gast to testify. Nor did he want to put Gast on the stand to combat the accusations of Minnie Butler. Morgan needed Gast — and he wanted them to work on the same side.

Morgan poured himself another cup of coffee before facing Gast. When he did, his voice was calm.

"Let me explain to you what we are trying to accomplish, Carl. I think you'll appreciate what I say, because you know the Gardner family and the Senator as well as anyone — at least you know the side of the Senator that I am concerned with."

"We are certain that Senator Gardner is responsible for the murders. You don't know all that we have learned about Senator Gardner — but let me say that we have some information that incriminates him beyond doubt — and this is information we have been unable to bring out in court."

"So what we are left with is to prove that Frank Gardner not only had reason to murder the Porters, but that he was the type of man to do so — or at least hire someone to do it for him."

Carl Gast listened, his scowl had disappeared, to Morgan's relief, and now he listened attentively. Morgan continued.

"We think that enough people are willing to believe Gardner had the Porters murdered because Dorothy was having an affair with Jas.

"Where does that leave us? It means we have to prove that Dorothy was having an affair with Jas Porter. We can do that. We have one witness who will swear to it in court. But that is just one witness. A lot of people will refuse to believe it — not because of their loyalty to Jas Porter or to Frank Gardner or even Albert, but because they are willing to give Dorothy Gardner the benefit of doubt. It's like stealing a young girl's virginity. Around here, once her reputation is gone — it's gone forever. It is not a decision that a jury or the public will take lightly. After they have decided that Dorothy Gardner was committing adultery, then the gossips and old ladies of Two Forks will revel in it forever — but that is later. I'm talking about now — and I'm talking about Frank Gardner."

Carl picked up his coffee again. He stared into it, elbows on his knees, "So where do I come in?"

Morgan looked at Crans. Their eyes met. Morgan nodded, indicating his pleasure, but Crans turned away and walked to the front of the room. A train whistle echoed through the valley and Morgan wondered if Crans would soon be going.

"That puts you on the witness stand, Carl. If you'll testify to your affair with Dorothy, then we'll have Gardner where we want him. The jury can then assume that Dorothy was also having an affair with Jas Porter. And the people of this town know Frank Gardner well enough to know that he wouldn't let something like that pass. Gardner found out about it. Gardner reacted."

Gast's head still hung over his knees. He shook his head slowly, "Do you realize what this will do to me — to Lona?"

Morgan's face went red, "Gast, I'm talking about a murder. No, eight murders. You have the chance to put Frank Gardner back where he belongs — to stand up to Gardner for the first time."

"It will ruin me."

"And what will it do to you if for the rest of your life you know that you let a murderer go free simply because you were having an affair with his daughter? It seems to me that would ruin you. You'd never be able to stand up to anyone again. Carl Gast would be a coward."

Carl Gast buried his face in his hands as he began to cry. He sobbed briefly. He looked up. Then he stood.

"I'll have to think about it."

"I'll need your answer tomorrow, Carl. I want you on the witness stand Wednesday."

"I'll let you know," Gast said as he walked to the door.

"Carl!" Morgan yelled.

"What?"

"Consider something else: you may be doing Lona a favor by exposing her father — and yourself. If you love her, then you'll testify."

Carl opened the door, "I'll let you know."

"I didn't want to bring Carl Gast into this. But I had to, so shut up about it."

Al Crans paced the floor behind Morgan who sat with his feet on the stove.

"That's right, you had to bring Gast in. You gallantly refrained from doing so, but now, for justice's sake, you have to."

"What are you saying, Al?"

"I'm saying if you can't prepare a case that will stand up in court, then get the hell off this case. You don't belong on it anymore."

Morgan remained calm, "Maybe I'll have a case. Maybe your boys will find the contractor and . . . "

"He's dead."

Silence. Morgan could see the flames through the small doors on the side of the stove.

"Your boys found him?"

"Yes. I got the telegram while you were waiting for Gast. Klaus Hartmann died in a train crash in California. He's been dead for two months."

Morgan did not respond. He looked at the flames through the hold trying to remember the countless setbacks and disappointments he had encountered over the past four years. Crans stared at him for a long time. He did not want to leave a sinking ship. But did this ship have any right to float? This was the end.

"Get the hell off the case, John. There's a train sitting at the depot now and I'm going to be on it. If you're smart, you'll ride out this trial, then join me in Denver if you still want to. I won't be a part of any of what I see coming in this case. Goodbye, John."

Crans waited. There was no response. He reached for his coat, swung it around him and opened the door. As he closed the door he heard the sound of hooves and carriage wheels on the brick paving. It was Frank Gardner's carriage. As it rounded the northeast corner of the Square, Crans saw that it carried two passengers. It was dark at the middle of the block so he could not make out who the passengers were. He waited until the carriage came to the intersection beneath the overhead light. As it passed, for a brief moment, the face of the two passengers were exposed to the light. He saw the man first. It was John Goodell. Then he saw the woman. He felt his heart throb stick in his throat. He backed into the headquarters in a mild shock.

"John. I just saw Gardner's carriage bringing John Goodell home from the train."

Morgan was too tired and depressed to get excited. "Wonder where he has been."

Crans shook his head, "Goodell wasn't alone, John. I'd say that he has been to New Mexico. He has your wife with him."

Morgan jumped. "My wife!" he looked at Crans fearfully, then his eyes relaxed. There was nothing he could do. He turned back to the stove. Presently he heard the door open and close. He heard the footsteps fade away. His old friend Al Crans had walked out of his life.

CHAPTER TWENTY-EIGHT

Kathy Gast was eight years old. She was in the fourth grade at the Twin Forks school. Kathy was not popular with the other children. Kathy dressed in the worn-out clothes of her sister, Alice. If she followed the pattern, Kathy would soon drop out of school, not willing to put up with the embarrassment any longer. She would become scornful of others, jealous of the more well-to-do, and then she would hate them as her brother Carl hated them.

She feared her father. Andy Gast would come home drunk. Sometimes he would beat her. Other times he would try to take advantage of her. Like her sister, Kathy was learning young how to fear and avoid Andy Gast. And like Alice, Kathy was learning that she was worth no more than the value others gave her — and as a Gast, that was not very high. She had once dreamed that she was a young lady of the community respected and sought after. Those kinds of dreams came less often now. Soon the fantasy would be twisted and soon she would be older. Young men of the better families would come to her to experience what was dishonorable for a good girl to give them. She would meet them. She would pretend they loved her and fantasize that some day one of them would marry her. And most important of all, Kathy would keep their secret or they would never see her again.

Today, on Tuesday, the first day of the final part of the trial, Kathy took her seat at the back of the school room.

Some boys were pushing and shoving each other in the aisles on either side of her desk. One boy fell toward her and she thought he might crash down upon her. She lifted her arms to protect herself.

When the teacher entered everyone scrambled for their seats. The room quieted. The teacher began writing on the blackboard. As usual, Kathy's mind had already began to wander. She looked at the early budding trees outside the window which reminded her that in another three months school would be out for the summer. She liked school. It was her only escape from the scrub farm her father rarely worked.

Kathy looked away from the window. Her eyes dropped to the top of her desk and fell upon a piece of paper that had been carefully folded twice. A prank, she thought. Some taunting message would be inside. Whoever had placed it there wanted to hurt her. She didn't know why. It seemed everyone wanted to hurt her.

Carefully, so that the teacher would not see her with the note, Kathy unfolded the paper. The words were too neatly written to have come from one of the children around her. A parent must have written the note — knowing this made the message even more frightening.

KATHY

DO NOT GO HOME TONIGHT. YOUR FATHER WILL KILL YOU. HE KNOWS YOU TOLD SOMEONE ABOUT THE BRIBE.

Kathy ran to the front of the room. She handed the teacher the note. The teacher's hand came to her mouth — "My God, Kathy. Run to the sheriff. He will know what to do. Run Kathy, run."

"I'd like to request a brief recess, Your Honor."

"How much time will you require, Mr. Potters?"

"About five minutes, Your Honor."

Judge Erwin looked to the back of the courtroom. Like all other eyes in the crowded courtroom, he saw the ragged Kathy Gast standing beside Russ Porter. The people of the court were murmuring among themselves. Heads popped up trying to see the little girl.

Morgan remained calm. He did not know what Kathy Gast had to say to the court, but he could see that Frank Gardner was not pleased. For the first time since the beginning of the trial, Senator Gardner was nervous. He stood up to see the girl, then sat down again stroking his grey beard nervously. Twice John Goodell pulled on his arm asking what the girl wanted, but Frank Gardner shook his head dumbfoundly. Whatever she had to say, Morgan thought, put her on.

"You have your five minutes, Mr. Potters."

"Thank you, Your Honor."

Five minutes later Katherine Gast was called to the witness stand.

The crowd hushed as the bailiff swore her in.

Amos Potters stopped at the defense table. He explained briefly to Morgan about the warning note Kathy had received. And that Sheriff Gustavson was to find her father and deliver him to the courtroom. Then he handed a folded piece of paper across the table.

"Here's a little present from Russ," he said.

Morgan scanned the note. He could not help but look over at Frank Gardner and was hoping to catch Gardner looking worriedly back at him. Squirm, you bastard, he thought.

"Now Katherine, you are the daughter of Andrew Gast, is that correct?"

"Yes sir."

"Where do you live?"

"On a farm east of town."

"East of Twin Forks?"

"Yes sir."

Potters returned to the defense table, rummaged through the papers on his desk until finally he picked up the note from the top of the pile.

"Now Katherine, will you tell the jury how it is that you are here today."

Kathy Gast glanced around the courtroom nervously, coughed to clear her throat and began,

"I went to school today and after we sat down I found a note on my desk warning me not to go home."

"Is this the note?" Amos Potters asked handing it to her.

"Yes sir."

"Will you read it to the court please?"

"Do not go home tonight. Your father will kill you. He knows you told someone about the bribe."

The audience whispered the message — bribe — bribe — bribe. Judge Erwin dropped the gavel. The crowd hushed.

"Can you explain this note, Katherine?"

"No sir. I don't know who sent it."

"We realize that. What I mean is, can you explain why the note was sent and in regard to what?"

"Yes sir. Last month I was riding on the wagon with my father. We were driving to town when Mr. Gardner rides up."

"Senator Frank Gardner?"

"Yes sir. He stopped us on Six-Mile Road."

"Go on please."

"He asked my father if he could use $500.00. My father said that he could and Mr. Gardner handed him the money. When my father took it, Mr. Gardner said that it was for him to stay quiet about my sister Alice."

Frank Gardner was visibly shaken. He leaned far forward in his chair stroking his beard quietly. Morgan looked back to Amos Potters.

"How did this involve Alice, Katherine?"

"I don't know, sir. I asked but my father told me to forget what I heard and not to tell anyone."

"But you have no idea?"

"No sir."

County Attorney Evers rose quickly from his chair. The crowd had anticipated some reaction. He rewarded them with a knowing shake of his head and a mocking grin.

"Your Honor, I must object."

"What is your objection, Mr. Evers?"

Evers raised his hands then let them drop to his sides in a helpless gesture. "This entire statement, Your Honor: first, we are asked to listen to a child testify against her own father, obviously without his knowledge and probably totally unaware of the criminal implications she is burdening on her father. Then, we are asked to believe a note from whom we know not it came. A note simply appeared on the child's desk in the middle of a crowded classroom — or possibly it appeared in the healthy and frustrated mind of an eight year old girl. Then, Your Honor, we are asked to believe that a conversation took place, a very short conversation of total incoherence, during which the rather large sum of $500.00 was exchanged. I suggest, Your Honor, that all this is far too much to accept and the entire statement of this young child be stricken from the record."

"What do you say, Mr. Potters?" Judge Erwin asked.

Amos Potters stood near the jurors. "Well, Your Honor, if Mr. Evers feels that the child may not be telling the truth, the normal procedure would be for him to find that out in cross-examination."

It was an obvious and weak stand. Evers jumped on it. "Your Honor, I suggest that cross-examination would simply add more attention to testimony that should not have been heard in the first place. If Mr. Potters has somewhere to go with this, then let him say so now, or retract her statements."

Judge Erwin looked up from his desk with studied calm. "Yes, Mr. Potters. The court would also like to know where you are leading."

Potters paused. Five seconds. Ten seconds. Fifteen seconds. The door to the courtroom swung open. The crowd turned to see who had entered. Their whispers roared a giant hiss.

Morgan saw Frank Gardner jump to his feet. He saw Gardner's face turn gray as he sat down again slowly. Morgan smiled when Gardner glanced in his direction.

Amos Potters returned to the table. "Well, John, I don't know what Andrew Gast has to say, but I guess we'll have to put him on the stand to find out."

Morgan nodded toward Gardner. "Our Senator just turned to stone, Amos. Put old man Gast on the stand. He's got a cannonball to deliver."

Potters bent low to Morgan's ear. "I must warn you, John, Russ said that you would not like some of what Andrew Gast has to say. He implied that it would effect you — personally."

Morgan looked at the old man at the back of the room. How could this stranger hurt him? Surely he would hurt no one but Frank Gardner. He turned to face the bench. "Put him on, Amos."

"State your full name."

"Andy Gast."

"Do you swear to tell the truth, the whole truth and nothing but the truth, so help you God?"

"I swear."

"You may take the stand."

CHAPTER TWENTY-NINE

"Objection, Your Honor."

Judge Erwin had been staring at Andrew Gast. Gast stood in the witness stand in the tops of his winter underwear striped by two tattered suspenders that held up a baggy pair of old trousers. He looked like a poor sharecropper up from the south — red-necked — three days without a shave and an hour without a drink.

"Yes, Mr. Evers. What is your objection?"

"Your Honor, I must object to these courtroom theatrics. Obviously, this entire scene has been planned and I don't see how we can be expected to put up with this — this show. It is degrading to my profession and to this court and the entire cause of justice we are seeking in this courtroom today. Yes, I do object, Your Honor."

Judge Erwin looked down at his desk. "Mr. Potters, do you wish to comment?"

Amos Potters stood beside John Morgan. "Your Honor, less than three minutes ago Mr. Evers was accusing us of dragging a young girl to the stand totally unprepared. Now he is saying that we carefully planned these happenings. I suggest, Your Honor, that it is

Mr. Evers who is unprepared today to fulfill his duty to his client and perhaps he is no longer qualified to conduct this case for the plaintiff."

The courtroom stilled while Judge Erwin pondered the issue put before him. Twice he checked his watch. Morgan noted that it was three-thirty. It would be a good time to break for the day — but not good for his side of the case. The audience was excited. The jury members sat erect and alert for the first time since the beginning of the trial. They were ready to rally behind John Morgan now, he thought. Tomorrow could be too late. It must continue. Please. God, please.

"Objection overruled . . ."

The audience exploded into cheers. They were so loud no one heard the judge say, "You may continue, Mr. Potters." But Amos stepped to face the jury while the crowd calmed. One by one their voices dropped until all were quiet again. Potters turned to the witness stand where Andrew Gast now sat. He had not known Andy Gast and for a brief moment the eyes of the two men met: Amos' old and wise and calm; Andy's hot and red and fearful.

"Andrew Gast."

"Yep. Yes sir."

"Are you the father of Katherine Gast from whom this court has just heard testimony?"

"Yes sir. She's my daughter."

"Do you have other children, Andy?"

"Yes. I have Alice and Carl — they's my oldest and then there's Kathy and two little young 'uns."

"How old is Alice?"

"Oh, 'round twenty-one or twenty-two, I'd say."

"And Carl?"

"He's 'round a year older than Alice."

Amos Potters wandered nearer the jurors. "You seem rather old for the three smaller children, Andy. Is there a reason for that?"

"Alice and Carl are of my first wife. Kathy and the two young 'uns are of my second."

"What happened to your first wife?"

Andy Gast shrugged his scarecrow shoulders and looked at his lap. His eyes and head were lowered most of the time. "She died.

I never could figger what she died from. It was winter and she died."

"When was that, Andy? What year did she die?"

"It was the winter of nineteen and two. I took me a second wife in nineteen and five."

Potters looked at the jury. Their faces were drawn and all eyes were trained on Andy Gast. They could not pull their attention from him. We all fear the beggar, Potters found himself thinking. And for the same reason, they fear the king — in this case, Senator Frank Gardner.

"Now Andy, I want you to tell this court: have you, at any time, discussed this case with me or discussed what we are going to talk about today?"

"I never seen you before this minute."

"And the defendant, John Morgan, have you seen him?"

"I seen him. Never talked with him though."

Amos turned toward the audience. He gave Dan Evers a triumphant nod and resumed his questioning. "Andy, your daughter, Kathy, has told this court today that she received a note in school warning her not to return home because you had threatened to kill her. Is this true and did you make such a threat?"

"I might of said something like that in the pool hall. I was plenty drunk, but I don't think I would kill her."

"Why would you threaten her like that, Andy?"

Andy Gast paused. He lifted his head to Amos then looked around the courtroom. Most of the faces he recognized —most of them he had hated for as long as he had known them. They enjoyed his suffering, he knew. They enjoyed it in that strange way people pity others. His head dropped again.

"I said it because I heard she'd been tellin' folks about the $500.00 Frank Gardner gave me."

Amos waited for the noise from the audience to subside.

"Let me get this straight: Senator Gardner paid you $500.00?"

"Yup. Cash."

"When did he give you this money?"

"A couple of, two or three weeks ago."

"That's a lot of money? Why did he give you the money? Was it for corn or was it a gift to help your family?"

Gast's head shot up. His face turned as red as his eyes which darted from Frank Gardner to Amos Potters. He yelled "Frank Gardner never done me a kind deed in my whole life. He came out and found me on Six-Mile Road and paid me $500.00 to keep my mouth shut."

Andy Gast was standing. His finger pointed at Frank Gardner, who met his glare with astonished disbelief.

"Frank Gardner has been blackmailing me for four years. He told me four years ago that he'd take my farm away from my family if I told anyone about my Alice and his son Albert. And he paid me $500.00 this month for that same reason."

"Order in the court. Mr. Gast, you'll have to take your chair if you want to be heard in this courtroom. Order in the court. I must have order or I'll clear this room."

The audience sank back into their seats as Andy Gast went down onto his own chair at the witness stand. A couple of minutes passed.

"Suppose you start at the beginning, Mr. Gast." With that, Amos Potters walked to the defense table and waited. He looked at Morgan, but Morgan did not see him. John Morgan was staring at Andy Gast. Morgan's heart was stopped in his throat. His mind raced. Andy Gast . . .

"I knew for a long time that my Alice was seeing Albert Gardner even after he was married. But I didn't do nothing about it." He began to cry. Stifled it. "I couldn't do anything about it. Nothing." He cried.

Under control again. "A couple of years earlier I lost my farm to Gardner. He was just the mayor of the town then but he owned the bank I owed money to. Instead of letting me extend my mortgage like anyone else would of done, he said he was foreclosing and was taking my farm. He did. The bank foreclosed on my farm and he bought it. That was toward the winter of nineteen and eleven and it was about then that Albert started nosing around my Alice. You see, Gardner wanted my land but he didn't want to farm it. He's a paper farmer. So he tells me I can stay on the land and he'd pay me twenty per cent of the crop. I stayed. I shouldn't of, but I stayed and I ain't too proud of that fact. And I didn't say nothin' to Albert neither. I should of, but I knew they'd throw me off my land. I let him come and my Alice would see him a few times each month. I beat her once, but it didn't do no good. He still came 'round and she couldn't stop him. But she's a good girl, my Alice. It's just that everyone shunned her because she come from a no-good family and she had no friends. Laying under Albert was better than nothin'. Then, about the summer of nineteen and twelve, Alice found out she was pregnant."

"Order. Order in the court. All right. Continue, Mr. Potters."

"Pardon me, Andy, you did say 'pregnant' didn't you?" Potters voice was suddenly old and hoarse.

"Yup. She was pregnant by a couple of months or more she thought."

"Did you tell Frank Gardner this?"

"Tell him? No — not for a day or so. Then I got to thinkin', well what the hell, his boy had been rootin' on my daughter and sure as hell he owed me something for that. It meant another mouth to feed for me, didn't it? Finally I got up enough nerve to see Gardner face to face."

"And how did Mr. Gardner receive you?"

"He laughed at me at first. He said he'd have twenty men testify that they had laid my Alice and bring disgrace down on my family's name. Then he said he'd take my farm away if I ever told anyone about it."

Morgan watched Frank Gardner. Gardner rocked back and forth in his chair, easing forward as if to hear better, leaning back as if to reject what he heard. Squirm, bastard, Morgan thought. He'd forgotten Russ Porter's warning. He was not ready for what was next to come.

"And you left the Gardner mansion, Andy?"

"No. I started to but Gardner called me back. When I got back up to his study Gardner had $400.00 in his hand and he was real friendly like. I asked him what the money was for."

Andrew Gast cried.

"What was the money for, Mr. Gast?" Amos asked the question softly.

"He said he didn't want no bastard grandson around Twin Forks haunting him for the rest of his life. He said that I should take the $400.00 and he would get a doctor to do an abortion on Alice."

Judge Erwin pounded the desk. "Order in this court! I say, order!" But the audience would calm only when they had repeated the word over and over again and became curious to hear the rest of the story. Frank Gardner looked around the room as if to find a place to escape. Desperately he buried his face in his hands then, composed suddenly, nervously, he stared at Andy Gast along with John Morgan and a thousand other eyes.

"I needed the money," Gast cried. "I needed my farm. Another baby — I couldn't feed another baby, especially without the farm. I ain't no good at no trade. So I agreed to Gardner's bargain. I sold my daughter's unborn kid."

"What was the bargain exactly, Mr. Gast?"

"I was to deliver my Alice to a place Gardner picked out on the first Friday of June."

Amos Potters held his hand in the air. "Let me see, that was June 7, 1912, three days before the discovery of the Porter bodies?"

"I guess so."

"I just want to make sure of that date, Mr. Gast. Do you agree it was June 7, 1912?"

"Yeah."

"All right. Continue."

"That's all. I was to deliver Alice to this place she would get the abortion. Then she'd stay there a few weeks until she got well."

"Who was the doctor who performed the abortion on your daughter, Mr. Gast?" Amos Potters yelled the question so that it rang throughout the shocked courtroom.

"It was Doctor Stewart."

"Doctor Stewart? Our County Coroner? The same Doctor Stewart who performed the autopsy on the Porter family and the Stills girls?"

"The same. Gardner said Stewart was his man."

Again the audience exploded as they conjectured the plot which Morgan had hoped they would. When they were quiet again, it was an impatient quiet, a respectful calm while they waited to be released so that they could spend the night discussing what they had heard today.

Amos Potters was also calm. He spoke in a conversational tone as if to say, all right, Andy, it is over, so let's wrap it up now.

"Why did you testify today, Andy? After all of these months why did you come forward now? You could have denied everything your daughter said."

Gast was not calm. He had bared himself to all and there was nothing left for him to hide. No shame. No pride. "Because I am a man. I may not look like it, but I'm a man, Senator Gardner. That's one thing you didn't count on — that Andy Gast would crawl out of a bottle and stand up to you."

He spoke directly to Gardner. "You took my farm, like you did the others and you ripped out my daughter's baby. You'll have us all Gardner, if someone don't stop you. Well, I'm stopping you now. You can take my farm. Take it away from me. But I got you, Gardner — you'll pay for my daughter's baby."

John Morgan relaxed. He dropped his head and listened to Andrew Gast proclaim his manhood. He had won. It would soon be over. Then he heard Amos Potters beside him.

"One more question, if I may, Your Honor."

"He is still your witness, Mr. Potters. Proceed."

"Andy, you said you were to take your daughter to a place Frank Gardner had picked out. Can you tell me where you took her?"

"I took her to the Widow Durham's place. I took her to Lorraine Durham's."

Morgan's face turned to steel. He did not see Amos Potters look at him. He could have stopped Amos, but he was frozen. His eyes were fixed on the whiskered mouth of Andrew Gast.

"Why there, Mr. Gast? Do you have any idea?"

"She was Gardner's woman. He used to go out there once a week. I heard she wouldn't see him any more after the abortion. But she was his woman until then."

"That's all, Mr. Gast."

"This court will adjourn until ten o'clock tomorrow morning."

CHAPTER THIRTY

It was late. Carl Gast had not returned to the hotel room. Lona had heard the news and was certain that Carl had not known about the abortion before today, just as certain as she was that he had undoubtedly heard the news today. Everyone was talking about it. Copies of the Yellow Sheet were selling for one dollar. They were everywhere. Three times she had gone to the bars along the Square, and in the excited, milling crowds she would find someone to enter the bars to look for Carl. But they could not find him.

Lona had been waiting alone in the room for over three hours when finally she heard Carl's footsteps on the stairs and she ran to the door.

"Carl!" She screamed his name as she threw her arms around him. "Carl, I thought I had lost you. I didn't know where you were."

Carl Gast walked sullenly into the room "I've been out. I walked and I thought. I suppose I should have just gone out and gotten blind drunk like my old man and called it good."

Lona sat on the bed beside him. She put her head on his chest and hugged him as she cried, "Oh Carl, I'm so sorry. I had no idea . . ."

"I know you didn't." He jerked away from her arms.

"Carl. Oh, Carl, I'm so sick about this. Forgive me. Can you do that for me? Don't let this separate us, not like this."

Carl knelt in front of her. She was soft now and weak, a little girl he loved. He put his fist beneath her chin and lifted gently. "Lona, I don't blame you for this."

"No. Don't blame me, Carl. Don't blame me — I love you."

She wanted to tell him he was the father of the baby inside her and how happy she was that he was the father. But not now, she thought. Not during this trial — and not with the word "abortion" still filling the air. Instead she pulled his head to her breasts and cried.

Carl pulled away, "Lona, I wouldn't hurt you for anything. But my father was completely disgraced today. I never thought I could give a damn about him, but to think of him doing that — he's my father, Lona, and she's my sister."

"Carl, what are you saying? Can't you still love me?" Lona felt her heart jump fearfully as she watched his eyes drop away from hers.

"I do love you. I could love you forever. But there won't be anything left between us . . . not after tomorrow.

"Tomorrow? Why . . ."

"I'm going to testify in court tomorrow. What I have to say is important to detective Morgan's case. I wasn't going to testify, but after today I have no other choice."

"I don't understand. What do you have to testify about? You didn't know about the abortion."

"It isn't about the abortion."

"What then?"

"Dorothy."

"What about Dorothy?"

Carl turned his back to her. He spoke through the window to the crowds he could see below on the street — the crowds that were there talking about his family's disgrace, the crowds he had scorned all his life.

"Morgan said that if he could prove that Dorothy had committed adultery, then the jury would be more able to believe that Dorothy was having an affair with Jas Porter. He said your father would have had the Porter family murdered if he found out — and I believe that is true. I believe Jas Porter and Dorothy were having an affair and your father discovered it and hired a murderer."

Lona shook her head, "Do you mean that you do know Dorothy was having an affair with someone, someone other than Jas Porter?"

"Yes."

"Who?"

"With me."

Lona felt her insides turn. She wished she could miscarry. She wanted to ruin herself. But it was her father's fault, she thought. Everything was her father's fault. Lona jumped to the door. Carl called after her as she ran down the stairs.

"Go away. Leave me alone," she cried and ran onto the Square.

Through the crowds, tears running down her cheeks, sobs emitting involuntarily from deep within, Lona ran across the Square to Third Street. She ran until her lungs ached from sucking in the cold air, but she kept running to the boulevard and to her father's mansion. The key, she thought. Dorothy had said there was a key to the Porter home in her father's desk drawer, if she could get hold of it . . .

She was halfway up the first-floor stairs when Albert appeared at the landing above her.

"Get out of my way," she screamed.

He grabbed her wrists as she tried to push past him. They struggled on the landing. Albert had pinned her against the wall when the door below them crashed open and Carl Gast rushed into the mansion.

"Get out of here, you bastard!" Albert Gardner yelled at Gast as Carl ran up the stairs to meet him. Albert tossed Lona aside. He jumped from the landing to meet Carl in mid-air. They fell against the bannister and as Lona hurried up the stairs she heard the sound of splintering wood followed by a loud crash as the heavy bannister and the two men hit the floor below.

The key, she thought. She had to have the key. Nothing else mattered. She ran the rest of the way up the flights of stairs to her father's study. There was no one in the study. Gasping for breath, Lona ran to the library table, ripped open the middle drawer and there she found the key. She paused a moment before picking it up. The key, she thought: it had opened the door to the Porter home that night. It had been there. Shaking herself free of the fear that had chilled her, Lona grabbed the key and ran for the stairs.

"Lona. Lona." She heard the voice call her name. "Lona. It's your brother. He's hurt — really hurt."

Lona looked at the door to the front lawn. Escape, she thought. Nothing else matters. Escape.

"Lona. He's going to die."

She came to where Carl knelt over Albert. There was blood pooling on the floor beneath her brother's body.

"I think there's a large splinter of wood gone through his back. Help me turn him over."

Lona put the key on the floor behind her and helped Carl roll Albert to his stomach. They sickened at the sight of the jagged end of a wooden splinter over an inch in diameter piercing Albert's back.

"There's nothing we can do. I'll go get Doc Stewart. He's still alive, Lona. He's still alive." Carl ran out of the door leaving Lona alone with her brother. She gazed at him for a long time. Poor Albert, she thought, none of this was your fault either. Finally she stood. The doctor would have to help him now. She bent for the key — it was not there.

"What . . ." Lona whirled around to find her father near the door. For the first time in her life she was not afraid of him. She pitied him. "What have you done with the key, Senator Gardner?"

Frank Gardner looked at his daughter. She was a stranger, he thought. He had never known her before.

Carl Gast, Doctor Stewart and John Goodell came into the room and went to work immediately on Albert. They paid no attention to Lona and her father at the bottom of the stairs.

They stared at each other. Father. Daughter. Presently Frank Gardner looked away slowly from his daughter and climbed the stairs to his study. Lona watched him disappear beyond the landing, then she, too, turned and disappeared into the night. They would never see each other again.

Lorraine sat at her table in the kitchen. Before her was a long sheet of yellow paper. It was the only Yellow Sheet she had purchased throughout the trial. This day she had been to town and although she was accustomed to the chill that always filled the people around her, this day she had noticed a greater rejection from the crowds. They parted in front of her as she went to the stores and did not close behind her, as if they did not want to step on the same ground she had just walked. At a corner, a boy was selling the Yellow Sheet. His voice was loud and clear as he sang out the day's happenings:

"Gast testifies to abortion!"

The sun had set beyond the western horizon. Dim twilight shadowed the little house.

Never had she loved a man as she had loved John Morgan. And now, with news of her part in the abortion and her involvement with Frank Gardner, John Morgan was gone. Gone forever from her life.

Lorraine pulled the sharp edge of the knife into her chest. It felt not nearly so bad as she had hoped. It did not destroy the pain in her heart. She withdrew the blade slowly. It came out red and sparkled in the twilight. Beyond, in blurred vision, she saw the low flames of the fire, and in front of it, the thick rug where she had lain with Morgan. She remembered the tender moments they had shared there. It was the last that she saw.

CHAPTER THIRTY-ONE

The last day.

Frank Gardner rose in the morning. He was not in a gay mood, nor was he depressed, for he had reached an important decision that lifted the world from his shoulders. As he dressed he yelled to his helper. "Provo, are you getting the carriage ready? We must not be late." He heard with satisfaction the heavy steps of Provo pounding down the stairs to follow his instructions.

When he had dressed, he went to the third floor where he met Doctor Stewart in the hallway.

"How is he, Doctor?"

Doctor Stewart cocked his head wearily, "He is not good, Frank. But I do think he will live. He's made it this far and I think he'll pull through now. It will take time, and there may be more wrong inside of him than we know."

"That's good, Doctor. Thank you. Let me be alone with him for awhile."

"He'll be asleep for another six or seven hours."

"I know. I just want to be with him before I go back to the trial."

Frank Gardner entered the room and closed the door behind him. He took the chair near the bed and looked upon his son's peaceful face.

"Well, son," he said aloud, "I am afraid I have protected you as long as I can. It is up to the jury, really. But if they find Morgan not guilty today — then everyone is going to think that I murdered the Porters. We cannot let that happen, Albert. Look at all we have built. Look at my position. Do you realize that I may be governor of this state some day soon?" He leaned across the bed to caress Albert's forehead. "No, son. I cannot protect you any longer — and lose everything that we have. If they find Morgan not guilty today, then I will have to tell them the truth about you. I know you'll agree with me."

Doctor Stewart tapped on the door. "Frank, your man is ready. If you want to reach the courthouse by ten o'clock you better be leaving."

"Yes. I am ready." Frank Gardner looked again at his son. A few seconds later he rushed from the mansion and climbed into the carriage.

In the morning the jury heard the testimony of Vina Thompkins and Carl Gast. The summations followed. For both sides they were brief and obvious. There was no cheering, however. Everyone was numbed by the recent happenings and now they came to see their saga end. They seemed to regret that it was about over. The jury received its instructions and court adjourned.

Four hours later the jury returned and waited patiently as the courtroom filled to capacity. The jurors sat stone-faced in their box. They looked neither at Frank Gardner nor to John Morgan nor the audience.

At four-thirty Judge Erwin stepped from the anteroom in his stately black robe.

"All rise."

Judge Erwin took his chair.

"Be seated."

The audience, the jurors, the plaintiff and the defendant collapsed into their chairs in one great roar of bodies meeting wood.

"Will the defendant please rise?" John Morgan and Amos Potters stood together.

"Have you reached a verdict?"

"We have You Honor."

"Will you tell the court what that verdict is?"

"Yes, Your Honor. We find the defendant, John Morgan, not guilty."

Frank Gardner stood calmly. He smiled when a photographer hurried into the courtroom to take his picture.

"Mr. Gardner," a reporter shouted above the crowd, "Do you have a statement?"

"Yes, I do have a statement," Frank Gardner said. "I have a statement for the press. If you'll wait a moment until the crowd is gone, I have something very important to say. What? Yes, I would like all of the reporters to be here. Yes."

He was smiling as more pictures were taken and more reporters gathered around him. Suddenly his smile faded as over the crowd he saw John Goodell pushing and shoving his way through the crowd to get to him. He watched.

"Mr. Goodell, what are you doing here? You are supposed to be with Albert."

"Sir. I have bad news. Albert is dead. He died an hour ago."

"Dead? No. That can't be. It can't be. What about my statement? They'll never believe me now. They'll think I am the murderer. Oh, god . . ."

"He is dead, sir."

The crowd gave way as Senator Frank Gardner left the courthouse. He walked across the brown lawn to where the carriage awaited. Over eight thousand people watched him drive away.

Amos Potters grabbed Morgan by the arm. "Where are you going, John? You're a famous man today. The press is going to want to see you."

Morgan smiled. "I'm in a hurry, Amos. Tell them I'll talk to them tomorrow."

"They'll want to know if you plan to charge Gardner with murder. Well, are you?"

"No way. We couldn't prove it anyway — right?"

"I'm afraid you're right. But I think we have proved enough, don't you?"

Morgan grinned. "Amos, I don't care. Gardner can go to hell, for all I care. Right now I'm going to see the only person in the world that means a damn thing to me."

"Lorraine?"

"That's right. If she'll have me."

THE END

EPILOGUE

December 18, 1937

Doctor Everett Stewart sat rigidly on the hard surface of the fireplace hearth, preferring the cold brick outside the perimeter of the flames to the soft overstuffed chairs that were arranged in a semicircle facing him.

At each quarter hour a giant grandfather's clock across the room chimed the passing and he checked it against the watch in his vest pocket. Outside the snow was falling. It had been building since midnight. It was now eleven-thirty in the morning and over six inches of white, fluffy snow had accumulated on the ground.

"As long as the wind doesn't come up, we'll make it back okay, Doc," the driver of the taxi had said. "Otherwise, you can forget it for sure." So far the wind had not come. The snow lay flat across the yard outside the window and packed heavily in the trees. So far. But this was Iowa. Whoever heard of a windless snowy day in Iowa? As the snow piled higher and higher on the windowsill, the doctor realized that he might never make it back to Twin Forks.

And if he did, he might be too late . . . all because of this damnable meeting.

At twelve noon he was to appear before "the Honorable Judge Mark Durham," grandson of the respected Sam Durham.

As he sat in the judge's library outside the private study, he wondered if the young man would make him wait until noon. It was not customary to stick to time schedules. Not if the meeting was urgent. And he wondered if the grandson would be similar to old Sam Durham. He'd know soon enough. Maybe too soon. At eleven forty-five he checked his watch against the great clock and looked at the huge double doors to the study, as if they had a time lock and would not open until precisely the right moment.

This was not far from the truth, he thought. The doors had closed on him twenty-one years ago, through mutual agreement, and each day since then all concerned parties knew the doors would not reopen until a time only destiny would determine. Frank Gardner's death. What he had not expected was that destiny would take Sam Durham's life before Gardner's. But, true to form, Sam Durham had anticipated even this and left his grandson the inheritance of a secret. Or, a covenant.

As he waited, he picked up the newspaper again and reread the front-page story. It was a fresh copy of the Twin Fork's "Clarion".

"Famous Axe Murder Mystery — Unsolved Forever?"

That was how it was supposed to be. A few questions. Romantic gestures and querying news stories. But no answers. A brief period of renewed but futile interest. And then it would be over. Over forever, finally.

Only one other detail was out of order: Frank Gardner was dying — but not yet dead.

"A memoir may exist . . . the possibility of a death bed confession."

But who would substantiate the memoir or be able to pass on a private confession to the public?

There was little doubt in the doctor's mind why the junior Durham had sent for him. As the large hand of the clock neared the vertical position, he found himself, to his own surprise, wishing that the time would pass more slowly. Hoping the telephone would ring and the voice of an old woman standing in the dark entryway of Gardner's mansion would sadly announce that "the Senator" had died in his absence. The moment they had all been waiting for had finally come and the fears he felt now had proven useless and unnecessary. "The Senator" had died in his sleep, silently.

There was a loud click followed by the sound of one of the large doors of gleaming black walnut sliding open. The doctor looked up, startled, surprised to see how similar young Durham's appearance was to his grandfather's thirty years earlier. He tried to retain his composure as he rose, walked toward the ominous black doors, and entered.

"Forgive me, Doctor Stewart, but we have come across some — unusual information — and I thought we should get together."

Doctor Stewart nodded in agreement and sat down in a hard leather chair in front of Durham's desk. His mind was befuddled. He had agreed — to what? It had been a long time since he had carried on a conversation that required any degree of wit or guarded reaction. Twenty-one years ago he had announced his semi-retirement, keeping only those patients he had already taken on. Now he was old and most of his patients had died of the same disease. Frank Gardner was one of those who remained in what could only derisively be called his "practice". Over the years his mind had slowed, his reflexes had become dull.

And yet, here was Mark Durham. A different Durham, but the same. A businessman in a dark, pinstriped suit and a large diamond ring that sparkled beneath a broad chandelier overhead. It was the same chandelier that had been here before, except light bulbs had replaced the tubular vases where candles once stood. Time, Stewart thought, had changed the Durham family only where convenient.

Behind the wide expanse of the desk that indicated no workload, Durham rested his elbows on the sides of his chair as he puffed on a giant cigar, the kind that are flown in from the east in tubes of grease.

"So . . .Frank is dying. Is that correct? All I know is what I've seen in the papers. I'd rather hear if from you then some wet-nose reporter picking up rumors on the street."

"It would appear that he's dying."

"When?"

Doctor Stewart was startled. He wondered if it was the question that startled him or the matter-of-fact attitude displayed by young Durham. He had never been like the Durhams or the others. Actions had been forced upon him.

Conspiracy. Conspiracy.

The word pounded in his mind. Here was Durham speaking to him like they were continuing a conversation cut short yesterday, not almost a quarter century ago, two generations removed.

"I can't be precise. He's been getting worse the past few months — and a few days ago he went lower than ever. I gave him some medicine to soothe the pain and let him sleep and then, yesterday, his servant summoned me. I would guess he'll be dead within three days."

"Three days." Durham stood and looked out the window with his back to the others. The snow was falling harder than ever now, diagonally across the window. The wind was picking up.

"How did news leak out he was dying?" Durham asked.

"I needed assistance. A neighbor lady was kind enough to help. She sat with him for a few hours yesterday morning and must have guessed the seriousness of his situation."

But Durham was not satisfied. He turned. "Why wasn't I told?"

"I saw no reason. I mean —" Doctor Stewart faltered as his voice cracked, "I just didn't think about it."

"No, I suppose there was no overt reason to inform me," Durham agreed. "At least none of which you were aware." he went to the deacon's bench in a corner of the room and returned laboring under the load of a heavy cardboard box.

It landed with a dull thud on his desk. Durham met Doctor Stewart's inquiring gaze. "The transcripts. They've been requested," he said simply.

"The trans . . ." The doctor felt his heart leap. For the first time the real issue was about to enter the conversation.

"Which ones?"

"All of them," answered Durham. "The murder trial, The slander suit . . .your coroner's inquest."

Silence followed as the younger man allowed time for the full impact of the news to sink in on Doctor Stewart. The possibilities — so vague — and astonishing.

"What are we going to do?" Doctor Stewart asked in a hoarse whisper.

"People will wonder what happened to them."

Durham shrugged. "We'll destroy them, of course. There's a pile of records down there in metal boxes — like this one." He indicated the brown box he had just placed on the table. It was soiled and the top flaps were chewed and dog-eared. The bottom was moldy and wet, would give way if the box was picked up by the sides and not supported from the bottom.

"It took two hours to find it," Durham continued. "No one would miss it if it were gone. And if they looked for it — they just wouldn't find it."

Doctor Stewart peered into the box. On top of the official papers was a small card with a picture of a handsome, powerful-looking man with immaculately groomed brown hair combed back from a high, wide forehead. Piercing, stern eyes looked out at him from the sides of a long, Roman nose. A beard and moustache were trimmed to perfection and added credence to the strict pose.

Beneath the picture in large bold type were the words: FRANK F. GARDNER — FOR SENATOR.

Doctor Stewart stared at the picture, his eyes transfixed on the image. He has lost track of all time, the face on the card reminded him. Of reality. Slowly he had watched Frank Gardner slip from youth to old age, good health to tragic illness. Not until now did he realize how pronounced the transformation had become.

The doctor returned the picture.

"We can burn them tonight. Everything. And no one will be the wiser. Every shred of evidence will be destroyed," Durham said.

Doctor Stewart disagreed. "Their absence alone will be evidence that there's a cover-up."

"So what?" Durham argued. "It just adds to the mystery. People will love it. But the proof will be gone. That's what counts."

The young Durham put a match to a half-smoked cigar, speaking between puffs of gray smoke.

"A wire requesting the transcripts was sent to the attention of the County Attorney of Davies County," Durham smiled. "It was sent by Lona Gardner. Apparently she has presumed that the Durham family doesn't pull much weight around here anymore."

Durham slapped the flat of his hand against the decaying box. "The point is we can destroy all of the junk before it can destroy us! And we damn well better do it tonight."

Why, Doctor Stewart wondered, was Durham so intent upon destroying the transcripts. The young man acted as if he had more to lose under close scrutiny than himself. Was he now over reacting to a fear that had built up inside of him over the years? A guilt complex that enlarged his sense of personal persecution.

The feeling was not unknown to the doctor.

Durham turned toward the doctor. "I've been trying to imagine why she wants these transcripts. What possible motive could she have? It would seem that she would have more to lose than anyone by rejuvenating the investigation, especially since there's only an outside chance that the investigation would put Frank Gardner in a somewhat better light. A very far outside chance."

"Anything it would add would be conjecture only — having to deal with. . ." The doctor glanced out of the corner of his eye at young Durham. How much had his grandfather passed on to him? How much did he really know?

If ever there was a time for honesty, he thought, this was the time. Tactfulness was too often misunderstood and, in this situation, a mistake in judgement could be fatal.

". . .having to deal with the last days of the slander trial," the doctor continued boldly.

"It hardly seems likely that she would suddenly be moved to action now by something that happened over twenty years ago. I was considering a more recent occurrence, what, I don't know, that may have happened," Durham said.

"Perhaps you're right."

"No. I cut you off and I'm sorry for that. Please continue so we can at least ponder your hypothesis."

Doctor Stewart took a deep breath, "I was summoned to the Gardner mansion the day before the trial. Lona, as you may know, left town on that day . . ."

"Yes. My grandfather told me she disappeared — leaving her father in the clutches. It looked like she'd deserted him, and did more for the case against him than all the witnesses or evidence. That was the same day Albert died, wasn't it?

He sat back in his chair, relit the cigar, and gazed contentedly for a few brief seconds at the ceiling. Those days provided a pleasurable memory — one of his grandfather's finer accomplishments. If there were masters of deceit, Sam Durham had been the headmaster. He enjoyed his work.

A manipulator of people.

The swivel chair creaked as he turned to look out the window.

"You were saying, doctor . . ."

"The night before the last day of the slander trial, I was called to the Gardner mansion. Lona was still there. Albert Gardner was out, but Frank and Dorothy were present, along with Martha, of course."

Repeating the names was difficult for Stewart. A few weeks ago he had climbed the cemetery hill in attendance at a funeral of one of his few remaining patients. It was a climb he had grown accustomed to over the years. When the funeral party left the gravesite, he had continued up the hill and found himself by the large plot reserved for the Gardner family. Martha Gardner had died a few months earlier. Beside her was the stone that bore her son's name. The son's death preceded the mother's by nineteen years. Albert would have been fifty-five, now. And then Dorothy Davies Gardner lay beside Albert. Something they could never do in life. Her date of death followed her husband's by thirteen months. Beside these were two more carved stones: Frank F. Gardner and his daughter, Lona Gardner.

On these two stones the dates of death were yet to be filled in. Ironically, as if the cemetery personnel had played a cruel joke on the dead, within eyesight of the Gardner plot were the graves of the eight axe murder victims of 1912. Most prominent was a large stone monument with six deep letters carved on its side: PORTER. A long rectangular block of stone, slightly tilted at the top, eighteen feet long and two feet wide extended from the larger stone with the names of the dead. A few feet away were two more graves. All eight markers had that same date of death. The graves brought back memories that filled his sleep with nightmares. Vividly.

"I arrived in the middle of a terrible argument between Lona and Dorothy. It had something to do with Lona leaving."

Durham wrinkled his brow ponderously. "And you think the happening of that night would have something to do with her renewed interest in the murder case?"

"I don't know. It's just a feeling I've had — that's stayed with me all theses years. That Lona knows something she decided to conceal, for reasons of her own. Then things got hectic. Albert had been badly injured. Frank was in low spirits. I spent the rest of the night trying to save the boy's life."

"As you know . . . I failed."

"There's no sense dwelling on the past," Durhams's voice was firm and disapproving. He had been studying the doctor's face: measuring each word and the sound of his voice. "It's the future we're concerned with now. Specifically, what happens in the next three or four days. A deathbed confession, we can take care of. Your presence in the home should be enough. You do have him sealed off, I assume?"

The doctor nodded.

"The memoirs bother me. Do you believe they exist?"

"I know they exist. Along with reams of newspaper clippings, he had notes of his memoirs stacked on his table. They are there."

"Have you read it? Does he go into . . .detail?"

The doctor shrugged. "I didn't dare read them. A neighbor claims that Frank told her he was working on them. That they'd 'set the record straight', whatever that means."

Durham's eyes widened. "Then you can destroy them."

"Probably," Doctor Stewart agreed.

"If Frank Gardner dies before someone else gets to them," Durham continued.

Behind his desk, Durham rubbed his chin while he considered the possibilities.

If the doctor knew of the memoirs, then so must Gardner's daughter, Lona. His eyes strayed to the large, deteriorated cardboard box on the desk in front of him. In neatly wrapped packages were the court dockets that, in a nutshell, recorded the history of the Twin Forks axe murders from the first day of the discovery when Martha Pinkerman became worried about the "strange quiet" at her neighbor's house, to the final day of the slander trial three and one-half years later.

And now Lona had requested copies of them. Was willing to pay eight hundred dollars to a typist who could reproduce them by the end of the week. Why?

One thing seemed certain to Durham, a deathbed confession or a memoir from Gardner would only be slightly harmful without more substantial evidence to back it up. Gardner had been suffering from a growing paralysis for many years. It had moved to his spinal column, a direct route to the brain. Whatever he said or wrote could be watered down as the ravings of an old man who was legally insane. Conversely, if Lona tried to cause problems, she, too, would have little to go on without some kind of contribution from Frank Gardner himself. Across the table, the doctor's eyes were fixed on the box of court testimonies.

"Our problem may be even more serious than you think, doctor. I'll bring you up to date on Lona Gardner's movements. That detective the Porters had hired . . ."

"Morgan."

"Detective John Morgan. He died eight years ago down in Louisiana. Two days after his death, someone broke into the shack he was living in, ransacked it, and according to a local prostitute, stole a ream of old papers and newspapers Morgan had kept with him. I had sent a man down to do the same thing, but someone beat us to it."

"The detective's notes on the case?" Doctor Stewart reacted to the news with a rush of fear. All these years his concern had been centered on one man, Frank F. Gardner. Now, to think that others might have been a greater worry — his heart pounded like a man who had calmly survived an accident just minutes earlier and didn't break into fear until after, when the message of peril reached his brain.

Frank Gardner had been obsessed with keeping track of the detective, and revelled each time the news showed that Morgan had slipped lower and lower into poverty and oblivion.

"That was eight years ago," Stewart whispered. That someone had been collecting material about the axe murder case not just recently, but as long as eight years ago, was a frightening realization.

Durham slid open the bottom right drawer of his desk and pulled out a thin yellow file folder. It contained a twenty-page typewritten report, stapled at one corner, which he handed across to the doctor.

"I hired a detective to find out who stole the papers," Durham offered in summation.

"The investigation ended at 210 Parker Place, New York City. Lona's residence."

Doctor Stewart thumbed through the pages and laid the report on the desk, hands shaking. "Is there more?"

Durham placed the crisp papers back in the file and placed the file back in the drawer. He took his time answering, pulled out a fresh cigar, snipped off an end with expert smoothness, and struck a match. "If she has that, then she probably has managed to collect other information. The point is — what's she up to? And can we afford to find out? Is she trying to hurt us or protect her father's name?"

As Durham posed the last question, the jangling of a telephone came from the library. It stopped. A maid in a light blue dress with white laced sleeves entered the double doors after knocking.

"Doctor Stewart's driver is on the line, Mr. Durham."

"Come on up," Durham said into the telephone. "The doctor will be waiting." He turned to the doctor, "Your driver is worried about getting back, so you'd better go now. He'll be out front in five minutes."

Doctor Stewart rose slowly from his chair. "Little difference it will make. There's nothing I can do for Frank. There never has been. It's a helpless feeling — to watch a man die."

For the first time since the doctor had entered the study, Mark Durham stepped from behind his desk and extended his hand. Doctor Stewart took it reluctantly.

"It's important that you are with him. I don't have to tell you how this territory would be affected if a deathbed confession or a memoir was known. It would be 1912 all over again. Everything we've worked for — our families, our reputation — everything is at stake. We must be positive that you and only you have access to Frank Gardner."

"What about . . . the others?"

"Not to worry. Now that we've talked, I'm sure everything will be fine. I can take care of them. If I need your help, I'll call you. Don't do anything until you hear from me."

"But . . ."

Durham turned toward the door. "Don't worry, doctor. Three days from now, everything will be just fine. Finished. The great mystery will go on forever."

"Over, at last," Doctor Stewart spoke as if in prayer.

"At last," Durham gave the benediction.

Five minutes later Doctor Stewart got into the taxi that was to take him back to Gardner's mansion. The wait would be easier now. Knowing that Durham was not worried calmed his nerves. The snow was lighter, but the wind had picked up to twenty miles an hour, which was worse than more snow. Out in the nine miles of open country between the County Seat and Twin Forks, the wind could easily drift over the narrow roads, making them impassable. It was futile to hurry only to sit at Gardner's deathbed for hours on end. As the taxi plowed through the new snow in Judge Durham's driveway and onto the street, the doctor peered through the frosted glass at the white columned house that was barely visible one hundred feet away. He wished he had Durham's faith that after all these years the axe murder case would come to a close, and they would emerge unscathed. He leaned back in the rear seat, a tired old man.

But Doctor Stewart had forgotten, or not imagined, that young Durham had inherited a great deal of Sam Durham's personality. The reason he was rich and powerful was not because he had faith in humankind, but because he never left anything to chance. His grandfather had taught him long ago that the only thing that could not be trusted was another man's emotions. The heart cannot be calculated.

Durham walked out of the study to one of the overstuffed chairs in front of the fireplace. New wood had been added while he had talked with Doctor Stewart. It popped an crackled. The flames were warm on his legs as he stared at them contentedly. It had been almost twenty-one years since his grandfather had spoken with Doctor Everett Stewart. A lot can happen to change a man in that long of time. He had to be sure. That was the reason for summoning the doctor in this miserable weather. But it had been worth it, for now he was sure: Doctor Stewart was the same man his grandfather had known in 1912. Age had made him older — but he was still a coward.

He would allow one hour for the taxi to reach Twin Forks. Four more hours for Doctor Stewart to sit by the deathbed of the man who could destroy him. And then he would place the telephone call ordering the doctor to kill the patient.

It would be so simple.

Death is simple.

And then the good doctor would destroy the memoirs. If they were nowhere to be found, then the mansion itself would burn to the ground. A dangerous undertaking? No. No action was too strong. The transcripts could be destroyed. Gardner's mansion could mysteriously, conveniently, catch on fire. Some would say that Gardner himself, in his insanity, had started the fire and then died in it, flames of hell scorching his body. A just reward. Even the visitors from New York could be taken care of if Lona Gardner decided to cause too much trouble. After all, this was the Twin Forks axe murders. An unsolved crime that had become folklore. People would delight in the added mystery. It would add to their confusion. Nothing. Absolutely nothing was impossible.

And chance could play no part in this, he thought, as the wind outside increased and the flames in the fireplace grew higher as he began the task of feeding it the transcripts. The man must die — without mercy. He relished the prospect, for Frank Gardner was a threat to the Durham family, and the family was everything. Five hours from now he would call the old doctor and drop the bombshell. "I know that my grandfather instructed you to kill Albert Gardner. I know you killed Martha Pinkerman in the same way. So now I'm ordering you, kill Gardner tonight and destroy those memoirs." There would be no guilt, for he did what he did out of necessity.

Frank Gardner would be the first to understand.

CRITIC'S CHOICE
The finest in HORROR and OCCULT

CRITIC'S CHOICE
Espionage and Suspense Thrillers

CRITIC'S CHOICE
The greatest mysteries being published today

CAPTURED by Michael Serrian	$3.95
THE ZARAHEMLA VISION by Gary Stewart	$3.50
THE TENTH VIRGIN by Gary Stewart	$3.50
ACADEMIC MURDER by Dorsey Fiske	$3.50
DEATH OF A RENAISSANCE MAN by Linda Uccello	$3.50
A TIME TO REAP by Michael T. Hinkemeyer	$2.95
FOURTH DOWN, DEATH by Michael T. Hinkemeyer	$3.50
THE KING EDWARD PLOT by Robert Lee Hall	$3.50
ONE-EYED MERCHANTS by Kathleen Timms	$2.95
HIS LORDSHIP'S ARSENAL by Christopher Moore	$2.95
PORTRAIT IN SHADOWS by John Wainwright	$3.50
THE THIRD BLONDE by M.S. Craig	$2.95
GILLIAN'S CHAIN by M.S. Craig	$2.95
TO PLAY THE FOX by M.S. Craig	$2.95
NEW YEAR RESOLUTION by Alison Cairns	$2.95
STRAINED RELATIONS by Alison Cairns	$2.95
A CHARMED DEATH by Miles Tripp	$2.95
DEATH ON CALL by Sandra Wilkinson	$2.95
MAGGIE by Jennie Tremain	$2.95
THOSE DARK EYES by E.M. Brez	$2.95
SOMEONE ELSE'S GRAVE by Alison Smith	$2.95
THE DOWN EAST MURDERS by J.S. Borthwick	$3.50
THE GLORY HOLE MURDERS by Tony Fennelly	$2.95
MACE by James Grant	$2.95
INTIMATE KILL by Margaret Yorke	$2.95

Please send your check or money order (no cash) to:

Critic's Choice Paperbacks
31 East 28th Street
New York, N. Y. 10016

Please include $1.00 for the first book and 50¢ for each additional book to cover the cost of postage and handling.

Name _____

Street Address _____

City _____ State _____ Zip Code _____

Write for a free catalog at the above address.

CRITIC'S CHOICE
Captivating historical romances